PRAISE FOR THE DARWEN ARKWRIGHT SERIES:

"An imaginative page turner that manages to be by turns spooky, suspenseful, and touching. . . . 'Brilliant!' as Darwen would say."
—*Kirkus Reviews*

"If your mirror suddenly turned into a window, and you could climb through it to an amazing—but dangerous—world . . . would you do it? Would you dare? If you answered yes, this is the book for you! Fantastic, surprising fun!"
—RL Stine, bestselling author of GOOSEBUMPS

"Great storytelling draws you into the book just as surely as Darwen— a Lancashire lad caught in the USA—is drawn through the mirror!"
—Joseph Delaney, author of *The Last Apprentice*

"A fantastic entry. . . . A.J. Hartley shows an uncanny, brilliant ability to shape the inner life of an unmoored child."
—*New York Times* bestselling author Eloisa James

"Impressive feats of imagination. . . . Young readers will certainly agree with the author's supposition that some teachers are simply inhuman."
—*BCCB*

"Hartley is most effective in creating an air of menace . . . along with an on-target satire of a school overly enamored with standardized testing."
—*Booklist*

"Jam-packed with action from the first to the last page. The characters are well drawn, the alternative world fully developed, and the situations deliciously scary. . . . An enticing selection for young readers who fell in love with *The Golden Compass* and The Chronicles of Narnia."
—*New York Journal of Books*

DARWEN ARKWRIGHT
ARKWRIGHT
&
the school of
SHADOWS

DARWEN ARKWRIGHT
& the school of
SHADOWS

a.j. hartley

razor bill

An Imprint of Penguin Group (USA) Inc.

A division of Penguin Young Readers Group
Published by the Penguin Group
Penguin Group (USA) Inc., 345 Hudson Street
New York, New York 10014, U.S.A.

USA / Canada / UK / Ireland / Australia / New Zealand / India / South Africa / China
Penguin Books Ltd, Registered Offices: 80 Strand, London WC2R 0RL, England
For more information about the Penguin Group visit penguin.com

Published simultaneously in Canada

Library of Congress Cataloging-in-Publication Data is available

ISBN: 978-1-59514-543-7

Printed in the United States of America

1 3 5 7 9 10 8 6 4 2

To Finie and Sebastian, to my parents, and to all those other parents, teachers, librarians, and booksellers who enact the conviction that good books make for good people.

Chapter One
The Five-Minute Mission

Darwen Arkwright stood in front of the shimmering portal on the floor of the chamber known as the Great Apparatus, Alex O'Connor on his left and Rich Haggerty on his right. The flickering doorway before them was one of a hundred arranged in a great circle around an outlandish contraption whose brass and copper surfaces were studded with elegant, if antiquated, controls. Darwen and his friends had crossed over into Silbrica many times before, but rarely had they done so with such a sense of dread at what would be waiting for them on the other side.

"Ready?" asked Darwen.

Alex—slim, black, her hair pulled away from her face with a spangled headband—scowled.

"Never," she said, "but we always go through anyway. How about you go through first and make sure it's safe? I can bring Rich through myself."

It was Rich's turn to scowl. He hadn't gotten over the fact that of the three of them he was the only one who couldn't open the portals into Silbrica by himself. Darwen had been the first—the true mirroculist—but somehow, no one knew why, Alex had picked up the gift during Hillside Academy's trip to Costa Rica. Rich didn't say much about it, but Darwen knew it rankled.

"No," said Darwen. "We go through as we always did: together. Rich," he added, "take this." From his pocket Darwen drew what looked like a toy gun fashioned from wood, copper, and brass, and placed it in Rich's large pink hand. "Weazen lent it to me," Darwen explained. "You have about ten shots before it will need recharging, so make them count."

"Why don't I get a cool blasty thing?" Alex demanded.

"Because you get this," said Darwen, handing her what looked like a miniature snow globe containing a watch mechanism.

"Ooh," she said. "Nice. What is it?"

"We're not supposed to be here," Darwen explained, staring at the shimmering rectangle of light in front of them, "and the portals will seal once Greyling detects us. We have five minutes from the moment we step through the first gate. That," he said, glancing at the device in Alex's hand, "will keep track of time."

"So it's a clock," said Alex, disgruntled. "Rich gets a blasty thing and I get a clock. Awesome."

"If it's any consolation," said Darwen, unfolding a square of grease-stained cardboard, "I've got nowt but this dodgy-looking map Weazen drew on a pizza box."

"*Nowt* means nothing," said Alex sagely to Rich. "One of his primitive Lancashire dialect words."

Darwen opened his mouth to protest but changed his mind. Alex didn't have the kind of filter that stopped most people from speaking their mind, but she never intended to be mean. "This is for Mr. Peregrine," he said. "So let's get it right."

Rich and Alex nodded seriously. It was Mr. Peregrine who had first shown Darwen the way into Silbrica, and since then he had been a mentor and friend to the three students. But sometime before Christmas, Mr. Peregrine had been replaced with a terrible insect-like creature disguised in a suit made of flesh. The real Mr. Peregrine—it turned out—

had been abducted by Greyling, once a member of the Silbrican Council of Guardians but now a powerful and ruthless villain whose armies of scrobblers and gnashers were bent on taking over the world beyond the mirrors. Darwen and his friends had been trying to locate Mr. Peregrine for months without success, but at last they had a solid lead.

"One more thing," Darwen said. "The loci we have to pass through will all be dangerous. Greyling has deliberately connected places to make it as difficult as possible to reach our destination."

"Wait!" exclaimed Rich. "What?"

"On three," said Darwen, not looking at them. "One. Two. Three."

Alex clicked the timer device and they stepped through the first portal.

There was a bright light and a buzz of power as they crossed over. They had to shield their eyes aginst the glare on the other side, so it took a moment for them to realize that they were standing next to a battered and ancient-looking boat on a beach unlike any they had ever seen. The sand was a brilliant blue and shifted beneath their feet, rippling like water. The water, by contrast, was a milky amber color and quite still.

"Okay," said Alex. "Fairly weird."

"It's Silbrica." Rich shrugged, stirring the air in front of his face with a broad, sweaty hand. "Of course it's weird. Weird is okay, though. I'll take weird over terrifying and deadly. Where to next?"

Darwen studied the pizza box lid. He could feel the sweat breaking out on the back of his neck. "That way," he said, pointing at an unlikely looking grove of palm trees. He took a step, releasing their hands, but the ground seemed to collapse beneath him and he sank into the sapphire-colored crystals up to his waist.

"Whoa!" exclaimed Alex, reaching out and grasping Darwen's flailing right hand. Holding his ground carefully, Rich did the same, bracing himself against the ancient boat.

"Still just weird, or are we getting close to terrifying and deadly?" said Alex.

"Just weird," said Rich.

"It's fine," said Darwen, trying to sound upbeat. "I'm nearly out."

"Let's make it completely out, shall we?" said Rich, his voice suddenly urgent.

"We've got loads of time," said Alex, checking the mechanism in the crystal sphere.

"No," said Rich, his eyes fixed on the blue sand about a hundred yards away, "we really don't."

There, between the palm tree grove and the edge of the unnaturally still water, something was stirring in the blue sand. Most of it was invisible, but poking through the water was what appeared to be a large, triangular fin.

"Shark!" shouted Alex. "Worse, Silbrican shark! Terrifying and deadly right on schedule!"

"Just get him out," Rich retorted, leaning back and dragging Darwen till the joint in his shoulder sang with pain.

Darwen glanced back. The shark—or whatever it was—had been tracing a slow semicircle through the blue crystals, but now it had locked onto them and was closing fast, leaving a long furrow behind it in the sand. Darwen tried to clamber out, but he seemed to sink deeper.

"Keep still," said Rich.

Darwen tore his eyes from the shark thing, which was getting faster, and locked onto Rich's. The bigger boy met his gaze levelly and, almost under his breath, said, "Okay, Alex, now!"

Darwen stayed quite still as they tugged, feeling himself sliding up and out.

"Into the boat!" said Rich.

They half clambered, half vaulted over the wooden side and in.

The shark thing almost broke the surface of the sand, showing a slick gray body speckled with leopard-like spots, and then it was diving, rubbing the hull of the boat so the whole thing rolled and threatened to capsize. A moment later the creature, whatever it was, was gone.

"Chuffin' 'eck," Darwen muttered.

"What is it with this place?" Alex demanded. "I swear it's designed to make you think everything is nice and happy, then WHAM. Where would you most like to go? The beach? Sure. But of course, this is a beach that can kill you, because it's Silbrica and that's just how we roll here."

"Those palms are a portal," said Darwen, wiping the sweat from his face. The heat was becoming unbearable. "We've got to get over there."

"Check this out," said Rich, taking a long pole of dark, lacquered wood from the floor of the boat.

"What's that, an oar?" asked Alex.

"More like a punt," said Rich, standing up. "Here goes nothing."

He pushed one end of the pole into the blue sand and shoved. The boat shot forward at an impossible speed, like a waxed sled on snow. Darwen found himself laughing with delighted relief as Rich fought to steady himself on the plank seats.

"This thing has some serious horsepower," Rich observed as he recovered his balance.

He punted twice more, trailing the pole in the sand to steer, and in moments, they were gliding into the grove, the unnaturally regular spacing of the trees leaving no doubt that what lay before them was actually a series of portals. Darwen checked the pizza box. "That one," he said.

Rich plunged the pole deeper into the sand and the punt glided slowly to a halt. He was about to clamber out, his broad pink face split by a contented grin, when Alex grabbed him.

"Wait!" she shouted. "Didn't your daddy tell you to look both ways before crossing the street?"

Rich gave her an incredulous stare, but Alex just nodded significantly at the undulating blue sand. As they looked, one of the ripples broke and another triangular, spotted dorsal fin crested above the surface for a moment, then sliced lazily down again.

"You can take your chances wading around among whatever they are," she said, "but I'd suggest getting the boat up against the portal and hightailing it through before they can take a chunk out of us."

"Agreed," said Darwen.

"Let's just hope they can't jump," Alex added darkly.

Rich nodded hastily, then used the pole to bump the punt right up against the palm trees framing the portal Weazen had indicated. Like other Silbrican gateways Darwen had seen over the last few months, the doorway looked like it had grown out of the very earth, but it was also studded with dials and controls, valves and levers, all made of finely wrought glass and copper and brass. He reached over, pushed a button, then pulled the lever next to it and waited as the portal hissed out a blast of steam and shimmered into golden life.

"How about I try this time?" said Rich hopefully.

"And have it fire you back yonder to be lunch for those sand-sharky things because you're not a mirroculist?" said Alex.

"Good point," said Rich. "Darwen?"

Darwen took their hands, and together they leapt out of the boat and through the glittering doorway.

They were standing in a muddy clearing surrounded by towering scarlet grasses whose feathery stalks reached twenty feet into the still, silent air. A damp path of beaten earth stretched ahead between the walls of vegetation. Somewhere in the distance something called, a ragged *kraaak* sound that Darwen thought was vaguely familiar.

"Ohhh-kay," Alex ventured. "Doesn't seem so bad so far. And at least we know where to go."

Straight down the path, no more than a couple of hundred yards away, they could make out another ring of portals, these fashioned into the braided hoops of the gargantuan grass.

"Let's do it," said Rich. He took a few steps along the trail and grunted as his foot splashed in the soft ground. "Marsh," he said, peering off into the red grasses. "There's probably all kinds of stuff living out there. Better stick to the path."

Darwen was gazing to the other side, his eyes locked sightlessly on a patch of particularly tall grass as his brain teased at the sound he had just heard. It reminded him of something. Not something in Silbrica, but something from home, from England, and his associations with it were good, even excited. He tried to summon the sound once more, and as he was trying to mentally re-create it, it came again.

Kraak!

This time he knew it. It was almost the same as the call of a great grey heron, a bird he'd heard when he'd visited the waterfowl sanctuary at Martin Mere with his parents. He remembered being in one of the hides watching a flock of pink-footed geese, a pair of miniature binoculars grasped tightly in his fingers. . . .

Suddenly, the gigantic red stalks he had been staring at shifted, interrupting his reverie, and he saw not blades of grass, but carefully camouflaged feathers of russet and crimson, a pair of bright, hard eyes, and a needle-sharp beak as long as a car.

He cried out, leaping forward just as the colossal birdlike creature lunged. Its bill stabbed into the sandy dirt only inches from where he had been standing. It was so big it plunged the whole path into shadow, and for a second Alex and Rich could only gaze up in rapt horror.

"Run!" shouted Darwen.

They didn't need telling twice. Alex was off like a shot, and Rich followed, his lumbering, pounding footsteps much noisier than the light, mincing steps of the bird on its telegraph pole legs. It lunged at Darwen's back, missing only by inches. Undeterred, it stepped over him with one immense stride, blocking him from the portal that was his goal. It turned its narrow face and unblinking eyes to face him. Behind it, Alex and Rich were off and running, but the heron thing had lost interest in them. Its focus was all on Darwen. Out here in the open, Darwen had no chance, so he did the only thing he could. He leapt sideways into the grass forest.

He landed in water up to his ankles, took three messy steps, and then stopped, eyes turned upward, waiting. For a moment nothing happened. Then, without making any sound at all, the great heron thing stalked slowly into view. It moved with almost impossible care, and was absolutely motionless between steps.

Darwen thought of Alex's little "clock." He was wasting time, and the longer he tried to inch toward the portal from here, the more likely the heron thing would get him. For a brief moment he wondered what that would be like, the spear-like beak stabbing at him from on high, but he pushed the thought from his mind, remembering something his father had told him:

Herons are stealth hunters. They aren't built for pursuit.

As the thought struck him, something moved in the grass a few yards from him. It was long and black, and reached through the stalks beside him to land carefully in the wet ground: it was one of the heron thing's feet. Darwen looked up again and saw the great bird, its head perfectly level, its bright, unblinking eyes fixed, gliding past like some lethal, animated crane on a building site.

It was now or never. He took three silent steps back toward the path, then pushed through the last of the grass stalks, turned up toward the portal where Rich and Alex were waiting for him, and broke into a flat run. He didn't need their cries of panic to know the bird was coming after him. He felt its shadow on him, felt the wind of its first lunging stab as it darted its beak into the silty ground, but he did not look back.

A couple of seconds later, he knew it had given up the chase. Darwen thought gratefully of his dad: without that memory of the two of them at Martin Mere, Darwen would never have tried to outrun the heron.

"Quite the safari we're on, huh?" said Alex as Darwen reached the portals. "Like being in Costa Rica all over again. Only instead of jaguars and snakes, it's giant, freak-show birds that are trying to kill us."

They both looked badly shaken.

"Well," said Rich as they prepared to step through the gate, "the next locus can't be as bad as this."

"I really wish you wouldn't say things like that," Darwen muttered. Then he led them through the shimmering rectangle.

They landed hard on cold, wet rock in a howling gale that blew rain in great horizontal sheets. They were high on a mountainside, which was treeless except for the twisted and misshapen trunks that formed the portal ring they had just come through. All three of them bent their heads and turned their backs into the wind.

"It's looking a bit black o'er Bill's mother's," Darwen remarked dryly.

"Huh?" said Alex. "Black or Bill's mother's what?"

"It's looking black *over* Bill's mother's *house*," Darwen explained. "Like you're looking out over the town and there are clouds overhead."

"What?" said Alex.

"It's an expression," said Darwen. "Means the weather is going to be grim."

"The weather *is* grim," said Alex.

"I know," said Darwen. "It's a kind of joke."

"Who's Bill?" asked Rich.

"No one," said Darwen. "It's just something mi dad used to say."

"I don't get it," said Alex.

Darwen had to shout to be heard. "Never mind," he yelled, checking the pizza box. "It's not important." Then, pointing right into the mouth of the gale, he called, "That way!"

"Of course," Alex retorted.

"How long?" Darwen called back as he trudged through the driving rain, already soaked to his skin.

Alex consulted the glass device, wiping the water away as best she could. "Three minutes," she said. "Greyling *really* doesn't want anyone finding a way through, does he?"

Darwen started walking faster.

They covered about fifty yards, but the rain was so heavy they could barely see ten.

"You sure this is right?" shouted Rich.

Darwen wasn't, but he said nothing and pressed on, eyes scouring the blasted windswept slopes for signs of another portal.

"Two minutes, twenty seconds!" called Alex.

Darwen gritted his teeth. There was nothing up here. They had taken a wrong turn.

"What's that?" demanded Rich. "There in the mountainside."

"It's nothing," said Darwen.

"No," Rich insisted. "There, see? Looks like a cave."

"I don't see it," said Darwen.

"Two minutes," said Alex.

"Follow me," said Rich. He pushed ahead, veering to the right and up a slope of ragged scree and scattered boulders. The wind seemed fiercer here, and Darwen was actually blown back a step. He stooped till he was almost bent double, and managed a few faltering steps. When he looked up, he could see that Rich was right.

It was a cave, Darwen supposed, but as soon as they were inside the opening, they could see that the walls pulsed with an eerie blue light as if the very stone was breathing. There were alcoves set into the wall, though whether they had formed naturally or been carved was hard to say. What was clear was the system of brass numbers set above them, and the ornate switch mechanisms that brought them online. Darwen rubbed the rain from his eyes, shuddered at the chill of the cave, and with one hurried look at his sodden cardboard map chose the third alcove. He pushed a button, grabbed Alex and Rich by their damp, cold hands, and stepped in.

As Darwen gaped, stricken with dread and fear, Alex leaned in and whispered, "It's looking black o'er Bill's mother's."

Darwen nodded seriously. It was.

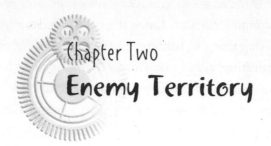

Chapter Two
Enemy Territory

They were indoors, but this was no cave, and the air was hot, thick with the tang of acrid smoke, and thrumming with the drone and clank of heavy machinery. They crouched together, huddled in the corner of what seemed to be a large factory, shielded by heaped crates and stacked metal refuse. Around them were brick furnaces with great iron hoods. Blackened, oily smokestacks rose up from filthy engines draped with chain and cable. There were trucks loaded with coal. There were nameless hulking pieces of equipment sprouting drills and funnels, plows and tendrils of wire. And there were scrobblers.

Lots of them.

They were lumbering about in their clumsy helmets, goggles over their bright red eyes, their huge muscles tight beneath their greenish skin, their yellowing, overlarge fangs showing between heavy, animal jaws.

Darwen tore his eyes away, his heart hammering. These were Greyling's servants and soldiers. The scrobblers were intent on their work, but he couldn't expect to remain undetected for long.

"We need to find *this*," Darwen hissed, showing the increasingly smeared and battered cardboard panel on which Weazen had scrawled something that looked like a flying saucer with a studded outer rim. "I need to pull one of these electronic box things from the edge and take it through to the next portal."

"Remember that little screen you had back in September when we first went into Silbrica?" Alex said, her eyes still fixed on the milling scrobblers. "The thing that meant they couldn't see us? That would be useful to have about now, don't you think?"

"It got broken, remember?" Darwen hissed back.

"So we brought a clock instead," said Alex, deadpan. "One minute, fifteen seconds, by the way."

"There!" said Rich, pointing between a pair of smokestacks.

Darwen stared through the industrial fog, swallowing back the urge to cough, and saw the dish-like apparatus, its rim pocked with metal boxes the size of his fist. "Cover me," he said, gathering into a racing crouch. "Then meet me on the other side. There should be another group of portals just like this. Be quick."

Alex stayed him with a hand. "I'm faster than you," she said.

"What?" Darwen sputtered. "No! This is my task—"

"No, it's not," said Alex.

"The Peregrine Pact, remember?" Rich agreed. "It's our fight too. If this could help save Mr. P . . ."

Darwen turned to look at him, and in that instant, Alex bolted out into the factory.

With a cry of surprised frustration, Darwen got to his feet. "Make sure she gets through," he said to Rich, who was already up and aiming Weazen's blaster.

A great bellow of rage went up from the nearest scrobblers as they spotted Alex. Then they were grabbing shovels and wrenches to use as weapons as they lumbered toward her. Alex bobbed and weaved, feinted right, then left as she shot through the factory. One of the scrobblers—clearly a guard rather than a worker—turned a long and lethal-looking energy weapon in her direction and fired. It shot a wandering shock of light that caught the edge of a furnace and exploded with a bright orange flare and a bellow of sound.

Rich ducked away, but a moment later he was up again, aiming Weazen's blaster with amazing composure. The weapon kicked once in his hands, and the scrobbler was thrown backward before it could get off a second shot.

Darwen looked for the other group of portals. Spotting them on the far side of the factory, he sprinted deliberately away from Alex, shouting to draw the scrobblers' attention. How long would she need? Ten seconds? Twenty? He looked over his shoulder once to see if she had reached the saucer apparatus, but when he turned back, two scrobblers were closing on him. One was squat and trailed a piece of heavy pipe in its massive fist; the other was bigger, rangier, and had a coil of steel cable that it was flicking back and forth like a whip. Darwen heard the crack of Rich's blaster somewhere close to Alex and knew he would be getting no help from that quarter.

The scrobbler with the cable lashed it suddenly in his direction, and Darwen flinched to his left, hearing the lethal snap of the thing inches from his face as he fell onto his side. The squat scrobbler took a couple of hasty strides and swung the pipe at his head. Darwen rolled, and the flagstone beside him cracked in a shower of grit.

Darwen skittered backward, struggling to his feet as the bigger scrobbler cocked his whip hand again. Darwen took a chance, lunging toward the other one. It pivoted, unsure what to do. As he heard the cable come scything through the air, Darwen dived and rolled on the hard floor. The whip flashed above him, lashing the other scrobbler hard across the face so that a great gash opened beneath its goggles. The creature shrieked with pain and rage and took a vengeful step toward its companion.

In that instant Darwen was up and gone.

All around him the reverberations of the machinery were now topped by the bellows of the scrobblers and the fizz and roar of weapons fire. As Darwen wheeled to the left, a truckload of coal beside him exploded into the air, showering him with hot sparks. He cried out and brushed them from his arms and hair, but he did not stop running. Rounding a corner, he saw Alex, perched on top of the saucer-shaped contraption, tugging something from the rim, while Rich stood beneath her methodically aiming and firing as the scrobblers emerged from cover.

"Got it!" Alex shouted, starting to climb down. "Catch!"

She flung it at Darwen, who reached for it with one hand as it sailed toward him. It bounced off his outstretched fingers, turning slowly in the air as he dived underneath it. It fell neatly into his stomach and he clamped it there, shooting a baleful look at Alex.

"What?" she said. "Oh, and by the way? Forty seconds."

"Go!" shouted Rich, still standing guard and loosing off another whistling shot that exploded somewhere deep in the factory behind them.

They ran, feeling the weight of the smog in their lungs, their knees unsteady with exertion and panic, till they saw the cluster of gates.

"Number four!" Darwen called to Alex, who got there first.

She was through before Darwen reached the portal. He reached behind him, snatching Rich's hand and pulling him into the shimmering curtain of light.

They were outside, surrounded by gusting, yellowish smoke that made it impossible to see much beyond the rough gravelly stone at their feet.

"Last one," said Darwen, coughing. "We have to get to a portal somewhere over . . ."

He paused, looking around.

The smoke was thicker than it had been in the factory, but it smelled different, like bad eggs.

"Sulfur," said Rich as the wind shifted, revealing a beaten ash path toward a precipice. He stooped and picked up an irregular pockmarked stone. "Pumice," he decided. "We're on top of a volcano."

"Great," said Alex, who was further up the path. "And you are really not going to like where this portal is."

Darwen and Rich took a few quick steps so they could see what she was looking at. They were standing at the very rim of the volcano crater. In front of them was a great rock bowl spewing smoke and steam from innumerable crags and gashes, and deep in the center was a thick black ooze that bubbled as they watched, the surface revealing a smoldering red heart. Spanning the crater was an iron bridge no more than three feet across, and in the middle was a wheel-like cluster of metal gateways where four huge scrobblers stood motionless in pod-like sentry boxes.

"Twenty-five seconds," said Alex.

"I'll lead," said Rich, readying the blaster.

But at that instant they heard the telltale noise of the portals they had just come through. The scrobblers from the factory had followed them.

"Cover the rear!" shouted Darwen, purposefully setting his foot onto the iron bridge. It stirred slightly beneath him, swaying against its cable suspension. As Rich hesitated and fired a preliminary shot back the way they had come, Darwen locked his eyes on the sentries up ahead. They still hadn't moved. He took a step, then another, and he was running now, pounding the iron causeway so that it rang beneath his feet, Alex hot on his heels, Rich a step or two behind her. Darwen was halfway across when he saw a greenish light begin to glow around the sentry boxes. Moments later, the scrobblers inside them began to move.

Darwen kept running, but only because he didn't know what else to do. He had no weapon, and he was sprinting right into the arms of the scrobbler sentries. There was no room to hide or dodge, and one wrong step would mean a terrible fall into boiling lava.

He risked a look back and Alex ran right by him. Rich, meanwhile, had stopped shooting. He turned and Darwen could read the anguish in his face: the blaster was out of power.

"Come on!" Alex urged. "Those scrobblers ahead. They're . . . I don't know. Slow. Like they're just waking up."

She was right. Instead of massing for assault, they seemed hesitant, uncertain, barely aware of what was happening. Darwen reached inside himself for another burst of speed and ran right between two of them and onto the central platform. One turned vaguely toward him, extending a heavily muscled arm.

Darwen shrugged it off, catching a glimpse of the monster's face. He was surprised to see watery blue eyes beneath the goggles. Every scrobbler he'd encountered before had had red eyes. But before Darwen could make any sense of this, the monster tried to clutch at him. He elbowed it hard in the ribs and the scrobbler staggered, misjudged its reach for the rail, and fell silently off the platform and down.

Darwen caught his breath, stepped into the inner circle of rusty, lifeless gates, and chose. He jammed the component into a socket above the controls and threw a lever. Slowly, very slowly, he heard the portal humming into life.

"Quick," shouted Alex, slithering between two of the sentinels as they reached for her. If they had indeed been asleep, they were waking fast. "And you have eight seconds!" she added, wide-eyed.

Darwen pushed a button and flicked a switch. There was a hiss of steam and something thunked into place. "Rich!" he called.

Rich was running along the bridge and the scrobblers were coming after him, shooting so that one of the cables popped from its bracket and the whole causeway sagged dangerously.

"Four seconds!" called Alex.

At his back, the portal flickered into life, and Darwen backed into it, arm outstretched. He felt Alex push past him and through. And then, as his vision filled with the blundering scrobblers trying to reach for them, Rich was grabbing his hand and pulling himself in.

On the other side, Darwen didn't even turn to see where they were before dragging a wire from the metal gate frame so that its energy died, and with it any opportunity for the scrobblers to pursue them.

And that's when they heard the most welcome sound in the world.

"Darwen Arkwright!" said a tiny, familiar voice.

Darwen turned, took in the rich green of the forest and its ornate fountain, then found the source of the voice hovering a few feet in front of him.

"Hello, Moth," he said.

Chapter Three
Lightborne

It had been the beginning of the school year when Darwen Arkwright moved from his home in a little northern English town to Atlanta, Georgia, following his parents' death in a car accident. That was also when he had discovered that he was a mirroculist, a person with that rarest of gifts: the ability to pass through certain mirrors to the land of Silbrica beyond. Central to this discovery was Mr. Octavius Peregrine, the old man who ran the odd little mirror shop in the mall close to Hillside Academy, where Darwen went to school. But while Darwen, Rich, and Alex had thwarted Greyling's plans in Costa Rica, they had not been able to prevent Mr. Peregrine from being captured, so that despite all they had achieved they had come home feeling defeated.

That had been two months ago, and the sense of failure had only gotten worse. Darwen, Rich, and Alex had searched in their own world and in Silbrica, but they'd turned up nothing. Moth's forest had been sealed off right after Mr. Peregrine's disappearance, so they were sure that the two events were connected. But no matter how hard they had tried to find a way into the forest locus and whatever clues it might contain, they had been unable to find a point of entry. Then, one Thursday night in May, just as the Atlanta heat had started to swell into the stifling beginnings of a real Southern summer, Darwen had been sitting at the desk in his room, toying hopelessly with some pre-algebra homework, when he had heard a stifled squeak from the closet.

He flung the closet door open and gazed into the reflective surface hanging behind it. Though the object appeared to be an oven door, it was actually a portal to Silbrica that Mr. Peregrine had sent him at Christmas. Now that the sun had just dipped below the horizon, activating the portal, Darwen could see into the metal chute that led down to the Great Apparatus.

He could also see an odd purple face with bright pink eyes. They were wide and staring, and the face looked scared, desperate even, as its gaze flicked from Darwen back down the chute behind it. The figure it belonged to was no more than the size of monkey, utterly bald, and clad in what looked like a miniature uniform of brown leather.

"Help me, Darwen Arkwright!" the little creature begged, its voice high and piercing. It looked crumpled with exhaustion and was holding its side as if wounded. "There are scrobblers in pursuit and they are equipped with terrible hunting creatures that already have my scent."

"There are scrobblers coming here?" Darwen demanded, careful not to touch the portal, since that would allow the creature to pass through.

The creature tried a different approach. "I bring news from the dellfey called Moth," it squeaked with another panicked look over its shoulder.

"Moth!" gasped Darwen. "Here."

And he reached inside.

The creature's transformation was instantaneous. It sprang forward, all injury or tiredness forgotten, and seized Darwen's fingers in a tiny but viselike grip. Then it turned slightly and called, "Forward!" over its shoulder. Darwen tried to pull away, but the creature's strength was remarkable for its size, and Darwen was distracted by the way the chute behind the mirror had filled up with identical little uniformed creatures with pink eyes.

They streamed up to the mirror and, as Darwen unwittingly held the portal open, hopped right into his bedroom and huddled around him, taking fast hold of his clothes. Their hands were no more than half the size of his, but they were strong, with long bony fingers ending in sharp little nails that dug in when he fought them.

The last of them to come through was the one that had pretended to be hurt, and it did a happy sort of skip around the room before huddling in with the others and getting a good grip on his jeans.

"Sorry!" chorused a dozen shrill voices.

"You lied to me!" Darwen exclaimed. "You don't know Moth!"

"Sorry, Darwen Arkwright," added the leader, climbing deftly onto the shoulders of his fellows so that he could reach up to Darwen's face, "but this is Necessary."

So saying, the creature clamped a hand over Darwen's mouth and held it in place. Darwen struggled again, but absurd though the little creatures were, they clearly meant business and were alarmingly strong. They had earnest, hopeful faces and wore worried smiles, even as they—seemingly reluctantly—gripped him mercilessly into stillness. Apart from their largely human faces and their minuscule pants, jerkins, and boots, they looked a little like cuter and more anxious versions of hairless cats, or skinny piglets walking on their hind legs.

Darwen pitched suddenly, throwing all his weight to his left so that he fell heavily, but his captors adjusted with uncanny speed, and none of them were caught beneath him. They then swarmed, pinning him to the ground as the Lilliputians did to Gulliver, so that Darwen wound up worse off than he had been when he was standing. For their part, the little creatures seemed positively delighted by this development and they squeaked and chirped as if this was all a great deal of fun.

"If you promise not to cry out," said the leader, looming over him and speaking in a high, squeaky voice, "we will let you speak."

Darwen considered trying to bite him, but thought better of it, and lay still. The purplish creatures watched him with slightly comic attentiveness and then, as one, took their hands off him.

Darwen considered yelling at them, but he did not want to disturb his aunt and, despite his outrage, felt that he had nothing to fear from these odd little visitors. "Thank you," he managed to say.

The one that had spoken licked its lips apprehensively, and then smiled so widely that its curious little face seemed to split in half.

"Moth was right!" the creature announced. "You are Nice."

He—or she, it wasn't clear to Darwen whether the speaker was male or female and they all looked pretty much the same—spoke with delight, clapping his minuscule hands together and beaming at him.

Darwen didn't feel remotely *nice*, but he focused on the purple creature and blurted, "So you do know Moth? Where is she?"

"That I am familiar with the dellfey in question I can veritably attest," said the other, nodding proudly. "That I know her current location is, alas, beyond the reach of my current intelligence."

Darwen blinked as he deciphered this. "What?" he said.

"I know her," said the purple pig thing, looking abashed. "I don't know where she is."

"Why didn't you just say that?" snapped Darwen.

"I would hate to be discourteous," said the speaker, giving a horrified look at his fellows—all nodding furiously—"particularly on this our first meeting."

"Whereas jumping on me and pinning me to the floor was really chuffin' polite," Darwen muttered.

"That was Necessary," said the lead piglet. "And now we will take you to the Guardians."

"You work for them," said Darwen sourly. "I should have known."

"Precisely so, Darwen Arkwright," said the piglet, as if Darwen had paid him a compliment. "We do, and when you are calm, we will escort you to your meeting with them."

He said it like this was something that had been scheduled weeks ago. Darwen bit his lip to keep from yelling or otherwise showing how far he was from calm. "Why are there so many of you?" he demanded, swinging his legs over the side of the bed.

"The Guardians feared you might show some reluctance toward accompanying us, so we were authorized to bring such numbers as might reduce difficulties."

"Meaning you're going to drag me to them whether I want to go or not."

"While I would hesitate to use such terms to so esteemed a guest of the council, your grasp of the situation is precise in all significant details."

Darwen rolled his eyes.

"Fine," Darwen snarled. "Lead the way."

The little purple creatures beamed with obvious relief and formed a line, moving in step like little piggy soldiers, waiting for Darwen to reach through the oven door and hold the portal open. One by one they hopped through the glass of the oven door and shot down the chute with giggly cries of *whee!* which did nothing for the aura of military precision they had been trying to convey.

"What *are* you?" Darwen asked after all but one of the creatures had gone through. "I mean, no offense or anything, and I know you work for the Guardians, but does your . . . er, species have a name?"

One of the uniformed figures turned, smiling proudly, and said as if it was obvious, "We are snorkies."

Again, Darwen blinked, but this time he also had to suppress a smile. "And you come from?"

"Silbrica," said the snorkie.

"Well, yes," said Darwen. "But where exactly . . . ?"

But the snorkie just grinned encouragingly and vaulted cheerily through the oven door and down the long slide, shrieking with glee as it went. Darwen sighed, wondering what Rich and Alex would make of the absurd manner of this kidnapping, and climbed in after it.

The chute emptied them out into the hall containing the Great Apparatus with its circle of a hundred portals, but the snorkie commander—who Darwen now saw wore little brass pips on the shoulders of his tunic—led them around to an imposing stone staircase and up to the council chamber, which sat directly above it. By the time he reached the top of the stairs, Darwen found the little purple soldiers huddled around a dark-haired man who was stooping to hear the chirping report of their mission. As Darwen approached, he stood up and turned.

It was Jorge.

Darwen stared. There was no mistaking the tanned, handsome face, though he had discarded the shorts and safari shirt he had worn as their nature guide in Costa Rica for a cream-colored robe belted at the waist and overlaid with a burgundy sash that hung diagonally from one shoulder. He was smiling.

"Welcome, Darwen," he said, glancing at the snorkies, who were hopping from foot to foot in delight at having completed their assignment. "I'm sorry for the manner in which you were brought here."

He smiled self-sconsciously and, in spite of himself, Darwen smiled back, before reminding himself who Jorge was, and the way that the Guardians had been prepared to sacrifice land and even lives to satisfy Greyling back in Costa Rica. He turned deliberately away to consider the council chamber and noticed the transparent globe covering the energy pool. When he saw it last, it had been purple, black, and dying, but it was now a deep amber, flickering red and gold. Around the covered pool were twelve stone thrones, all occupied, save the one Jorge had vacated and one other right next to where Darwen was standing. What had been a circle, however, was now a V shape and Darwen was standing at the open end, facing the point where one throne was a little larger and a higher than the rest.

In it sat an old man with long white hair, bright blue eyes, and a kindly smile. "Please," he said, and his voice was clear and calm. "Have a seat."

Darwen glanced at the empty throne beside him and hesitated, remembering the last time he had been in this chamber, and the way Alex had seemed to fall into a deep sleep when she had sat in one of those stone chairs.

The old man seemed to read his thoughts and chuckled softly. "It is quite safe," he said, "thanks to you. See the energy pool? Full of life and power. You did that."

He smiled so genuinely that Darwen's outrage faltered. But he didn't sit down. "You abducted me," he said. "Like Greyling abducted Mr. Peregrine."

He watched the old man's face for a sign of anger, but his smile only broadened. "I would hardly compare the two," said the old man, shooting an amused glance at the snorkies, who were now watching the conversation with comic anxiety. "Greyling's operatives are rather more . . . er, forceful."

The snorkies nodded furiously and Darwen felt a little more of his anger drain.

"So, Darwen," said the old man, ignoring the fact that Darwen was still standing. "You don't mind if I call you Darwen, do you? Mr. Arkwright seems so formal."

"Yes," said Darwen, flustered. "I mean, no, I don't mind."

"Excellent," the man replied, with another twinkling smile. "And I am Lightborne. My first name is Reginald, but I don't seem able to get anyone to call me that."

The people seated in the other thrones—all of whom wore robes that matched Jorge's—smiled bashfully at one another.

This, Darwen thought, *is all very strange.*

"Jorge, you already know," said the man called Lightborne, "and when we are done talking, you can congratulate him on his promotion to the council. There has been, as you can see, some restructuring in recent days: a measure taken to combat the threat Greyling poses to our two worlds."

"What do you want?" Darwen said. The words just sort of slipped out, and as soon as they had, he felt the urge to apologize for his rudeness.

The man who called himself Lightborne seemed unabashed and merely smiled wider still. "A fair question," he said, "and one I would expect given our recent dealings. There have, I am very sorry to admit, been some serious miscommunications between us, Darwen. Many things lost, as it were, in translation."

"You gave in to Greyling," said Darwen, unable to stop himself. "You would have let him take land, take *children*, if my friends and I hadn't stopped you."

The old man was still smiling, but it was a sadder, more apologetic smile, and he nodded slowly before answering. "You are quite right," he said. "I referred to misunderstandings before, but I'm afraid it went rather further than that. We made, I am ashamed to say, some bad decisions, prompted by fear and desperation." As he said this, he looked around the seated council, and they all looked suitably chastened. Some nodded, others hung their heads.

"But these matters have been resolved," Lightborne continued. "Albeit with some difficulty and with the aforementioned restructuring of the Guardian Council."

"Greyling said there was no council," said Darwen, still defiant in spite of himself. "He said there was a new council with him at its head, that the old council was defeated, gone. . . ."

"And yet," said Lightborne, smiling again. "Here we are. Grey-ling, as we have all learned to our cost, tells lies, Darwen. That is his primary talent." He nodded at the empty chair. "Are you sure you won't have a seat? I don't mind if you would rather stand, but I think you would be more comfortable sitting, and I would feel less like a school principal talking to a student who has been sent to his office."

He smiled his twinkling smile again, and Darwen was unsettled at how much the old man's manner reminded him of Mr. Peregrine. He sat down. Immediately he felt a surge of relief that was almost physical, as if the weariness of the day was being drained away and new energy pumped into him. Jorge patted his shoulder reassuringly and returned to his seat.

"There now," said Lightborne. "That wasn't so bad, was it?"

Darwen did not know what to say. A part of him wanted to tell them all exactly where they could get off, but another part was desperate to have the council on his side again.

Still, there were things he needed to know, things he needed to hear them admit.

"When I first came to America," he said at last, "you already knew who I was, didn't you? Mr. Peregrine called me by name the first time I met him. You knew I might be a mirroculist."

Lightborne's eyes narrowed. He hadn't expected this, and the question seemed to put him on his guard. "One of the tasks of the gate-keepers is to be alert for a new mirroculist," he said, studying the backs of his hands, "or someone who might become one, particularly if something has happened to the current mirroculist."

"Like what?" asked Darwen.

Lightborne shrugged, something of his smile returning. "Any num-ber of things," he said. "No one lives forever, Darwen, but usually the mirroculist simply grows out of his gift."

"Grows out of it?" Darwen echoed. "What do you mean?"

"All good things come to an end, Darwen," said Lightborne. "You know that. The mirroculist is on his way to becoming an adult. The gift comes during the transition but fades as that transition completes. You cannot become a mirroculist till you are eleven, but by the time you are sixteen, the gift will have passed to another. This should have been explained to you before. I apologize."

"I don't understand," gasped Darwen, hating the words even as he said them. "I could just *lose* it? I could just go back to being . . . what I was, without any warning? One day I'll just be me again?"

"As you say," said Lightborne. "But you will have had adventures others could never even imagine, and you can do great good for your world and ours so long as you have the gift."

Darwen felt sick. No more portals, no more Moth, or Weazen, no more forests just beyond his closet, no more adventure, no more of that private, secret sense of home, no more being . . .

Special.

Anything.

"Sixteen?" he said, and it was like saying the word began a stop-watch in his head, a rapid counting down to the day he would no longer be able to cross over through the mirrors.

"By sixteen, yes," said Lightborne. "But that's still four years of wonders in store for you, Darwen, isn't it?"

Four years. Four minutes. Darwen's head was spinning. He was glad he was sitting down. He just wished they all weren't looking at him. Darwen stared at Lightborne, saying nothing, blinking as his vision began to swim. Lightborne lowered his eyes, gazing at the eddying currents of the energy pool, and most of the council members did the same. The polite, awkward silence extended to minutes.

"So," Darwen managed, clearing his throat when the word stuck, "what do you want from me?"

"We want to make amends," said Lightborne. "Heal our alliance so that we can work together against our common enemy."

"Greyling," said Darwen.

"Greyling," repeated Lightborne. "We see now that what he attempted in Costa Rica was only the beginning. He is gathering forces, taking over areas of Silbrica and—we think—establishing operations bases in your world too. We do not completely understand how he is able to use some of the portals connecting our two worlds, but there is no doubt that he has found a way. And these are no minor incursions. He is preparing for large-scale invasion, and he will not stop until both worlds bow before him. War is coming, and we would like the mirroculist to help us stand against him."

"I'll bet you would," said Darwen.

Lightborne shifted in his chair, but his benevolent smile did not stall.

"You need me," said Darwen. "For now. There are still things only I can do, and I'm guessing that I'm not the only one who isn't too happy about your recent strategies and decisions."

Jorge shot Lightborne a look, and the whole council seemed tense and watchful, but Lightborne's smile grew wider, and he nodded thoughtfully.

"You are wiser than your years, Darwen Arkwright," he said. "You are essentially correct. And I will extend your realization further: we are preparing for war, and we need allies. The Guardians are considerably stronger with the mirroculist standing beside them. You have friends in Silbrica who could be of great value to us in the weeks to come, and there are many others you do not yet know who must be persuaded to stand with us against Greyling. You will make a better envoy to them than anyone sitting on the council. So yes, we need you. Will you stand with us, flawed as our behavior has been, for the sake of Silbrica and the ruin Greyling will bring to it?"

Darwen almost said yes right away, but though he was still reeling from what Lightborne had told him about his gift, he managed not to. There were two other essential demands he had to make while his position was still strong.

"What about Mr. Peregrine?" he asked. "Did Jorge tell you about what happened to him?"

"Yes, Jorge has informed us of everything he learned in Costa Rica," said Lightborne. "Recovering Octavius, whatever his condition, will be our first priority if you agree to join us. We will give you every assistance in finding and rescuing him."

"With my friends," said Darwen. "My human friends, I mean. Alex and Rich."

Lightborne frowned and tipped his head on one side. "We do not think it wise," he said carefully, "to involve civilians in this enterprise."

"That's a deal-breaker," said Darwen, his resolve stiffening. "Everything I do involves Rich and Alex or I don't do it at all."

There was a long, thoughtful pause and Darwen felt that some form of communication passed wordlessly among the Guardians. Eventually, Lightborne nodded.

"As you wish," he said. "You will need to assemble them immediately. You will be our ambassador to all in Silbrica who will unite against the threat Greyling presents."

"And Mr. Peregrine?" Darwen prompted. "You said finding him was your first priority."

"Indeed it is," said Lightborne. "We do not know where Mr. Peregrine is being held, but we have found a way to reach a Silbrican forest locus that had previously been sealed off by Greyling. This, in itself, had struck us as suspicious, but when we learned of the creatures inside—dellfeys, Darwen—and heard that one of them was your friend . . ."

"Moth," said Darwen, the name escaping from his lips.

"Yes, well, it struck us that she might be in possession of information about Mr. Peregrine's abduction. After all, why else would Greyling go through the trouble of sealing off her locus? Unless of course he was simply trying to taunt you." Lightborne paused. "And frankly, that seemed excessive, even for him."

Darwen nodded. The same thought had been running through his head for months. "How can I get to her?"

"Well," Lightborne said tentatively, "all we have is a partial way around the seal."

"Meaning?"

"We have only some of the necessary informations," said Jorge. "A friend of yours has the other informations, but he would tell us nothing until you agreed to work with us." He turned and raised his voice to address the seats, which rose up around the chamber like the stands of a sports arena. High up was a little figure Darwen had not noticed till now, a furry creature munching on what was clearly a slice of delivery pizza. "Are you satisfied, Peace Hunter?"

Weazen rose, though he was so small that didn't make much difference, and nodded. He ambled down toward the center of the chamber, licking cheese off his claws. At the bottom, he belched, grinned his ferrety grin at Darwen, and said simply, "Aye, I'm satisfied."

"Can he come with me?" Darwen asked, all other concerns forgotten.

"Nah," said Weazen before the Guardians could say it for him. "This one is on you and your pals. Keeping the peace sometimes entails stopping people from getting what they want. Once," he added, starting to grin, "I was in a forest locus where this giant slug called Kialblad had taken to eating the eggs of all the Dingle Naiads. Now, Kialblad was *really* fat . . ."

Lightborne coughed discreetly, and Weazen shot him a look.

"Right," the ferret-like creature conceded. "Not relevant. A tale I'll save for some long winter evening in the future. The point is that not everyone in Silbrica is quite so well disposed to yours truly as you. It's just possible that I could make things worse, if you catch my drift. But I will give you this."

It was one of his ornate little blasters.

"Ten shots only," said Weazen. "So make 'em count."

"And this will help you keep track of time," said Jorge, not to be outdone, rising from his seat and producing a crystal sphere full of dials and cogs from somewhere inside his robes.

"So we are agreed," Lightborne said. "The journey will be extremely perilous but with luck . . ."

"Just show me where to go," said Darwen. His delight at seeing Weazen had turned all his other feelings into determination. He needed to be doing something. Now.

"These are the portal numbers we know," said Jorge, producing a crisp piece of paper on which numbers had been carefully inscribed in an elaborate copperplate script. "The problem areas are between this gate and this one."

He showed the list to Weazen, who rubbed his muzzle, then tore the cover off the pizza box, snatched a stub of pencil from his belt, and scribbled the sequence onto the box, filling in the gaps with numbers of his own.

"Good pizza?" Darwen muttered to Weazen, grinning.

"All pizza is good pizza," said Weazen. "It's finding a broken portal close enough to a restaurant that's the trick. Here," he said, handing the greasy cardboard panel to Darwen. "That should do it."

"Very well," said Lightborne, rising and shooting the pizza box a slightly distasteful look. "Then we will await news of your investigations. And Darwen?"

"Yes?"

"Be sure your friends understand the danger they are stepping into if they go with you. Greyling's power is rising. There is much we do not know about what he is doing, but his plans are clearly beyond ambitious. They are massive. Reckless. You have thwarted him twice and both of you have survived. This time, I fear, defeat will bring greater consequences. For the sake of both our worlds, we—and I suppose I really mean *you*—must win. Do you understand?"

Darwen could think of nothing to say to that, so he just nodded, gave Weazen a half smile, and tried to ignore the cold, hollow feeling in his belly.

Chapter Four
Moth's News

And so the five-minute mission had begun, the culmination of which had been Darwen, Rich, and Alex's finding their way to Moth, who now hovered in front of them, the wings of her flying harness whirring like a mechanical dragonfly.

The forest locus had not fared well since it had been sealed off. Many of its trees were spattered with oil and smoke, or raked with gouges as if great machines had blundered around the woods, stripping bark and snapping off branches. The dellfeys themselves looked sooty, and some of them sat on the ground, the wings of their flying devices bent into uselessness as if swatted by some massive scrobbler fist. Darwen frowned, remembering the way they normally flitted through the forest like glimmering fireflies, their elegant copper wings a hummingbird blur.

He should have guessed it would be like this, he told himself—Greyling never left the habitats of the creatures who stood in his way unharmed—but he was angry all the same. Darwen's eyes swept over the ravaged forest and found Rich kneeling in front of the portals Greyling had disabled, seeing if there was a way to get them back online.

Yet, despite the damage to her locus, Moth was smiling.

"You knew Greyling had taken Mr. Peregrine?" asked Darwen.

"Immediately," Moth said.

"That's why Greyling blocked the way in." Alex nodded. "Didn't want you telling us that the Mr. P with us in Costa Rica was really one of those suit things containing the Jenkins insect."

"And you know where he is now?" Darwen pressed.

Moth shook her head sadly, though she was so small that Darwen could hardly see the gesture in the low light.

"I do not," she said. "He came here, but the scrobblers followed. We could do nothing to stop them. They took him, ravaged our forest, and sealed us in. I am sorry."

"It's not your fault," said Darwen, struggling to keep the deflation out of his voice. He had felt sure that if they could get to Moth, there would be a clear trail to wherever Greyling was holding Mr. Peregrine.

The green light in the middle of Moth's flying apparatus had dimmed somewhat, and sensing her weariness Darwen put out his hand so she could settle on it.

"The Guardians have been good to us, Darwen Arkwright," she said. "But we are small and unimportant. They need to send their more powerful agents to stop Greyling."

"Agents?" echoed Rich, looking up from his work on the portals.

"Like secret agents?" tried Alex. "Like black ops and all that?"

"They have the Fixer," said Moth, as if the name would be familiar.

"Who is that?" asked Darwen, considering her closely.

"No one knows," said the dellfey, "but in times past he has put things right for the Guardians."

"How?" said Darwen. Though Moth's tone was approving, she looked uneasy.

"Whatever way he thinks necessary," she said carefully.

"That doesn't sound good," said Alex.

"It is!" said Moth. "The Guardians are Silbrica's friends."

"So what is it about this Fixer that bothers you?" asked Darwen.

35

The dellfey looked at her hands and shrugged. Then, speaking in a small, halting voice that Darwen had to strain to hear, she said, "Some say the Guardians do not ask enough questions about how the Fixer gets the results they want."

Darwen peered at her, but she stepped off his hand, her wings buzzing. She clearly wanted to say no more on the matter.

"The point," said Darwen, closing his eyes for a moment as he pushed these other concerns away, "is that we have to find where Mr. Peregrine is. We figure Greyling kept him alive, that he had to be alive for that flesh-suit thing the Jenkins insect wore to work properly, right? I mean, it's not just a body. That thing moved like Mr. P, even talked like him. We're betting the suits maintain some kind of link to the abducted person."

"But knowing that doesn't really help us find him," said Alex. "So what do we do next?"

"Well," said Rich, standing up and slipping a pair of pliers back into his pocket. "I think I have this portal working again. Should take us directly to the Great Apparatus, so no more sand sharks and scrobbler hangouts on the way back."

"Nice going, Rich!" said Darwen. "Weazen and the Guardians have been trying to pull that off for weeks."

"Huh," said Alex, eyeing him shrewdly. "I knew there was a reason we kept you around."

Rich flushed and stared at her.

"What?" she said. "I was paying you a compliment, man. You thought I was making a crack about you not being a mirroculist?" She rolled her eyes and sighed theatrically. "Nope. Not this time. I swear: no one gets me."

Rich shrugged and nodded. "Actually it wasn't that hard," he said. "Apart from a few snipped wires, all it really needed was the kind of muscle you aren't going to get from a hundred dellfeys."

He said it unselfconsciously, but blushed when Moth gazed at him, impressed, and Alex rolled her eyes.

"Good," said Darwen. "But now we have to find Mr. P. We just have no chuffin' idea where to start looking."

There was a lengthy silence.

"Have you tried his house?" asked Moth.

Darwen, Rich, and Alex stared at the tiny dellfey, speechless.

"His house?" Alex repeated at last.

"We don't know where he lived," Rich admitted, sounding amazed by his own ignorance. "How do we not know where he lived?"

"I always assumed . . ." Darwen began, but couldn't think of how to end the sentence.

"That he lived in the mirror shop?" Alex completed. "We've been in there. Apart from that little kitchen in the back, there was nothing. He must have had a house somewhere. I can't believe we never asked him where it was."

"I may know where he lived," said Moth, "though I do not know how to get there."

Darwen held his breath.

"It is a curious locus," she said, "and it is not in Silbrica, but in your world. A structure. How you might find it, I cannot say, but perhaps this code will help." She screwed her eyes up and recited in a singsong voice, as if the words held no real meaning, "472 West Paces Ferry Road Northwest, Atlanta, Georgia."

Again, the three humans stared at her, humbled.

"Yeah," said Darwen, grinning. "That might help."

Darwen, Rich, and Alex clambered up the metal chute that led from the Great Apparatus to the oven door in Darwen's bedroom. They had been gone almost an hour. Darwen pressed his ear to the door.

His aunt was clearly on the phone: work.

"Get changed," said Darwen.

They had all brought overnight bags with extra clothes, which was just as well. Their Silbrican adventure had left them wet and filthy.

"Turn your backs," Alex commanded.

Moments later, they were ready.

They opened the bedroom door and filed into the kitchen. Honoria was just hanging up the phone and she looked tired. She was wearing a trim black business suit and the silver necklace she always wore at work, but she couldn't hide her irritation and it made her look like someone else entirely.

"Ready to head out?" she asked. "I'll call Eileen."

Eileen was the teenage babysitter who didn't like kids. They all loathed her.

"You aren't going to drive them?" asked Darwen.

"I just don't have time tonight, Darwen," his aunt replied, glancing at where her laptop sat, waiting.

"It's fine," he said. "Eileen. Great."

His aunt closed her eyes again as if she had a headache. "I'm sorry," she said. "But look. This arrived today. I ordered it weeks ago. I have no idea why it took so long. . . ." Some of the irritation was creeping back into her voice, and conscious of it, she stopped and pushed the cardboard parcel over to Darwen. "You are always saying how much you miss British candy, so I thought I'd get you some."

Darwen tore open the box and drank in the contents with his eyes. Bounty bars (both milk chocolate and dark chocolate) and Lion bars with crispy rice, honey sweet Crunchies, and several different kinds of Yorkies.

"Wow!" said Darwen. "Thanks." Then, without a second's hesitation, he pushed the box toward Rich and Alex. "Here," he said. "These are the best."

Rich hesitated, checking Aunt Honoria's face.

"This is special stuff for you," Alex said. "You don't need to share it."

"But I want to." Darwen shrugged. "It's like a bit of where I come from. Try one of these."

They didn't need much persuading, and for the fifteen minutes it took before Eileen arrived, they sampled the candy, compared notes, and laughed happily while Aunt Honoria tapped out e-mails on her laptop.

Darwen took the elevator down with Rich and Alex, and since Eileen was staring blankly ahead, nodding to the music streaming through her earbuds, he muttered, "We'll talk about getting to Mr. Peregrine's house tomorrow at school, yes?"

Alex shot Eileen a glance, then, used to the teenager ignoring them, nodded.

"I'll Google the address tonight," she said. "See how easy it will be to get to. Maybe we could take MARTA and walk."

MARTA was the Atlanta light-rail system.

"We'll need a reason for staying late," Rich added. "Special archaeology club meeting?"

"What about me?" Alex demanded. "Nothing will rouse suspicion more than announcing I've joined your idiot digging club."

"We found scrobbler bones!" Rich protested.

Darwen cut him off. "Just say you have a chorus meeting or something," he said to Alex. "Something that will go late."

"Deal," Alex agreed.

When the elevator doors opened and everyone else stepped out, he stayed where he was, and when he started to say that he wasn't going to come with them, Eileen turned before he had managed to get the sentence out.

"Yeah," she said. "Bye."

Chapter Five
Ghost Stories

"**S**chool," Alex mused as they sat in homeroom the next day. "Some days I can only go on by pretending I'm somewhere else."

"Always so dramatic," said Rich, rolling his eyes as he absently wound his old-fashioned watch. "Let's just get through the day. Then we can check out that address. . . ."

"That's what's so maddening," said Alex. "We have serious stuff to do. Important stuff. But we can't do it because we are stuck here all day. Look around you!" Alex went on, gesturing so wildly that Naia Petrakis and Simon Agu flinched away. "Hillside Academy, ladies and gentlemen, the reason people invented truancy. And what will we be doing today? Well, I'm glad you asked. First we'll march to an assembly where we will see if Principal Thompson has mastered his impression of a robot with hair, and then we'll form another little zombie procession to our first class: English, taught by the oh-so-gifted Rumpelstiltskin—"

"Miss O'Connor," said Miss Harvey, the homeroom teacher, "if I hear you making fun of Mrs. Frumpelstein's name one more time, you will be in detention for a week."

"Sorry, ma'am," said Alex brightly. "I get confused. Every time I take my essays to her office, I expect to find her spinning straw into gold."

"Miss O'Connor . . ." Miss Harvey warned, though Darwen could have sworn he saw the corner of her mouth twitch into the hastily terminated beginnings of a smile. Darwen had not liked Mrs. Frumpelstein since she had set out to rid him of his Lancashire accent, and he sometimes thought the other teachers weren't too keen on her either.

The assembly bell chimed and the students began their march down to the great hall, where they lined up again, and stood in silence while Principal Thompson talked about the installation of a new computer and communication system and the end-of-year talent gala. During this "celebration of all that Hillside is," whatever *that* meant, a new stained glass window would be unveiled, and the students would perform for their parents "in ways befitting their creative gifts and proclivities." Darwen thought it sounded ghastly, but he was not surprised to find Alex's mood much improved.

"Maybe I'll sing," she was musing as the students lined up in the hallway. "Or dance. Or both. Maybe I could do a dramatic scene where the performance involved acting, singing, *and* dancing: you know, show my range."

"It's not a freak show, O'Connor," remarked Nathan Cloten. "We're supposed to be impressing our families with all the skills we've learned so they'll keep paying Hillside's ridiculous fees, not make them run screaming for the exits."

"I don't know, Nate," said Chip Whittley. "The school could probably raise a pot of money just putting her in a tent and charging admission. What do you suppose people will think she is?"

"Yeah," said Barry "Usually" Fails, "some kind of mutant thing from the planet of the . . . *things.*"

"Real witty, Barry," Alex shot back. "I assume there'll be a lack-of-talent gala as well, in which you three will be headlining. What will you be doing? Juggling with one ball, perhaps, or counting to ten with your hands in your pockets? Since y'all have the mental agility of mountain goats, you could demonstrate reading without moving your lips, but we've only got a few weeks to prepare, so we shouldn't be too ambitious."

Barry, who apparently hadn't heard anything after "mountain goats," was now stalking about with his arms spread like a tightrope walker.

"She said *mental* agility, Usually," said Nathan lazily.

"Who's mental?" snarled Barry, dropping the high-wire routine and giving Alex a menacing glare.

"Come on," said Darwen, leading Alex away.

"What *are* we going to do?" asked Rich as they moved off down the hallway, leaving Barry, Chip, and Nathan snickering behind them.

"What do you mean?" asked Darwen.

"The principal said *everyone* had to participate in the gala; weren't you listening?"

"Apparently not," Darwen admitted. He had spent the whole assembly thinking about what they might find at Mr. Peregrine's address.

"Yes," said Mr. Sumners, the math teacher, who happened to be passing. "I couldn't help wondering what your dazzling contribution would be, Arkwright. I assume you have a talent of some sort, yes?"

"Sir, I don't know, sir," Darwen muttered, avoiding the teacher's smug gaze as he had done so many times before.

"Oh, yes," said Mr. Sumners, swaggering cheerily away. "This year's show will certainly be worth the price of admission."

"Maybe I could do a lecture on science or archaeology," Rich said, a slightly panicked look on his face.

"I suppose," said Darwen. "But what am I going to do? Apart from being a mirroculist, I'm rubbish at everything."

"No, you're not," said Rich.

"Yeah?" said Darwen. "What else am I good at?"

"You're a decent soccer player," said Rich.

"Not really," said Darwen. "Not like dazzle-the-parents-with-my-ball-juggling-skills kind of good."

"Then you could . . ." Rich tried.

"What?" Darwen pressed.

For a moment Rich just stood there, thinking furiously, but in the end he just gave a defeated shrug.

"Exactly," said Darwen. "Give me portals to Silbrica to open, or I'm chuffin' useless." He felt his stomach clench because if Lightborne was right, he wouldn't be doing that much longer either.

His gaze slid through the window to the central quadrangle, where the grass was partly covered by a scaffold erected against the clock tower, which was to be home to the new stained glass window. Darwen suspected it would represent something impressive and inspiring—or what Hillside thought was inspiring anyway, like the cringe-worthy statue of "Learning" in the entrance lobby—and it would probably make Darwen feel more than ever that he didn't belong. He was starting to feel that Alex was right: they had real work in Silbrica to do. Being trapped in school, worrying about some ridiculous talent show, felt like a huge waste of time.

The sixth graders filed into their English class and took their seats, chattering about the upcoming gala and how they would dazzle their families. Mrs. Frumpelstein told them to settle down, though she seemed less keen to stomp out the conversation than Darwen would have expected. It was soon clear why.

"Some of you might be looking for ideas for the talent show," she said, smiling with barely suppressed excitement. "We'll have a conversation about what everyone is planning to do. And—for those who are undecided—I have some suggestions for dramatic scenes and monologues."

Alex gave Darwen a look, one eyebrow arched high. Alex had long maintained that Ada Frumpelstein was actually an alien from the Crab Nebula. Rich groaned. He wasn't the only one.

"Is this going to be on the test?" said Barry.

"No, Barry, it's not," said Mrs. Frumpelstein with a sigh.

"Phew!" said Barry, leaning back.

"Mr. Fails," said Mrs. Frumpelstein, "not everything is about tests. Some things are about building you as human beings and giving you the knowledge civilized people are meant to have."

Barry frowned comically, then held up his cell phone. "I don't need to know stuff," he said, quite cheery. "I have Wikipedia."

Mrs. Frumpelstein stared at him, lost for words, then turned for inspiration elsewhere. She found Naia Petrakis.

"Naia," she said, like a woman recently washed overboard and looking for someone to throw her a life preserver. "What are your plans for the talent show?"

"I'm going to sing some Athenian folk songs—in Greek, of course—and perform an ancient dance welcoming the summer after a long, hard winter."

Alex rolled her eyes, but Mrs. Frumpelstein beamed with delight.

"Bobby," she said, turning to Bobby Park, a quiet boy, friendly enough in his way, but private. He never spoke in class unless he was called upon. "What are your plans?"

Bobby shrugged and looked down. "I was going to play my violin," he said. "But I don't have anywhere to practice."

"You stay late at school, don't you?" the teacher asked.

Bobby nodded. "My dad picks me up after work."

"So, why don't you practice in the music room?" asked Mrs. Frumpelstein.

"Yeah," said Barry. "Violins are music, right? So play it in the music room."

Bobby didn't look up. His shoulders moved in a kind of shrug, but he kept his eyes down. Sensing he was upset, the class became quiet.

"What's wrong, Bobby?" asked Mrs. Frumpelstein. "Is there something you want to talk about?"

Bobby shook his head emphatically.

"Come now," said Mrs. Frumpelstein. "It can't be as bad as all that."

Bobby took a little shuddering breath and, without raising his head, whispered, "The music room is haunted."

Nathan Cloten gave a great bark of laughter, and as some of the tension evaporated, Barry started making stupid ghost noises and menacing the girls closest to him.

"There's no such thing as ghosts," said Chip Whittley scornfully.

"What?" Barry exclaimed. "Ghosts are totally real! There's this one guy in London who walks around at night with no head and tries to bite you—"

"With what?" asked Chip Whittley in his usual lazy drawl.

"What do you mean?" said Barry. "With his teeth."

"Which he keeps where, in his pocket?" Nathan scoffed. "He has no head, remember?"

Barry looked uncertain.

"Maybe he carries his head around with him," Barry tried, "or throws it at you, like a bowling ball with teeth. That would be cool."

"Mr. Fails," said Mrs. Frumpelstein wearily. "That's enough." She turned her attention back to Bobby Park, her irritation shifting to concern. "Has someone been telling you stories, Bobby? Trying to scare you, perhaps?"

"No," said Bobby Park. "The room is haunted. I know it is."

Now he sounded both nervous and defiant. Everyone turned to look at him.

Mrs. Frumpelstein leaned forward. "You have some good ghost

stories from your home country, Bobby?" she asked. "Stories your parents tell you?"

Bobby's parents were from Korea.

"I guess," said Bobby, his eyes momentarily confused, "but this was different."

There was a pause. The classroom had become tense and expectant. Bobby still looked uneasy, even scared, and would not make eye contact with anyone.

"Go on," Mrs. Frumpelstein prompted carefully. "We're all friends here. I'm sure there are lots of fun stories about Hillside—" she began.

"I'm not talking about stories," Bobby insisted, his voice only just in control, his face set.

"Not stories?" said Princess Clarkson, smiling sympathetically and moving so that she was almost in his line of vision. "Then what, Bobby? Come on. You can tell us."

Bobby blinked, and Darwen was shocked to see his eyes were shining with unshed tears. Bobby glanced at Princess, who had her actress mother's good looks and blond, wavy hair, then muttered something Darwen couldn't hear.

"What, Bobby?" asked Princess, beaming angelically. "I didn't catch that."

"It wasn't a story," said Bobby through gritted teeth. "I saw it."

Again the tension seemed to escalate like the surge of energy before one of the portals in the Great Apparatus opened.

"Where?" asked Melissa Young, craning to get a better look at Bobby.

"When?" asked her friend, Jennifer Taylor-Berry.

"Two nights ago," Bobby whispered. "After school. I was in the music room practicing Haydn's Serenade. I had played the whole thing through twice, and I was just turning the page to start over when I looked up, and there it was."

"What did it look like?" asked Melissa, her voice hushed.

"Did it have a head?" asked Barry.

"Shut up, Usually," said Jennifer.

"It was shaped like a person," said Bobby, his eyes still down, "but it wasn't solid: just soft gray light. I could make out arms and legs and bits of the face, but I could see the whiteboard and the music stands and the computer screen right through it."

"What did it do?" asked Princess.

"It stayed still for a while," Bobby answered. "Then it moved, sort of walking, but sort of drifting too, like its feet weren't really on the ground."

"Maybe it was like a radio-controlled hovercraft thing," said Barry. "Did it try to bite you?"

This time half the class told him to shut up.

"It didn't make a sound," said Bobby. "Just sort of moved around the room, like it was . . . I don't know . . . exploring it or something, and then it saw me."

Jennifer gasped.

"How do you know?" asked Rich, who looked unnerved by the whole thing.

"It just sort of stopped," said Bobby, "and turned to face me. Looked at me. Then it started coming toward me."

"And?" prompted Melissa.

"And I ran," Bobby said, his eyes wide as if he were there again, seeing it all afresh. Sweat broke out on his face despite Hillside's frigid air conditioning. "I took off. Left my violin and got out of there. Didn't stop running till I got to the front lobby and waited there for my dad to pick me up."

There was a respectful silence, but then Chip Whittley shrugged and grinned at Nathan. "Probably nothing," he said. "A weird reflection off a car outside or something."

"It wasn't a reflection," said Bobby forcefully, his eyes flashing up and latching onto Chip's so that the other boy raised his hands in mock surrender.

"What do you think it was?" asked Genevieve gently.

At first, Bobby just shrugged, but then he swallowed and spoke. "It wasn't real clear, but I think it was a girl, and I *think* she was wearing a Hillside uniform."

Chapter Six
The Peregrine Mansion

For the rest of the day, it seemed that the ghost of Hillside was all anyone could talk about. By lunchtime several students had performed Internet searches of local newspapers for articles about ghostly activity at the school or evidence of past tragedies involving its students, but nothing relevant had turned up. Rather than killing the debate, however, this merely seemed to fuel more speculation.

"Maybe she died when she was older, but her ghost wanted to return to when she was a schoolgirl," Melissa suggested.

"Because her time at Hillside was the happiest in her life?" Alex said wryly. "I know I'd *definitely* want to stay here even after I'm dead."

"Me too," agreed Melissa, missing Alex's joke.

"Maybe she never got into the school and killed herself," said Jennifer, "so her ghost wears the uniform she never got to wear in life."

This was too much for Alex. "Maybe she's still waiting for her acceptance letter," she said.

Melissa nodded thoughtfully.

"Man," said Alex as soon as she was alone with Darwen and Rich. "These kids will do anything for a bit of drama."

"You think Bobby is making it up?" asked Darwen. "He looked pretty rattled."

"You're thinking it's something to do with Silbrica?" asked Rich.

Darwen shook his head. "Ghosts?" he said. "Doesn't sound right. Especially that bit about the uniform. Either it's just in his head . . ."

"Or?" Rich prompted.

"I don't know," said Darwen. "Maybe the school *is* haunted. Stranger things have turned out to be true about this place. One more thing to ask Mr. Peregrine when we find him."

Eileen, when she arrived, was wearing oversized sunglasses that hid half her face, shorts, flip-flops, and a pink halter top with sequins on it. Her earbuds were, as ever, jammed in place, and she was chewing gum, occasionally blowing hard little bubbles and bursting them loudly. She didn't speak to Darwen, Rich, and Alex, but unlocked the car doors and sat there, waiting for them to get in.

"Could you take us to this address?" asked Darwen, avoiding the blank stare of her shades and drawing a slip of paper from his pocket.

"What?" said Eileen over the sound of her iPod.

Darwen tried again, but she still couldn't hear and yanked the earbuds out irritably.

"You really aren't supposed to have headphones on while you drive," said Rich quietly.

Eileen shot him a look in the rearview mirror, and he turned quickly away.

"How can anybody go so red that fast?" Alex mused, grinning. "You look like a genetic experiment gone wrong: half man, half fire truck."

Rich opened his mouth, presumably to explain how you couldn't cross a person with an emergency response vehicle, but caught Darwen's scowl and changed his mind.

"I said," Darwen tried, pulling the conversation back to Eileen, "could you take us to this address?"

"Not a cab, you know," said Eileen.

She stared at the paper, eventually snatching her sunglasses off to get a better look. Her eyes scanned the words Darwen had written out, and she looked suddenly very focused. Darwen was about to say something when the car lurched out into the surging Atlanta traffic in a blare of horns.

Ten heart-stopping minutes later, they were there.

"Well, that was bracing," Rich remarked as they screeched to a halt.

"You getting out or what?" Eileen demanded.

Darwen slid awkwardly off the sticky seat and out into the hot Atlanta air. It wasn't even summer yet and it was already hitting ninety degrees, the kind of heat Darwen had barely been able to imagine in England.

Eileen did not speak, and the car pulled away the moment the door latched shut. Darwen watched her drive off, and it was a moment before he realized that the others were silently staring up at the house to which Eileen had brought them.

"This can't be right," said Alex eventually.

"The address is correct," Rich mused. He sounded dazed.

Darwen immediately understood their confusion. The house was huge: not so much a house, really, as a mansion, sprouting whimsical turrets with leaded windows and elegant, conical slate roofs. It had odd wings and crazy additions, such as a largely glass conservatory tacked on seemingly at random. The overgrown garden was surrounded by iron railings and contained massive sprawling trees and a dry fountain on the formal approach to the stately front porch. The paint was peeling and the whole place looked shabby and forgotten, but it was clearly worth a fortune, especially in this fashionable downtown district.

"You know what this lot alone is worth?" Rich mused.

"A couple million dollars," Alex said. "Maybe more. You could build a condo complex on this ground and charge whatever you liked."

Darwen couldn't think about money. His eyes traced the house's ancient timbers, its walls hung with sheets of ivy, its dark, enticing windows promising a labyrinth of passages and countless rooms all waiting to be discovered. Some of the upper windows had balconies and one little tower had a door that opened onto a railed walkway that wrapped all the way around the outside. It was, he thought, what houses should be, rambling and strange, but somehow homey and layered with age.

"Those trees," Rich mused. "How old do you think they are? How old do you think the house is?"

Alex's brow creased, and for once, she was silent for a moment but gave Rich a significant look.

"Are you thinking what I'm thinking?" said Rich.

"Pre–Civil War," said Alex with a slow nod. "But it can't be."

"What do you mean?" Darwen asked. "People lived here before the Civil War, right?"

"Oh, yeah," said Rich. "But when the city fell to the Union armies, Sherman ordered it evacuated, then torched half the city. This house, in this location? It's impossible."

"Then we'd better go inside and see what other impossible things it has to show us," Alex reasoned.

They moved in silence up the broad, weedy driveway, skirting the dry fountain—Darwen had seen smaller swimming pools—and into the shade of the mansion itself.

"Check out the watchtower," said Darwen, gazing up at the turret with the railed balcony.

"They call that a widow's walk," said Rich.

"Not sure I like the sound of that," said Alex.

Slowly they climbed the steps to the porch with its screened veranda and paused over the spidery writing on the card above the bell push: MR. OCTAVIUS PEREGRINE.

"I can't believe we didn't know this place existed," Darwen whispered in wonder.

Rich tried the tarnished brass door handle and scowled when it wouldn't turn. "Don't suppose anyone has a key?" he said.

Darwen shook his head, but Alex stepped forward. "Let me try something," she said, taking hold of the handle and turning it easily, so that the door shuddered slightly and swung open with a long, ominous creak.

"How did you do that?" Rich demanded.

"I'm a mirroculist too, remember?" she said, though she said it simply, apparently trying not to make Rich feel bad.

"So this is a portal?" he asked.

"I don't think so," said Darwen, peering into the dim hallway with its threadbare Oriental rug and faded paintings on the walls. "Just a Silbrican locking mechanism. The house inside looks real enough."

"One way to find out," said Rich, bracing himself. Being careful not to touch the other two—and thereby take advantage of their mirroculist powers—he stepped cautiously through the doorway and into the house, paused to see if anything happened, then smiled and took a deep breath. "I guess we're in," he said.

What they were in was far from clear. It was, as they had gathered, a very old and very large house, but it looked unlived in, and there were no obvious signs that Mr. Peregrine had spent any time there. The hallway led to an impressively spacious foyer and a broad staircase that branched into two and climbed up to a railed landing and corridors lined with doors. The foyer walls were interpersed with life-sized stone figures of women on plinths, their hands above their heads as if they were holding up the second story.

"Cool," said Rich, inspecting them. "The ancient Greeks used these on their temples sometimes. They're called caryatids. They look like decoration, but they are actually structural, like pillars."

Alex, who didn't need decoration to be structural, stood on her tiptoes so she could look the nearest caryatid in the face, then she stuck her tongue out at it. "They look like Miss Harvey," she decided. "No fun at all."

At first they picked their way cautiously around the first floor together, finding a formal dining room with a long, polished table, now layered with dust, then a huge kitchen complex hung with copper pans and riddled with chill, stone-flagged pantries with undersized doors. There was a circular library whose high shelves were stuffed with leather-bound books, and what they could only describe as a ballroom, vast, open, and hung with chandeliers. Upstairs they found bedroom after bedroom, though each one resembled a carefully maintained exhibit in a museum and showed no signs of recent habitation, so that after a while Darwen found that the edge to his search had dulled. Soon they took to wandering off by themselves, calling out what they stumbled upon.

"A music room!" yelled Alex, punctuating her announcement with a few plinky notes on an out-of-tune piano.

"Another bathroom!" returned Rich. "Even bigger than the last one!"

Darwen took a few more steps down a long hallway, opened another door, and peered cautiously in. The first thing he saw was an ancient rocking horse, then two stuffed bears—one with an eye missing—and a wooden clown on wheels.

A playroom, he thought, then as his eye settled on the dusty crib at one end, he revised the term and called out, "Nursery."

There was a long silence, but then he heard footsteps in the hall outside and Alex stepped in. "Did you say—?" she began, but her eyes drank in the room and she didn't need to finish the sentence.

Rich was at her heels.

"Mr. Peregrine had kids?" he asked.

Darwen shrugged, small and embarrassed. He didn't know. He hadn't asked.

"Man," said Alex, picking up the wooden clown. It had a bright red, slightly chipped nose and staring glass eyes. "Who would give a kid this? Nightmare central, or what?"

Darwen shuddered as he considered it sideways, remembering the clown mask Greyling had adopted when they'd met in Costa Rica.

"I don't think this was his place," said Alex. "I mean, he might have lived here, but it feels like one of those rentals where all the furniture is already there and they bill you if you leave cigarette burns in the armchairs when you leave."

Rich gave her a questioning look.

"My mom used to smoke," she explained, "and we had an apartment for a while when my parents first split up. It wasn't bad, but my mom was terrified of scratching the coffee table or whatever 'cause the landlord was always looking for reasons to charge us extra."

"If this stuff was here when he moved in," Darwen mused, "then either the house was empty for a long time or Mr. Peregrine is really old."

"He is pretty wrinkly," Alex agreed. "His hands look like one of those maps with the wiggly lines that show hills and such. What do you call them?"

"Contours," said Rich.

"Right," said Alex. "Contours. His hands are like that. Just the backs. Not the palms. The palms feel like paper when he touches you."

And suddenly, she stopped, and the three of them, gazing at the curious room with its ancient toys, felt Mr. Peregrine's absence in ways they hadn't before, and a sadness passed among them.

"It's like we didn't know him at all," Darwen said finally, staring at the empty crib. "He's gone, and we're trying to get him back, but all we've found so far is that we know nothing about him."

"We've only been looking five minutes," said Rich, taking a deliberately cheery tone. "There's tons of the house we haven't seen. Every room so far has been in the center."

"How do you know that?" asked Alex.

"Simple," said Rich, nodding at the walls of the nursery. "No windows."

"Huh," said Alex, turning on her heel and striding out and down the hallway.

Darwen heard her trying door handles, then closing them again, each time calling sharply, "Nope!" He and Rich went after her, Rich opening other doors as they went.

"I'm turned around," Darwen admitted. "Which way is the front, the side we came in?"

Rich started to point decisively, but his face clouded, and he shrugged. They followed the corridor at a brisk walk. It turned sharply left, then right, and along the way, they passed three more rooms, including two tiny bedrooms and an ancient walk-in closet, but they saw no windows, and Darwen could tell that Rich was getting agitated.

"Doesn't make sense," he was muttering. "Should have seen one by now. The house is big, but it's not *that* big."

"Where's Alex?" asked Darwen.

They had been right on her tail, but as they made the last turn of the hallway, there was neither sight nor sound of her.

"Alex!" called Rich.

His voice sounded unnaturally loud in the tight and dusty hallway, where it seemed no one had spoken for decades.

"Alex!" he called again. "Don't be fooling around now. I'm serious. Where are you?"

But there was no sound.

Darwen tried another door, which stuck and only yielded judderingly when he leaned his weight upon it. It opened with a high-pitched squeal, revealing a bathroom with an antique, claw-footed tub and no sign of Alex. He stepped out, dragging the door closed behind him.

"Not in there," he began, then caught himself and looked wildly around. "Rich?"

But Rich was nowhere to be seen either.

"Not funny, Rich," he said, opting for bravado. "Come on out."

Nothing.

Darwen took three hurried strides down to the next corner and rounded it, half expecting to see both of them huddled together and giggling, but there was only more of the same moth-eaten carpet and blank wooden doors. No people. No windows. No way to gauge which way he should go.

Darwen pressed on to the next corner, the next door, behind which he found bunk beds and a nonsensically massive chandelier right in the middle of the room, then doubled back, his heart starting to race.

He was lost, and alone.

He tried another door and found himself on the edge of an impossibly large and empty swimming pool, lined with cracked tile. The room on the opposite side of the hall contained a huge snooker table with a polished bar at one end with high stools. When he came out, he tried finding his way back to the bathroom with the claw-footed tub, but he couldn't remember which way he had come. There was no sign of Rich or Alex anywhere.

Not good, he thought. *Not good at all.*

He ran back around the corner to a T junction, which he was sure he'd seen earlier, but now a pair of those women statues that Rich had called caryatids stood on either side, and Darwen was certain they had not been there before. He considered them warily, studying their blank stone faces and closed eyes, while he chose which way to go. They were elegant and their stone clothes hung in finely chiseled folds, their heads bent slightly below their out-turned elbows, as if focused on the weight they were bearing, but there was something about their stillness that unnerved him. They wore belts from which hung long stone swords, and while they were only carved, they looked curiously sharp. It took him a moment to realize that though Rich had said the caryatids were structural, these two—though they had their hands above their heads like those in the lobby—weren't actually supporting anything at all.

This, he thought, *doesn't feel right.*

Darwen edged around them, moving to the right, and called for Rich and Alex in a loud, slightly unsteady voice. No one replied.

There were no doors on this hallway so Darwen moved quickly until he came to a rickety-looking staircase. There was nowhere to go but back, so he began to climb, each step creaking beneath him as if he was the first person to tread on it for years. He was halfway up the square spiral when he heard something on the stairs below and behind him: a creaking footfall and a curious rustle as of fabric. Darwen stopped moving to listen, conscious that the hairs on his arms were prickling upright. When no sound drifted up to him, he took two hurried steps down and peered around the corner.

Where there had been nothing but the angular twist of the stairwell, there was now a single caryatid. The statue was motionless, caught in the moment of climbing the stairs, her arms no longer above her head, the long, keen-looking sword now held in front of her in one elegant stone hand. Darwen gasped, staring into the blank face with its closed eyes, but it did not move and gave no sign that it had not been standing in that very position for decades. Very slowly and carefully, making as little noise as possible, he began walking backward up the stairs, his eyes locked onto the caryatid till the corner of the stairwell hid her from view. Only then did he turn to face the right way and run up the steps two at a time.

He climbed ten, twenty steps, then stopped. In the sudden silence he heard the creak of a step below him, the familiar swish of fabric for a fraction of a second before it too fell utterly still. He took two steps down and peered around the corner, a throbbing sense of dread making his arms and legs tremble. He knew what he was going to see but couldn't stop himself from looking.

There, frozen mid-stride, was the caryatid, sword drawn back this time as if she was going to bring it slashing down, eyes still closed, body utterly motionless, even the material of her dress seemingly carved from solid rock.

Darwen didn't wait. He hurried back up the stairs, sure now that he was ascending one of the house's towers, perhaps the tallest one, the one with the door onto the balcony. He was suddenly desperate to see outside, even if he would be too high to make his escape that way. He rounded two more corners as he climbed, his legs starting to wobble with panic. There was a door at the top. He reached out to press the latch, and as it clicked home, he heard the rustle of fabric once more, this time right behind him. He turned quickly, and there it was, inches from where he stood, the stone woman with her sword raised over her head.

And this time, the eyes were open.

Chapter Seven
The Watchtower

Whatever the rest of her was made of, the caryatid's eyes were not stone. They were amber and alive, and fastened on him with something like fury. Darwen was momentarily spellbound, then the caryatid came to lethal life, the sword swishing savagely through the air. He leapt backward through the unlocked door as the blade sliced into the doorframe, scattering splinters.

Darwen fell backward into the room, landing heavily on a stained hardwood floor. His eyes were locked on the figure in the doorway, which was poised to stride in and skewer him where he lay. He tried to get to his feet, but he was almost paralyzed with fear and couldn't wrest his gaze from the stone figure with the blazing eyes.

The caryatid straightened up, filling the doorway with her impossibly fluid stone form. Then, without warning, she turned her back on him, becoming still as a sentry as she blocked the door.

Darwen realized he had been holding his breath. He blew it out and inhaled deeply, finally managing to scramble to his feet, his eyes never leaving the caryatid's back. She did not move, and the sense of her being somehow on guard insisted itself to Darwen's mind ever more sharply.

But guarding what? Keeping others out, or keeping him in?

Darwen moved as far back as he could, then did a quick scan of the chamber before returning his gaze to the caryatid. The room was circular, or very nearly, and there were indeed windows all the way around it. Darwen thought Rich would be relieved, though the windows did seem curiously dark. Could he have been so lost in the house that he had lost track of time and it was now after sundown? That seemed unlikely, but then everything about this place was unlikely. He turned slowly, keeping the caryatid in the edge of his vision, and risked a closer look at the nearest panes of glass. He suppressed a gasp as he realized that they were not, in fact, windows at all, but floor-to-ceiling mirrors, a dozen of them.

No comfort for Rich after all, he mused.

Darwen checked the caryatid again, but it was still as any statue, so he dared another look around the chamber.

In the middle of the room was a bed with a nightstand on which stood a glass of water. The bed was the only thing he had seen in the house so far that did not look like it belonged in a museum. Yes, it was as old as everything else in the mansion, but its covers had been kicked half off, and there was a clear depression in the pillow. Someone had slept in that bed recently.

Mr. Peregrine?

It might stretch his sense of *recently*, but Darwen hoped so. The caryatid still hadn't moved, so Darwen began to cautiously walk the perimeter of the room. At his back was a door—presumably the way to the balcony he had seen from the outside—next to which was a tall grandfather clock, its hands set to twelve and its mechanism silent. But Darwen wasn't interested in that. All his attention was on the dark mirrors, through which he could see other places entirely.

And *hear* them too.

As he got over the panic of running from the caryatid, he became aware of irregular noises coming from the various mirrors: movement, distant machinery, even snatches of what sounded like conversation.

He became still again, terrified of giving his own presence away, and edged closer to a mirror that showed what he could only describe as a laboratory whose walls were lined with machinery, much of it hooked up to a series of coffin-like metal pods, each with a window about head height.

Darwen tested the surface of the mirror and, when it did not give to his touch, flattened his face against it to get a better look at the image on the other side. There was light inside the pods, and by that light he could make out strange faces. He gazed at them and then something in his brain clicked into place and he recognized what were surely . . .

Scrobblers!

There could be no doubt. They were huge and greenish, with protruding tusks, but they were also still, as if they were sleeping or dead. It took Darwen a moment to realize why he hadn't recognized the scrobblers for what they were at once: they wore no goggles. He shivered and double-checked that there were no controls around the mirror he might accidentally trigger if he wasn't careful. Fortunately, there weren't any; these were portals for looking through, hearing through, but you could not pass through them. Mr. Peregrine—if this was indeed his room—had used this place as a kind of observatory, not a means of transportation.

Before Darwen could examine the other mirrors, he heard footsteps on the tower steps: clumsy, running footsteps.

Rich and Alex. Darwen spun around. His friends were about to run right into the caryatid at the top of the stairs.

He dashed to the doorway and called over the armed statue's shoulder. "Rich? Alex? Don't come up any higher. There's something waiting for you!"

"Like a big stone something with a sword?" Alex's voice countered.

"Yes," Darwen shouted back. "How did you know?"

"'Cause we got two more behind us," she shouted. "Two behind, one ahead. You do the math."

"No!" Darwen shouted, but he could hear them coming up. With no other choices to pick from, he prepared to grab the caryatid when it attacked them.

Fat lot of good that will do, he thought.

But before he could devise an alternate plan, he saw Alex's anxious face peer around the corner. The stone of the caryatid seemed to ripple, and it came to life, the sword blade sweeping wide. Alex ran right at the door, Rich stomping up in her wake, and Darwen got a glimpse of the other caryatids that pursued them. He grabbed at the one in the doorway, trying to stay its sword arm, but the statue was impossibly strong, the flesh as cold and hard as granite. The caryatid didn't even bother shrugging him off, but it did step to the side, leaving the doorway wide open. Alex and Rich threw themselves into the room, and the three caryatids immediately turned their backs on them and became still.

"I don't think they can come in here," said Darwen.

Rich, who looked sweaty and alarmed, stared at what were now three stone sentries and shook his head.

"I don't think it's that they can't come in," he said. "I think they wanted us in here."

"Like it's a prison?" asked Alex.

"Maybe," said Rich. "But I'm not sure they were really trying to hurt us."

"What?" Alex demanded. "Are you forgetting the whole chasing-us-with-giant-swords thing?"

"I'm saying they kind of herded us up here," said Rich. "Like dogs moving sheep."

"You calling me a sheep?" Alex said warningly.

"Hold it," said Darwen. "Rich may be right. I think those things are like guards, but I don't know that they mean us harm. In fact, they brought us to the one place that seems like it really has a connection to Mr. P. Look," he said, nodding at the unmade bed.

"But even if this was his room," said Alex, "how does putting us in here help us or him?"

"Not sure yet," said Darwen, "but check out these mirrors. I don't think they're portals, just sort of viewing points. We can see and hear through them, but I don't think there's a way for us to pass through."

"You're right," said Rich. "This must be a surveillance room. Or, better yet, a watchtower. I'm guessing this was where Mr. P kept an eye on things in other places."

"Why these?" said Darwen. "I can't tell what I'm looking at. This looks like some kind of lab with scrobblers in it."

Rich peered over his shoulder and they both stared into the glass and the dimly lit chamber beyond. Each of the windows had a brass plate inscribed with a four-digit number, but there seemed to be no connection among the various codes.

"Guys," said Alex from the other side of the room. "I think you're gonna want to see this."

As they crossed to her, she did not take her eyes off the mirror she was gazing into, the plate above which read 8449. "There," she said, pointing.

It was, Darwen supposed, another kind of laboratory, though it was quite different from the one they had just been looking at. There was movement inside: two men, one in a white coat, the other in greasy overalls. Not the headless gnashers with their shark-mouth chests and snake tongues. Not the brutal scrobblers that were Greyling's soldiers: ordinary men.

"You think they can see us?" Darwen whispered.

Alex and Rich just stared in silence.

The man in the lab coat had a clipboard and was making notes while the other lugged a coil of heavy wire to a set of tanks filled with green fluid in which odd shapes floated.

"Not that one," said the man in the lab coat, pointing. "*That* one."

Darwen winced at the sound, but neither man showed any sign of awareness that they were being watched.

"What difference does it make?" said the other gruffly, plugging the wire into one of the pods.

"Trust me," said the one in the lab coat, his voice lilting with a curiously musical accent that Darwen found vaguely familiar, "it makes a difference, look you. Just do as you're told, for once."

"Or what?" said the bigger man. "You think the odd bods will take your word over mine if you go whining about my work? Fat chance."

Only then did Darwen process the tanks of liquid that Alex had been staring at. They were the size of Darwen's bedroom and, had they been at the Georgia Aquarium, would have been large enough to hold a dazzling array of colorful fish and even a couple of small sharks. But they weren't full of fish.

Floating motionless inside, his face slightly flattened against the glass, was Mr. Peregrine.

It was too awful. The shopkeeper looked impossibly old, haggard, faded somehow. He was naked except for a series of straps and a metal contraption fitted about his head, half tiny cage, half bridle—from which wires ran to equipment outside the tank. His usually bright eyes were closed, and his wispy hair drifted back and forth in the currents of the bubbling tank. It was, Darwen thought, the saddest thing he had ever seen.

"He's dead," said Darwen.

Alex silently took his hand and squeezed it, but Darwen couldn't look away.

"He's not," said Rich. "That makes no sense."

"Doesn't have to make sense," said Alex. "Look at him."

"If he was dead, why would they keep him in there?" Rich persisted. "He's not dead. He's in some kind of stasis."

Darwen wrenched his gaze from Mr. Peregrine's lifeless face and looked into Rich's eyes, searching for any sign that this was just wishful thinking. Rich stared back at him and his gaze was level, determined. He believed he was right.

"Alex?" asked Darwen. "What do you think?"

"Makes a kind of Silbrican sciencey sense," she said. "Can't say I like it, but it's better than the alternative."

"So we just have to get there," said Darwen, considering the two men. The one in the lab coat was studying his clipboard while the other paced silently, occasionally tapping on the glass of the tank like a kid in the zoo. Why were there people—humans—monitoring Mr. Peregrine?

"Where is it, though?" asked Alex, as if reading his mind. "I mean, is it Silbrica or our world?"

Darwen was forced to shrug. He suddenly felt tired and defeated. "I don't know," he said. "He's right there. If we could just step through . . ."

"What was that?" asked Rich. He had straightened up and his head was cocked on one side, listening intently.

"What was what?" asked Alex.

"Shh," hissed Rich.

"Excuse me?" said Alex, putting her hands on her hips.

"Alex," said Rich, eyes squeezed closed, "for once in your life, shut up."

Alex's eyebrows just about climbed off her head, but she said nothing, and at that very moment, the house shook with a deafening animal bellow from below. It was as if an impossibly oversized grizzly had roared immediately below them. Darwen put his hands to his ears and winced, as if the whole place was exploding, but the noise stopped as quickly as it had come.

"Oh, *that*," said Alex. "Yeah, I heard that."

Rich took a step toward the door. All but one of the caryatids had gone.

"Something's coming," said Rich.

And now they could all hear it, a dragging groan of a sound, like something huge pulling itself slowly through the house. There were footfalls within the noise, vast and heavy and slow, like the steps of an elephant, but there was also a strange scraping that didn't stop, as if the sides of the creature—whatever it was—were rubbing against the walls as it moved. They heard the creak and snap of breaking furniture, the shattering of falling pictures and crockery as it shambled inexorably through the house. Darwen was sure the sound was getting louder.

"Whatever it is," said Rich, "it's big."

Then there was another earthshaking roar, followed by a terrible wailing scream that lit the air for a moment, and then was gone.

"The caryatids," said Rich and Darwen at the same moment.

"Can statues die?" asked Alex, her face pale. "Because I think one of them just did."

Instinctively they edged away from the door.

"What do we do?" asked Rich. "Anything that can take down one of those statues . . ." He looked at Darwen and the fear in his eyes was infectious. Darwen shook his head. He had no idea. There was no way out of the room but down a confining stairway right into the path of whatever was coming. They had no weapons of any kind.

"What's through there?" asked Rich, indicating the only other door, the one beside the long case clock, which Darwen had assumed opened onto the balcony outside and the widow's walk.

He rushed to it and threw it open.

"A bathroom," he groaned.

"Windows?" asked Rich, hurrying over.

"No," said Darwen. The room was tiny, barely larger than a broom cupboard. There was an ancient sink and a toilet. Nothing else. Certainly no way out onto the roof.

"Maybe it—whatever it is—won't come up," said Alex.

Darwen turned to her to answer but saw that she had her eyes shut tight, fists clenched till the knuckles blanched.

"Maybe the staircase is too narrow," said Rich.

Darwen nodded desperately. "It won't be able to get up," he agreed.

But the dragging scrape and slow, heavy tread that made the house creak was getting louder.

"We should go down," said Rich. "Try to slip past it and out. If it traps us up here . . ."

"But Mr. Peregrine," Darwen began, throwing a hopeless look at the mirror that showed the awful laboratory with its tanks of colored liquid.

"We can't get to him from here," said Alex, whose eyes were open again. "Rich is right. We should go."

Darwen looked at each of them, knowing they felt the same anguish he did, then nodded. "Go," he said.

Rich went first, gingerly stepping out onto the stairs, Alex right behind him. The lone caryatid moved, or rather Darwen assumed it moved, though it happened so fast he didn't actually see it. One moment it was standing beside the door, the next it was barring their path.

"We have to go," Rich said to the stone, expressionless face. "You have to let us get down."

But then there was another roar from below, followed by two more of the dreadful, keening screams, and suddenly the caryatid blocking the stairs wasn't there anymore.

"It's gone to help the others," said Darwen. "Now's our chance."

They rushed down the stairs unimpeded, but when they reached the bottom, Rich paused. He was looking at what appeared to be a slightly misshapen soccer ball that had rolled to the foot of the stairs, but as Darwen examined it closer, he realized it was the shattered remains of one of the caryatids' heads, now just a hunk of carved rock. As they hesitated, there was a crash from down the hall and more stone fragments came flying out, pelting them where they stood.

Darwen blinked, and when he opened his eyes again, wiping the grit from his face, there were two caryatids in the hall, their backs to him, their swords drawn. One of them leapt around the corner with impossible speed, and there was another bellow of rage from their massive adversary, but he could not see what happened.

Then two things happened at once. First, Darwen heard hurried footfalls and grunts coming through the house: scrobblers. Naturally. Whatever the monster around the corner was, it wasn't alone. Getting out was going to be a lot harder than they had thought.

Second, and almost worse, was that the last remaining caryatid turned to them, its head moving slowly. Its eyes opened, showing the same amber fire, and with its sword arm it motioned them deliberately back up the stairs.

"It wants us to go back to the watchtower," said Darwen. "It's going to try to hold them off by itself."

"There's no way," said Rich.

But before they could debate the matter further, the thing with the voice like thunder came around the corner, and they no longer needed persuading to run back upstairs.

Chapter Eight
Under Attack

Darwen had known it would be big, but he was unprepared for the way the thing filled the hallway. Its face was reptilian, eyes small and black, snout turning into a long, cruel beak that gaped, showing a cavernous, pink throat. The creature looked like some colossal snapping turtle, though its shell was segmented, skin hanging in leathery folds between hard panels the size of car doors. Walking on its back two legs, dragging a squat tail that ended in sharp spikes as it moved, the monster hunched around the corner before resting on the elbows of its forelimbs as it considered the remaining caryatid. It unfurled its massive front fists, and the nails that flashed into view looked like foot-long fishhooks. Then it looked past the caryatid with hard, deliberate eyes and saw the three of them huddled behind it. Lowering its head and opening that terrible mouth so wide that its eyes disappeared, it bellowed.

The volume was almost physical. Darwen could feel it in his chest like a shock wave. He clasped his hands to his ears again and took an involuntary step backward. In the same instant, the caryatid lunged forward with its sword and stabbed the monster just beneath its armored shoulder. The stone blade found a space between the shell plates, sliding in deep. But though the strike had been impossibly fast, the caryatid seemed to linger in its victory, and one of those dreadful claws swept across its sword arm, shattering it.

With its remaining hand, the caryatid lashed its splayed fingers toward the creature's face, but the huge maw snapped, severing the stone hand just below the elbow. The caryatid hesitated, but the battle was clearly lost, and anything it did now was only to buy them time.

But time for what?

The monster filled the corridor. There was no way to go but back up the stairs. The others came to the same realization as soon as he did, but Darwen stalled as they began to climb up to the tower, watching as the caryatid was flung with unimaginable force against the wall, where its body broke apart. The amber eyes found him on the steps for the briefest moment, and then they were just stone again. As the monster roared its triumph and came surging down the hall, crushing the stone fragments beneath its massive feet, Darwen, Rich, and Alex fled.

They took the stairs two at a time, feeling the rumbling vibration of the tower as the creature surged after them. Darwen risked only one look back as he rounded the second story, hoping against hope that the staircase was indeed too narrow for it to get up. But the narrowness of the hall barely slowed the monster down. Its skin was like elastic, and it was able to squeeze up the stairwell, as if the very sockets of its bones were dislocating so that the beast became almost formless. As Darwen ran wildly up the stairs, he remembered Rich saying something about snakes that could eat prey larger than they were by unhinging their jaws. . . .

He was the last into the watchtower. Rich was flat against the furthest wall while Alex had thrown open the door to the tiny bathroom and was now staring desperately around, as if there might be something—anything—that would help. There wasn't. She slammed the door shut and turned to the others just as they got their first glimpse of those reptile claws dragging the beast up around the corner and into view. The head peered into the room, hard black eyes shining, and then it roared again so that the room shook.

Alex, Rich, and Darwen shrank back against the wall, clutching each other, but there was nothing to be done. With sudden and astonishing clarity, Darwen saw that he was about to die, and there was nothing he could do about it.

"Sorry, Mr. P," he muttered, his head sinking to his chest. "We tried."

For a moment his eyes closed, and when they opened again, that serpentine head was pushing itself into the room, its clawed hands holding onto the doorjamb as it pulled its massive bulk inside. The room seemed to halve in size as the monster came in, pushing aside Mr. Peregrine's bed like it was a toy. The beak mouth gaped one last time, but it did not roar, and the only sound was a satisfied hiss, which might have been a laugh. The eyes locked onto them and the claws swung back to strike.

There was a sudden flash of light, a bang, and a whiff of electricity in the air.

The monster stood motionless for a long second, then its eyes rolled back in its head, and it fell heavily forward, crashing to the floor so that Darwen had to leap to the side to avoid being crushed.

There could be no doubt that the creature was dead.

But that was nothing to what they saw behind it.

Standing in the doorway straddling the monster's scaly tail was a figure in a pink halter top and bright green shorts, with a rhinestone studded purse slung over her shoulder. She had sunglasses pushed back on her head, and her eyes were still focused down the barrel of the oversized blaster she had been aiming with both hands.

It was Eileen.

Chapter Nine
Eileen

"**S**he's one of those suit things, like the Jenkins insects!" shouted Darwen, reaching for the glass of water on the nightstand and flinging its contents at the thing that had taken the shape of his babysitter.

The water hit her in the face and splashed all over her cheery pink top. For a split second, she just stood there, then she considered her shirt and stared at Darwen. Rich pointed out the obvious.

"She's not dissolving."

"Give it a second," said Darwen, lamely flicking the last drops from the glass in her general direction.

The thing they had thought was Mr. Peregrine, the thing that had turned out to be a flesh suit containing a giant insect, had been vulnerable to water. Eileen, on the other hand, merely looked irritated.

"Another breathtaking insight," she observed, in a voice so precise, so unlike her usual vacant tone that the others stared at her. "This is Mr. Peregrine's crack mirroculist and his sidekicks? No wonder Silbrica is falling apart."

There was so much wrong with this remark and the careless way in which she delivered it that for a moment Darwen could think of nothing to say. Eileen, he noticed, was studying the weapon in her hands and frowning. The blaster looked like something halfway between a shotgun and a bazooka as fashioned by some mad Victorian scientist: all copper pipes, brass cogs, and intricately inlaid wood, ending in three different barrels, one with a tiny red light at one end, another studded with holes, and a third that flared like the horn of a trumpet. There were three blue lightbulbs set up above the trigger mechanism, but only one of them was lit.

"We have to get out of here," said Eileen, to herself as much as to the others.

"Can't we just, you know, shoot our way out?" Rich suggested, looking hopefully at the weapon in her hands.

"*We* can't," said Eileen pointedly, "because *we* only brought one blaster between four of us and *we* have already used up most of its power getting in. The terrapods always fight in threes, and each one will have a platoon of scrobblers in support. There's no way we're going back down those stairs."

"What's a terror pod?" asked Rich.

"*Terrapod,*" said Eileen, nodding hurriedly to the reptilian creature whose body almost blocked the door. "That. Not real bright, but strong, and tough to bring down."

"I thought it was, like, a dinosaur or something," said Alex, trying to sound flippant.

Eileen gave her a withering look and started scanning the mirrors on the walls.

"Who are you?" Darwen demanded.

"I'm Eileen," said Eileen. "Your babysitter. Remember? I also work for the man you know as the owner of a little mirror shop in the unfashionable end of a trendy mall. None of which matters right now, so can we get on?"

Rich gaped at her.

"Is there a way through these?" Darwen asked, determined to seem like he knew what he was doing. "I might be able to open them if—"

"Of course not," said Eileen, as if he was being stupid on purpose. "This is Octavius's observatory. You can look through them, hear through them, but they aren't portals."

"Octavius?" Darwen echoed.

"Mr. Peregrine," snapped Eileen. "Now give me a moment's silence and let me think?"

As she spoke, the house seemed to tremble with a roar from below. She was right. Another terrapod was making its way through the halls below, and by the sounds of things, some of the scrobblers had already reached the stairs.

"Think," Eileen muttered to herself.

"You're sure there's no way to open these observation window things. . . ." Darwen tried, pressing the surface of one that showed what looked like a stone circle on a rainy moor.

"I told you," Eileen shot back without looking at him. "Will you please be quiet?"

Darwen felt himself flush and, catching glances from Rich and Alex, looked down. Given how close he had come to dying, it seemed amazing that he should be left feeling so stupid, useless, and afraid.

Eileen had flung open the door to the tiny bathroom, checked inside, and slammed it hard with a grunt of frustrated disgust. The door failed to latch and bounced half open, juddering as it hung.

"Why does it say twelve noon?" asked Alex, considering the grandfather clock that stood beside the bathroom.

"What?" snapped Eileen. "Who cares? It's wrong, okay? Just let me figure this out. . . ."

"But it's not just wrong," Alex persisted. "It's said that time since we got here."

"So it stopped," Eileen shot back, her voice rising. "Big deal! Octavius has been gone for weeks. No one wound it. Of course it's stopped."

"Where's the pendulum?" asked Rich, who was squatting in front of the glass panel in the lower part of the clock's case. "I don't see a pendulum. I see gears and workings and stuff, but they shouldn't be down there, and they sure as heck-fire don't look like a regular clock."

"Will you all just STOP TALKING!" shouted Eileen, turning so swiftly toward Rich that her blond hair whipped around, her eyes widening as they fell on the top of the stairs.

She dropped to one knee, made a rapid alteration to the settings on the blaster, and unleashed five quick shots that lit the room like yellow lightning. The two scrobblers that had been inching their way up the stairs dropped, and at least two more ducked back around the corner.

Eileen checked the blue light on the side of her gun, and her anger was replaced by something like despair. They were running out of time.

"What if it's not a clock?" said Rich, who—amazingly—had not taken his eyes from the hands on the dial despite the shooting. "What if it's a control mechanism?" And then, as if answering his own question, he added, "But for what?"

"The door," said Alex, pointing at the bathroom door Eileen had failed to shut. "Close it."

Darwen did so, hoping she had some idea what she was doing.

"Now move the hands on the clock," said Alex.

"To what?" said Rich.

Alex shrugged. "Till you find something that works," she said.

At the head of the stairs, Eileen fired twice more, but at the roar of another terrapod somewhere below, she backed into the room, looking haggard. As if for the first time, she noticed what Rich was doing. He had opened the glass window on the clock face and had taken hold of the long hand. He glanced at Darwen and shrugged.

"Set it to eleven," said Darwen, stepping back from the door and considering the clock thoughtfully. He had no idea what he was doing, but someone had to make a choice.

Rich wound the long hand backward, and the hour hand edged back with it. "Done," he said.

Eileen was now watching Rich closely as he reached for the door handle. He tried to turn it, but it wouldn't move.

"It's locked," he explained.

"Maybe it needs the hand of a mirroculist like me to open it," said Alex with a would-be careless air aimed at Eileen.

Eileen gazed at her, her face hard to read. "You really are—" she began, then stopped herself.

"Oh yeah," said Alex. She took a couple of confident strides toward the door. She was reaching toward the handle when she was snatched backward by a massive greenish fist.

Darwen whirled around, but it was too late. As they had been focusing on the clock, the scrobblers had gotten up the stairs. Two of them were already inside and three more were coming. Behind them, pulling itself up the stairs like a wall of leathery flesh studded with two hard black eyes, was another terrapod.

Darwen flung himself at the scrobbler who had caught Alex, Rich at his heels. Eileen dropped and fired twice more toward the head of the stairs, but Darwen had no idea if she hit anything.

He and Rich hit the scrobbler just as Alex stamped on one of its heavy boots. Darwen punched twice into the creature's stomach, feeling pathetically small. With its hands full, the scrobbler lowered its goggled face and opened its mouth wide, showing boar-like tusks. It was going to bite him, and the sheer horror of that loosened Darwen's grip. He fell back to the floor.

"The door, Darwen!" yelled Rich. "Open the door!"

Darwen rolled to his feet and scrambled to the bathroom door, standing and yanking it open in one move.

It was immediately apparent that their hunch had been right. Where the little bathroom had been there was now a long carpeted hallway lit with wall-mounted oil lamps that burned amber. Darwen had no idea where it led, but it would get them out of here, and if you had to be a mirroculist to go through, then the scrobblers couldn't follow.

That also meant he couldn't go through alone without abandoning the others. Alex would be okay if she could get free, but since Rich and Eileen weren't mirroculists, Darwen would have to be touching them.

He turned back to where Alex and Rich hung on the arms of the massive scrobbler that was trying to shake them off, only to find that the other had shouldered its way past Eileen and was right on top of him.

He shrank into the corner. With one wild swing, the scrobbler slammed the portal closed. To make matters worse, the entrance to the stairwell was suddenly darkened by a massive reptilian head with the sharp beak of a snapping turtle: the second terrapod had made it up. Darwen dropped into a squat, and through the legs of the scrobbler standing over him, he saw Eileen hopelessly fiddling with her blaster as she retreated from the stairs into the room.

The scrobbler swung at Darwen with what was probably a tool but might just as well have been a medieval mace. He dodged and a portion of the wall behind him exploded in a shower of plaster dust. As he tried to run, the scrobbler caught his shoulder with one gnarled, claw-like hand and squeezed. The pain was intense and Darwen collapsed, dimly aware that the scrobbler was raising the mace over his head.

And then the room exploded with the roar of the terrapod and everything seemed to stop. The scrobbler winced, its grip slackened, and Darwen rolled out from under it. Alex and Rich had broken free too and were already at the portal, which Alex had opened.

"Go!" roared Darwen. "I'll bring Eileen."

They ducked inside, but as Darwen crossed to the portal, the terrapod managed to squeeze in from the staircase. Darwen didn't see the slash of its talon, but he felt it open a cruel gash along the side of his thigh. He kept moving, feeling nothing but a curious cold deadness in his leg, which suddenly turned to fire. He tried to take a step toward Eileen, reaching for her with all his strength, and for a moment he saw her face quite clearly, as if he had never seen her before. All her teenage nonchalance, her irritation, her permanent disapproval had gone, and she looked very young, and very scared. She was still clutching the blaster in one hand, but she was no longer trying to shoot, and though one of the scrobblers had her about the waist, she was reaching with her free hand toward Darwen.

They were only inches apart. For a moment he thought he could reach her, but then he felt the impact of the terrapod's fist, and he spun backward, falling through the portal and onto the carpet of that impossible hallway. The shock of the blow left him dizzy so that for a single, blessed moment he was able to forget that he had left Eileen alone in the room.

He called her name, but he knew that without being able to touch her, she couldn't get through the portal, and try as he might, his legs just wouldn't let him go back. He put a hand to his thigh and felt it come away warm and slick with blood.

Then Rich was pulling him along the hallway.

"Eileen?" called Alex from somewhere down the hall. "Where's Eileen?"

Rich leaned into Darwen's face. "She's still in there?" he said, looking wildly back to the watchtower.

"I couldn't reach," Darwen murmured. "I tried, but I just couldn't. . . ."

And then Rich was climbing over him, grasping one of his hands and stretching till he was close enough to the portal. Then he was gone.

"No!" called Darwen and Alex at once.

It was suicide to go back in there. And even if he could get to her, Rich wasn't a mirroculist. He'd be trapped with the scrobblers and the terrapod.

"Rich!" called Darwen. He tried to stand, but the pain in his leg flared like he had been kicked, and he crumpled, his eyes closed tight. When he opened them, he saw Alex looming over him.

"One of us will have to go back in to get him," she said.

Darwen could only nod, and then suddenly, impossibly, Rich was back, dragging a battered-looking Eileen through the portal behind him.

"What?" gasped Alex. "How did you . . . ?"

Rich, for all his exertion, managed a shy smile.

"Guess I'm one of you now," he said.

Chapter Ten
Revelations

"How's the leg?" asked Eileen.

Darwen wasn't sure how long it had been since they had made their escape: twenty minutes? Perhaps more. Eileen had recovered much of her composure, but she was quiet, and the irritation that had characterized his babysitter as long as he had known her was gone, so that he found himself gazing at her, struggling to accept the idea that this was the same person who had bossed him and ignored him and generally treated him like an unpleasant inconvenience for the last nine months.

"A little better, thanks," he said.

Rich produced an oversized handkerchief and Alex wound it tightly from Darwen's knee to his hip.

"You blow your nose on this?" said Alex to Rich. "It looks like a tablecloth, man."

Darwen grinned in spite of himself. The wound still hurt a great deal, but the bleeding seemed to have stopped.

The portal had taken them into a Silbrican version of the same mansion. The rooms were roughly identical to those on the Atlanta side, but this one had large, glorious windows overlooking acres of immaculate, manicured garden, which reminded Darwen of a stately home he had visited in England with his parents. No one had stepped outside yet, but they could make out lawns and flower beds and carefully clipped hedges laid out in geometric patterns as far as the eye could see.

Darwen was lying in a sunny sitting room on a pale couch, his feet up, while Eileen paced and Rich and Alex relived their escape from the watchtower. Rich seemed to have grown a couple of inches, the way he carried himself now. He could barely keep from laughing with delight at somehow having become a mirroculist, and no matter how much Alex teased him for being pleased with himself, he couldn't stop grinning.

"So you can open portals," she remarked. "Big deal. I could do that months ago. You gonna start singing and dancing like me too, copycat?"

"No one wants to sing and dance like you, Alex," said Rich, unoffended.

"They want to," Alex rejoined. "They just can't."

"I think I'll take opening dimensional portals over being one of your backup singers," Rich quipped, gazing out at the garden through the tall windows.

Darwen smiled because he knew how delighted Rich was, how proud, but he couldn't help wondering where this left him. Darwen had mockingly imagined opening portals at the school talent gala because, as Mr. Sumners had shrewdly pointed out, he didn't have any other talents. Now even this had been taken away from him.

No, he reminded himself, *not taken away. I can still do it. For now. It's just that other people can too. And that's good because they are my friends and it makes them happy.*

Or so he told himself.

"Rich Haggerty, the mirroculist." Alex sighed. "Must be some kind of mistake. Like the Guardians wanted to give me even more power and some of it landed on you. Something like that."

"This just eats you up, doesn't it?" Rich cooed, grinning sideways at her. "No more waiting for you to open the portals for me. *No thanks, Alex, I got this one. . . .*"

"You're quite the comedian," Alex muttered, trying to hide her smile. "You should get yourself a red nose and some clown shoes. Man, the Guardians' standards sure are slipping. I guess they let *anyone* become a mirroculist these days. . . ."

"No," said Eileen, absently, but so thoughtfully that the others stopped sparring to look at her. "They don't. There should be one mirroculist. That's how it works. One. Not two, and certainly not three. It doesn't make any sense. Mirroculists aren't made, they just are. One at a time."

She looked more than serious. She seemed almost sad.

"How does that work?" asked Darwen, sitting up awkwardly. "I mean, it's not destiny, right? Because I don't believe in destiny."

"I'm not a philosopher," said Eileen.

Yesterday, Darwen thought, that statement in his babysitter's mouth would have struck him as extraordinarily funny, but now he didn't know what to think.

"All I know," said Eileen, ceasing her pacing and sitting in a large wing-backed leather chair, "is that for centuries there has been one mirroculist. After each one lost the gift, another would be discovered, but sometimes it took time. There have been years when no one could open the portals between our world and Silbrica."

After each one lost the gift.

The phrase rang in Darwen's head like a mournful bell in the distance.

"How long have you been working for Mr. Peregrine?" asked Rich.

"For the last three years," Eileen replied.

"But you're . . . you know, human, right?" Rich pressed.

"Obviously," said Eileen, a flicker of her former irritation coming back into her face.

"Three years?" said Darwen, sitting up properly now.

Eileen shot him a look, and there was something a little hunted in her expression, like she wished she hadn't said that.

"So when you started working for my aunt, you already knew Mr. Peregrine?" he pressed.

"Sure." She shrugged, as if the point was of no consequence, though Darwen thought she avoided his eyes.

"Wait a minute," said Darwen, giving her a hard look. "You knew the day I met him, the day he gave me the mirror. Right?" His voice had an edge to it. "You told him who I was, or maybe he told you? Maybe he got you to apply for my aunt's babysitting job, yeah? Was that how it worked? She never told me how she met you."

Eileen said nothing, and Darwen felt the color in his face rise.

"All that time I thought you were ignoring me, talking on your phone and stuff," he said, "you were spying on me!"

"I did what Octavius asked," said Eileen.

"And you somehow connected me with him," said Darwen, trying to make sense of it all, astonished as the pieces fell into place.

"The moment you came to Atlanta, he was going to connect with you," said Eileen, suddenly frank and forceful. "That wasn't me. I just told him where you would be and when. He released the flittercrake into the mall to lead you to the shop, not me."

"He *led* me to the shop?" Darwen gasped. Rich and Alex were frozen in silence, watching.

"He had to!" Eileen replied. "Everything suggested that you would be the new mirroculist. He had to meet you to be sure."

Ask him how he knew your name, Darwen thought. Those had been Scarlett Oppertune's last words. Mr. Peregrine had known who he was, known what he might be, and the gift of the mirror had been a test, plain and simple. Lightborne had admitted as much.

"Wait," said Darwen, shaking his head, like he was trying to clear it. "How did he know I was going to be a mirroculist?"

"The Guardians had been . . ." Eileen hesitated, picking her words carefully. "Monitoring you."

"But I was just a normal kid!" Darwen shot back. "This mirror stuff didn't start till I came here!"

"The abilities of the mirroculist," Eileen recited, as if she was remembering something she had read long ago, "don't start at birth. They begin as the subject crosses into adulthood."

"I'm not an adult!" Darwen shouted back. "Look at me! I'm a kid."

"Sometimes," Eileen said, even more carefully, her eyes fixed on the carpet, "an emotional trauma accelerates the process."

Darwen was about to yell back at her when the weight of the words struck him and he fell silent. Alex was also looking down. Rich was staring at him, his mouth open, his face a mask of shock.

"Emotional trauma," Darwen repeated.

"Yes," said Eileen. "I'm sorry, Darwen, but it's true. You might never have become a mirroculist if it wasn't for the road accident that killed your parents. It pushed you over the edge and activated your abilities. No one could have known that for sure, but when the Guardians learned that a possible mirroculist was coming, we had to find out. I was positioned to keep an eye on you and make sure you met Mr. Peregrine. I'm sorry that I couldn't tell you. It was for your own protection."

Darwen said nothing. For a little while Silbrica had been a kind of home for him, a refuge from his loneliness and sadness; it had been an enchanting secret, a place where he was special. But now it seemed that had only been possible because of what had happened to him, what he had lost. In a moment of startling clarity, he saw that he would give it all up—the portals, Moth's forest, all the beauty and adventure of Silbrica—to have his family back the way it had been.

"My aunt," said Darwen at last. "Did she know?"

This took Eileen so completely off guard that she actually laughed.

"Not a clue," said Eileen. "As far as she was concerned, I just showed up at the right time and was far more flexible than the other babysitters she interviewed."

"But you seemed so . . ." Darwen tried to find the word.

"Uninterested," Rich supplied.

"Obnoxious?" offered Alex. "Insufferable? Jackassy?"

Eileen gave a half smile and a nod of acknowledgment. "Gonna be a theater minor when I go to college," she said. "If I ever get to."

"Majoring in what?" asked Alex, skeptical.

"Physics, I think," Eileen said with a self-deprecating shrug.

"Yeah?" said Rich, pleased and impressed. "Cool."

"But wait," said Darwen. "If it's so rare to be a mirroculist, and my gift was triggered by some emotional trauma, what about them?"

He nodded at Alex and Rich, who returned his gaze a little guiltily.

"No idea," said Eileen, and there it was again in her face: that deliberate blankness, as if she was hiding some feeling even from herself. "When the Guardians heard that you opened a portal," she said to Alex, "they went nuts. First they didn't believe it. Then they went into full-on research mode trying to figure how it was possible, but no one came up with anything. When they find out he's a mirroculist too . . ." she said, glancing at Rich. The sentence trailed off, and she just shrugged and shook her head.

"So," said Darwen, "you're still working for the Guardians?"

"Right now," said Eileen, "I just work for Octavius. He was my link to the council. Since he disappeared, I've communicated with them only once, through a Spanish agent of theirs. . . ."

"Jorge," said Alex and Rich together.

"Right," she said. "You know him?"

"Let's say our paths have crossed," said Darwen. "What did he tell you to do?"

"Keep you safe," said Eileen. "Help you find Octavius, and help you gather allies to stand with us against Greyling."

She sounded uneasy, even a little resentful that after her years of service, Darwen—who was no more than a kid in her eyes—was in charge.

"So Greyling hates you too," said Alex, grinning. "I'm pretty sure he hates us more, but at least we're on the same side."

She said it so easily, reveling in it like it was a badge of honor, that all the tension evaporated. Eileen started to laugh and soon they were all laughing with her. For a moment all the danger they had passed through, all the terrors surely to come, seemed no more than a game, a bit of fun in which they got to be the good guys and nothing serious could possibly happen to them. They were just sitting in a fancy living room, basking in the softening light from the windows and chatting as if they were swapping stories from books. Darwen was the first to stop laughing, and he did so with a sudden sense of dread that made him wince with a pain as clear as that in his thigh.

"Well, one good thing's come from all this," said Eileen.

"What's that?" asked Rich.

"I get to see Silbrica again," said Eileen, beaming so that she looked like a completely different person.

"Mr. Peregrine didn't bring you across much?" Alex asked.

"What?" said Eileen, the smile evaporating. "No. He wasn't a mirroculist."

"Isn't," said Darwen, firmly.

"What?" asked Eileen.

"Mr. Peregrine *isn't* a mirroculist," Darwen spelled out. "Not *wasn't*."

"Right," said Eileen. "Of course."

He managed not to add that it was starting to seem like the old shopkeeper and Eileen were the only people who weren't mirroculists, because he didn't want to rain on Rich's parade. And it was, perhaps predictably, Rich who seemed most keen to press on.

"So now that we're here," he said, "what are we going to do? Is there a way to find where those places we could see in the watchtower actually are? Mr. Peregrine was in one of those labs—"

"What?" snapped Eileen, so brusquely that Darwen glimpsed the old babysitter he had loathed for months. "You saw Octavius? Where?"

In all the confusion of the fight in the Atlanta mansion, Eileen had not had a chance to study the windows in the observatory. Now she was eager to learn all they had been able to see, after which her pacing took on the feel of a tiger in the zoo, glaring.

"Maybe we should go outside," suggested Alex, who was also starting to get antsy.

"This is Silbrica, remember?" said Darwen. "Who knows what's out there?"

Normally this remark would have had a serious, weighty quality to it, but with the windows showing only the early evening falling softly on acres of manicured gardens, even Darwen knew he sounded paranoid.

"You don't even know that those gardens are real," he insisted. "Might be a trick of the windows, an effect to make the house feel nicer. Maybe if you step outside, you're actually in some underground cave crawling with monsters."

"One way to find out," said Alex, moving to the French windows.

"No!" said Rich. "Not yet. We should see what there is to find here before we go wandering off into whatever dangers are waiting out there."

"Right," said Alex, considering the view from the window. "Wouldn't want to risk the perils of a formal English garden. We could prick ourselves on a rosebush or have to run from servants trying to serve us cucumber sandwiches." She turned abruptly to Darwen. "I take it you didn't have a garden like this at your house?"

"No," said Darwen flatly.

"Huh," said Alex, as if this was disappointing but to be expected. "The version of England you came from sure isn't like the movies."

"Right," said Darwen. "'Cause all English people live in palaces or thatched cottages, and take tea with the queen." He rolled his eyes. "*Americans,*" he muttered.

"Hey!" protested Rich. "What did *I* say?"

Darwen picked at his bandage.

"He's just feeling a bit less special than he did before you became a mirroculist," said Alex with a careless shrug.

Darwen saw the hurt confusion flash through Rich's face and shot Alex a murderous look.

"What?" she remarked. "I'm just sayin'."

"Well, don't," said Darwen. "It's not that, Rich. It's just this stuff about how I became a mirroculist. And my leg," he added for good measure.

Rich didn't look completely convinced, but he nodded.

"We should search the house," said Eileen, as if coming to the end of a private debate. "There must be clues as to where we should go, portals, perhaps."

"I know we have to find Mr. P and all," said Alex, "but what about going home? Our families are going to start looking for us about now. If we're not back in an hour or two, my mom will call out the national guard."

Darwen hadn't thought of this.

Eileen frowned as if just remembering what a pain it was to be dealing with kids who couldn't drive wherever they wanted to go at any time.

"Well," said Darwen, "we can't go back the way we came. The

Atlanta mansion clearly isn't safe. We're going to have to find another way, so I say we start looking. We're supposed to be connecting with allies to stand against Greyling, remember? Maybe we can learn about where Mr. P is at the same time."

"So we split up and search the house first," said Eileen.

"No way," said Alex. "When we split up in the other house, things got bad faster than Rich's dad at an all-you-can-eat barbecue."

Darwen shot Rich a glance to see if he was offended, but the other boy just shrugged. "The man likes his pork," he said.

"Together then," said Eileen. "Darwen, can you walk?"

"Not right fast," said Darwen, getting to his feet, "but yeah."

"Okay," said Eileen, her face set grimly. "Let's do this."

Chapter Eleven
The Map Room

It took ages to search the mansion. The building was, at least structurally, an exact copy of the Atlanta building, so that by the time they were done, the light in the gardens outside had dropped to almost nothing. There were caryatids holding up the second story of the lobby, and the house had the same sprawling and irrational collection of rooms. But there were differences. Apart from the windows lining the perimeter walls, the Silbrican version of the watchtower was quite empty: no bed, no observation mirrors, no bathroom door beside a long case clock. So far as they could see, there were no portals of any kind anywhere.

Back downstairs they found another room that had no parallel in the Atlanta house. It stood at the end of a wide hallway hung with brownish paintings of distant hills and waterfalls, behind a pair of polished oak doors. They had seen nothing like these doors in the other mansion, and Darwen instinctively knew that they had found what they were looking for. There was a momentary hesitation as he, Rich, Alex, and Eileen decided they were ready for whatever they would find on the other side; then Eileen, still cradling the almost empty blaster, pushed the doors open.

The room on the other side was one of the oddest Darwen had ever seen. It was circular, and sunken, so that the landing on which they emerged was actually a kind of second story that ringed the chamber below like the gallery in a round theater. Along the rail of this gallery were set copper plates marked with numbers, each one with a pair of buttons beside it, one red, one black. The room below was empty except for a curious tiled floor overlaid with a giant spiderweb of copper wire and hundreds, perhaps thousands, of old-fashioned lightbulbs set into the ground, each one marked with a four-digit number.

"It's a circuit board," said Rich.

"It's a map," said Alex.

"It's both," said Darwen, pushing one of the red buttons on the rail. On the floor below, an amber bulb came to life and throbbed softly. Darwen looked at the plaque next to the button.

"It says 5547," he read. "Wait. I know what this is. It's a plan of all the gates in Silbrica! Look there, in the middle! That's the Great Apparatus: a circle of a hundred portals." He pressed the black button, and as the amber bulb died, half a dozen others in different parts of the room lit up. He frowned thoughtfully. "What does that mean?" he mused.

"Let me try," said Alex, punching buttons at random so that half the floor seemed to glow.

"Stop that," said Rich. "We can't learn anything if you push things willy-nilly. We've got to be scientific. Everyone stop pushing buttons!"

Grudgingly Alex obliged, though she mouthed *willy-nilly?* in disbelief.

"Okay," said Rich. "So the red buttons light one bulb, which marks a portal. But the black buttons light up . . . well, it varies. Sometimes it's only one or two, sometimes it's more, and they aren't all grouped together. That light over there comes on when I hit this black button *and* when I hit this one, but the other lights that come on at the same time are completely different."

Rich scowled.

"Isn't it obvious?" said Alex.

"Not to me," said Darwen.

"The red button shows the location of the portal," said Alex. "The black button lights up wherever that portal leads."

Rich's scowl deepened. "Maybe," he said, "but how can we be sure?"

"Simple," said Alex. "Look. Push this black button for portal 2339, five lights come on. One of them is—let me see—4231. Okay, find the buttons for portal 4231."

Eileen and Rich walked quickly along the great circular walkway, scanning the controls on the rail.

"4231!" shouted Eileen. "Got it."

"Push the black button," said Alex.

Eileen did so and eight lights came on, including . . .

"2339!" Alex confirmed. "Easy peasy. So this should give us a way to get to every single portal in Silbrica."

"The observation windows in the watchtower all had numbers!" shouted Darwen. "Including the one where we could see Mr. Peregrine."

"Don't suppose you remember the combination?" asked Rich, who looked a little shamefaced.

Darwen flushed and shook his head.

"Try 8449," said Alex.

Everyone turned to look at her.

"You think that's right?" asked Darwen.

"Pretty sure," she said.

"How on earth did you remember that?" asked Rich.

"My birthday is in August," she said, as if that made everything clear.

"So?" said Rich.

"August is the eight month, half of eight is four, plus another four to get us back to the eight, then add one for the final number, nine. See?"

Rich's eyes narrowed. "That makes no sense at all," he said.

"Works, though, doesn't it?" said Alex.

"But there's no system," said Rich. "It's just random."

"Guys," said Darwen, and everyone stopped and looked. He had pushed the red button beside the plate reading 8449 and a crimson bulb had come to life over on the far side of the room. "That's where he is."

"If we can trust Alex's completely arbitrary method for remembering stuff," Rich qualified.

"That's where he is," said Alex with such certainty that even Rich let it go.

"Why is the bulb red?" Rich asked, but no one answered.

"So how do we get there?" asked Eileen.

"Should be easy enough to find out," said Darwen, pushing the corresponding black button with a rush of hope he hadn't felt for weeks.

That hope stalled immediately.

No lights came on.

Darwen pressed the button again and again, but nothing happened.

"Maybe the map is broken," said Rich.

"Let's see," said Alex, hoisting one leg over the rail and dropping softly to the floor below before anyone could stop her.

"Careful!" shouted Rich as she began picking her way across copper wires on her tiptoes.

"Good suggestion," said Alex dryly. "'Cause I never would have thought to be careful with all these little glass bulbs and an electric current down here."

"Fair point," said Rich.

"I see the problem," said Alex, squatting delicately close to the only bulb that was still lit, the bulb for portal 8449. She pointed, tracing the spiderweb strands of the copper wire out from that one glowing red spot. "These have all been cut," she said. "Every wire connecting to this bulb has been clipped. Why would the Guardians do that?"

Darwen's heart sank.

"If we assume the map represents the actual setup of the gates," said Rich, thinking it through, "then the portal where Mr. P is being held was once on the Guardians' grid, but there's no way to reach it. In fact, that entire section has been cut off. Why?"

"Greyling," said Darwen. "So we're stuck. We can't reach him."

"We could get in from our world," said Rich.

"But we don't know which part of our world connects to the portal!" Darwen shot back, his temper getting the better of him. "And even if we did, we have no chuffin' way of reaching our world from 'ere anyway." He slammed his hands against the rail, and the sound reverberated around the room like a shot. "We fought our way through 'ere," he shouted, "and nearly got chuffin' killed in the process— *again*—and what do we have to show for it, eh? Chuff all. We're no nearer to finding Mr. Peregrine, and we've got NOTHING!"

That last word bounced around the room like an accusation, and for a long moment no one spoke. They all stood still, looking at the floor. Then Alex looked up.

"You done?" she said.

Darwen nodded once.

"Good," she said quietly. "And we don't have nothing. Look what I found."

She held up a battered and stained notebook the size of a paperback. It was brown, dotted with reddish wax and soot, and bound shut with a leather thong. On the cover someone had sketched in spidery black pen the image of an elaborate doorway surrounded by intricate scrollwork.

"What's that?" asked Rich as Alex untied the thong and flicked through what looked like columns of numbers.

"It's basically this," she said, gesturing at the floor map. "Tables of portal numbers so you can figure out how to get from one gate to the next. Pretty useful, huh?"

Rich agreed that it was, then looked to Darwen, who nodded.

"So now what?" asked Eileen.

"We've searched the house," said Alex, climbing back up to the gallery, the notebook in one hand. "Darwen's right: there are no portals. So now we go outside and see what we can find out there." She nodded at the darkened French windows and the night beyond, and as Darwen winced with apprehension, she led the way outside.

But once they were out in the gardens, they found only the beautiful rolling lawns, carefully clipped hedges, and extravagant fountains with elegant spouting statues. In spite of the darkness, it was peaceful, even beautiful.

"I bet this is what Versailles is like," said Alex happily as they moved down the long, straight gravel path that led from the front steps of the house out through the grounds. "That's in Paris. Have you been?"

"No," said Darwen.

"Even though it's in Europe and you're from Europe," Alex said, something she had observed several times in the past.

"There are a lot of things in Europe," said Darwen testily.

"Most of which you haven't seen, apparently," Alex agreed.

"These gardens go on forever," Rich mused. "I wouldn't want to mow this lawn. It would take days. And what kind of grass is this? It ain't Bermuda or fescue."

"*What kind of grass?*" Alex reposted. "It's grass. What's the difference?"

"Well, Bermuda dies off in the winter," said Rich, "and spreads by surface runners, whereas fescue—"

"I didn't mean *what's the difference* as in *please explain all about* the different types of grass," said Alex, shaking her head. "I mean I don't care."

"If you worked for a lawn care company like my dad's, you'd care," Rich grumbled.

"You got that right," Alex muttered darkly.

"What's that supposed to mean?" Rich returned.

"Will you two give it a rest?" said Eileen. "I'm looking for clues that might lead us to Mr. Peregrine. You two are doing nothing for my inner calm."

Darwen grinned at her in spite of himself, the first time he had ever done so. Eileen, realizing as much, looked surprised, then flushed so that he thought her cheeks turned pink in the low light.

Rich was right. The gardens just seemed to go on forever, and as the house got lost in the dark trees behind them, Darwen began to think that the locus might somehow be infinite, or some kind of loop like Moth's forest, where if you kept walking, you would eventually come back to where you started. But even as he thought this, he saw an elegant array of pale columns arranged like a miniature version of an ancient Greek temple, and he immediately recognized the colonnade for what it was.

"Portals!" he said, pointing.

"Maybe," said Eileen.

"No," said Darwen, not sure how he knew. "Definitely."

Eileen frowned but said nothing, and when they got close enough to see the elegant controls set into the colonnade, she gave a grudging shrug of acknowledgment. "We don't know where they lead though," she said. "They have no numbers."

"Not sure it really matters at this point," said Darwen, "so long as we can get back. We're supposed to be exploring Silbrica anyway. Looking for clues and allies, right? That's what I promised the Guardians."

"It just seems a bit random," said Rich.

"While wandering the Infinite Garden is making real progress, you mean?" asked Alex.

"Let's at least look," said Darwen.

Eileen shrugged again, and Rich, nodding, offered her his hand. Once they were all touching, Darwen led them through. There was more marble on the other side, a once elegant walkway lined with statues of noble-looking beasts, now smashed, spattered with oil and disfigured by large, greasy handprints. There were carefully laid out gardens here too, but the lawns had been churned to mud by the treads of some huge-tracked vehicle. The flower beds had been tramped under foot and the ornamental trees had all been axed or pushed over. Why was anyone's guess, though the damage looked less like construction and more like vandalism.

"More of Greyling's handiwork," said Darwen, biting his lip. "He's probably trying to disrupt the way the Guardians communicate by having his scrobblers destroy as many portals as he can get access to. Do any of these still work?"

Apart from the gate they had just come through, all but one pair of columns were broken, and the mechanisms set into them had been smashed in. The surviving portal was carved with the numbers 2713.

"Let me look it up," said Alex, thumbing through the notebook from the map room. "No way!" she exclaimed.

"What?" asked Darwen, who was considering a fractured statue of a girl hanging a picture frame a little outside the portal ring.

"This goes right to the Great Apparatus!" she exclaimed. "Perfect. We can be home before anyone misses us."

"But we haven't made any new allies or learned anything about where Mr. Peregrine might be," said Darwen, splaying his fingers and holding up his hands in exasperation.

Alex looked at the shattered columns on the ground. "We should leave," she said. "Before Greyling's uglies come back."

"I think they're done here," said Darwen.

"This portal might be okay," said Rich, studying one of the marble columns. "I need to reconnect these wires, but otherwise it looks usable."

"I don't like it," said Eileen. "Why would they leave one intact? Either wherever it leads isn't worth visiting, or it's a trap."

"Not necessarily," said Rich, stripping a wire with his teeth. "The scrobblers aren't exactly careful workmen. They may not have realized how easy this was to fix. There." He pushed a button and the portal shimmered into life. "See? Good as new."

"I don't know," said Eileen warily. "Seems like taking an unnecessary risk."

Everyone looked at Darwen, waiting, and he considered the flickering light of the portal thoughtfully. A part of him just wanted to go home, but he knew in his heart that he couldn't do that. Not yet.

"Yes, it's risky," he said. "But we have a job to do. And if it doesn't look like we're going to find anything useful . . ."

"Or if it looks too dangerous," Alex chipped in.

"We'll get out fast," Darwen concluded. "Okay?"

Eileen looked ready to protest, but she glanced at the others and snatched Rich's hand, stepping into the portal with a muttered "Fine."

And for a moment, it looked like it was.

Chapter Twelve
A Cold Reception

The temperature dropped to freezing. A howling wind whipped at their hair and clothes and they immediately turned against it, their feet crunching in deep, crystalline snow.

To his left, Darwen saw black, leafless trees and then only an expanse of open, snow-covered land running to where wrinkles of blue ice rose up like something between a mountain and a frozen waterfall.

"That's a glacier, that is," said Rich. "Cool."

"Probably," said Alex, dry as a bone, but Darwen just nodded, smiling and hugging his arms to his chest. The place was—in a wild and chilly way—quite beautiful. He was considering the glacier when something large moved between the trees, something big enough to momentarily blot out everything beyond it entirely, but pale and formless as the empty sky.

"Whoa," he exclaimed. "Did you see that?"

"There was *something*," said Alex.

Eileen checked her blaster anxiously.

"Where?" asked Rich, stamping his feet in the snow. "I didn't see anything. In those trees?"

And then there was another one moving in the same direction, vast and slow. Rich gaped. "Dang."

The huge creatures were the size of double-decker buses. They were white and hung with shaggy, matted fur, which blended so well into the snowy landscape that their precise shape was hard to make out. Each one had huge, curved tusks that looked like they were made of glass and a pair of similarly elephantine trunks that swept the ground as they walked. In the middle of their towering backs, the beasts had a pair of camel humps, and between those humps, sitting astride each creature, was something like a small man, wrapped and hooded in white fur.

As Darwen watched, the immense creatures swung around to face them and doubled their speed.

"Mutant mammoths," whispered Alex, her breath pluming like fog. "Will they spear us to death on their tusks or just trample us into little red pancakes? I, for one, can't wait to find out."

"Dulovune herders," sighed Eileen. "That's just great. No wonder Greyling didn't bother disabling the portal properly."

"Why?" asked Darwen quickly. "What are they?"

"Let's just say that they like to be left alone," said Eileen, her eyes flashing from the massive beasts to the men who sat astride them. "And because of what happens when people don't leave them alone, everyone generally does. We should leave. Now."

Five of the huge animals and their riders pushed through the trees, snapping heavy branches as they came on. The lead mammoth seemed to reach back with its trunks, one to each side, and then stretch them forward again like cannons.

"Run or fight?" asked Rich.

The mammoth took their decision out of their hands. It seemed to inflate slightly, and then from the extended trunks came a jet of aquamarine fire that arced over their heads and pooled on the ground a few yards behind them. Rich and Alex cried out and ducked.

"I think we stay where we are," said Darwen. "We're trying to make friends, remember?" As the others sputtered their doubts, he took a step toward the lead beast and raised his arms in the air.

"Yo, D," said Alex. "Much as I like the new decisive you—very impressive and all—I'd prefer to see you making decisions like what you want for lunch rather than, you know, stuff that might get us all killed horribly."

"My name is Darwen Arkwright," Darwen called, ignoring her, gazing up into the still-smoking trunks the mammoth had aimed directly at him, "and I come as envoy from the Guardian Council."

The five colossal white mammoths formed a loose semicircle around Darwen and the others, their twin trunks extended with obvious menace.

Up close they really were immense, and it was clear that if the huge animals took so much as a few sudden steps, Darwen and the others would all be crushed. They also stank like a barnyard on a hot day, a smell so powerful that Darwen actually took a step backward and covered his mouth. He turned to get a breath of air, glancing behind him to where the torrent of blue fire had left a smoking hole in the snow, then forced himself to look back at the mammoths and their riders.

Behind each rider was a complex array of crates, bags, and barrels, all wood but bound in copper. The barrels seemed to contain whatever flammable liquid the dulovune—to use Eileen's term—had shot at them. He could smell it now, a sharp gasoline aroma just discernible over the musky stench coming off the shaggy white beasts. Alex made a gagging noise, but Darwen didn't dare turn to stare her into silence. The riders all wore some kind of veil bound tight over their noses. Darwen got another whiff of the mammoth's potent odor and decided he couldn't blame them.

To Darwen's relief, Alex seemed to get the message all by herself. For a long moment, no one said a word, the tension as sharp and cold as the wind. The dulovunes' eyes were barely visible beneath the masses of thick hair, but their mouths moved constantly, a slow cow-like chewing that left ropes of spit trailing to the ground. Their double trunks were fitted with a device at the end of which burned a tiny bluish flame.

The dulovunes' riders were no taller than Darwen, but they looked wild. Their skin was a rich purple that seemed to shift in the light, like tiny fish scales, and their long copper-colored hair fell about their shoulders like coarse wire. Beneath their furs they wore body armor fashioned, Darwen guessed, from the shaved skin of their mounts. At their waists they carried ivory knives of strange, irregular shapes. They sat quite still, their black eyes boring into Darwen's, saying nothing.

"Er . . . hi," said Darwen, who was trying not to stare at the mammoths' glassy tusks, each ending in needle-sharp points.

The riders didn't utter a word, but one of the mammoths shook its pale head and a clump of snow fell from its fur.

"*Hi?*" muttered Alex. "Really? You figure that's how the secretary of state addresses the United Nations? *Hi?*"

"Shh," said Eileen. "Let him talk."

"My name is Darwen Arkwright," said Darwen, flustered into repeating himself, "and I am the mirroculist."

This time the riders did respond, their bodies tightening as they shifted in their saddles. Two of them exchanged slow, even glances.

"What is that to us?" said the lead rider at last. He spoke reluctantly and his faced creased into a sour frown, as if the very act of using words left an unpleasant taste in his mouth. English was clearly not his first language.

"War is coming," said Darwen, relieved that he could make himself understood at all. "I come on behalf of the Guardians to stand against Greyling. Can we count on your support?"

"You sound like a door-to-door salesman," muttered Alex, her eyes cast down. "You are trying, right now, to stop him from killing us, not trying to sell him magazine subscriptions."

Darwen shot her an irritated glance, but he knew she was right. The mammoth rider was continuing to stare silently down at him from inside his fur-lined hood.

"Greyling is destroying Silbrica," Darwen tried, trying not to show how much the biting cold was getting to him. "We have seen what he is doing to other loci," he explained, thinking of Moth's mutilated forest. "You can't ignore it."

A soft grunting sound came from the riders. It took Darwen a moment to realize that they were laughing.

"We can," said the leader, "and we will. Other loci mean nothing to us. We are secure. We are alone. None enters here without our permission—permission you do not have. Go back the way you came and bother us no more. Or face the consequences."

"You don't understand," Darwen began. "If you don't take our side, you may as well take Greyling's and even if he leaves you alone for a little while—"

It happened with astonishing speed, cutting Darwen off midsentence.

Three of the riders hopped over the heads of their mounts. Each mammoth instinctively lowered one trunk so that its rider could slide deftly to the ground, while the other trunk stayed aimed at Darwen and his friends. By the time the riders hit the ground, they had all readied a spear-like weapon whose tip had a cluster of lethal-looking points, all of which pulsed with electricity.

Cattle prods, thought Darwen, judging by the look of them. These, though, were bigger and probably packed a serious punch, assuming the spear points didn't just skewer you on the spot. Instinctively he raised his hands and took a step backward. The others did the same.

The wind gusted, blowing snowflakes in his face, but Darwen kept his gaze focused on the lead herder, who was staring in frigid silence. When Darwen opened his mouth to say something—anything—those three spears flinched, ready to strike home. With his arms still raised in surrender, he began walking silently back toward the portal.

"Next time," said the herder, his voice raised over the storm, "there will be no *conversation*." He said that last word as if it was particularly distasteful and pointed his spear meaningfully to underscore the threat.

Darwen just shook his head, then led the others through the portal.

"Okay," said Alex as they reached the columns and formal gardens on the other side. "That went well. When he hears of our diplomatic skill, Greyling will be shaking in his boots."

"Always helpful, Alex," said Rich.

"Well," she said, "at least we can breathe the air here. Man, those things *stank*! I don't know why they bother with weapons. The funk could knock down a grown man at fifty paces. No wonder no one wants to go there."

Alex stepped toward the portal that led back to the Great Apparatus. But before she could go through, Darwen interrupted her.

"Did you look at that one, Rich?" he asked, indicating the fractured statue of the girl in the process of hanging a picture frame in midair. One of her marble arms and half her face had been smashed off, but the picture frame itself was apparently intact, as were the controls that studded one edge of the frame. It was set a little apart from the others, but it was clearly a portal. "I noticed it before but didn't look at it closely. Kind of small, but it seems to be still in one piece, right, Rich?"

"I thought we were going home?" said Alex.

"But we're looking for clues and, you know, allies," said Darwen. "Maybe we should try this one."

"Are you forgetting the great white stink beasts that just threatened to flatten us if we so much as put a foot in their locus again?" asked Alex.

"No," Darwen returned, feeling flustered. "I just don't think that everyone we find will want to electrocute us. Some of them will know what Greyling is, what he's capable of. They'll join us."

"You sure about that, man?" asked Alex. "Because we have no idea what's on the other side of that portal. None at all. It could be worse. We can't just go into random loci blind, Darwen. We need to go back, talk to the Guardians or Weazen or someone and choose places where we think we'll make some real progress. Picking portals at random is . . ."

"What?" Darwen demanded angrily. "Stupid?"

"I was gonna say risky," said Alex. "Dangerous, even."

"Which *means* stupid," said Darwen.

"No, it doesn't," said Alex, not backing down. "But whatever. You're just mad because we're not getting anywhere and you feel like it's your fault."

"And maybe saving Silbrica is starting to look a little dangerous to you so you'd rather go home," said Darwen, giving her a hard look.

Alex put her hands on her hips and glared at him.

"Ex*cuse* me?" she said. "You sayin' I'm a coward or something, Darwen Arkwright? Because I will slap you upside the head, so help me Jesus."

"He's not saying that," Rich inserted, turning from the broken statue and looking anxiously at him. "Right, Darwen? You're not."

Darwen took a breath and closed his eyes for a moment. Even through his irritation he guessed that she was right. He was annoyed by their lack of progress and was taking it out on her.

"No," he said at last. "I'm not saying that."

"Well, all right then," said Alex, relaxing a little.

"It's late," said Eileen wearily. "I think Alex is right. We should go home for tonight."

Darwen bit his lip but said nothing, trying not to show how much his failure hurt.

"Okay," said Rich. "We can come back tomorrow. Yeah, Darwen?"

"Yeah," said Darwen, very quietly.

Darwen barely spoke again for the remainder of the journey back to the Great Apparatus and up the chute to his bedroom. He was still avoiding Alex's eyes when they rode the elevator down with Eileen.

"See you at school," said Rich, trying to make up for the fact that no one else was talking.

Darwen just nodded.

Chapter Thirteen
Plans and Specters

"What do flies wear on their feet?" said Darwen.

"I don't know," said Alex and Rich together.

"Shoos," said Darwen.

It was the end of the school day and the three of them were sitting at a desk piled with exercise books in their homeroom. The tensions of the previous day were forgotten, but Darwen had found something else to worry about.

"What?" said Alex. "Flies wear shoes? I don't get it."

"Not shoes," said Darwen, wafting the air vaguely, *"shoos."*

"Oh," said Alex. "Now I get it. But it's not funny."

"She's right, man," said Rich. "That's bad. What else do you have?"

"I'd tell you the story about the broken pencil—" Darwen began, but Rich cut him off.

"But it had no point?"

"Right," said Darwen.

"That's just sad," said Alex. "I thought English people were famous for their sense of humor."

Darwen sat down and put his head in his hands. "Guess I can't be a comedian in the talent show," he said.

"Wait," said Alex, "that's what this was? You were testing out material you were thinking of doing *in public*? Yeah . . . no. Never tell jokes again. Ever."

"So what am I going to do?" Darwen pleaded, his eyes flicking across a wall collage featuring all the students in the class. Somehow they all seemed to be brandishing trophies or holding up awards. "I've been so busy thinking about how to save Mr. Peregrine and find allies for the Guardians that I haven't given any thought to the stupid talent show. Not that it would have made any difference."

"Trust me, though, Darwen," said Rich. "What flies wear on their feet is not the answer."

"See," said Alex, "even if the jokes were funny, you have no presence. You've got to have presence to be a comedian."

"What is she talking about?" Darwen asked Rich.

"No idea," said Rich.

"Stage presence," said Alex. "You've got to own the room. Check this out."

And she began to sing.

Except that *sing* didn't begin to do it justice. She didn't just sing. She transformed into an entirely different person, a beaming superstar who sashayed around the room, looking them right in the face as she belted each word.

When Alex was done, she turned back into her usual self and said simply, "See?"

And the annoying thing was that Darwen *did* see. Alex was a performer. He wasn't. It really was that simple.

Rich looked positively unnerved by the whole display. "She's pretty good," he conceded as she went off to the bathroom. "I thought it was all just, you know, *Alex*, but she has actual talent."

"Good thing to have for a talent show," Darwen agreed, his head in his hands. "What's everyone else doing?"

"Jennifer Taylor-Berry is doing baton twirling," said Rich.

"What?" asked Darwen. Baton twirling wasn't big in Lancashire.

"You know," said Rich. "You have one of these little chrome poles and you spin it around and throw it in the air and what have you. Sort of cheerleader—marching band stuff. Kind of pointless, but difficult, and therefore impressive."

"I heard Naia's Greek folk songs," said Darwen. "I didn't understand a word, but she's really good too. Melissa Young does gymnastics and Genevieve Reddock has been playing the bassoon since she was three. I don't even know what a bassoon *is*."

"Kind of a weird-looking oboe thing," said Rich.

"Well, good for her," said Darwen. "I can't even play the kazoo."

"I was in a jug band when I was eight," said Rich. "You have these big old jugs and you blow into them. Can sound pretty good if you know what you're doing."

"And did you?"

"Nah," said Rich. "We were terrible. Sounded like a room full of kids farting. Not what the Hillside elite want to sit through."

"We can't be the only people with no recognizable ability at anything," said Darwen. "What's Barry Fails doing?"

"Turns out Usually can get out of knots," said Rich. "You tie him up and he escapes."

"Really?"

"Yeah, he's like Houdini except that he just breaks the rope. There's no real skill involved, of course. But he's really strong, and it's kind of amazing to watch."

"Great," said Darwen. "Just great. We have saved the school— twice—but compared to Usually—*Usually!*—we're going to look like gift-less idiots."

That was when they heard the first scream.

"Alex!" said Rich, getting up so fast he turned his chair over. They blundered to the door, tore it open, and stepped out into the hallway, turning in the direction of the girls' bathroom.

That was as far as they got.

They saw Alex standing quite still, her back to them. A few yards ahead of her was a girl. Or something like a girl. She was no more than a pale and shimmering form, the hallway beyond her visible through her body. Her feet drifted three inches above the floor, and at first Darwen thought the ghost—if that was what it was—was motionless, but then he realized it was turning very slowly to face Alex. Its countenance was a silvery blur and he could not see where it was looking, or if it could see anything at all, but he felt in his gut that it was aware of them, if dimly.

The apparition completed its slow rotation to face them and stopped, its head angled slightly to one side as if thinking. Then it raised its right hand slowly till the extended index finger was level with the specter's shoulder.

It was pointing directly at Darwen.

Darwen felt his skin crawl, and a chill ran through him as if his veins were pumping ice through his whole body. He took an involuntary step backward and felt Rich do the same. Alex, by contrast, seemed transfixed, immobile as a rabbit mesmerized by a snake. It wasn't until the ghost drifted suddenly forward that she leapt hurriedly aside with a cry of panic. The figure moved quickly, its legs quite still, but its hair seemed to stream behind it like tendrils of pale smoke.

It slid through the air toward Darwen, and as it came close, he backed up further, till he was against the wall with nowhere to go, his eyes locked on the silvery phantom as it surged toward him. Its mouth was moving, as if it was speaking, but no sound emerged, or nothing that Darwen could hear over his own cry of horror. In seconds it was almost upon him, almost close enough to touch him with that one extended hand . . .

And then, quite suddenly, it was gone.

It didn't merely vanish so much as fade quickly, breaking upon him like cloud, so that for a moment there was a pearly white after-image, which then melted into nothing at all. Darwen stood there, breathless, his heart racing.

"What on earth is going on out here, Mr. Arkwright?" said Miss Harvey, rounding the corner. "I could hear you shouting on the other side of the building. Come on—out with it! You look like you've seen a ghost."

Eileen picked them up at school, and they bombarded her with accounts of the Hillside specter, but she was at a loss to explain it. At length she suggested they try to forget the ghost and focus on their plans for the evening: searching for allies and clues to Mr. Peregrine's whereabouts in Silbrica.

"Forget about the phantom that attacked us?" mused Alex with a little shudder. "That might take a little doing, but we'll give it a shot."

"Good," said Eileen. "For all we know the ghost has nothing to do with what we are doing. We need to stay focused. Yes?"

"Yes," said Darwen.

They waited till the sun went down and—after Eileen had confirmed that Aunt Honoria wouldn't be home for at least two hours—climbed through the oven door and down to the Great Apparatus.

They made their way to Moth's forest—Rich had mended the portal on their last visit—and found the dellfeys working on their wings with tiny hammers, still repairing the damage the scrobblers had left in their wake.

"We need to start talking to people in Silbrica . . ." Darwen explained to Moth a few minutes after greeting the dellfey.

"Or creatures," added Alex, who was surveying the oil-spattered damage to the trees. The dellfey had obviously been busy cleaning the place up, but there was still a lot to do, much of it too big for Moth's friends to complete alone.

"Or creatures," Darwen agreed, "who might join us in a fight against Greyling before he can take over both our worlds."

"We were trying to decide if this portal here is safe," added Alex, showing Moth the notebook she'd been carrying with her ever since they visited Mr. Peregrine's house. "It's small, so we figured that while not many creatures could use it . . ."

"You might know," Darwen completed for her, smiling at the dellfey.

Moth smiled back, proud to be considered helpful, but her face fell when she looked at the book. "I do not know these markings," she said.

"They're numbers," said Rich, "Like the ones in the address you gave us."

"The portal looks like a statue of a human child, a girl, holding a picture frame about this size," said Darwen, gesturing with his hands.

"Oh yes!" said Moth, delighted. "This is a very good place to go. It is where the zingers live."

"Zingers?" said Alex, sounding skeptical. "Are they comedians?"

Moth gave her a baffled look. "They are friends of the dellfey," she said, "and will be your friends as well."

"Good enough for me," said Darwen.

"Mr. Peregrine liked them," Moth added. "I think they have something of his that you might find helpful."

"What is it?" asked Rich. "A weapon of some kind?"

Moth looked affronted. "It is his whistle," she said seriously.

"His what now?" asked Alex.

"His whistle," said Moth, as if this was obvious.

"And what does that do?" Darwen coaxed.

The dellfey shrugged minutely. "Nothing," she said, "but I think he liked it."

"Right," said Darwen. "Great. Thanks."

It took three portals to reach the fractured colonnade in the gardens of the Silbrican mansion, but though the journey went without difficulty, they were tense and jumpy. In one locus dominated by curiously square-sided rock formations, Alex shrieked as something like a giant green crab scuttled by. The crab took off at high speed the moment it realized they were there, and they burst out laughing, partly with relief, partly because it kept bumping into things in its rush to get away.

They passed through the final portal and reached the half-broken statue of the girl with the picture frame without seeing another living thing.

"Not sure I can fit through that," said Rich, eyeing the portal.

"Sure you can," said Alex. "It's about the same size as Darwen's oven door, right, Darwen?"

"I guess," said Darwen, remembering the way the snorkies had tumbled through the portal into his bedroom, "but why would the scrobblers leave this one intact?"

"You're worried because the last one took us to the land of the killer ice elephants," said Alex wisely. "Maybe they just ignored it 'cause it was little. Come on, man; time's a wastin'.'"

Darwen said nothing. Instead he approached the statue, placed one hand on the lower edge of the empty marble picture frame, put the other on the statue's broken left arm and—trying not to look at the unnervingly blank look on the broken face—boosted himself through.

For a moment he saw leaves, but then he was through them and falling through nothingness.

Chapter Fourteen
Zingers

Darwen landed awkwardly on the silver bark of a massive tree limb. He threw his arms around the smooth branch, its bark cool to the touch and concrete-hard, and stared wildly down. He was in a cloudless blue sky. The ground was too far below to be visible. Darwen hugged the branch for dear life, only remembering a moment later to call back up to the portal he had fallen through with a desperate "Watch it!"

Too late. Rich came crashing through the leafy canopy and hurtled toward him. Darwen rolled a fraction but didn't want to lose his purchase on the branch, so Rich still hit him hard, knocking the wind out of him. As he gasped for air, he saw Eileen and Alex tumbling out of the portal above him.

Somehow they managed the descent with more grace than either he or Rich, and they landed on the branch as if they had been on some kind of amusement park ride, startled but grinning.

"Where are we?" asked Alex brightly.

"In a tree," muttered Rich, rather less enthusiastic.

"Well, *duh*," said Alex. "But what's the locus like?"

Darwen had no clue—he'd been trying so hard to keep his eyes fixed on the branch that he hadn't gotten the chance to take a good look around. Feeling the entire tree sway fractionally, he hugged it all the tighter and said nothing. Alex, who had landed on a limb a little higher than the one Rich and Darwen were clinging to, leaned out and peered down through the leaves.

"Wow," she said, pleased. "We're really high. What do you think, Eileen? A hundred feet? Two hundred?"

"Something like that," said Eileen. "I can barely see the ground!"

"Thanks," said Rich, whose normally ruddy complexion had turned the color of sour milk. "What kind of place is this? No wonder the scrobblers didn't bother to shut it down. Step through a portal and fall out of a tree? It's a death trap. Why didn't Moth warn us?"

"Because she can fly," said Darwen. "It probably never occurred to her."

"Smells nice," Alex remarked. "Guess there are no stinking furry elephants up here."

"In the tree," said Rich dryly. "Not big tree climbers, elephants. You're right about the smell, though. Pretty nice."

But it was more than *nice*. The tree hung with a powerful scent, sweet and fragrant, so that Darwen was suddenly reminded of shopping for his mother's Christmas present at the perfume counter of a department store back in England.

"No wonder," said Rich. "Check out those blooms."

He was gazing to where a flower hung inches above Darwen's head. It was the size of a soccer ball, bulb-like in the center but with huge open petals around the edges, which, as he looked, shifted from white to pink, and finally to a deep crimson, before cycling back to white again. As the colors changed, the aroma became so strong that Darwen began to feel himself losing focus.

"What are you doing, man?" called Rich.

Darwen came to with a start and grasped the branch with renewed vigor. He had relaxed so much he had been close to letting go. He shook his head.

"It's the chuffin' perfume," he said. "Sort of . . . distracted me."

He gazed at the flower in disbelief, trying not to breathe in its fragrance. As he was considering the massive bloom, he caught a thrumming whir above him: a bird, as big as a pigeon but a bright, irridescent green color, and hovering like a hummingbird. It was watching him, and when Darwen met its gaze, he could see that it was not precisely a bird at all. It had slender arms and its beaked face held something human about the eyes that reminded him of the bat-like flittercrake that had led him to Mr. Peregrine. This, however, was something different entirely.

"Hello," Darwen ventured, still clinging to his branch.

The bird thing stayed suspended in the air, its wings a blur of movement. Then it opened its beak, and in a shrill scream, it called, "Scrobblers!"

It swooped up and away, but there was suddenly movement all around the tree. More of the bird things were massing as if poised to attack.

"No!" shouted Darwen. "We're not scrobblers! We're people. I'm the mirroculist, Darwen Arkwright."

But the bird things—at least a dozen of them—were already in their attack formation and swooping through the branches.

"Big deal!" shouted Alex. "You think we can't swat off a few sparrows? Bring it on!"

But instead of diving right at their hands and faces, slashing with their sharp little claws or stabbing with those dagger-like beaks, the birds suddenly pulled up and soared away again. It took Darwen a second to realize that they had each dropped something, like a squadron of tiny bombers. He barely saw the tiny ball-like containers—miniature barrels—raining down around him, but as soon as they hit the tree and split open, he knew what they were, and he panicked.

"It's nectar from the flowers!" he called as the perfume exploded on his hands and clothes like a cloud. Immediately he felt his mind gliding up and away on a tide of exotic fragrance. It was a glorious feeling. He was no more than mist, drifting up through the leaves, a bodiless essence carried on a wave like a dream, and all around him was color and scent and beauty and . . .

"Darwen, look out!"

Rich had clawed his way along the branch and was holding him in place, the crook of his arm clamped over his nose so that he was breathing through his shirt. Darwen was barely aware of him and still felt he was drifting, groggy and confused, like waking up at the dentist when he'd had a tooth removed.

"Focus," said Rich, "and try to breathe through your mouth."

The birds came again, but this time the boys were huddled over, their faces buried in their clothes. Darwen caught a whiff of the potent fragrance all the same and held his breath for as long as he could. Dimly, as through a fog, he saw Eileen and Alex up on the branches above them, one hand over their faces, the other waving the birds away. When he could hold it no longer, Darwen blew the air out of his lungs and took another shallow breath. Immediately he felt his head swim and darken, but he gripped the branch and tried to balance himself so that if he lost consciousness entirely, he wouldn't fall.

And then, without warning, the attack stopped. The birds wheeled off into the upper parts of the tree and vanished from view.

"So these are zingers," said Eileen, when they finally got used to the stillness. "Moth's account was . . . incomplete."

"Not what you'd call friendly, are they?" Rich muttered.

"Maybe with good reason," said Eileen. "The scrobblers have been here. Look."

She was pointing to where something hung from the bough she and Alex were straddling. It looked a little like an old lantern, forged from blackened metal and suspended from a heavy chain.

"What do you suppose that is?" asked Alex. "Let me see if I can get a better look."

"Careful," said Darwen.

"Relax," said Alex, her old self again. "This is nothing. These branches are thick enough to walk on."

And she stood up, arms outstretched.

"Don't touch it," said Darwen.

"I wasn't going to touch it, smart guy," said Alex, inching along the branch and rolling her eyes. "Hey, it's making a noise. Can you hear that? A whiny sound like a mosquito or something. It's getting higher as I get closer. You think it's reacting to me getting near to—"

But she didn't finish the sentence.

There was suddenly a crackle of energy, and a fork of miniature lightning shot from the lantern directly at her. It hit her squarely in the chest and seemed to flicker with electricity, convulsing as her hair stood on end. For a moment she stood there, dazed, and then, very slowly she tipped backward and fell.

Darwen threw one arm out, but he couldn't reach and she dropped past him, down beyond the tree's thick branches and away. "Alex!" he cried, but there was nothing he could do. She turned slowly as she fell, the ground racing to meet her and nothing to break her fall.

Chapter Fifteen
Making Friends

And then there was a blur of metallic green like a cloud plummeting from above toward Alex as she fell. The cloud moved impossibly fast, knifing through the air until it had reached her. It seemed to flicker and still itself, and now it wasn't a cloud at all, but dozens of zingers that had attached themselves to her. Darwen wanted to shout out that they should leave her alone, but then he realized that her terrible fall had slowed and stopped. The bird things had caught her.

Then they were raising her up again, their tiny hands gripping her arms, her legs, her clothing, so that it wrinkled and hitched in ways that looked incredibly uncomfortable, though Alex's face showed only a frozen shock, eyes wide, mouth open, body stiff as if the slightest movement might send her tumbling down again.

The birds raised her up to Darwen's branch and lowered her into place.

"Is she okay?" called Eileen.

"Whoa," said Alex in a thick, dazed voice. Her hair was smoking slightly from the electric charge. "I got bug zapped. Then the bugs rescued me."

"Are you all right?" asked Darwen.

"I'm a little ticked," said Alex thoughtfully, "but yeah. I'm okay."

Slowly, carefully, she turned to consider the silent, watchful cloud of zingers, which still hovered in place just above her. "Thanks," she said.

"You are not scrobblers," said one of them. The voice was lilting and musical but so high that it was hard to listen to. "If you were, you would not fall prey to their traps."

"True story," Alex agreed.

"But you are large," said the zinger.

"Hey!" said Alex.

"He's just saying they thought we were scrobblers because we're big," Eileen said.

"Speak for yourself," said Alex. She still looked dazed and a little scared. "So no more pelting us with perfume bombs, yeah?" Alex asked the lead zinger.

"No more for now," said the bird thing, bobbing in place.

"I guess we'll take that," said Darwen. "We are looking for a friend of ours: Mr. Octavius Peregrine, a gatekeeper of the Guardian Council."

"We know your Mr. Peregrine," said the bird thing, "but we have no dealings with the Guardians. This locus is our own and none come here except those who mean us harm. The scrobbler devices have killed several of my people."

"So rule one of wherever we are," said Rich, glancing around. "Stay clear of the lantern things."

"You think?" said Alex, shooting him a withering look that was somehow intensified by the wisps of smoke that still came off her head. "You smell that? That's me burning. First scrobbler I see, he's gonna get a piece of my mind."

"You don't hang onto that branch," said Rich, "and it won't just be your mind they get pieces of."

"The scrobblers are our enemies too," said Darwen to the zingers, shooting Rich and Alex a look that told them in no uncertain terms to shut up. "They are threatening my world as they threaten yours."

"It is not the scrobblers themselves who come here at night and plant their traps," said the zinger. "They are too big to fit through, so they send the smaller ones."

"Smaller scrobblers," said Alex. "You mean scrobbler children?"

"The scrobblers have no children," said the zinger.

"Well, they must at some point, right?" Alex persisted. "Else there wouldn't be any adult scrobblers, would there?"

"Let it go, Alex," said Rich.

"I'm just saying . . ."

"Let it go," Rich insisted.

"The small creatures that plant the traps are not like scrobblers," said the zinger. "More like insects."

"Oh, great," said Alex, looking hurriedly around as if one of them might be close by.

"Anyway," said Darwen, "I'm saying we need to band together to protect Silbrica."

"We can defend our locus," said the zinger, puffing out his tiny chest and increasing the beat of his wings so that they hummed slightly.

"For now," said Darwen, "I'm sure."

He let the phrase hang there, watching as some of the zingers started to bob and weave in the air with agitation. "But they will come back," he said. "They always do. And they will bring machines to protect themselves from whatever weapons you have. They want your land. We have seen it before. They will cut down your trees."

The buzz of unease instantly became a torrent of angry zingers shouting their defiance and outrage as they flickered into Darwen's face and back. They looked furious.

"For future reference," said Alex, "let's not talk about cutting their trees down."

"It's not us who will do it!" Darwen protested, but the zingers were clearly incensed. "It's the scrobblers! We're not them, remember?"

The zingers seemed not to hear him, and the more they chattered angrily among themselves, the more they seemed less like a flock of birds and more like a swarm of colossal wasps.

"I think we should go," said Eileen.

"Just let me talk to them!" Darwen protested.

"I don't think they're in the mood," said Alex. "Start climbing."

They did so, one eye on the angry zingers, who were zipping around them, surely only moments from commencing another attack, and one eye on the black lanterns that hung from the tree branches like lethal fruit.

"Keep your distance and keep going," said Rich, hoisting himself up onto the next branch. "The portal is about twenty feet up that way."

And so they climbed, and the zinger swarm moved with them, their eyes bright with fury, their bills sharp as needles. But when they reached the portal, and the sense of failure and futility rested on Darwen's shoulders like a heavy, sopping coat, he found he had to try one more time.

"Listen," he said. "I'm sorry if I offended you. Really I am. But please, listen to me for a moment!"

The buzzing slackened off, and some of the zingers poised in midair to look at him. Darwen didn't wait for them all to pay attention and started talking.

"I'm just warning you of what will come," he said. "Not from us. We're on your side. We want to protect Silbrica from the scrobblers, from Greyling. But to save you all, you may have to fight *outside* your locus. We have to band together. We have to take the battle to him."

He paused. The sound and fluttering about had dropped to almost nothing. Above him, Eileen, Rich, and Alex were poised to squeeze through the tiny portal, but they were watching him closely.

"We do not leave our locus," said one of the zingers at last. "We will defend our home to the end, however bitter, but we do not leave this place."

"If you are going to live, you may have to," said Darwen.

"Then we will die," said the zinger. "But we will die fighting."

Darwen looked into the bird creature's earnest face for a long moment and then nodded. "If we can help you," Darwen said, "we will."

He nodded a farewell, and the zinger in front of him gave a fractional bow before turning and calling to one of the others, which flew forward, cradling something in its arms. The object was brass and no more than two inches long with holes at each end and a slit in the middle.

"This was left with us," said the lead zinger. "Perhaps it will be useful to you."

Darwen took it gratefully. It was the whistle Moth had mentioned.

"Thank you," he said, but the zinger was already flying away. After a moment, the others followed.

"What does the whistle do?" asked Rich excitedly as soon as they had all made it through the portal. "I mean," he said, "if it belonged to Mr. Peregrine, it must do something cool, despite what Moth said."

"Maybe it creates portals," said Alex.

Darwen doubted it. He put it to his lips and gave it a long, hard blow.

Nothing happened.

"Maybe it's broken," said Alex.

"It's not," said Eileen. "It's just not that useful."

"What is it?" asked Darwen.

"It's like a dog whistle, but for flittercrakes."

"Oh," said Darwen, deflated.

"Those are the bird things with the ugly old man face?" asked Alex. "Yeah, let's not blow it again. Those things give me the willies."

Darwen pocketed the whistle and hung his head.

"Still," Alex said, looking around the garden. "Better than nothing."

Darwen nodded thoughtfully but kept silent.

"You did well, Darwen," said Eileen. "I thought we were just going to leave with another enemy, but we left with an ally."

"An ally who won't actually fight with us unless the battle takes place in their tree," Darwen said.

"An ally nonetheless," said Eileen. "Right now we take our victories where we can find them."

Again, Darwen nodded and said nothing, but this time, he smiled a little.

The sun was almost down in the gardens as they considered their next move.

"We could go back to the Great Apparatus and pick another portal," said Alex, "though we haven't really explored this area beyond the route to the house."

"What's that over there?" said Rich. "There's a gravel path that leads through those trees." He started along the path and the others followed, peering ahead through the low light, which dropped still further as they entered the shadow of the trees. "Hmm . . . it's a building," Rich murmured, answering his own question.

Darwen caught a glimpse of brickwork through the bushes ahead and thought at first that they had found their way back to the mansion. Quickly, however, he realized that they hadn't—this was something quite different. Still, the scene felt oddly familiar.

The shrubs parted before them and there it was: a crumbling brick structure with leaded diamond-shaped panes of glass set into windows surrounded by flaking, faded frames. The edifice itself was a strange enough sight in the middle of the woods of Silbrica, but it was the hand-lettered sign that hung above the front door with its worn brass latch that made their mouths hang open in disbelief.

MISTER OCTAVIUS PEREGRINE'S REFLECTORY EMPORIUM: MIRRORS PRICELESS AND PERILOUS

Darwen stared.

"Well, I'll be," gasped Rich.

Standing before them was the shop from the mall, exact in every detail, except that there was no mall, just more gardens, the store sitting there as if it had been left by someone who didn't know where to put it.

Darwen found that he was rushing to the front door and that, without saying a word, the others were doing the same. This was Mr. Peregrine's shop . . . in Silbrica. There had to be a clue here, a portal, maybe, something that would get them to where he was now. . . .

But the shop was dark and empty. The little bell over the door jangled as they went in, and though the floor plan was the same, there were no mirrors, no sign in fact that anyone had ever been inside. It resembled a model or a film set, a shell that looked perfect from the outside but felt completely unreal up close.

Darwen slumped dejectedly to the floor by the counter. There was no antique cash register, no night-and-day clock, no messaging system like the one Mr. P had once used to alert his friends the Jenkinses that he was coming to visit. Darwen remembered that awful night at the Jenkins house and the things that had emerged from what had seemed to be just a kindly old couple. He wondered what had happened to the real Jenkinses and if they were being held somewhere with Mr. Peregrine. . . .

"Come look at this," called Rich from the stockroom in the back.

Darwen's heart quickened and he got to his feet, but Alex and Eileen still beat him there. Rich had his face pressed to a tiny window in the rear wall. Rich was staring at a series of distant silhouettes in the night.

"Those trees," he was saying. "They look familiar to you?"

"This again?" said Alex, rolling her eyes and grinning. "You're gonna lecture us on how your daddy would prune a crepe myrtle?"

Darwen hung his head.

"They're not crepe myrtles," said Rich. "They're eastern red cedars."

"Wait," said Darwen, remembering something Rich had told him on only his second day at Hillside, a tale Rich had said attested to the school's *deep weirdness*. "Are you sure?"

"Pretty sure," said Rich. "And see how regularly spaced they are? Like they were deliberately planted like that."

"When we were walking around in those gardens back there for the last fifty years or so did you, like, open your eyes at all?" asked Alex, very politely. "Only everything was regularly spaced and deliberately planted because that's what formal gardens are."

"And how many eastern red cedars did you see out there?" asked Rich, turning from the window, his eyes bright with excitement.

"I don't know," said Alex. "You tell me."

"None," said Rich. "Because red cedars are not formal garden material. They are trash trees, and they pop up all over Georgia."

"But they were planted by Native Americans to mark ritual spaces," said Darwen, catching some of Rich's enthusiasm. "And there's a ring of them around Hillside."

"Which, if we were in Atlanta," mused Rich, nodding at the trees through the window, "would be in that direction, and exactly that far away. There's a Silbrican version of Mr. Peregrine's mansion, and a version of his shop. What if there's also . . . ?"

He didn't have to say anything else. The four of them moved hurriedly to the door and out, the bell tinkling as they ran around the back of the building and made for the trees.

"Well, that's just plain unsettling," said Alex, who had come to an abrupt halt between two of the massive cedars.

Darwen pushed through the trees' hard green boughs and stared into the gathering darkness.

Unsettling was right.

Directly ahead of them was Hillside Academy, or rather a very strange version of it fashioned roughly out of—what? Stone? It looked like it. The school rose up from the ground like it had been molded or carved by someone who couldn't picture all the details. The buildings were all there, the steeply sloped roofs, the clock tower, but everything looked slightly irregular and unfinished. Darwen could just make out the faint tracing of lines between what should have been bricks, but the walls looked like they were just slabs that had grown up out of the ground, the brick pattern just a surface treatment to fool the eye. He remembered the gates of the Great Apparatus, composed of tree jambs rooted into the very ground, and he had the powerful impression that this replica of the school had not been built at all, not really, but had somehow *grown* there.

"I was never a big fan of Hillside," said Rich, "but this is quite a bit worse."

Darwen knew what he meant. The night, the silence, the uncanny rough-hewn version of the buildings in front of them made the school feel *off* somehow, familiar, but alien, and just plain . . .

"Creepifying," Alex whispered aloud, completing Darwen's thought.

"We should go in," said Eileen.

Alex gave her a wide-eyed stare.

"Might not be that easy," said Rich. "Check it out. There's a fence."

It was almost too dark to see the wires, but set a little back from the trees, Darwen could just make out a series of posts along which cables were strung. On top of the posts were tiny lights.

"It's electrified," said Rich. "Or worse."

"Anyone got any better ideas?" asked Darwen.

"Better than being fried on an electric fence, you mean?" asked Alex. "Yeah, I got a few ideas. How about not being?"

"We have to see inside," said Darwen, adding—hurriedly, and with a half look at Eileen—"it might help us find Mr. Peregrine."

"What if the fence is alarmed?" asked Rich.

Eileen checked her triple-barreled blaster. "I've got another couple of shots left in this thing, but that's all," she said. "If I set the power real low, I might get a few more, but it won't be firing much more than light at that point."

"There's a gate over there," said Alex. She was pointing to what—in the real school—would have been the main drive. It passed through two metal scaffolds that looked like sentry boxes, and the air between them seemed to thrum with power.

"Some sort of portal," said Rich.

"Built by Greyling," added Darwen, "judging by the technology."

Anything built by the Guardians tended to be old: wood and brass and copper. Only Greyling's scrobblers built from iron, and where the Guardians' work was elegant and sophisticated, scrobbler construction was clumsy and functional.

They approached the gate cautiously, glancing around for signs of guards, but there was nothing. Darwen's eyes fell on a statue—or what would have been a statue at the Atlanta version of the school, specifically the one where he'd spotted a flittercrake on his first day at Hillside—but here the sculpture was little more than a stalagmite twisting up out of the ground.

"If it's a portal," Rich whispered, "we should hold hands."

Eileen shot him a look and Rich blushed. "Otherwise you won't be able to get in," he explained hurriedly.

Eileen held his gaze for a second, then nodded once and took his hand. For all the tension, Darwen thought Rich failed to hide how much this pleased him.

Darwen was about to speak when Alex stopped him. "And if you ask if I'm ready to step inside this spook-infested Silbrican nightmare of a school, I'm gonna whup you, got it?"

Darwen merely squeezed her hand, took Eileen's, and led them through.

Chapter Sixteen
The Shadow School

There was a faint bluish fizz from the gateposts, a ripple of the air as they crossed over, then silence closed over them again. They released each other's hands, Rich letting go of Eileen's last, but quickly, like it had grown too hot to hold. They walked up to the main entrance, climbing the steps that seemed to have formed from some impossible geological accident.

"This is beyond weird," muttered Alex.

There were no doors, no windows, so the structure felt like one of the ruined medieval castles that Darwen had so loved back in England, hollow shells that dripped with age and deeds long forgotten. The floor of the entrance hall was uneven, the statue of "Learning" a great stone blob that would have been unrecognizable if they hadn't known what stood in its place on the other side. Alex considered it, her head cocked onto her left shoulder, her eyes almost closed.

"I can almost smell the sappiness of the original," she said. "If I stood here long enough, I might get the urge to take a hammer to it."

"I think our time might be better spent exploring," said Rich.

"What are we looking for?" asked Eileen.

"No idea," said Darwen. "Something connected to Mr. Peregrine, I guess, but . . . what was that?" He stood quite still. For a second, off in the shadows to his left, he thought he had seen movement. He stared past the rising rocky growth that echoed Hillside's main staircase but could see nothing.

He shrugged.

"Trick of the light, I guess," he said.

"Trick of the dark, more like," muttered Alex. "And can we agree right now that if we see something terrifying, you don't try to make friends with it, 'cause so far . . ."

"There!" said Rich. He was pointing to the other end of the hallway, his face pale, his eyes wide and fixed.

"What is it?" asked Eileen.

"Looks like . . ." Darwen hesitated, unable to say the word.

"A ghost," said Alex.

It did. It was a smear of pale gray light, roughly human in shape, and it flickered as it drifted toward them.

"Here as well?" gasped Darwen.

"It's coming," hissed Rich.

They backed away, but it came on, and though it clearly wasn't solid, the figure did have legs and was walking, albeit soundlessly, right at them. And then, all of a sudden, it wasn't. The specter shifted direction, hesitated, and moved off down the steps into the grounds.

Darwen shuddered.

"What *was* that?" demanded Eileen. Though she had been completely unfazed by the scrobblers and the turtle-like terrapod back in the Atlanta mansion, the ghostly apparition seemed to have unnerved her quite badly.

"This is Silbrica," said Rich, who hadn't taken his eyes off it. "So who knows? Could be anything."

"But it looked like what we saw at school," said Darwen. "Like a ghost."

"There's no such thing," said Rich.

"'There are more things in heaven and earth than are dreamt of in your philosophy,'" said Alex. "That's Shakespeare, man. *Hamlet.*"

"She has a point," said Darwen. "We've seen lots of stuff no one would believe in. Compared to gnashers and flittercrakes, ghosts sound pretty plausible."

Rich shrugged and nodded, grudgingly.

"Weird, though," said Alex. "Here and at Hillside? Can't be a coincidence."

"Let's get moving," said Rich, his face pale and tense in the dark.

"Where to?" said Darwen. "The clock tower basement?"

Rich nodded and led the way. "This is seriously strange," he whispered as they paced the curiously cave-like corridors. "You think this was where Greyling's army gathered at Halloween before coming through to Hillside?"

"Maybe," said Darwen, taking in the eerie silence of the place. "There must be a way to cross into the school directly from here."

"How about we talk about happy things?" said Alex, glancing uneasily into the shadows around her. "Like my dog, say. Let's talk about Sasha."

"Okay," said Darwen, who was feeling the same nervous apprehension. "Tell us about your dog."

Alex hesitated thoughtfully. "She would really hate this place," she said.

Rich considered this for a moment, inching along the near black hallway. "Smart dog," he said. "Er, guys," he added. "Are your watches being . . . I don't know, weird?"

Darwen glanced at his. The digital display was flickering, but it was impossible to read the numbers. "Yes," he said. "What's yours doing?"

Rich held out his wrist and Darwen stared at the hands of his old-fashioned watch. The hour hand was inching visibly around the dial while the minute hand was positively spinning.

"Ohhh-kay," said Alex. "What does that mean?"

"Nothing good," said Rich.

"Time can be slippery in Silbrica," said Eileen. "I think it's passing faster here."

"So it's like four in the morning back home?" gasped Alex. "You have *got* to be kidding!"

"Four?" exclaimed Darwen. "My aunt will go nuts."

"Start picking out the flowers now, boys," said Alex, "'cause we are *so* dead."

"We have to find a way back," said Rich.

They moved slowly and in silence till they came to the first classroom on their right, and Darwen heard Eileen gasp.

Inside the room, visible through the uneven space that should have been a doorway, two more ghostly figures drifted soundlessly. One was barely visible, the merest pearly smudge like smoke that didn't dissipate, but the other was clearer, more obviously human in shape, and when it revolved to face them, its pale face came into view. It was vague and the features seemed to swirl and blur as the figure moved, but there was no question that it was a human face. If Darwen had to guess, he would have said it was a girl.

"We really have to get out of here," said Rich, speaking for all of them.

"Just keep moving," said Darwen, trying to ignore his pounding heart and the way the hair on his arms and the back of his neck was standing on end.

He traced his fingers along the rock wall so he could feel where he was and realized that there was wood in there too, gnarled rope-like roots and coarse bark: the structure was indeed growing, though instead of feeling the throb of life and energy such as he had felt in the Great Apparatus, Darwen felt only the wrongness of the place, as if the force that coursed through the tree trunks, through the veins in the rock, was somehow poisonous. He took his hand away and moved closer to the others.

"There are more ghosts in the other classrooms," Rich said in a hushed, breathy voice. "Some of them are so faint they're barely there. Others look almost solid."

"So long as they stay away from me," murmured Alex.

But as she said it, one of the figures emerged from the far end of the hallway and even at this distance they could see that it was altogether more substantial than any they had seen so far. There was nothing wispy about it at all. It had the same pallor as the others, but where the previous apparitions had looked like smoke and vapor lit softly from within, this looked like a person, though his face and clothes held no color.

Darwen thought *his* because he was sure it was a man, or rather a tall boy, and there was something familiar about him, something that Darwen did not like, even though he couldn't put his finger on what it was. Worse, while the other specters seemed to go about whatever they were doing seemingly at random, ignoring the presence of Darwen and his friends, this one stopped quite still and stared at them. It wasn't just facing in their direction. It was looking at them, seeing them. Darwen was sure of that even before it raised an accusing hand and pointed their way.

But his terror did not fully engage until the apparition began to scream.

It was a terrible sound, high and keening, full of rage and hatred. It stretched the figure's mouth wide and kept coming long after any living person would have had to pause for breath.

And then the pearly shadows in the rooms around them seemed to hesitate too and turn in the direction of the sound. There was an awful pause, then they started moving out into the hall.

"They're coming after us," gasped Rich. "All of them."

They weren't the only ones. Darwen heard a series of distant bangs out near the perimeter fence and heard grunting voices. *Scrobblers*, he thought. *Probably other things too.*

The alarm had obviously been raised. Now they really did have to get out.

"This way!" shouted Darwen, sounding braver than he felt, particularly since his first few steps actually took him closer to the shrieking ghost before they could cut left into the open space of the quadrangle and the great black hunk that was this world's equivalent of the Hillside clock tower.

The tower reached up into the night sky, immense and threatening, but up just beneath where the clock face should be, Darwen could see lights, and leading up to it was an iron staircase that zigzagged its way down to the ground. He peered into the blackness, deliberately not looking to the classrooms where the ghostly figures were now drifting out into the corridor, as if gathering to attack. He tried not to listen to the panicked sounds of Alex's stuttering footsteps, Rich's labored breathing, and what might have been a sob from Eileen, all of which were almost drowned out by the dreadful cry from the ghost boy at the end of the hall. At last Darwen could just make it out: an archway that maybe, just maybe . . .

"There!" he yelled, pointing. "Up those stairs. I think it's a portal!"

Alex led the way, leaping ahead through the night like a gazelle with a lion on her tail. Rich and Eileen followed, and only when they were safely past him did Darwen risk a look back into the corridor.

He had been right. Beyond the throbbing ghost forms, he saw large, solid figures stomping into view. A pair of scrobblers with more behind, and at least one gnasher. They were coming fast. Maybe too fast for him to get away.

The thought had just occurred to him when there was a sudden explosion from behind the scrobblers and one of them fell hard. Just visible in the brief muzzle flash of his blaster was a small ferret-like creature.

Weazen!

"All right there, Darwen?" called the Peace Hunter, quite unfazed by being in the middle of a battle. "Moth said you were snooping in the neighborhood, so I thought I'd check in. Rather hoped I wouldn't find you here, to be honest. Not what you'd call the most pleasant of places."

He fired twice more as if to make the point. The scrobblers hesitated, turning to face their new adversary, and Darwen knew that would buy him just enough time to get out. He turned back to the iron staircase, grateful for Weazen's timely appearance, and was alarmed to find the screaming ghost was actually closer now. Close enough that Darwen could see his face.

It was like being slapped hard. For a moment he stared in baffled shock and horror. But then he heard Rich calling to him from the metal stairs and he forced himself to move, though he was walking blind, his head twisted back toward the screaming boy and his terrible face.

It was a Hillside student, but it was also, somehow, a scrobbler.

Or some dreadful echo of one. The face was pale, the eyes dead, the jaw heavy and studded with tusklike teeth. It oozed malice and cruelty.

But there was something else in the face, something he almost recognized. Someone he felt he should know . . .

After an impossibly long and horrified moment, Darwen was able to look away and stumbled up the steps, gripping the rail as his injured leg groaned with pain. In the structure below, there were more explosions, more shouts, and now a stream of ghostly forms was flowing into the quadrangle, moving as if with one mind toward the staircase. Darwen looked wildly around for signs of Weazen, but the little creature was nowhere to be seen.

"It's a portal," snapped Rich as Darwen reached the top, "but I don't think it's finished."

The scaffold platform was littered with heavy tools and tangles of wire.

"We can't get through?" gasped Alex, desperately glancing from the swarming enemy to her speeding watch. She squeezed her eyes shut and a single tear rolled down her cheek.

"I don't know," said Rich, pointing to a set of terminals, only some of which had cables plugged in. "There's power running to parts of it, but not everything has been hooked up and I don't know what that means. It might not be stable. Might not work at all."

"Do we have any alternatives?" asked Eileen, her eyes fixed on the swelling tide of ghost figures coalescing at the foot of the stairs.

Among them was a small, lithe figure, which fired two more quick shots through one of the windows, forcing a heavily armed scrobbler to duck back before it came bounding up the stairs. For all his dread at what was happening, Darwen sighed with relief.

"That's Weazen," said Rich to Eileen. "He's on our side."

Eileen just nodded and when Weazen saw her, he returned the nod, more formally. For all the panic and fear, Darwen was almost sure that the emotion in Eileen's face was something quite different, something more like a momentary but acute sadness. It was there in her eyes as she looked at Weazen, and then—as suddenly as it had come—it was gone.

"I suggest you use that gate," said Weazen. "Or we're all, you know, dead."

"Good point," said Rich, taking one last pained look at the spinning hand on his watch. He pulled a lever and the portal arch filled with blue flickering light.

"Can anyone use this, or just mirroculists?" asked Eileen.

"Better be on the safe side," said Rich. "You come through with me. You two bring Weazen."

So saying, he took Eileen's hand and stepped into the portal. There was a flash, and they were gone. Alex went next. Darwen looked at Weazen, then stooped, and the little creature leapt onto his shoulder, firing his blaster at the gnasher that was pulling its blind way up the stairs.

Together they stepped through.

That they had escaped should have been an immense relief. But Darwen instantly knew that he was now in trouble of an altogether different kind.

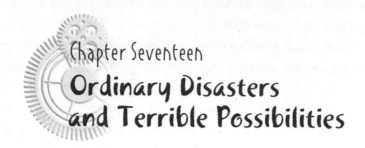

Chapter Seventeen
Ordinary Disasters
and Terrible Possibilities

It was daylight, and after the darkness of Silbrica, the bright, hard sunlight made Darwen wince. It also revealed the full horror of his situation. Alex was quite still, staring down, speechless. Rich was still holding Eileen's hand, and both were equally frozen. They were standing on the platform built around the school clock tower for the workers installing the new stained glass window, and the entire school—newly released from morning assembly—was flattening its collective face to the windows of the quadrangle and staring up at them. The principal was leading a gaggle of other teachers, including Miss Harvey, Mr. Stuggs—the barrel-shaped PE teacher—Mr. Sumners, and a baffled-looking Mr. Iverson—the science teacher who Rich especially liked—marching across the grass to the foot of the scaffold.

Time had indeed moved faster than usual.

"Oh," said Alex, finally finding her voice. "This is going to be bad."

It was.

They had been out all night, which would have been enough to get them in serious trouble. But, to make matters worse, they'd also been found trespassing in an "out-of-bounds" portion of the school, apparently vandalizing the new window installation while—according to Mr. Stuggs—trying to smuggle a raccoon into the tower as some kind of "sick practical joke." Darwen was just relieved that Weazen did his best to look like a harmless animal they had trapped in the grounds, instead of speaking in his own defense.

Darwen pocketed Weazon's blaster, being very careful to power it down before anyone noticed, though he couldn't get the creature's leather backpack off him. Eileen's blaster was too large to conceal, so she just dangled it from its strap, trying to make it look like it was unworthy of attention. Somehow, Darwen didn't think that was going to work.

The three students and Eileen—who no one knew quite what to do with—were marched to Principal Thompson's office, where they waited for their families to arrive. Darwen's first thought was that this would mean dragging his aunt from some crucial boardroom meeting, but when she reached the school in under ten minutes, he realized that she had not gone into work at all, which was considerably worse. When she came in, she looked both haggard and hard, her mouth the thinnest of lines, her eyes bloodshot from crying but now bright and hard as diamonds.

The first thing she did on walking into the principal's office was to shoot Eileen the most brittle of looks and say, in a voice that was leaden with a calm that clearly took immense effort: "You're fired. After this meeting, I don't want to see you again, and if I hear you've been near Darwen, I'm calling the police."

Eileen looked stunned, but she just inclined her head fractionally, and though Darwen thought she spoke, he couldn't catch the words.

"What is that thing?" demanded Mr. Stuggs, peering at Eileen's blaster.

"Paintball," said Rich.

"Laser tag," said Darwen.

"Nerf gun," said Alex, all at the same time.

Eileen just shrugged, looking ashamed, and said, "Just a toy," in a voice so small Darwen could barely hear it.

"Get the foreman to inspect the window," said the principal. "I want to know how much damage has been done and how much it's going to cost to fix it."

The first part of this sentence was directed at Mr. Stuggs, who lumbered off, smirking, but the latter part was given to the students' families. Rich's dad was looking uncomfortable in a hastily tied tie of bright green, while Alex's mom—despite an initial bout of relieved hugging when she saw her daughter was alive and well—had become frostily silent, something the principal's talk of money did nothing to thaw.

"And call animal control!" he called after Mr. Stuggs. "I want this creature out of my office. And why does it have a backpack? Is this supposed to be funny, Arkwright?"

Weazen looked into Darwen's face and blinked. Rich was trying not to stare at the Peace Hunter, but his concern was obvious. Even without the backpack, no one from animal control would think Weazen was a raccoon, and if there was one thing they didn't need right now, it was more awkward questions.

They had already been subject to a battery of them—mostly on the lines of where they had been all night and what they'd been thinking—and had not been able to say anything. They'd had no time to rehearse a story, so they improvised something badly between them. Rich said they had stayed in school last night to work on their talent show acts, though he couldn't explain why it had taken so long or why they hadn't thought to alert their families. Eileen added that she had come to pick them up but had had a problem with her car and couldn't drive home. She hadn't been able to call anyone because her phone was dead, she said, at which point it rang, and she had had to make up some nonsense of how it must have recharged overnight.

All told, it was a train wreck.

The students hung their heads as they were berated for recklessness, selfishness, and "behavior unbecoming Hillside students" while their families stood stoically by, barely containing their anger and embarrassment. The only upside was the report, brought by a slightly disappointed Mr. Stuggs, that the tower window showed no obvious signs of damage. Even that was tempered when, after a phone call from the office downstairs that animal control had arrived, Weazen promptly bit Darwen on the finger.

Darwen yelped and dropped him. For a moment all the adults shrank back as Weazen chose his route to the door and bolted. Mr. Stuggs shot Darwen a furious look and wobbled out, though there was no way he was going to catch the lithe little creature.

Darwen was sent to the nurse, who said that the cut on his finger was not bad but should be treated as if the "raccoon" was rabid. The wound was washed thoroughly, and despite Darwen's protestations that he was sure the animal was uninfected ("And how would you know that?" demanded the nurse), he was then given a painful vaccination right into his injured finger. Throughout this, Darwen was very careful not to show the nurse that he was carrying a rather nastier cut to his thigh.

When this was done, he was returned to the principal's office, where everyone but Eileen—who had already been dismissed—was still waiting for him.

"You have behaved extraordinarily poorly," said the principal to the students. "You will leave the school premises immediately."

Rich gaped. "But morning classes are just starting!" he protested.

"Not for you, Mr. Haggerty," said the principal.

"We're being expelled?" Alex sputtered. "You can't! That's not fair!"

"You are being suspended for the day," said the principal. "You can come back tomorrow, when we will discuss your punishment further."

Alex opened her mouth to speak, but her mother's glance at her was swift and murderous. For once, Alex said nothing.

Darwen had just decided things couldn't get any worse when something distinctly odd happened. It began with a sound, a distant hum that rose in pitch till it was a shrill whine that—had it been louder—would have been painful to listen to. In the same instant, the lights in Principal Thompson's office flickered and dimmed, and Mr. Stuggs reentered, slamming the door shut with such a crash that everyone jumped. The PE teacher lowered his head and snarled, grimacing like a wolf, his teeth bared. Darwen took a step back, pressing into his aunt, but then he heard something like a growl from her as well, and turned to look into her face.

It was still her, but the expression on her face was unlike anything Darwen had ever seen. Her eyes were hard and malicious, her lips trembling, teeth locked together like a pit bull about to pounce. He flinched away and she raised her right hand as if she was going to strike him, something she had never done before. Actually it was worse than that. Her fingers were slightly bent, her nails poised as if she was going to slash his face with them.

And then the lights came back up and the moment, whatever it had been, passed. Honoria blinked and lowered her hand. Her face—though still angry—returned to normal, so that if Darwen hadn't seen the alarm on Rich and Alex's faces as well, he might have believed he had imagined the whole thing.

As they left the office a few minutes later, Darwen thought he heard Aunt Honoria murmur a thank-you to the principal, but the walk to the car—made in complete silence—had never seemed so long. The drive home was no better. Still, it took a while for Darwen to realize that while his aunt had been upset with him before, this was different. Usually she would read his failings as hers, turning in on herself and worrying about the kind of job she was doing as a parent. But though she had been upset by his disappearance, she was—this time—

just plain angry, so angry, in fact, that she didn't trust herself to speak to him.

It was unnerving, and when they got home and she ordered him to bed immediately with the stern promise that they would talk about all this later, Darwen was actually relieved. He retreated to his room, shamefaced, and lay on the bed listening to her clatter around the apartment before making a series of irritated phone calls to work. She should really have been in the office, but since she had just fired his babysitter, she was stuck at home, and that wasn't going to improve her mood.

Darwen felt more lonely and homesick than he had in months. He wished he could talk to Mr. Peregrine, or that he could hang out with his friends with no thoughts of what lay on the other side of the mirrors. Most of all, and for the first time in a long while, he wished he had never left England, that he still lived in his little Lancashire house with his parents, and that the last year had simply never happened. He sat on his bed, trying to read or rooting disconsolately through his old things, but he couldn't relax.

At last, he turned on his computer and went online. Without really deciding to do so, and with a sense of nervous apprehension, he entered the date of his parents' death into the search bars of various Lancashire newspapers. He had never done this before and didn't really know why he was doing it now, but when the stories started to appear on the screen, he found that he could not look away. He found brief accounts of the car accident, how it had happened, and the terrible consequences, one of which was the bitter remark that "the Arkwrights left a ten-year-old boy, Darwen, who was in school at the time of the crash."

There were pictures too. Wreckage, mainly, and policemen moving bystanders out of the way. A woman with a shopping bag was staring from across the road, and there was a green Fiat parked close by, which had, perhaps, been driving right behind his parents when the accident occurred. Darwen tore his gaze from the twisted metal and more closely examined the faces in the pictures for some sign of the grief that seemed appropriate, but everyone just looked curious.

He turned the computer off and lay on his bed, facedown, thinking of nothing, and eventually the exhaustion of the night caught up with him, and he fell into an uneasy sleep. He dreamed he was in the back of a car, driving along a dark road lined with buildings that looked like they were carved out of the living rock, but he couldn't tell if people lived in them because he was watching the green Fiat behind. Darwen couldn't see the driver, something that made him increasingly uneasy even as the car seemed to get faster and faster. . . .

He awoke to find his aunt standing over him with a plate of sandwiches and a glass of juice. Her face looked troubled, but still hard, and she received his thanks without a word.

"It wasn't Eileen's fault," Darwen said as she was turning to leave. "She just did what we asked her to, then sort of got stuck."

"I don't want to discuss her, Darwen," said his aunt. "She is no longer a part of this family."

"Will you get another babysitter?" asked Darwen.

"That depends," said his aunt. "In the short term, probably, but in the long term . . . I don't know. I need to think this all through."

Darwen heard the defeated frustration in her voice, and he felt a surge of panic. "But I'm staying with you, right?" he said. "I mean, that's not going to change, is it?"

She hesitated a fraction too long before saying, "No, that's not going to change."

She left without another word and Darwen set his sandwiches down, his mind racing. She couldn't seriously think about giving him up, could she? Because he got a one-day suspension from school?

But it's not just last night she's upset about, is it? he reminded himself. *She's been worried about this ever since you came to her, that she wasn't a good guardian, parent, or whatever. Every time she thinks you are making progress, you do something to smash it all up. She never wanted you here in the first place. She's doing your dead parents a favor, and it's screwing up her career, her life, in the process. But that's not why she might look to hand you off to someone else. She's not thinking about herself. She's thinking about you, wondering if you might be better off in another home. . . .*

But where? Were there orphanages in Atlanta? He supposed there were, the idea settling in his stomach like a cold and cavernous space. Or maybe he'd go to foster parents or get adopted. Maybe they'd send him back to England and he'd have to start all over again, trying to make friends, knowing no one. . . .

His pulse was starting to race as if he was being chased by scrobblers. If only he could explain to her that he wasn't acting out because he was sad or disturbed. If only he could take her by the hand and lead her through the oven door and into Silbrica. Then everything would make sense to her and they would be okay again. Perhaps he could just explain without actually trying to make her believe it all. But that would be just the push she needed to convince her that he was delusional and in need of help she couldn't give, the kind of home she could never provide. . . .

The bedroom door opened again, and his aunt's slim form appeared in the hall.

"I have to go in to work for a couple of hours," she said. "Can you be trusted to be left alone?"

"Yes," said Darwen. "Of course."

"There's no *of course* about it, Darwen," said his aunt, her face impassive. "No video games, no TV, no talking to your friends on the phone, no guests, and absolutely no leaving the apartment, you got me?"

"Yes, ma'am," said Darwen, watching her carefully. The memory of the way she had raised her hand at school, the half snarl he had heard in her throat suddenly leaped to the front of his mind.

Normally his slightly pathetic, apologetic tone would have brought an affectionate smile to her face, but not today.

"See that you do," she said, setting a sheaf of papers on the bed. "Homework," she said, before turning and closing the door. He could hear her talking irritably on her cell phone even before the front door banged shut behind her.

Darwen sighed and flopped back on the bed. The worst thing about it was that she was right. He was a screwup, and if she had known that he had been out all night trying to assemble allies and rescue Mr. Peregrine, then she'd know that he'd failed at those things too. He wasn't even the only mirroculist anymore. In fact, what had looked like a unique gift actually seemed to rub off on anyone who spent any time in Silbrica. It was no wonder she was considering giving him up.

He thought of the Peregrine Pact. Rich was clearly the brains of the outfit, though Alex had her brand of smarts too. But she also had nerve and creativity. And Darwen contributed what exactly? Even Eileen had turned out to be more crucial to Mr. Peregrine and his plans.

He leafed through the homework assignments and groaned. This was going to take all afternoon.

It did. He had barely put his books away when he heard his aunt return. She put her head around the door—clearly just to ensure he was still there and hadn't set his bed on fire or something—and then ordered Chinese food for dinner. She didn't ask him what he wanted.

After dinner Darwen sat in the glow of his computer once more. He tried inputting portal numbers, references to the flesh suits and the laboratory where the conversion process was engineered, as if somewhere there might be some obscure conspiracy-theory site put together by people who'd had brushes with Silbrica, but there was—predictably—nothing. He went back to scanning newspaper accounts of his parents' death and found different images of the crash site taken a little while after the wreckage had been removed. It was hard to believe that something so terrible could be cleaned up so quickly and completely. The people in the photos were going about their business as if nothing had happened.

All but one.

The only thing that was the same as the earlier pictures was the little green Fiat. The picture was too grainy to see much, but this time, at least, he could make out the driver. The man appeared to be in some kind of strange getup, as if he was wearing something over his head, a helmet perhaps, or some kind of mask that had built-in goggles. . . .

His aunt tapped on the door and poked her head in to say good night, so Darwen closed the browser window hurriedly. If she saw him reading up on his parents' death, it would confirm all her worst fears.

"Bed," she said crisply. "School tomorrow."

Darwen braced himself for the lecture, but she said no more, and as the door snapped shut behind her, he felt his mind racing. He stared at the image on the computer screen, the peculiar man in the car, the gas-mask-like face, and he could make no sense of it.

He got into bed—unassisted for once by his aunt, who normally tucked him in so tightly that he could hardly move—and lay there, thinking furiously. He had been told his parents' death was an accident. Could that be wrong after all? Who was the strange man in the car? Was it even a man at all? Because that gas mask raised an awful, baffling possibility in Darwen's mind, a possibility that hinged on a word he had not even known the day his parents died.

Scrobbler.

Chapter Eighteen
Hillside Gets a Mascot

Darwen marched from school assembly in an exhausted daze, unable even to respond to the snide whispering of Nathan, Chip, and Barry about how he was sure to be expelled by the end of the week. Rich and Alex weren't much better, each moving in a surly fog of their own, grunting their hellos and then falling sulkily silent as they went from homeroom to classes, listening to the rumble of a gathering thunderstorm outside. Evidently they had all come up with the same strategy: *Keep your head down and just get through the day.*

But that, apparently, was too much to hope for.

They were in Mr. Iverson's science class, a place Darwen usually felt pretty comfortable, partly because Mr. Iverson had always been nice to him, and partly because if the work got too tricky, Rich could steer him around the curves. So his guard was down as Mr. Iverson put safety goggles on over his glasses and owlish eyebrows in preparation for the day's experiments. The teacher lit his Bunsen burner and arranged his glass beakers of colored fluid before indicating a piece of equipment Darwen had never seen before. It looked like a large glass cabinet surmounted by electronic controls.

"This," said Mr. Iverson, "is our brand new fume hood, for which we were just able to find room in the end-of-year budget. It's the finest piece of equipment in the lab—a very expensive device—and I think you'll find it very exciting."

And they did. Because at that very moment there was a crash of thunder, the whole cabinet wobbled, and something sat up inside the glass box. It looked at them: a furry face with a dark mask.

Weazen.

Half the class shrieked and several fell out of their chairs in shock. Mr. Iverson staggered back, knocking over two of the beakers of liquid and, as he tried to catch the third, the Bunsen burner. Immediately, it ignited whatever had been in the beakers, so that rivers of fire coursed over the work top. Weazen's eyes fastened on the flames, which were perilously close to the fume cabinet, and he leapt. The cabinet shook alarmingly.

"Get Mr. Stuggs!" shouted Mr. Iverson. "Call animal control!"

Chip Whittley bolted for the door.

"And close the door after you!" Mr. Iverson added. "We mustn't let it out of the room."

"It's kind of cute," said Princess Clarkson, putting one hand up to the glass and waggling her glittery nail-polished fingers in greeting. "Maybe we could keep it as a pet or a mascot."

But at that moment Weazen hurled himself at the glass again, and this time the expensive fume hood—the finest piece of equipment in the lab—swayed, teetered for an agonizing second, then crashed to the ground. The glass exploded in all directions, and the students shrank back. Genevieve Reddock screamed, not because she had been cut, but because Weazen had come rocketing out of the wreckage directly at her.

She leapt onto her desk, and soon half the kids in the class were up on theirs too as Weazen looked madly around for an exit. Princess had abandoned the idea that he was cute and was up on her chair with the rest looking panicked.

"It's that raccoon you brought!" roared Nathan, pointing at Darwen.

"It's not a raccoon," said Bobby Park. "It's a ferret."

"Who cares what it is!" shouted Barry. "Kill it."

So saying, he flung his book bag at Weazen, who dodged easily and shot between the legs of Barry's chair, just as lightning outside flashed through the room, followed by a deafening crash of thunder.

"You're scaring it!" shouted Alex. "Be quiet!"

But that wasn't going to happen.

"It's got rabies!" shouted Barry. "It will kill us all!"

There was a sudden whoosh as the last remaining beaker caught fire, so that there were now two separate mini-infernos raging at each end of the teacher's desk. Mr. Iverson leapt back, his hair smoking. The shattered fume cabinet gave an ominous pop and added a little smoke of its own.

"This is your fault, Arkwright!" yelled Nathan, hopping onto his chair as Weazen shot past.

The Peace Hunter's eyes were wide and fixed as he sought for an opening, however narrow, that he could shimmy through. He was still wearing his backpack, but otherwise looked exactly like a cornered otter might: all trace of intelligence and his usual easy deliberation gone. Alex was right. He was out of Silbrica and he was scared. As Nathan tried to trap him in his carefully flung blazer, Darwen had an idea.

He turned to Alex.

"Diversion," he said. "Quickly."

"A diversion from what?" asked Alex, her eyes flashing from the shattered fume cabinet to the burning desk and the screaming children dodging the careening Weazen. "There's already quite a bit going on."

"Get their eyes off him," Darwen replied, nodding to where Weazen was now feinting and dodging as Barry Fails tried to corner him with a chair, like an old-fashioned lion tamer.

Alex got up without another word, leapt onto the counter in between the fires that burned at each end, muttering, "Never got to do this with special effects before," and then she began to sing.

Well, I've got your attention now
You've gotta be wondering how
You never saw till . . . pow!
I got your attention now.

And she did. The class gaped at her stupefied as she crooned and danced between the little towers of flame. Mr. Iverson's mouth hung open, and he wasn't the only one.

"She really isn't bad," Rich admitted.

Darwen wasn't watching. He had managed to catch Weazen's eye and had slipped his right arm out of his blazer suggestively. The little creature needed no further invitation. It dashed across the classroom and leapt into Darwen's lap. Darwen rotated slightly and Weazen vanished up the back of his jacket, clinging to the sides of Darwen's shirt with claws that made him wince.

Darwen bit back the pain and tried to sit very still as the class, recovering from the strangeness of Alex's impromptu performance, went back to hunting for signs of the supposedly rabid animal.

"It's gone!" said Simon Agu, sounding quite pleased. "It got away."

"Can't have," said Nathan. "There's nowhere for it to go."

"Maybe it caught fire," said Barry eagerly. "Just, you know, burned up to nothing."

"Don't be stupid, Usually," said Nathan. His eyes came to rest on Darwen. "Where did it go, Arkwright?"

"I didn't see," said Darwen.

"This window was open," said Rich, who had slipped to the back of the classroom in the confusion. The rain was coming down in sheets outside, but one of the windows was indeed open.

"No way," said Nathan. "You just opened it."

"No, I didn't," said Rich, flushing flamingo pink.

"Miss O'Connor, get down from there immediately," said Mr. Iverson, who was directing the pale smoky jet of a fire extinguisher at the little infernos on the desk. "Mr. Haggerty, did the animal escape through the window?"

"I'm not sure, sir," said Rich, who looked almost hot enough to set his shirt on fire. "I wasn't really looking."

At that moment the door cannoned open and Mr. Stuggs, almost as red-faced as Rich and breathing twice as hard, blundered in.

"Where is it?" he demanded. He was carrying a large wire trap that was almost too big to get through the door and a pole with a loop of cord at one end. "Where is the beast? I'll have it now."

"Gone," said Mr. Iverson. "We think."

"Gone?" repeated Stuggs, fury and disappointment chasing each other through his fat face.

"Through the window," said Nathan.

"Perhaps," added Mr. Iverson. "Close the window, Mr. Haggerty, and let's double-check that it's not still in the classroom."

Mr. Stuggs turned his eyes onto Mr. Iverson as if noticing him for the first time, saw the wreckage of the fume hood and the smoldering remains of the experiment on the desk, and said, "Just what kind of classes do you teach in here?"

"Can I go to the bathroom, sir?" said Darwen.

It was a terrible excuse, but his head was empty of everything but the desire to be somewhere else. He felt Weazen dig his nails deeper in his back.

"Bathroom?" repeated Mr. Iverson, whose hair was still smoking.

"I'm bursting, sir," said Darwen, grimacing at the pain of Weazen's claws.

"Oh, very well," said Mr. Iverson. "But close the door properly behind you and get back here in a hurry."

Carefully, Darwen got up, walking stiffly so that Weazen wouldn't be dislodged and trying to not to present the bulge under his blazer to the class as he walked. Mr. Iverson watched his pained movements and almost smiled. "If you're that desperate, boy, you might want to go a little quicker," he said.

"Right, sir," said Darwen, opening the door, sidling through, and closing it quickly behind him.

He began to run. "Where to?" he muttered.

Muffled words came from the small of Darwen's back.

"What?" Darwen demanded. "I can't hear you . . . ow!"

Weazen scrambled up the back of Darwen's blazer and then stuck his head out of the collar so that his bristly snout was right against Darwen's neck. "Same place we came in," said Weazen. "The window. It's not online to non-mirroculists yet so I need you to open it."

Great, thought Darwen. *The most visible place in the school: a platform overlooking the quadrangle, the place where I got caught and suspended twenty-four hours ago . . .*

"Where do you think you're going, Arkwright?"

Darwen stopped and turned, feeling Weazen shrink back into the cover of his blazer, clawing at his back as he went. It was Chip Whittley.

"Bathrooms are that way," he said.

Darwen just stood there, feeling a rising sense of dread in his chest. Something about Chip reminded him of the shadow school, and though he couldn't pinpoint why, he felt an unexpected sense of alarm.

"What are you looking at, Arkwright?" Chip demanded.

"Nothing," Darwen managed, his skin crawling as the other boy got close enough to touch him.

"Nathan's right," said Chip, eyeing him knowingly. "You brought that thing here. But it's not a raccoon, is it?"

Darwen was cold. Chip's voice was low and his gaze was watchful.

"What do you mean?" Darwen said.

"You know what I mean," said Chip. "It's not from around here. You brought it from . . . that place."

Weazen had become very still. Darwen's mouth was dry.

"What place?" he said, willing his brain to come up with something. This was not good at all. They had always wondered just how much Chip remembered from that awful night on the school trip when Darwen and his friends had freed several children from Greyling's generators.

"From Costa Rica," said Chip, extending one foot and putting it carefully down on top of Darwen's right shoe, then putting his weight on it till Darwen winced. "You brought it back from the jungle somehow, didn't you? It's one of those coatis or something, isn't it?"

He pressed harder with his foot, and Darwen felt his eyes prickle with pain. Chip grinned, a hard little grin that did not reach his blank eyes, so that for a moment Darwen saw something cruel and heavy in his face.

"Exotic animal trafficking," he continued, twisting his foot slightly so the pain in Darwen's flared. "Which is illegal, so you're trying to get rid of it. Sell it maybe, you and your pauper friends. That's right, isn't it?" He pressed harder with his foot. "Isn't it?" he insisted.

It was a strange moment, and in spite of the pain, Darwen found he was more confused than angry or afraid. Because the more Chip said, the more Darwen was sure the other boy didn't really believe it. He had other suspicions that he wasn't saying, suspicions he didn't want to think about, memories, perhaps, memories of a terrible night in an impossible place. . . .

"Don't tell anyone," said Darwen. "I found a buyer, but the coati escaped, so I'll lose the money."

Chip grinned, pleased by Darwen's misfortune but also—just maybe—by something else, by the idea that this was all rational and didn't reinforce those awful half-remembered images that had been rattling around in his head since Costa Rica. He removed his foot from the top of Darwen's shoe, momentarily satisfied, even relieved.

"We'll see," said Chip, back to normal and laughing his woodpecker laugh. "Maybe I'll tell, maybe I won't. Better be on your best behavior, Arkwright."

So saying, he turned and made back for the classroom, whistling through his teeth.

Darwen shuddered as he watched him go, then made for the clock tower as fast as he could, desperate to get Weazen out from under his jacket before things got any worse.

"Here," he muttered, fumbling for the miniature blaster in his pocket and thrusting it up the back of his jacket where Weazen snatched it. "You'll need that."

"Thank you, Darwen Arkwright," said Weazen, wrenching his head out of the blazer again. "And you will need this."

He produced first the little brown notebook inscribed with the image of the gate.

"I was holding this for Miss O'Connor," he said, pressing it into Darwen's hands. "The numbers are no use to me. Only the mirroculist can use these portals."

"Well," Darwen muttered, "there are a lot more of those than people seem to think."

"No," said Weazen. "Only one."

Darwen looked into the animal's bright eyes and nodded once.

"And as you gather your allies, watch for the Fixer," said Weazen. "Moth was right to warn you about him. Even as a Guardian employee, he is dangerous, but it may be that he is now working for himself or—worse—with Greyling. I've heard odd stories. If he is on your trail, you'll need to be very clever and very quick to stay ahead of him."

Darwen nodded in understanding, but there was one question he still had to ask.

"You know about mirroculists," said Darwen. "Is there a way to keep the gift forever? You know, *not* grow out of it?"

"No," he said. "It's just how it is. You don't want to lose it. Understandable, but . . ." He shrugged and glanced sideways into the rain. "Can't be helped. All mirroculists grow out of their gift. Some hold onto it longer than others, several years, sometimes, but eventually it goes."

Darwen looked away, unable to speak, blinking at the rain.

"But you are still the mirroculist, Darwen Arkwright," Weazen added. "For now. All Silbrica, and maybe your own world, will be depending on you as much as is Mr. Peregrine. So gather your allies. Anyone who will stand with you against Greyling. I have written about one in that notebook."

"Who is it?" asked Darwen.

"You can read all about it," said Weazen. The little creature looked unusually twitchy.

"What?" said Darwen. "What aren't you telling me?"

"It's all in the book," said Weazen, glancing uneasily about. "Well, good luck."

"What about this ally? What are you afraid of?"

"It's in the book," said Weazen with finality.

Darwen opened his mouth to protest, but Weazen merely scanned the empty quadrangle and said simply, "Now."

Together they sprinted outside into the driving rain, then across the slick grass to the scaffold around the clock tower. Darwen carried Weazen up, not daring to look to see if they had been spotted, not slowing till they reached the curious window at the top.

"It's not night!" he exclaimed. "How am I going to open it?"

"This is one of Greyling's portals. Works differently, right?" shouted Weazen over the storm. "Just try."

Darwen set the creature down on the platform, feeling the rain dripping off his nose and running down the back of his neck. Then he considered the window, trying to look past it into another world, to the dark and irregular tower in the shadow school beyond. For a moment his eyes almost closed and then he could see it.

He stooped, not taking his gaze from the window that was now a portal as he reached for Weazen's tiny paw. Then, as the Peace Hunter took his hand, they stepped through.

The darkness around them was just as it had been the last time they were here, and Darwen felt a dread of the place and the things that lived there, the scrobblers and gnashers, of course, but also—especially—the ghosts.

Weazen released his hand and was off, running into the dark craggy echoes of the school buildings Darwen had come to know so well. Watching him go, Darwen was relieved to have nothing to do but return to Atlanta, the storm, and whatever new trouble was waiting for him in school.

Yet as he got out of the rain and made his way slowly back to Mr. Iverson's science class, Weazen's words hung in his mind like a sword suspended by a slender thread above him. He was the mirroculist for now. But one day he would wake up and find that the mirrors were just mirrors. The thought settled on him like the chilling, soaking rain that ran down his face.

Chapter Nineteen
Clues

Darwen expected the gossip to be all about Weazen's escape, but the students had other things on their minds. Alex overheard Melissa and Jennifer discussing how upset Princess was about what had happened to her while she had been rehearsing her dance recital for the talent show.

"Something was in the gym with her," said Alex. "She was halfway through her routine—very glam, by the way, but you'd expect that—"

"And?" Darwen prompted.

"And this thing came in through the wall," she said. "Pale, floaty. A ghost. Just a light, at first, but then got kinda more human: still just like light and air but clearly a kid, and she thinks it could see her. Moved right up to her across the gym while she was dancing. Freaked her out big time."

"Sounds like what we saw," said Rich.

"Which is a lot less comforting than you might think," said Alex. "I'm staying out of this place at night, that's for sure."

"But what does it mean?" asked Rich.

Darwen shook his head.

"I wish Mr. Peregrine were here," he said. "Something is going on. I can feel it. I just don't know what."

"Then we need to go back and get him," said Alex. "And do it right this time."

Darwen thought for a moment. He didn't know where to start. He was afraid of what they would find if they went back into Silbrica now, and if they were caught or even delayed so that someone noticed his absence, he might be thrown out of school. He could even lose his place in his aunt's home. But the thought of the old man trapped floating in that awful tank was too much to bear.

"Yes," said Darwen simply. "We need to get to him and we need to do it right."

Darwen spent his last minutes of homeroom studying the little book Weazen had given him, keen to find out what potential ally the Peace Hunter had been too anxious to even name. He had been about to tell Alex and Rich all about it when he stumbled on the key pages, which were covered in tiny, scratchy writing and included a picture. Darwen closed the book hastily. He was going to need to think about how to raise this with his friends.

The light dimmed fractionally. He looked up, vaguely aware of a high-pitched whine coming from somewhere outside the room. He got up, glancing around, but as he did so, Miss Harvey turned on him suddenly.

"I was just wondering where that noise—" he began, but he didn't get the sentence out.

Miss Harvey, who was generally strict but pleasant, was staring at him as if she had never seen him before.

No, Darwen corrected himself. She was looking at him as if she *hated* him. Her head was lowered bullishly, and her eyes were fixed unblinking on his as if she might leap forward and snap at him with her teeth. From deep in her throat came a rumbling growl like some great and terrible beast contemplating its attack. . . .

And then it was gone: the sound, the dimmed light, and whatever had come over the homeroom teacher. But if Darwen had any fear that he had imagined the whole thing, Rich soon set him straight.

"So I was helping Mr. Iverson clean up just now," he said, "and he got really weird. Just for a moment. But he was glowering at me, and he had this beaker in his hand and I was sure he was going to throw it at me."

Other students had similar stories. Mrs. Frumpelstein had hissed at Genevieve Reddock like she was a cat, and Mr. Stuggs had actually pushed Nathan Cloten against the gym wall and stared into his face as if he was going to punch him. Stuggs could be a bit of a bully, but he never took it out on his lacrosse players.

Nathan, for his part, was most indignant about the episode. "I'll be talking to my father about this," he warned.

"Far be it from me to think ill of anyone who makes Nathan Cloten miserable," said Alex, "but this is getting a bit weird, even by Hillside standards."

As his aunt drove him home from school—no replacement for Eileen had yet been found—Darwen gazed out of the window at the Atlanta streets, shrouded with wet trees whose limbs were impossibly green in the post-rain sunlight. He had been watching his aunt closely, but she seemed her usual self.

"Can Rich and Alex come over tonight?" he asked. "They are both at Alex's place until Rich's dad can get over to collect him. If we called before he left work, they could drop by and—"

"No," said his aunt.

No discussion, no explanation, no *We'll see if you're good*, or *What do the parenting books say?* Just: no.

All day he had been going back over his memories of that terrible mirror in the Atlanta mansion through which he had been able to see Mr. Peregrine suspended in that tank of liquid while another flesh suit was being grown. He tried to recall something—anything—he had seen that might give him a hint as to where the locus was, but the lab contained only Silbrican technology, which told him nothing.

Well, he thought, *it had contained one other thing: people. Humans.*

He tried to remember what they had looked like, one in overalls, one in a lab coat, but he couldn't remember their faces. Not that that would have helped. It's not like people could read the town you were born in from your face, like it was a sign around your neck.

"Better day at school today, Darwen?" asked his aunt carefully.

"Aye," Darwen replied absently, still gazing out of the window. "It were all right."

"Excuse me?"

"I mean, yes, ma'am," said Darwen.

"Mrs. Frumpelstein is right, Darwen," she replied, shooting him a look in the rearview mirror. "I'm sure you'd fit in better if you could neutralize that accent of yours. Sometimes I have to guess at what you're saying."

Darwen bit the inside of his lip and said nothing. His dialect was part of who he was. He knew it would fade over time, but he had no interest in speeding that process up so that the likes of Nathan Cloten would find him more palatable. Darwen liked his accent, liked what it reminded him of, liked the thought that it kept him tied to that little Lancashire town, to its streets and fields, to his parents. It was a badge of identity, of honor, and he would hold onto it.

A badge. Like a sign around his neck . . .

Accents!

He remembered the two men in the watchtower window. He couldn't recall their faces, but their voices had stayed with him. The sound had struck him as musical and familiar. What had the man in the lab coat said? Something like, "Trust me, it makes a difference, look you."

Look you.

He was sure of that. He could hear the lilting sound of the sentence, the way it turned up at the end of certain words, almost like a song. They were speaking English fluently, naturally, but the accent . . .

Look you.

Suddenly he was sitting in the living room in his little Lancashire house and his father was in the next room listening to that old record of his, the funny little radio play he loved so much, by a poet called Dylan Thomas, about a town where the houses were blind as moles and there were dogs in the wet-nosed yard, down by the slow, black, crowblack, fishingboat-bobbing sea. . . .

Over and over his father had played the scratchy old record on his ancient turntable, reciting chunks along with the voices.

Tears started unexpectedly to Darwen's eyes at the memory, but at the same time, he started to chuckle, so that his aunt half swiveled in her seat, causing the car to swerve dangerously, till at least three cars blew their horns.

"What?" she demanded. "What's wrong?"

"Nothing," said Darwen. "Just figured something out. A homework problem."

"What's the answer?" asked his aunt, her eyes returning to the dreaded rush hour traffic.

He recalled the musical language of the radio play and he knew with absolute certainty why the dialect he had heard from the man in the watchtower had sounded so familiar.

"Welsh," he said, smiling to himself. "The answer is Wales."

What Darwen was to do with the discovery he had made he wasn't sure. It was possible, of course, that the Welsh accent he had heard was a red herring, an irrelevance. After all, Welsh people could be found all over the world, and perhaps scattered across Silbrica too. But it might also mean that Greyling's lab was staffed by workers who lived close by. Darwen couldn't be sure if the locus he had seen was in Silbrica or in the human world, but he was prepared to bet there was an access point very close to it in Wales.

Did it matter that Wales was only fifty miles or so from the town where he had grown up? Probably not, but the idea that he had a legitimate reason to go back, to breathe that damp air and walk those dark hills, filled Darwen with a secret joy. How he was going to get there was far from clear, but his journey surely began with the oven door inside his closet and the chute down to the Great Apparatus. Maybe he would have time to speak to the Guardians again about what it was to be a mirroculist and, more urgently, what it meant to lose those abilities. He didn't know what else they could tell him that would make the truth of the thing more bearable, but he wanted— *needed*—to talk about it.

Back in his room, Darwen went online, resisting the urge to go back to the newspaper reports of the car crash. He spent an hour researching Wales, moving at random from page to page, perusing dry statistics about population and exports and watching videos of male voice choirs and rugby matches. Next, he typed "weird things in Wales" into his search engine. Not a very promising line of inquiry, he knew, but he hit the enter key and watched the screen fill up. Most of it was just odd facts and figures, but there were also tales of inexplicable experiences and ghost sightings.

Ghosts again? he thought, remembering the dreadful phantoms he had seen in the shadow school and the strangely similar apparitions other students had glimpsed around Hillside.

Darwen read hungrily, but none of it sounded right. Most were vague accounts of strange presences, while others were clearly folk tales. Nothing helped.

He ate a somber dinner with his aunt, who spent most of the time tapping at the keyboard of her laptop, something she normally—if reluctantly—refrained from doing during meals. She barely made eye contact with him, and Darwen had the curious feeling that the more he ate, the emptier he felt.

"Can Rich and Alex come over tomorrow night?" he ventured. "We need to work on our talent show act."

"Which is what?" asked Honoria.

"Kind of a secret," said Darwen in a way he hoped was appealing. "You'll have to wait and see."

"I'm not sure I can come to the gala," she said. "I'm very busy at work. But okay, they can visit for a spell, if you are all on your best behavior."

"Okay," said Darwen. "And since you've not found another babysitter, maybe you could give Eileen another try. It really wasn't her fault that—"

"No," said his aunt, with such finality that Darwen winced. He started to say something apologetic, but she cut him off. "I would prefer not to discuss the matter further, Darwen," she said, "and I really need to finish reading this report."

Darwen returned to his room and went back to poking around on his computer, but since he was getting nowhere—beyond finding a video clip of some Welsh kid who could hum through his nose—was about to shut the thing off when he caught a headline that intrigued him.

"Peregrines hunting Welsh castle grounds?"

It was the first word that caught his attention, but he knew the article referred not to their missing friend but to peregrine falcons, one of the birds that had always fascinated him. He loved their speed, their agility, their rareness. He had never seen one in real life.

The article had three pictures. The first was of the bird in close-up, proud and beautiful. The second was an image of a castle rising up over a modern town with flat open sea on one side.

"Conwy," read the caption.

The article described how the numerous pigeons that haunted the medieval fortress were apparently being hunted in the evening by falcons nesting in another part of the bay. Castle workers regularly found pigeon bodies reduced to little more than wings and backbone, though no one had actually seen the peregrines hunting. Nevertheless, the falcons were, according to local experts, the most likely culprits, certainly more likely than the creature featured in a third blurry photograph sent in by a local teenager, which, said the experts, was surely a hoax.

The picture showed a bat-like animal perched on the edge of a stone block and looking down. Its face was vaguely human, except for the long, cruel beak. . . .

There was no doubt about what the creature in the image was: a flittercrake. And if a flittercrake could hunt pigeons at Conwy castle, then a portal was very close by—a portal that might just lead them to Mr. Peregrine.

Darwen, it seemed, finally had a place to start hunting. He just needed to figure out how to get there, and that meant that it was time he treated the Guardians as the allies they claimed to be.

As soon as the sun was down, he slipped through the oven door and down to the Great Apparatus, wishing he had been able to bring Rich and Alex with him. But when he entered the council chamber above it, the seat that had been occupied by Lightborne was empty. Darwen coughed awkwardly, and the other members of the council opened their eyes dreamily.

"Sorry," said Darwen. "I don't mean to disturb you and whatnot. I was wondering where Lightborne was."

"The head of the council is inspecting the damages performed by Greyling," said Jorge from his chair by the energy dome. "You may find him at portal number 32."

Darwen thanked him, but the Spaniard's eyes had already closed as if he had forgotten Darwen was even there. His manner reminded Darwen uncomfortably of the first day he had been in this chamber, when the council had been in something like a coma, oblivious to what Greyling was doing.

Portal 32 took Darwen to one of the strangest loci he had yet seen, and for a moment he looked wildly around for something to hold onto. He seemed to be standing on solid air: glass or crystal of some sort, no doubt, hard as stone, but so utterly transparent that you couldn't actually see it at all. Below was a rolling purple ocean flecked with pinkish foam over which graceful, black-winged seabirds skimmed and dived. Here and there, columns of some curious seaweed rose above the water like palm trees, and in their delicate, windswept tresses, the birds roosted between flights. Lightborne, his long silver hair stirred by the breaze, was leaning on a kind of rail made of the same invisible substance as the platform on which they stood, gazing out over the waves and watching the sun dip slowly into the horizon in a blaze of amber and scarlet.

He half turned at the sound of Darwen stepping through the portal, smiled, and returned to considering the view. "Remarkable, is it not?" he said, his blue eyes sparkling.

"Yes, sir," said Darwen, meaning it. "It is."

"For all its unique perils," said Lightborne, "Silbrica remains a place of extraordinary beauty, something we need to preserve. Greyling's machines had contaminated the water of this locus, but, as you can see, we have been able to rectify the situation quite satisfactorily. It is good to remember such small victories when things seem hopeless." The old man turned from the dark water, and as his gaze fell on Darwen, he smiled self-consciously. "But I suspect you came to discuss more important things."

Darwen wasn't sure he had much to say that was worth more than this breathtaking view, but he launched into an account of all he had done so far, trying to make it sound like they were making progress.

Lightborne listened in silence, nodding occasionally, but did not look at him until he was finished. "So you need to get to Conwy," he said. "There was indeed a portal there, but it has not been on the Guardians' grid for some time. I can show you how to reach it less directly, but part of the journey will have to be made overland in Wales."

"That's fine," said Darwen, thrilled by the possibility. "And I also need to go here." He showed Lightborne the page of the notebook on which Weazen had scribbled. Lightborne's eyebrows went up.

"Are you sure?" he asked. "This is an extremely dangerous place. The creature Weazen has described . . ." He hesitated. "There are few deadlier beasts in all of Silbrica."

"I know," said Darwen. "But I have to try."

Lightborne considered him carefully, then gave the smallest of nods. "Very well," he said. "I'm glad that your search for Octavius is not clouding your sense of our larger Silbrican concerns. And I can show you how to move from this portal through to those that will lead you—eventually—to Conwy. I hope your hunch is right."

Darwen nodded gratefully as Lightborne added some portal numbers of his own, but when he showed no sign of leaving, the old man gave him a searching look and Darwen was struck once more by how much Lightborne sometimes resembled Mr. Peregrine. "There is something else?" he said.

"Not really," said Darwen. "But . . . well, yes."

"Please," said Lightborne, watching one of the birds wheeling effortlessly overhead. "What is on your mind?"

"It's just this business about growing out of being a mirroculist," Darwen said, the words tumbling out before he could think them through. "I don't get it. Why does it have to be like that? And how do you know when it's starting? Finishing, I mean."

Lightborne smiled a distant and knowing smile. "Nothing lasts forever, Darwen," he said. "And that is not necessarily a bad thing. In time you would get used to your gift, bored of it even—"

"Never," Darwen inserted. "Sorry. I mean, I don't think . . ."

"I know," said Lightborne. "But being a mirroculist is to have a great deal of power, Darwen. No one should wield that for too long. It's not good for them."

"Why?" said Darwen, trying not to sound like a kid who was having a toy taken away. "I'm not going to do anything bad with my ability, am I?"

"People never think so," said Lightborne.

"But they do?" said Darwen. "Mirroculists go wrong somehow, bad?"

"Sometimes," said Lightborne. "Often enough for it to be a good thing that the gift is comparatively short lived."

"How?" asked Darwen, fascinated and horrified. "If they misuse their power, I mean. What do they do?"

"They stop caring about the needs of Silbrica in their rush to please themselves," said Lightborne. "They start to believe that they are better than everyone else and that abuse of their gift is therefore justified."

"What?" exclaimed Darwen. "That doesn't make any sense."

"Can you think of no mirroculist who came to think he knew better than everyone else?" said Lightborne, fixing Darwen with a hard stare. "No one who put his own will for power over the needs of Silbrica and all who lived there?"

"No," said Darwen, feeling both righteous and baffled. "Anyone who could see Silbrica would want to preserve it. No one would try to . . ."

He stopped. Lightborne was still looking at him levelly, but the old man's expression had changed. He looked surprised now, and cautious, and Darwen was sure that the council leader had referenced something he had assumed Darwen knew.

"What?" asked Darwen. "There's something Mr. Peregrine didn't tell me, isn't there?"

"I'm sure he had his reasons," said Lightborne. "I should say no more."

Darwen thought furiously, determined not to miss the opportunity to learn something of his predicament, but sure that Lightborne would offer nothing unprompted.

"Tell me," he said. "I have a right to know."

"When you find Mr. Peregrine," said Lightborne, "you can ask him."

"No," said Darwen. "Wait. Are you saying . . . ?"

"Let us leave the matter," said Lightborne.

"Greyling," said Darwen at last, his voice hushed. "Greyling was a mirroculist." Only moments before the idea would have been inconceivable, but now it seemed obvious. "That's it, isn't it? He went bad, and no one wanted to tell me because they thought I'd freak out. Mr. Peregrine probably thought I'd panic, that I'd worry about turning into Greyling, or something like him."

"And will you?"

"Will I turn into him, or will I worry about it?" asked Darwen.

"Either."

"No," said Darwen. He said it firmly, like it was obvious. "Never." He needed it to be true.

He turned quickly and stepped through the portal, before the head of the Guardian Council had a chance to read the doubt and anxiety in his face.

Chapter Twenty
That Which Eats

It was night in the Silbrican desert. The still air was unexpectedly cool, and the pale sand glowed beneath their feet like silver. Distant ripples of blue-green streaked across the darkened sky in a constant but never repeated pattern that reminded Darwen of the northern lights. These, however, were slower, more wavelike, undulating in the sky like liquid in a glass that was being gently rocked back and forth.

Darwen, Rich, and Alex had been at school all day, a typical day for Darwen in that he had spent most of it trying not to be noticed—particularly by Mr. Sumners in math class—but a day in which he had also been avoiding his friends. There were things about tonight's mission he had not dared to tell them.

"What are we looking for?" asked Alex, who had grown tired of his evasion hours ago.

"Two things," said Darwen, trying to sound casual. "There's a portal here that will take us to the human world close to where I think Mr. Peregrine might be."

"And the other thing?" asked Rich, watching Darwen closely. "What else are we looking for?"

"A friend," said Darwen carefully. "Kind of."

"Which means what?" asked Alex, giving him a level look so that Darwen glanced away.

"An ally," he said.

"And does it know it's an ally, this kind-of friend of ours," Alex pressed, "or is it the kind of pal who might stab us to death if he doesn't like the color of our sneakers?"

"It's not so much a *he* as an *it*," said Darwen, gazing at the odd lights in the sky as if they were absolutely fascinating.

"Fantastic," said Alex dryly. "Does this *it* have a name?"

"Not one you'd find helpful," said Darwen.

"Try me."

"Some call it simply That Which Eats," said Darwen.

"What?" said Rich.

"Or the Death Dreamer," said Darwen, leading them along the crest of a long, pale dune. "Or the Consumer of All Things. See," he added. "I told you the names weren't helpful."

"They helped me make up my mind that I'd like to leave now, please," said Alex. She stopped walking by a patch of thin, dry grass that rose up from the sand like reeds.

"If we can get this thing on our side," Darwen insisted, "it could be a powerful ally against Greyling."

"And if we can't?" asked Rich.

"Well," Darwen hedged, "we'll cross that bridge when we come to it."

"You notice people always use that phrase," Alex said, "when they know the bridge is going to fall apart as soon as you put your foot on it?"

"So this Thing That Shall Not Be Named," said Rich. "What does it look like?"

"Okay," said Darwen, turning to him, "now you've not to freak out on me, all right?"

"Oh, this just gets better and better," said Alex.

"I mean, it's fine," said Darwen, "but Rich might not like it very much."

"Why me?" asked Rich. "Why will I like it less than Alex?"

He caught himself and stared at Darwen. "It's a snake, isn't it?" he said.

Rich's fear of snakes had been well established in Costa Rica.

"Kind of, yeah," said Darwen. "Just bigger than usual."

"How much bigger?" asked Alex, who was starting to pick up some of Rich's anxiety.

"Oh, you know," said Darwen, "a bit. Hundred feet or so. Nothing we can't handle."

"*Nothing we can't handle?*" Alex shot back. Even in the low light, Rich was looking very green. "A hundred-foot snake?"

"I told you," said Darwen. "It's an ally. Or at least it will be. And besides, it doesn't eat people. Not usually. It eats antelope. And scrobblers," he added grudgingly. "Sometimes rhinos."

"Oh, you have *got* to be kidding," said Alex.

Rich was looking wildly around, muttering to himself: "Shouldn't be too hard to spot: hundred-foot snake . . ."

"Well," said Darwen, "it kind of moves through the sand. It has low-level telepathic ability that it uses to home in on its prey."

"Wait a sec. It can hear us thinking?" said Alex. "Then it just pops out of the sand right in front of us and swallows us whole for a snack to tide it over till the next rhino comes by? I don't think so. Darwen Arkwright, we're going home."

"It can't hear us thinking," said Darwen. "It sort of senses us a bit, and it sends out its own thoughts."

"I thought it was just a snake," said Rich. "It thinks?"

"It just looks like a snake," said Darwen. "It's very old and yeah, it thinks more like a person than an animal, I suppose."

"So," said Alex, "about our going home?"

"Not yet," said Darwen.

"Not till we've been eaten, you mean?" Alex shot back.

"Look over there," said Darwen, pointing.

"Is that it?" asked Alex, looking around for cover and seeing none.

"Of course not," said Darwen. "Look. Antelope."

"Those are antelope?" said Rich. "They are huge."

They were. On a rocky ridge overlooking the dunes stood three antelope the size of horses, each with a single spear-length horn like a narwhal's spiraling from its forehead.

"The snake thing eats those?" asked Alex in a hushed voice. "Those horns could skewer an elephant."

"Yes," said Darwen, "but the fact that they are here and calm means that it isn't around, right? In fact, Weazen said there hasn't been a sighting of That Which Eats for weeks."

"So it might be dead," said Rich, clearly relieved.

"Or it might have joined Greyling," said Alex.

"Weazen says that's unlikely," said Darwen.

"Why isn't Weazen here himself?" said Alex. "It's not because he's scared of it, right? Because Weazen isn't scared of anything in Silbrica. He's the Peace Hunter. Nothing frightens him, does it?"

"Let's just see what we can find," said Darwen, avoiding her gaze.

Alex just stared at him.

"This way," said Darwen.

"How do you know?" asked Rich.

"Those lights in the sky," said Darwen. "They aren't supposed to be here. They first appeared about three weeks ago. They might be connected to our mission."

"I hate it when he talks about missions," Alex muttered darkly. "He gets all Commander-in-Chiefy and you just know Terrible Things are going to happen."

They walked for ten minutes across the sand and saw nothing save two more of the antelope, grazing on dry grass at the foot of a rocky escarpment. One of them looked up and watched them and then, suddenly spooked by something only it could see, leapt forty feet in a single bound.

"Ohhh-kay," said Alex. "So long as they keep jumping *away* from us, I'm good. Not keen on those horns."

"I wish Eileen were here," said Rich.

Since she had been fired, Darwen felt that any contact with her at all would prompt too many awkward questions. But Rich was right. After all they had been through together, it felt odd to be venturing into Silbrican peril without her.

"We're getting close," said Darwen. "Look! The lights aren't coming from the sky at all. They are coming from the ground, somewhere over that rise. They are just reflecting off clouds."

"Great," said Alex. "Can we go home now?"

Darwen just kept going. Walking on sand was working different muscles than usual, and he could feel an ache spreading through the backs of his legs. He hoped he didn't have to do any serious running anytime soon. He was still thinking this when he crested the ridge and saw the source of the lights laid out on the desert floor before him.

It was, he supposed, a sort of cage, but vast—the size of a soccer field—and its bars were made up of coursing pulses of energy that lit the whole area and bounced off the clouds above. The light was dazzling, so that he had to look away and was not able to see if there was indeed something trapped inside.

He sensed it, though, a silent but ceaseless moan of pain and hunger and misery. "Can you feel that?" he asked the others.

He needn't have; their faces told him that they could. Alex's fearful anxiety was gone, replaced by anguish, while Rich looked horrified—not scared of the beast in the cage—but appalled by what had been done to it.

Darwen wasn't sure if it was the creature's telepathic energy, but he was suddenly certain of something else. Greyling had ordered this. It wasn't just a tactic to keep a powerful creature from disrupting his plans. It smacked of cruelty, even of pleasure. There was a mad, vengeful impulse behind the act, and Darwen found himself wondering what could make anyone do such a thing. "Why didn't they just kill it?" he hissed through clenched teeth.

"Maybe they couldn't," said Alex, shading her eyes so she could study the electric cage. "Or maybe they hope to use it somehow, like they did the Bleck."

"How do we turn that thing off?" asked Rich.

Alex turned to him, and some of her nervousness was back.

"You think we should just let it out?" she asked. "I don't know, man. I mean, I hate what they're doing to it, but anything that needs that kind of cage has got to be pretty horrendous. You really want to just turn it loose?"

"Yes," said Rich. "We can't keep it in there. It's barbaric."

"We didn't put it in there," said Alex. "It's not our fault."

"It's our fault if we leave it now," said Rich. "And besides, Darwen wants to talk to it, don't you, Darwen?"

Darwen had caught some of Alex's unease and was far from sure what he wanted. Rich's faith in him gave him a kind of strength, however, and he nodded and said, "Sure," in a voice he hoped sounded convincing.

"So we just have to figure out how to shut the cage down," said Rich to himself. "Disconnect it from the power source and we should be good."

"You think it knows we're here?" asked Alex.

"I don't know," said Darwen. "Seems like it's in a lot of pain."

"Assuming we can trust the feelings it's broadcasting," said Alex. "Assuming it's not just luring us into letting it out so it can start eating its way through the world, beginning with us."

Darwen couldn't think of anything to say to that, but Rich was already walking the pulsing perimeter, casting long hard shadows on the green and blue sand. "There's a receiver of some sort here," he said. "That's where the power is coming from. Disable that and—"

He stopped suddenly, staring at something on the ground.

"What?" called Darwen and Alex at once.

"I think the thing in the cage put up a fight," said Rich, a little less sure of himself. "We've got two dead scrobblers down here. Judging by the state of the bodies, I'd say they've been here awhile."

Darwen approached cautiously, but he felt oddly relieved to have something else to think about before they had to commit to shutting the cage off and dealing with whatever was inside. Rich was right about the bodies. They had been parched by the desert sun over some time, and beyond the brass helmet and the shredded and bleached fabric of their boiler suits, little but bones remained.

Darwen considered one of the skeletal faces by the strobing light of the cage. "Huh," he said.

"What?" asked Alex, her face screwed up in an expression of disgust.

"Aren't the tusks usually bigger?" Darwen said. "The skull more ridged? I mean, it's obviously not a man, but it's less scrobblerish than usual, wouldn't you say?"

"Darwen!" exclaimed Alex. "Look at its pocket!"

Sticking out of the skeleton's jacket pocket was a pair of gold, half-moon spectacles, one lens missing. Darwen stooped and drew them carefully from the pocket. A fold of cardboard came with them and fluttered to the desert sand.

"You think they belong to—" Alex began.

"Mr. Peregrine?" said Darwen. "Yes, I think so." He picked up the piece of cardboard and frowned. "Railway ticket," he said, reading the torn fragment of lettering. ". . . *iniog*. Weird."

"You guys ready?" asked Rich. "I've found which wire to pull."

Alex said nothing but braced herself. Darwen took a breath and nodded.

Rich got a tight hold of a cable and pulled on it with all his strength. For a moment, nothing happened, then the lights flickered, and Rich fell backward to the sandy ground, the plug torn from its socket. The wall of brilliant light died without a sound, and the darkness was so complete that Darwen could see nothing at all.

It took several seconds for his vision to return, and in the meantime he felt the change in the creature that had been caged. Its sadness was gone, its pain suppressed, but its hunger burned bright as lightning. Darwen looked to where Rich lay, and that was when he finally saw it.

It was at least as big as Weazen had said, vast and crimson and shining, its body drawn up, its massive snake head suspended above them, gazing down at Rich's prone body. Its black, unblinking eyes were hard and fixed as glass.

Chapter Twenty-one
Space

"**G**ood colossal snake," cooed Alex in an unsteady voice. "*Nice* terrifying monster. Hungry? Why not get yourself a burger. Hmmm," she said, smacking her lips. "Or a massive unicorn-antelope-thing! Yum, right?"

"Quiet," said Darwen gently. "It's thinking."

Rich was lying faceup, staring motionless at the giant serpent looming over him. Its jaws opened, like the hatchback of some terrible car, and Darwen saw not the massive, folding fangs he had expected, but rows of serrated teeth like the edge of a saw: teeth designed for holding prey.

"It's a constrictor," Rich whispered.

Even in the terror of the moment—perhaps because of it—Darwen was impressed by Rich's ability to analyze the creature that might be about to kill him.

The snake hissed, and as it flicked its forked tongue blackly into the night, Darwen felt it again, that sense that the creature was thinking, considering even. And then he felt its question:

What do you want?

The words were familiar, a phrase you might say when you opened the door to a stranger, perhaps, but this was no casual inquiry. It was asking what they most desired, trying to get a handle on who or what they were. The question was a test, Darwen was sure. He was also sure that it was directed at Rich, whose life now hung in the balance, the snake poised to strike as sure as if an ax was raised above his neck. Darwen hoped beyond hope that Rich knew the right answer.

For a long moment, however, Rich said nothing; and there was silence in the desert. Then it came again.

What do you want?

Darwen braced himself, willing Rich to speak, but far from clear what he wanted his friend to say. Knowing Rich, it would be something long and precise, something with lists and subtle scientific distinctions, something complicated. Rich leaned back, his eyes tightly closed, and somehow, Darwen wasn't sure why, his answer appeared in the snake's mind so that Darwen could hear it as clearly as if it had been spoken aloud.

Space.

That was it. One word.

Darwen felt his muscles tighten as if he might have to leap to Rich's defense or merely spring out of the way of the snake's attack. Space? What did that even mean? He felt Alex shift from foot to foot uneasily. She had obviously heard it too.

Space.

Darwen heard it again, but this time it was clearly the voice of the snake, a slow, pondering echo of what Rich had said. And then there was more than the word, there were pictures in Darwen's head: a vast, open sky full of stars and patches of cloud uncolored by the blue-green light of the electronic cage in which the snake had been trapped. He saw the wide expanse of the desert, vast rolling dunes stretching as far as the eye could see, and tussocky bluffs where antelope grazed. He saw the vastness of the sky and the land, and he felt the thrill of movement through empty air without shackles or restraints, and then there were meadows and forests and oceans from Silbrica and their own world, and through them he saw people and animals of every kind wandering free. He saw the land where Rich's dad lived, the little field and the woods beyond where the creek ran, and for a moment it was like they were all little kids running barefoot through the wet grass. There were no scrobbler devices, no armies, no hint of Greyling's presence. No cages.

The snake reared higher still, its great reptilian lips gasping a long sibilant hiss somewhere between a sigh and a laugh, and then it was plunging down toward Rich, diving.

Darwen flinched, and Alex clapped a hand to her mouth, but Rich did not move, and the great snake slammed into the sand only inches from his neck and tunneled straight down. A plume of dust and grit rose like a funnel cloud as the huge crimson body arched into the ground like a torrent of water breaking over a precipice, and then it was gone.

If it had been a test, Rich had passed.

Darwen helped him to his feet. Rich was speckled with sand and he looked rattled and jittery, but he was smiling.

"That was amazing!" said Darwen. "How on earth did you come up with that? Space? Really? I would never have thought of that."

"It was weird," said Rich, who seemed a little stunned by what had happened. "I tried to think of something it would want to hear, but I could feel how smart it was, how old. Did you get that? It felt like it had been around for centuries. And I knew that if I tried to play it somehow, it would know. So I was just, you know, honest."

"That was pretty cool," Alex said, considering him in the low light.

"What?" said Rich, his smile broadening. "No cracks about my hillbilly family and my hankering for the great outdoors?"

"I'm just glad we're alive," said Alex. "You can't argue with survival. Still, not sure I'm comfortable being inside your head. One more reason to steer clear of hundred-foot telepathic snakes."

"Agreed," said Darwen. "But apart from the survival thing—

which is great—I'm not sure what we achieved other than letting loose a monster."

"True," said Alex. "We probably didn't make a lot of antelope friends just now."

"I don't know," Rich said musingly. He had been reflective since the snake left. "I wouldn't say we made a friend exactly, but he doesn't think of us as the enemy. Might be useful."

"He?" said Alex. "You mean the snake?"

"He," said Rich with certainty. "Yes."

"Well, I guess that's good," said Alex as they trudged back across the desert sand. "We met a monster that doesn't want us dead. Makes a nice change."

Back at the portal, Darwen checked his notes from Lightborne and said, "Okay, now to find Mr. Peregrine."

"Will there be more monsters?" asked Alex with a formidable glare.

"No," said Darwen. "We will be leaving Silbrica."

"And going where?" asked Rich.

"Wales," said Darwen. He recounted the strange sightings around Conwy and the accents of the men monitoring Mr. Peregrine. "Lightborne told me about an active portal in Wales. It's close to Conwy."

"It's not much to go on," said Alex.

"It's all I've got right now," said Darwen, "and I really don't want to go alone."

Rich shrugged. "I have a few more hours before anyone notices I'm gone," he said.

"And you promise a total absence of monsters?" said Alex.

"Cross my heart and hope to die," said Darwen, grinning.

"Hmmm," Alex mused. "Not a phrase to fill me with confidence in our safe return, but what the hey. I'm in."

"Okay," said Darwen, activating the portal. "Here goes."

Chapter Twenty-two
Blodwyn

For a moment all was dark on the other side of the portal, then a dazzling light arced around and Darwen looked hurriedly away. He found they were standing in a cramped round room with huge diamond-shaped windows that rose from shoulder height all the way to the ceiling, glittering blackly in the night. In the middle of the tiny room, sitting on a green-painted metal base, was a great glass box containing complex equipment and, at head height, the source of the brilliant light. It came in slits from behind a curious array of curved glass panels that might have been lenses or reflectors, and the whole thing was rotating slowly. The light took up so much space that the rest of the room was little more than a metal walkway around its edge. Outside, a full moon rode, and by it, Darwen could just make out the wide, black ocean far below.

"This is *our* world?" said Alex. "You sure?"

"I know what this is," said Rich.

Alex looked around, taking in the fact that there was no door into the room at all, only a tight metal staircase that came up through the floor, and suddenly, it dawned on her as well. "It's a lighthouse," she said. "Darwen? Why are we in a lighthouse?"

"Chuffed if I know," said Darwen. "No idea."

"Okay," Alex pressed. "Then where is the lighthouse located?"

"Again, not sure," said Darwen.

"Is someone up there?" called a voice from below.

Rich froze.

"Yeah!" called Alex, meeting Rich's exasperated stare and hissing, "You see somewhere to hide up here that I don't?"

Rich shrugged, conceding the point.

At that moment a woman's cautious face appeared in the stairwell. She was middle-aged, with a slightly florid face, and beneath her understandable wariness at the prospect of finding three kids at the top of a lighthouse in the middle of the night, she looked kind.

"What on earth are you doing up here?" she asked, pulling herself up the steps with large, strong hands. "Have you been hiding since the last tour?"

Darwen gave an apologetic half nod.

"That's a long time to be up here by yourselves," she said, "and it's really not allowed. I hope you haven't been messing with anything."

"No, ma'am," said Rich. "We were just looking."

"Ma'am, is it?" she answered, amused and impressed. "Well, you can't stay up here. I was about to lock up. It's a good thing I heard you when I did or you would be stuck here till morning. I'm normally good at keeping track of the tour groups, but I was watching the puffins. We've got three pairs nesting on the cliffs."

Her voice had a familiar musical lilt to it, cycling up and down and up again.

The slow, black, crowblack, fishingboat-bobbing sea.

"Wales," said Darwen, smiling. "We made it."

"Well, yes," said the woman, looking slightly bemused, snapping a walkie-talkie off her belt and setting it down. "Anglesey to be specific. Welcome to South Stack. The lighthouse is fully automated now, but— as you probably heard on the tour—when it was first built over two hundred years ago, everything was done manually and the lighthouse keeper who lived in the rooms below had to light twenty-one separate oil lamps backed by reflectors almost two feet across—"

"This is all very interesting," Rich cut in, uncharacteristically, "but I really have to go down. Not a big fan of heights or tight spaces."

Darwen was keen to be gone too. There was clearly no other portal up here. Darwen wasn't certain how he knew it, but he felt sure that if there was a Silbrican gate other than the one they had come through, he would have felt it somehow, sensed it. The glass surround of the great light *was* the portal: they were standing in it, and it went to only one location. That meant they were going to have to make their next move overland as Lightborne had suggested. He gave Alex a nod, then considered Rich, who was gripping the ledge below the glass with both hands and looking slightly green.

"Afraid of heights?" said the woman with a grin. "How did you get up here? Better question: how on earth did you cross the bridge or come down the four hundred steps?"

"Four hundred steps?" Rich repeated.

"From the cliffs," said the woman. "Only way down."

"We have to climb down this metal tube sticking out of the ocean," said Rich carefully, his face ashen, "and then we have to climb four hundreds steps up those cliffs just to get . . ."

"Anywhere, really," the woman agreed, beaming. "Yes."

"Conwy, for instance," Darwen said, trying to sound casual. "How far is that?"

"Thirty miles or so," said the woman, rubbing at a smudge on one of the great windows with her sleeve. "That where you're going next? Conwy is on the mainland. Is someone driving you? Where are your parents?"

Alex and Darwen looked at each other. Rich had closed his eyes and was squatting on the floor, still holding onto the ledge above his head. Not for the first time, Darwen wished Eileen was with them, and not only because three kids traveling alone together looked suspicious.

"It's just us," he said, smiling as if this was merely a fun adventure, not something that merited a call to the police. "We're kind of . . . backpacking."

"Only without backpacks," Alex added. Rich opened one eye and gave her a look.

"It's bit late for backpacking, don't you think?" said the woman. "I suppose you could take the train from Holyhead. That will take you to Bangor, across the straits. Then you can go up the coast to Conwy. It's a tidy walk to the station from here, though, and there are no taxis. Couple of miles at least, and that's after the steps."

"Better get going then, huh," said Rich, his eyes closed again.

Darwen gave the woman an apologetic shrug and helped Rich—eyes still shut—to his feet.

"I still don't know how you got past me in the first place," the woman remarked. "When I heard you moving around, I thought it was the ghost, but he's usually outside at night."

"The ghost?" said Alex.

"I really need to go down," said Rich.

"In a minute," said Alex. "What ghost?"

"Supposed to be the ghost of old Jack Jones," said the woman, leaning in and grinning, glad of the chance to tell her story. "He was the lighthouse keeper killed during a terrible storm here in 1853. He was coming down the cliff walk when he was hit by falling rock. He managed to drag himself across the bridge but couldn't get into the lighthouse. Took him two weeks to die, poor man. Or so the story goes. They say he bangs on the door at night, trying to get inside." She said the last words very slowly and seriously right into their faces. For a second she held their uneasy gazes, then laughed suddenly, straightened up, and gave them a wide smile. "You go on ahead," she concluded. "I have to make a phone call."

Despite the woman's cheery face, Darwen found himself chilled, and when Rich begged to go down once more, he agreed, winding his way down the stone and metal corkscrew staircase with exaggerated care.

"More ghost stories," muttered Alex as the woman ducked inside one of the rooms below the main tower to make her call. "Just what I need."

"What do you make of it?" Darwen asked as they threaded their way through the rooms at the bottom.

"I'd make nothing of it," said Rich, "except that we just came in through a portal at the top, and we're obviously not the first to do so, and we've heard a lot about ghosts ourselves lately. Seen a few too. I'd say odd things have been seen or heard here for a couple of centuries, and folk tradition has fastened on this dead lighthouse keeper as a kind of explanation. What actually came through," he concluded, "I couldn't say. But I'll be glad to be out in the fresh air."

The air outside was indeed fresh, a stiff sea breeze that whipped at their clothes from every side and carried the tang of salt to their eyes and lips. Even at night the place was alive with seabirds: gulls, but also guillemots and razorbills, which peppered the cliff walls and occasionally fluttered out over the churning black ocean below. The metal walkway across the chasm was positively hair-raising—and not just for Rich—and the zigzagging stone staircase up to the headland took an age to climb. Darwen was glad of the moonlight, without which it would have taken them twice as long.

At the top, they sat while they got their breath back, looking down to the ghostly white lighthouse and the dark sea beyond.

"It would be night," said Alex.

"The trains probably aren't running now," said Darwen, "and even if they were, we haven't any money."

"I have a few bucks," said Rich, searching his pockets.

"*English* money," Darwen said. "Dollars are no use here. We'll have to find a bank."

"Not necessarily," said Alex, producing a wallet and flipping it open.

"You have a credit card?" asked Darwen.

"I don't," said Alex, "but my mother does. Several. I figure we'll get one use out of each before they get frozen. Better use automated systems like ticket machines so we don't have to deal with awkward questions."

"You stole your mother's wallet?" said Rich, aghast.

"Borrowed," she said with a pointed stare. "I'll pay her back."

"How long have we been gone?" asked Darwen.

"Not long enough to have been missed yet," said Alex, plucking a cell phone from her pocket. "Time to make some calls. See if we can head off the panic."

"That your mom's too?" said Rich, regarding it warily, like it might explode.

"That's right. Check it out."

And without another word she scrolled through the phone's menu—its glow lighting her face—pushed a button, and waited for the call to be answered.

"Is that Rich's dad?" she said, in an uncanny imitation of her mother's voice. "Hi, this is Gloria O'Connor, Alex's mom? Listen, is it okay with you if Rich stays over here tonight? He and Darwen are doing one of their sciencey-experiment things and they think it's *really* important that they get to finish it. . . . I know, kids, right? Did we do this stuff when we were their age? I blame the interwebs."

Darwen and Rich stared at her in disbelief. The impersonation was extraordinary. Alex had her mother's manner down to the last detail. It was totally convincing.

"Is there anything he can't eat?" Alex continued. "Good, he and Darwen can sleep in the living room. I have a pull-out couch I got for Alex's uncle Bob. . . ."

A minute later, it was done.

"Okay," said Darwen, "so Rich is covered. My aunt thinks I got an early night. Unless she checks on me, I have a good eight hours. Alex?"

"I left my mom a note right about the time I lifted her purse," said Alex.

"What did the note say?" asked Darwen, impressed.

"'Uncle Bob is coming over tonight.'"

The boys stared at her in confusion. "That doesn't make much sense," Rich replied.

"Believe me when I say that what I wrote really doesn't matter."

Darwen frowned, but if Alex was upset by how little attention her mother paid to what she did, she shrugged it off. "So we've bought ourselves some time, but we need to make the most of it."

"*You* bought us time," said Rich. "That phone call was pretty amazing."

"We all have our talents," said Alex.

Darwen, who wasn't so sure about that, looked down, his smile stalling. He was startled from his reverie by a car horn. A green mud-spattered Land Rover had pulled up beside them and someone was winding down the window.

"Hop in," called the woman from the lighthouse, smiling wide as a church door. "I knocked off early, like. Can't have you wandering around the countryside in the middle of the night, can I? Can give you a lift as far as Menai Bridge. You can take the last train to Conwy from there, but we'll have to be quick."

Darwen looked at the others.

"Would save us some time." Alex shrugged. Rich considered the long road snaking through the darkened fields and nodded.

Darwen, relieved, smiled, not so much at not having to walk, but at the idea that someone was helping them. Lately it had started to feel like the world was conspiring against them, when all they'd wanted to do was rescue Mr. Peregrine. He climbed up and into the front, belting himself in as Rich and Alex got in the back.

"Blodwyn Evans," said the woman, offering him a large pink hand.

"Darwen Arkwright," said Darwen, shaking it.

"Hello," said Rich from the back. "Thanks for the ride."

"It's no problem," said the woman. "It's on my way, near enough. Mind if I drop something off en route? I'll still get you to the station in time."

"That's fine," said Darwen. "Thanks."

"So, Blodwyn, eh?" said Alex. "Interesting name."

Darwen turned and gave her a warning look, but the woman seemed unoffended.

"Shows my age, doesn't it?" she said. "Not many little Blodwyns around these days."

Before Alex could say anything else, Blodwyn's radio crackled and she snatched it from under her seat.

"*Ie,*" she said, "*fi wedi eu gyda mi yn awr.*"

"Welsh, I take it," said Alex.

"Yep," said Darwen.

"Another European language you don't speak, even though you were born, like, a hundred miles away."

"Less," said Darwen, unoffended.

He gazed out of the window at the moonlit hedges and fields as they flashed by. Once away from the coast, they moved quickly through a little town that merged into a bigger one with an industrial-looking port and a major railway station, and then they were on ever-narrowing country lanes, sometimes barely wide enough for a single car.

"What happens if something comes in the other direction?" asked Rich.

Blodwyn, who had finished on the radio, grinned. "We all take a deep breath," she said, "and hope for the best."

They paused once to navigate a bus that squeezed implausibly past them, the hedges rattling the passenger-side windows, until, just outside Menai Bridge, they reached a deserted gravel parking lot off a winding country road and came to a stop.

Blodwyn got out, leaving the keys in the ignition and snapping on a large, rubber-clad flashlight.

"So these errands you had to run...?" Darwen began as they climbed out of the car. There were no houses or shops to be seen, no streetlamps, nothing around them but fields and stands of trees divided by dry stone walls. The road they had come in on was deserted, and the only eyes watching them belonged to shadowy cows, gray in the moonlight.

"Have to check on the cattle," said Blodwyn, crossing the road and making for a narrow footpath.

Darwen glanced at Rich, who just shrugged back.

"Checking on the cattle," said Alex. "Rich, you ought to be right at home."

"We never kept cows," said Rich. "Too much work."

They walked for a while in silence, following Blodwyn, watched by the bright, glassy gaze of the cattle, which stood chewing thoughtfully by the fence. Alex moved away from them.

"Scared of cows?" asked Rich.

"Things are big, man," said Alex. "Never really been up close to them before."

"Nearly there," said Blodwyn, taking a left on a plank bridge over a little stream.

It was beautiful, this countryside, and it reminded Darwen of the fields and walls and hedges that surrounded the little town he'd come from. Seeing it at night, though, was eerie. *Is that why you feel something isn't right?* he asked himself.

"That sign back there," said Rich. "Said Bryn Celli something. What's that?"

"Bryn Celli Ddu," said Blodwyn without turning around. "It's a Neolithic burial mound. You'll see it in a moment."

Rich's face lit up, but Darwen felt his footsteps slowing. He was sure. This wasn't right.

"You know," he said, "I really think we should be getting back. I don't want to miss that train."

"Nearly there now," said Blodwyn, still not turning, not slowing. "Just round this corner."

As they came around the next bend, they saw a little metal gate and beyond it—unearthly in the moonlight—a miniature dome-shaped hill covered in green turf, around which was a ditch and a series of irregular standing stones.

"Oh, yes!" said Rich. "Can we go in?"

"Certainly," said Blodwyn.

Rich jogged across the ditch toward the grassy dome. "Cool," he called back. "There's a passageway into the hill. It's a tomb!" He stood, pointing happily inside the dark interior, the door to which was braced with large slabs of stone.

"Wait," said Darwen. "Rich! Stop." He waited till the other boy turned to face him, then said in a low, serious voice, "That's a portal."

"Darwen!" gasped Alex, flashing a glance at Blodwyn before hissing, "She'll hear."

"She already knows," said Darwen. "Don't you?"

Blodwyn had been standing quite still with her back to him, but now she turned very slowly and her broad, friendly smile was gone. In its place was something more cautious, puzzled, as she found him with her flashlight's beam. "Now," she said, "how on earth do you know that?"

Darwen just looked at her, conscious that Rich and Alex were exchanging panicked glances. Blodwyn held his eyes for a long moment, then said, "You're right. It's a portal, but how did you know? Mirroculists can't sense them."

"I can just tell sometimes," said Darwen. "Just recently. I don't know why. So who are you really?"

A version of the woman's smile came back on, and she looked quite harmless, even as Rich and Alex drew closer to him, as if bracing themselves to fight.

"I am Blodwyn Evans, like I said," she answered. "Really and truly. And you, Darwen Arkwright, are looking for an old friend of mine, Mr. Octavius Peregrine."

"You're a gatekeeper, like he was," said Rich, his eyes sparkling with excitement at the realization.

"And still working for the Guardians," said Alex.

"Right and correct both times," said Blodwyn. "I'm sorry about the cloak-and-dagger routine, but I needed to be sure you were who I thought you were. I've had a few thoughts of my own that I want to talk to you about. About something bad from long ago that needs stopping."

"We have come to find Mr. Peregrine," said Darwen. "We need to get to Conwy."

"Well," said Blodwyn, "I think your task and mine might be related. Solving one mystery might well solve both, if you know what I mean. But you'll need to know what to do, so I've asked for someone from the council to have a word with you. I'm not sure who the Guardians will send, but they should be here any minute, so have a seat. Won't take but a minute."

They sat cautiously, eyeing one another, finding spots on the turf and the lower standing stones. Blodwyn paused, then resumed her narrative.

"See, long ago, the Guardians had a problem. Running Silbrica took work, and I don't just mean mental work, I mean the kind of work that took muscle. Now the Guardians themselves are thinker types as you have probably noticed, so . . ." She paused, considering the burial mound. "Told you they wouldn't keep you waiting. Here they are now, look you."

There was a pulse of bluish light from inside the tomb, bright as the glare of the lighthouse in the night, and before it faded completely, Darwen could just make out the silhouette of a man-sized figure with a strangely distorted head.

He first thought it was a scrobbler, but then it stepped out into the moonlight, and Darwen could see that it was not as big as a scrobbler. He—if it was a man—was wearing a long coat and something over his face, something Darwen found awfully familiar.

It was a gas mask, and it was exactly the same as that worn by the man he had seen in a newspaper photograph of a small green Fiat. . . .

No. It couldn't be.

The mask had green lenses that covered the wearer's eyes and a miniature flashlight attached to the side so that he directed a hard, bluish beam of light wherever he looked. Something in his hand was smoking, producing a thick green fog that billowed around him.

For a moment there was silence, then Blodwyn took a cautious step forward. "You?" she said, aghast. "What are you doing here? They're just kids!"

The figure turned his ugly glass-and-rubber face toward her and pressed a button on the smoking device in his left hand. Blodwyn's flashlight bulb popped and went out. As the darkness thickened, the man drew something from his right-hand pocket. It looked like an old flintlock pistol, but the long barrel was surrounded by a basketlike metal mesh. Blodwyn turned back to face him, her face now wild with panic and dread.

"Run!" she shouted.

Rich didn't need to be told twice. He stumbled backward, eyes on the figure in the mask. Darwen, meanwhile, just stared, horrified.

Before Blodwyn could say more, the odd-looking pistol in the man's hand flashed once with a sudden whooshing sound that sent crows crying from the trees nearby. Something struck her, and her body flickered with electricity.

Blodwyn's face tightened, and she dropped to the grass.

For a second, nothing happened. The three children just stared at the woman where she lay.

"He shot her," gasped Alex, numb with shock. "He just shot her."

Then the masked man stepped clear of the dispersing gas cloud and the full horror of the situation hit Darwen with almost as much force as what had happened to Blodwyn.

There could be no doubt. He knew that mask. It was the man who had been driving behind his parents on the day of their accident.

Which meant . . .

Terrible things. Awful things that turned the world upside down. Greyling had been hunting him for years. And now his agent would finally kill them all.

Chapter Twenty-three
Driving Lessons

Darwen took a step toward Blodwyn, who lay motionless, but his eyes slid onto that blank, gas-masked face as its owner came striding toward them, mechanically resetting his weapon and raising it to fire.

They had to get out of here. Darwen grabbed Alex by the shoulders and started to run. He wanted to say something but could find no words, so he just dragged her after him, praying that Rich would follow.

They sprinted back the way they had come. Darwen heard the gun fire twice, heard the shrill fizz of electricity flashing off the stone wall to his right, and he ran harder, faster, his heart racing, his eyes wide and streaming.

But to where?

He checked over his shoulder once and was relieved to see Rich lumbering only a few yards behind as Alex streaked past both of them. Greyling's masked henchman was walking purposefully through the night. The gun was down by his side and he carried a briefcase in the other hand. He was coming after them, but his manner, though purposeful, was slow and assured. He wasn't going to waste energy shooting at this range, but he was absolutely confident that he would get them.

"Where do we go?" Darwen shouted as they left the cow pasture behind and reached the empty road. The man in the gas mask was still following.

"Car," Alex called back.

"What?" Darwen returned, panting. "What good does that do us? We can't drive."

"Rich can," said Alex, crossing into the parking lot. "Keys are still in it."

"You can drive this?" Darwen gasped, staring at Rich as he reached them, pink and scared-looking.

"No!" he answered. "Of course not."

"It's a stick shift," said Alex, throwing open the driver's door, then stepping aside. "Pretend it's a tractor or a ride-on lawn mower."

Darwen looked at Rich, whose eyes were flashing over the car's controls uncertainly.

"I could try," he said.

Darwen looked back over the road. The man in the gas mask was less than a hundred yards away. "Try," he said.

"Belt yourselves in," said Rich, climbing into the driver's seat. "Okay, so the gearshift is here—"

"Quick," said Darwen.

Greyling's agent had reached the gate.

"Clutch," he muttered. "Where's the clutch? Maybe this." Rich turned the key and the engine caught.

"GO!" shouted Alex from the back.

The man in the gas mask was crossing the road, his gun hand rising.

And then, suddenly, it wasn't. There was the blare of a horn and he stepped back as a car shot past in a blaze of headlights.

Rich shifted gears, grinding them, then twisted in his seat to look backward. The car shot forward, hitting the stone wall with a dull crunch.

"Reverse!" shouted Alex.

"Trying," he answered, pushing the gearshift and sending the car shooting backward, kicking up a cloud of dust and gravel. He swung the Land Rover around as it moved till they were facing the exit to the parking lot, an exit now dominated by the masked man and the business end of his weapon.

"Get down!" shouted Darwen.

The electric flintlock flashed and the windshield was suddenly a maze of cracks with two holes in the center, around which blue energy flickered briefly like lightning.

Rich slammed his foot down and the car rocketed forward. The man in the gas mask held his ground for one more shot, then leapt sideways as the Land Rover missed him by inches, slewed across the road, and sped back toward Menai Bridge with a scrape of gears.

"Everyone okay?" asked Rich, whose face and voice had both taken on a grim calm.

"Yes," said Darwen.

"Never better," said Alex. "Nice job."

"It's actually not that hard," said Rich, just as a bus came speeding around the corner and right at them.

"Drive on the left!" shouted Darwen.

Rich twisted the steering wheel hard and the Land Rover swerved across the road till it brushed the hedges. The bus blared its horn, but they stayed on the road. "Okay," said Rich. "Not so bad."

"And put your lights on," said Alex.

"Find them for me," he said.

Darwen reached over and messed with the controls. The radio crackled and the wipers leapt into action, but he eventually found the headlights.

"I can do this," said Rich. "But no one talk to me for a while."

That was fine with Darwen. There was too much to say and not enough words in the world to say it. But the silence lasted only a couple of minutes.

"Blodwyn . . ." said Alex, her voice taut.

"I know," said Darwen.

"It was so casual," she said. "So ordinary."

"I know," said Darwen again.

"She saved us," said Rich, not taking his eyes off the road. "She didn't know she was leading us into a trap and, when it counted, she chose to save us."

Darwen just nodded.

"How did you know it was a portal?" asked Alex.

Darwen shrugged.

"It was a guess, right, Darwen?" said Rich, shooting him a quick sideways look. "Because it was an ancient place, like the ring of cedars at Hillside, somewhere people have associated with mystical power for a long time, yeah?"

"Yeah," said Darwen, avoiding his eyes. "That must have been it."

Alex didn't let him out of her gaze. "That's not it, though, is it?" she said.

Darwen hesitated, then shook his head slowly. "Partly, perhaps," he said. "But not really, no. I can't explain it. I just felt it was a portal. I don't mean that I had some sort of mystical experience or something. It was more like . . . I don't know, like a smell."

"It *smelled* like a portal?" Alex repeated. She didn't sound skeptical or mocking so much as concerned, like she was trying to clarify something that bothered her.

"It wasn't *actually* a smell, no," said Darwen, struggling to find the words. "But it was that kind of feeling. An ordinary sensation, like touching something, or seeing. I could just tell."

Alex continued to watch him thoughtfully, and then she nodded, accepting his answer. She said no more, though Darwen glanced at her in the rearview mirror and thought she looked troubled.

"How long before we get pulled over by the police?" Darwen wondered aloud. "Think we can make it to Conwy?"

"We should be okay," Alex remarked. "Good thing Rich is twice the size of every other sixth grader in the world."

"Good thing it's dark," Rich added. "Still . . . Conwy," he mused, shifting. Darwen saw that his friend's knuckles on the steering wheel were white though the speedometer read only thirty miles an hour. "That's like a big town, right? I'm just about managing to keep us on the road. Not ready to handle a city or serious traffic. I really wish Eileen were here."

"It's late," said Alex. "Traffic shouldn't be too bad. But the guy in the mask is bound to be coming after us. Can we go faster?"

"Not if you want to get there alive," said Rich.

"Slow it is," said Alex. "You got a map up there, Darwen?"

Darwen wasn't listening. He was staring out of the window at the hedges flashing by, nothing in his mind but the newspaper article about his parents' death, and the photograph of the masked man sitting in the driver's seat, moments after he had done the job for which Greyling had employed him.

Had Greyling thought Darwen was in that car? Had it been an attack on the kid who was to be the next mirroculist? An attempt to wipe him out of the wars to come before he even developed his gift? If that was the case, then Darwen's parents had been killed for him. It was his fault.

"Darwen?" said Alex. "Map?"

"What?" he said, as if waking up. "Right. Hold on."

He opened the glove compartment and pulled out a dog-eared map, which he proceeded to rotate, feeling lost and stupid.

"Okay," he muttered. "Where are we?"

"You have it the wrong way up," snapped Alex. "Give it to me."

Darwen handed it to her, glad to go back to his own thoughts, and she studied it by the glow of her cell phone. "Right," she said. "We want the A55. Yeah, that way," she said, pointing.

Rich pulled the wheel hard and the Land Rover's tires squealed.

"Easy there, big fella," said Alex. "This ain't Talladega. Okay, now you know how you said you weren't ready for city traffic or major roads?"

"Distinctly," said Rich.

"How d'ya feel about bridges?"

"Not good," said Rich.

"Well, you might want to rethink that," said Alex. "'Cause Anglesey is an island and we have to get off it and . . . uh-oh."

The bridge in question was directly ahead. It was very long, very narrow, and very busy. There was a long drop to the dark water below.

"I can't do it," said Rich, braking so that a car behind beeped its horn.

"Yes, you can," said Alex. "You've *been* doing it. Just stay on the left and go straight."

"And if I can't?"

"It's a long way down," said Alex, peering over the side.

"Maybe if I go really slow . . ." Rich wondered.

"Let's not attract attention, okay?" said Alex. "Just do what everyone else does and maybe no one will notice that a kid is driving."

A kid is driving, thought Darwen. *Driving a car stolen from a woman who was shot dead in a field . . .*

How had things gone so wrong so fast?

Another horn blew at them and Rich sped up a fraction. He was gripping the wheel hard with both hands, leaning forward over it, his face rigid and sweating.

"Nearly there," said Alex as cars shot past in the opposite direction.

"On the other side we're going to turn left onto the North Wales Expressway. That should take us pretty much to Conwy. There should be a right turn onto the A547."

"I don't need to know the numbers," said Rich through gritted teeth. "Just tell me when to turn."

An ambulance sped past, sirens screaming and lights flashing, followed by a police car marked with fluorescent yellow stripes.

"I wonder if that's for—" Alex began.

"We need to get rid of the car as soon as we can," said Darwen, amazed that so ridiculous a statement actually made sense. "The police will assume that whoever killed Blodwyn stole it."

So now they were on the run from the police too. It was a disaster, and again, he thought, the idea settling hard and cold in his empty stomach, it was his fault. As the others focused on getting the car into Conwy without killing anyone or getting arrested, Darwen brooded in silence, oblivious to everything. He wanted to tell them about the man in the mask, about his parents . . .

And he would. But not yet.

When they stopped, he looked up, surprised. The headlights splashed across the stones of an ancient fortified wall. Darwen craned his neck to the castle battlements he had seen in the newspaper photographs of the story about the falcons and said the first words he had spoken in half an hour.

"We're here."

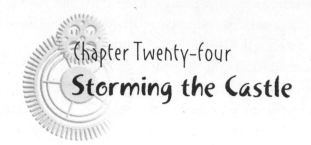

Chapter Twenty-four
Storming the Castle

The castle loomed over both town and harbor, lit by powerful lamps that made its impressive battlements and towers look romantic and impregnable. It was linked to a perimeter wall that encircled the whole town and sat right next to the railway tracks, which were carried across the estuary to the north via a monumental bridge whose turrets had clearly been designed to match the castle. The main entrance had closed hours ago.

"How do we get in?" asked Rich.

They had parked the car on a side street, its back end sticking out onto the sidewalk. Rich had done an excellent job getting them here, but parking clearly wasn't his strong suit.

"Think we could climb the wall?" asked Alex, not sounding hopeful.

"No," said Rich and Darwen together.

"Maybe if we walk around the outside, we could find a tumbled-down bit," said Alex.

"Man," said Rich, gazing at the great round towers and crenulated battlements. "I know we're in danger here and all, but did you ever see anything so cool in all your life? Unreal. You can feel the history, you know? The knights who used to patrol those walls, the archers and crossbowmen who would have stood right there . . ."

"Yeah, yeah," said Alex. "It's an old castle. Very nice. And it might as well still be guarded by knights and who-all 'cause we can't get in."

"Huh," said Darwen, checking his wrist. "My watch stopped. Is this another weird time thing like at the shadow school?"

Alex looked at hers.

"Mine's dead too," she said. "About forty minutes ago. My mom's cell phone's dead as well. Man, she'll have a cow."

"Mine is still working," said Rich, pressing the old-fashioned watch he always wore to his ear. "Still ticking away."

"But yours is a wind-up," said Darwen. "No electrical parts. I'll bet whatever the man in the gas mask used to knock out Blodwyn's flashlight fried any circuits that were close by."

"Good thing the car was over the road," said Rich.

The car, Darwen thought. *Is that how he killed Mum and Dad? He used some Silbrican gadget to mess with their car as they were driving?*

"You think Mr. P is inside?" asked Alex, gazing up at the castle.

"No," said Darwen. "Not in this world. But there is a portal here that the Guardians told me they don't use. Might lead right to him, but we'll have to force it open."

"Oy," said a man's voice. "What do you think you're doing there? Castle's closed."

Darwen turned to find himself looking into the keen eyes of a man in black trousers and a matching sweater. He wore a name badge and brandished a flashlight. A security guard.

Great . . .

"You have keys?" asked Alex. "To the castle, I mean."

"Of course I have keys," said the man, affronted. "I'm the guard, aren't I? *Do I have keys?* What's it to you?"

"We were inside earlier and I dropped my passport," said Alex. "We're supposed to be leaving in the morning, but if I can't get my passport . . . I won't be able to get home."

Amazingly, her eyes shone with unshed tears, and as one broke and ran down her cheek, she put her head in her hands.

"Steady on there," said the man, rather less assured. "I'm sure you can talk to your consulate or something. American, are you?"

Alex nodded, sobbing. Darwen and Rich just stared.

"School trip, is it?"

Again, Alex nodded.

"Teacher know you're out at this time?"

"Teacher said it was my own fault and they'd have to leave me, so I sneaked out to look," said Alex. "They came to help," she added, glancing at Rich and Darwen, who nodded their agreement stupidly.

"You sure you lost it in there?" said the security guard, nodding at the castle.

"Positive," said Alex. "I know where I put it down and everything. If you could let us in for a minute . . ."

"More than my job's worth to let you in now," said the security guard. "Probably got turned in to lost and found. It will be in the safe. I can't get into that."

"We were, like, the very last to leave," Alex improvised. "They were locking up as we left. I don't think anyone would have had time to find it. My mom will kill me if I have to stay here another day while they get me a new passport. And I'll have to pay for a new flight! You know what that will cost?"

She began crying again, this time grabbing hold of the security guard and burying her face in his ample middle, something that turned the man rigid with terror.

"Where do you think you left it?" he managed, his eyes wide, discomfort coming off him like a smell.

Alex turned to the castle, picked a tower, and pointed, managing to give a secret wink to a stunned Darwen as she did so.

"That one," she said. "I put it down to take a photograph. Just set it down on a ledge and then forgot it. I'm such an idiot. It's so beautiful here. So full of history. You can almost see the knights and archers on the walls. I can't believe I ruined it."

"There, there," said the man, patting her head awkwardly as Rich stared at her. "Let's see what we can do. Now, we can only look for a minute, and if it's not there—"

"Excellent," said Alex, cheering up a little too quickly. "Thanks."

The security guard fished in his pocket, produced a ring of keys, and unlocked the door.

"Maybe you two should wait outside," he said to Rich and Darwen.

"Out here by ourselves," said Rich, trying without much success to sound younger and smaller than he was. "In the dark?"

"And I need to go to the toilet," said Darwen.

The security guard scowled, then sighed. "All right," he said, "But stay where I can see you and don't touch anything in the gift shop."

He led them through the entrance hall and the store, which was crammed with books and souvenirs, then waited while Darwen descended to the bathrooms. He didn't need to go to the toilet, but the prospect of trying to force open one of Greyling's portals was making him anxious. For a moment he stood nervously in front of the mirror over the sinks, trying not to think about the agent in the gas mask, staring at his reflection as if—if he looked really closely—he might actually see himself aging. His parents hadn't just died in an accident. They had been murdered, and that act had somehow made Darwen a mirroculist.

But only, he thought bitterly, *for a while*.

Was his gift fading even now? Would Rich and Alex have to carry him back because he could no longer open any of the portals?

After a couple of agonizing minutes, he rejoined the others. The security guard led them through another door to a bridge over the street and up a long ramped approach that climbed to the remains of a gatehouse. There was an open area on the top flanked by two massive towers and the main door through a thick stone wall surmounted by battlements. Rich gazed up.

"Murder holes," he said, eyeing the chute-like openings over the doorway. "They could drop rocks, or shoot arrows, or pour burning oil on you as you tried to batter your way in," he added, though his smile faded when he caught Darwen's look.

Murder holes.

Darwen thought of Blodwyn, of his parents.

Not now, he thought. He had to to focus on finding that portal and Mr. Peregrine.

He concentrated, reaching out with his mind as they crossed the threshold into the castle proper. They were in a grassy area, open to the night sky, the interior walls with their high arched doors and windows extending out toward the battlements and the sea. Darwen pivoted, scanning the layout. There were eight huge towers, but the four closest to the water sprouted smaller turrets that went even higher, like round chimneys with crenulated tops.

"I'm turned around," said Alex, giving him a pointed look. "Which tower was it again, Darwen?"

Darwen thought. He could feel the cool night air, smell the seawater, hear the distant traffic on the roads outside. Rich was right. You could almost sense the age of the place. But there was something else, like a sound on the very edge of hearing, or a memory, triggered by an old song, a dim awareness of something that did not belong in this world . . .

"Over there!" he said, pointing ahead and slightly to the left. "The one right on the far corner."

"That's the Chapel Tower, that is," grumbled the security guard. "I thought you said it was that one back there? Well, all right. But get a move on. I can't stay here all night. Five minutes, I'm waiting. Five!"

Darwen led the way at a jog. The security guard, he was relieved to note, did not follow.

They moved into the depths of the castle, passing through a heavy interior wall into a well-preserved section where the fractured walls rose up high around them and the darkness deepened significantly. Darwen felt himself drawn all the way to the back of the castle—the closest point to the sea—and then to the left and into a tower. A few steps up he found a round room with a deep, half-moon alcove on one side, its walls fluted with stone buttresses aside three tall lancet windows, their tops curved into points. The buttresses continued up into the half-domed ceiling, where they met.

"The chapel," said Rich.

"You sure this is the place?" Alex asked Darwen. "How do you know? Gotta say, man, you're starting to freak me out a bit."

"Hey, check it out," said Rich, squatting to a slip of thick gray paper on the ground. "A railway ticket. You think it's the same as the one we found on that scrobbler's body?"

But Darwen didn't answer. He was gazing at the arched recess, trying to decide if this was the portal they had been seeking ever since Costa Rica, when they had realized Mr. Peregrine had been taken. If it was, he thought, picturing the dead bulbs in the corner of the mansion's map room, it was one of those that had been taken off the Guardians' grid years ago. He looked around it for any sign of a control mechanism before realizing that the stone inside the recess had a slight sheen to it as if it had once been polished. When he tipped his head slightly to one side, he could just make out a shadowy reflection on the wall. It wasn't a mirror, exactly, but it was close enough.

Darwen reached out with his mind, trying to stir the ancient portal into life.

At first nothing happened, but as his eyes slid shut, he was struck by a sudden weariness, as if something of his own energy had left him.

He swayed where he stood, but then felt a shift of the light through his eyelids. Alex gasped, and Darwen opened his eyes. A radiant curtain of blue light streamed across the dark stone of the chapel like a movie projector, dividing into two distinct arches.

"How did you do that?" asked Rich, but Darwen just shrugged, breathing deeply and considering the two portals, trying to decide which was the right one. It had never occurred to him that there would be more than one. They didn't have time to make the wrong choice.

As if to emphasize the point, there came a curious whooshing sound. It wasn't close, but it was still loud, and if they hadn't heard the sound already once tonight, they probably wouldn't have known what it was. It was that strange-looking flintlock pistol with the basketwork mesh.

Rich gasped. "Blodwyn's killer," he said. "He's here."

Alex was staring at nothing, horrified. "The security guard!" she said. "God, no. We need to see if he's okay."

"There's no time," said Rich. "We have to get out of here. Which gate is it, Darwen?"

But Darwen didn't know. He tried to focus his mind, but the sound of the weapon still rang in his head, and he could almost see the security guard, slumped against a wall, a man who had been killed because he chose to help three kids from America. . . .

"Darwen, which portal?" Rich insisted.

"I don't know," said Darwen, pressing his fists to his eyes.

He's coming for us now, Darwen thought. *Hunting us. He won't talk. He won't ask questions or offer deals and promises. He'll just raise that energy weapon of his—*

"Darwen," Alex pressed, "which portal?"

He'll be in the castle by now, walking up the ramp in that steady, unhurried way of his, the way he once walked up to the door of a little green Fiat and climbed inside. Maybe he's already through the gatehouse—

"Darwen!" Rich said.

"You have to choose!" Alex urged.

"Can't," he muttered. He stared at the two shimmering portals, but he felt nothing from each of them, his mind full of the imagined crunch of gravel under the agent's shoes as he paced through the castle toward them.

And then, without warning, he wasn't imagining it at all. He could hear even footfalls only yards away. They hesitated, then changed, echoing on the stone steps of the tower.

"He's here," Rich hissed.

Even in the moment, stricken by his own terror, Darwen was conscious that he had never seen his friends look so scared. But he just stared, unable to choose, and then he was being dragged by the hand as Alex seized Rich and dragged them both into the left-hand portal.

Chapter Twenty-five
Problems on the Home Front

They were standing in the center of a ring of intricately carved wooden gates on a hill overlooking the sea. Darwen knew at once that they had made the wrong choice.

"What did you do?" he gasped at Alex.

"She saved our lives," said Rich.

"Not if he follows us through," said Darwen.

"He's not a mirroculist," said Alex.

"Didn't stop him coming through at that burial mound where he killed Blodwyn."

"So close it," Alex insisted.

"I don't know how I opened it in the first place," Darwen admitted. "How am I supposed to close it?"

"I suggest you try," said Alex. "And quick."

Darwen turned to the flickering gateway and extended his hand toward the curtain of light, closing his eyes and reaching with his mind for what he thought of as the switch. He pictured it and then, as if in a dream, reached for it and flipped it. Again he felt some of the life drain out of him, but he knew immediately that it had worked.

When he opened his eyes, what had been a portal was nothing more than empty air. But the effort of closing it had taken more out of him than he realized. He felt light-headed, and sat down quickly before he lost his balance.

"Where to next?" asked Rich. "You okay?"

Darwen nodded and pulled the notebook with the gate codes from his back pocket, thrusting it at Rich. "Here," he said. "See what will get us back to the Great Apparatus. I just need to get my breath back."

As Rich flipped through the book, Alex watched Darwen, frowning. "What's happening to you, Darwen?" she asked.

Darwen just shook his head slowly. It felt impossibly heavy.

"This one," said Rich, checking the number.

"Okay," said Darwen wearily. "Let me try." He was able to open the portal, but it wasn't easy, and closing it behind them was more difficult still. It took three more portals to reach the Great Apparatus, and by the time they got there, Darwen was so exhausted he could barely stand.

They crawled up the chute to the oven door, but at the portal into his bedroom, Darwen hesitated. "Hold my hand," he said.

"What?" asked Alex. "Why?"

"I'm tired," Darwen snapped. "I can't do it by myself."

The gift is leaving me. I can feel it.

Rich and Alex exchanged looks but then nodded.

"That was a disaster," he said.

They had learned nothing from their excursion to Wales, and they had watched Blodwyn Evans—one of those rare allies they had been trying to recruit—get cut down in front of them. As Rich and Alex discussed their plans to slip out unseen, Darwen sank onto the bed and put his head in his hands. He didn't notice the precise moment that they left.

Darwen watched Aunt Honoria over breakfast for any sign that she had noticed his absence the night before, but she was merely clipped and businesslike, one eye on her phone at all times as she had been since the day she had fired Eileen. Though it was a relief not to be in trouble, Darwen found himself oddly disappointed, as if a part of him wished she had been paying more attention. She sighed when she realized it was time to take him to school and muttered something about needing to find a new babysitter.

"I'm all right by myself most of the time," said Darwen, in a voice that was supposed to sound encouraging. "And when it's just the two of us, that's, you know, nice."

He had avoided her eyes, slightly embarrassed by what he had said, but when she said nothing, he looked up to find her studying the screen of her laptop.

"Things are very busy at work right now," she muttered absently. "Did you take the homework sheet? I signed it last night and put it by your door. Did you not pick it up? Really, Darwen, you need to take responsibility for this stuff. I can't be late today."

"Right," said Darwen, feeling lost and sad for reasons he couldn't pinpoint. "Sorry."

"I thought this school would be good for you," she said, as much to herself as to him, smoothing her black pantsuit in the mirror and adjusting the silver necklace. "Maybe we'll try somewhere different next year. Somewhere more reasonably priced."

Stunned, Darwen just stared at her.

"Come on," she said, irritation wrinkling her brow as she held the apartment door open. "I'm going to be late."

"Tonight I'll be working after school," Darwen improvised as they rode down in the elevator. "Preparing for the gala."

Yesterday the very thought would have been absurd, but Darwen suddenly found he wanted to talk to her about it.

"The what?" asked his aunt, checking her watch.

"You remember," said Darwen, trying to sound cheery, "the end-of-year gala and talent show. I'm working with Rich and Alex."

Even though he would have no answer for her, he suddenly wanted her to ask what they were planning to do.

"Oh," said Aunt Honoria. "That."

"It's tomorrow night and we have to practice."

"Till when? And I won't be able to drive your friends home."

"I'm staying with Rich tonight, didn't I tell you?"

"Okay," she said as the doors opened and she stalked out.

"I could have Rich's dad call you—"

"It's fine. Walk a little faster, Darwen."

"And you'll be at the gala, right?"

"What? Oh. Well. I'll try. Maybe I'll make it for the end, but things at work are—"

"Busy," Darwen completed for her. "Yeah, I know."

Darwen was quiet all day. Their failure to reach Mr. Peregrine hung about him like a cloud, but it was more than that. His aunt's lack of interest, his anxieties about his own fading gift and, by extension, his own importance to the Peregrine Pact left him feeling as isolated and homesick as when he had first left England. He thought of those Welsh fields and the little roads that reminded him of the villages close to his hometown and it occurred to him that he belonged nowhere, that he was suspended between worlds, always just out of the reach of the people he cared about.

Though they had made it home without incident or awkward questions, Rich was tired and subdued. Even Alex, usually a force of nature, was quiet and introspective. Darwen guessed she was thinking about the man in the gas mask, about Blodwyn, about the security guard they had left behind at Conwy castle. And she would be thinking of Mr. Peregrine, who seemed as far away as ever, and of Greyling's power rising, something they seemed completely incapable of slowing this time. The very last thing any of them wanted to think about was their contribution to tomorrow's talent show.

"Everyone else has some kind of talent listed," said Mr. Sumners, studying his clipboard with a satisfied smile as he made the homeroom rounds at the end of the day. "But not you three. Trouble identifying your particular area of genius, Arkwright?"

"Just been busy, sir," said Darwen.

"So I hear," said Mr. Sumners, his smile tweaking slightly. "I look forward to what you do tomorrow night. Up there on the stage. With all your friends, family, and teachers looking on. I'm sure it will be dazzling."

"Boy, are we screwed," muttered Alex as he sidled away. "We should have just picked a song and you could have been my backup dancers."

"No," said Rich and Darwen together.

"We could do something with computers," said Rich, watching the workmen running wires for the new school network.

"Like what?" said Darwen.

"I don't know," said Rich. "We could write a program or something. Something with lots of pictures and noise. People like pictures."

"We have—" Darwen checked his watch, realized that it was still broken, and cursed. "A day," he concluded. "And I'm useless with computers."

"I'm not," said Alex.

"Yes, you are," said Rich. "Unless it's picture-editing and stuff, which doesn't count."

"Then doing *something with computers* wasn't much of an idea, was it?" returned Alex tartly.

"We need to get back to Wales," said Darwen, lowering his voice. "To the castle. Try that other portal."

"And walk into the guy in the gas mask who is waiting for us?" said Rich. "He's bound to be there, Darwen. He knows what you are trying to do."

"How?" asked Alex.

"What do you mean?" said Rich.

"I mean that you are right," said Alex. "That he knows what we were trying to do and he knew where we would be. Blodwyn was expecting someone from the Guardians, but the guy who showed up has to be working for Greyling, right?"

"I don't see who else he could be working for," said Rich.

"I mean," Alex continued, "we trust the council, right?"

Rich frowned, then nodded. "Yes," he said. "We have to. And Blodwyn worked for them, so they wouldn't attack her."

Darwen said nothing. All he could think of was the image of the masked man sitting in the driver's side of the little Fiat, and though he wanted to tell his friends, he knew he wasn't ready to put it into words.

"Which leads us back to my original question," Alex continued. "If this gas-mask guy is working for Greyling and came after us specifically, how did he know where we were?"

Rich's frown deepened.

"You think someone on the council is a spy?" he asked.

Alex shrugged. "Blodwyn thought we were going to have a chat with someone from the council," she mused. "But instead, right on time, we get gas-mask guy coming out shooting. Something isn't right."

Gas-mask guy.

Darwen had not told them about the pictures of the man in the Fiat. For all Rich and Alex knew, the man in the gas mask was just another of Greyling's agents like the scrobblers and gnashers they had encountered before. They didn't know why he felt so different to Darwen, why Darwen's fear of him was touched with hatred. Darwen didn't like keeping it from them, but he couldn't talk about his parents. Not yet. He pushed the thought to the back of his mind and kneaded his temples.

"Maybe I could ask Moth for advice?" he ventured. "Or Weazen?"

"Weazen!" said Alex. "He would be perfect."

"For what?" asked Rich.

"The gala, obviously," Alex said with withering scorn. "We do an animal act. Weazen pretends to be, like, a regular otter or whatever he is, and we make him do tricks. Weazen walks on his hind feet! Weazen jumps through a hoop!"

"Weazen shoots us with his blaster for even suggesting it," inserted Darwen.

"No," said Alex. "Weazen's sweet. He'd help us out. It would look like we'd been training him for months."

"And then Mr. Iverson remembers that this 'otter' destroyed his lab and mysteriously escaped," said Rich, "and we're out of here before you can say 'expelled.'"

"I might be out of here anyway," Darwen blurted before he could stop himself.

"What?" said Alex.

"My aunt isn't happy with my progress," said Darwen. "And things are rough at work. Money's tight and this place is kind of . . ."

"Expensive?" Alex supplied. "Exorbitant? Extortionary?"

"Well, it's not cheap," said Darwen.

"Ah," said Alex, "the great British art of understatement. *Not cheap.* No, it's not. Try *preposterously, outrageously overpriced.*"

"I can't afford any more screwups," said Darwen miserably.

"Guess we better find ourselves a talent," said Alex. "Blowing off the gala might be just what your aunt needs to drop-kick your sorry tail out of here."

"Okay," said Rich, "but no animal acts."

"I could bring Sasha, my dog," Alex suggested, ignoring Rich's comment.

"What can she do?" asked Darwen.

"Oh, you know," said Alex. "Dog stuff. Sit. Walk around. Lie down."

"When you tell her to?" said Rich, his eyes narrow.

"Not as such," said Alex. "But if you're fast, you can order her to do something as she starts doing it so it looks like she's obeying you."

"Next idea?" said Rich to Darwen.

"We're not done with this one," said Alex.

"We really are," said Rich. "Next?"

"You both covered for tonight?" asked Darwen, changing the subject.

"My dad thinks I'm staying with you," said Rich.

"My mom thinks I'm doing a sleepover with Genevieve Reddock."

Darwen pulled a disbelieving face.

"What?" said Alex. "It's possible."

"It's really not," said Rich.

Genevieve, like Nathan, had much cooler friends than Alex and thought her a bit of a goofball. Alex looked away and didn't speak for almost a minute.

"And we have permission to stay at school for a while at least," said Rich, breaking the silence. "I told Mr. Iverson we were having an archaeology club session. He thinks it's connected to our talent event."

"You're staying here tonight?" asked Simon Agu as he passed, carrying a stack of books. "After what happened yesterday? You're braver than me."

"What happened yesterday?" asked Darwen.

"You're kidding, right?" said Simon. "Naia, Melissa, Jennifer, and Bobby Park all saw ghosts. *Separately*. Naia saw two at the same time. They were in our homeroom. She was just finishing up some work and there they were: two of them. Floating about."

"What did they do?" asked Rich.

"Do?" said Simon. "They scared her half to death is what they did."

"Just by being there, though, right?" Rich pressed. "Not by attacking her or something."

Simon was affronted. "There were two ghosts in the room with her!" he exclaimed. "One of them had this really weird face with big teeth. That's not scary enough?"

At the end of the day, as the other kids filed out to their clubs and the waiting cars driven by their attentive parents, Darwen, Rich, and Alex found themselves alone in the very homeroom class where Naia had had her spectral encounter.

"Just close the door when you're done," said Miss Harvey, who seemed more cautious than usual. It was rumored that the janitor had reported seeing a spectral apparition in the basement of the clock tower and that he had discussed it with Mrs. Frumpelstein, who had confessed to glimpsing something similar while she was grading papers after school the previous evening. Even the teachers were getting nervous. "Don't get in the way of the workmen," said Miss Harvey, "and if you see anything . . . out of the ordinary, stay together and call the principal's office. Principal Thompson will be working late this evening."

"Right, miss," said Darwen, eyeing the scaffold in the quadrangle, where two men were hoisting tools up to the new window in the clock tower. "I mean, ma'am," he added to her retreating back.

They listened to the clack of her heels down the hall.

"She seems back to normal," said Alex. "I mean, normal for here."

"The Hillside teachers aren't *that* weird, Alex," said Rich. "My dad says you have an unhealthy fixation with everyone around you being strange."

"Your dad said 'unhealthy fixation'?" said Alex, dubious rather than offended.

"Got it off some TV show," Rich began, stopping when he realized that Alex was looking past him to where a face had appeared in the glass panel of the classroom door.

"Eileen!" Darwen exclaimed, getting to his feet as she came in. "What are you doing here?"

Rich nearly fell out of his chair. He stood hurriedly, his face flushing.

"Hi," said Eileen. She looked small, Darwen thought, and a little sad, as if their last disastrous return to the school was still on her mind. "I'm sorry. I just wanted to see whether you guys were making any progress with regard to Octavius. I can't go to your place anymore, so I figured I'd try to catch you here." She had a huge canvas duffel bag slung over her shoulder. To Darwen's inquiring look, she just shrugged. "Blaster," she said. "Only has a few shots left, but I take it everywhere now. Paranoid, I guess."

Eileen set the bag on a nearby desk, and Rich immediately opened it and began studying the blaster. "I can't get any more power to this," said Rich, looking up from the triple-barreled blaster, "but if you adjust these gauges here, I'll bet you could get one big punch out of it. 'Course, it may just turn it into a giant flashlight. . . ."

Before Eileen could respond, the classroom door cannoned open and Mr. Stuggs lumbered in. He was stooping, his head thrust forward in a way that looked oddly bearlike, his beady eyes scanning the students as if choosing which to go after. Eileen took a step back, snatching up the blaster, and Stuggs advanced on her, his arms bent and fingers spread like a wrestler in his fighting stance. Rich stood too, ready to step into the teacher's path if he attacked, and Mr. Stuggs considered him, snarling. Darwen was the furthest away and could only watch anxiously. Stuggs's eyes had none of the casual smugness they usually held: they were mad and cruel. This was going to be bad.

And then the electric light in the room brightened and the distant humming sound they had barely been aware of went away. Mr. Stuggs considered his hands for a moment, bemused, then straightened up and ducked out of the room quickly, as if embarrassed.

"An unhealthy fixation, huh?" said Alex.

Rich said nothing. He was trembling with tension.

"It's getting worse," said Darwen. "Whatever it is, it's lasting longer."

"Yes," said Rich. "The lights dimmed, did you notice?"

"They did before too," said Darwen. "So that means what, that it's electrical?"

"Or spectral," said Alex. "Maybe there's a link to the ghost stories. Some kind of energy spike."

"I don't believe in ghosts," said Rich.

"Got any better ideas?" asked Alex.

"Actually," said Rich, "I might." He went to the door, angling his head so that he could see across the corridor and into the quadrangle beyond, where the workmen were carrying tools and spools of wire. "What exactly are they doing out there?" he said. He was looking through the classroom door and out to the quadrangle, where a man in blue coveralls was unrolling a spool of cable across the grass at the foot of the clock tower.

"Supposed to be a computer-and-communication system, right?" said Alex with a shrug. "They are probably connecting speakers out there. If the weather is fine, that's where they'll be holding the gala. See? They're building a stage."

"The cable could be for the PA and lights," said Rich thoughtfully.

"But we already know that that window is a portal to the shadow school," said Darwen. "So laying lots of cable round it worries me."

"It's not just around it," said Rich, peering out. "It's up the whole tower. Could they be doing something that is causing these weird moments with the teachers?"

"Not just the teachers," said Darwen. "It affected my aunt too."

"Doesn't make any sense," said Rich. "I gotta check this out."

Without waiting to see what the others thought, he stepped out into the hallway and made his way around to the door into the quadrangle. Eileen shoved her blaster back into her duffel bag and followed.

"Uh-oh," said Alex, watching Rich. "Captain Science smells adventure. Look at him. He's like Sasha when my mom fries bacon: hotter than a dancing bobcat."

"Hotter than what?" Darwen asked, following.

"It's a well-known Southern phrase," said Alex.

Darwen gave Eileen a glance and she just shook her head as if to say, *No, it's not.* Darwen grinned and Eileen managed to return something similar.

They all spilled out onto the quadrangle lawn, where they found themselves gazing up to a stage built just beneath the still-draped stained glass window.

"You kids can't be out here," said the man in the coveralls. "It's dangerous."

"We're just researching a report for the school paper," said Alex easily. "Can I have your picture?"

The man's attitude changed immediately. He looked far less grumpy and puffed his chest out. "School paper, huh?" he said.

"Yeah, but the local NBC affiliate follows us pretty closely," Alex lied.

"Yeah?" said the man. "No kidding?"

"Fancy school gets new technology while the public schools are bursting out of trailers," said Alex with a knowing look. "You know the kind of thing."

"Right," said the man. "My name's Ed McGinnis. Two *n*'s."

"Got it," said Alex, producing her mother's dead cell phone. "Say *cheese.*"

He did so and she mimed taking a picture.

"I'm about done for the day," said Mr. McGinnis, "but if there's anything I can tell you . . . ?"

"What are those wires for?" said Rich, pointing.

"Power supply," said McGinnis.

"To what?" Rich pressed.

"Those," he said, nodding to each side of the stage, where two open wire racks sat. Darwen thought they looked like satellite receivers or the kind of radar dishes you saw rotating in old war movies.

"What do they do?" asked Rich.

"That I couldn't tell you," said McGinnis, looking slightly abashed and checking Alex to be sure she wasn't recording. "I just install 'em."

"Great," muttered Rich sarcastically.

"Yeah, that's great!" said Alex, very cheery before McGinnis could grasp Rich's tone. "That's really helpful. I'll try to make sure NBC interviews you when they take the story for *Eleven Alive*."

"Not that I *want* to be on the news or nothing," McGinnis lied, "but sure. Right. Well, I'll leave you to it. Don't touch anything."

"Wouldn't dream of it." Alex beamed.

He got his tools together and left, walking through the quadrangle without even glancing back.

"He's very trusting," said Eileen.

"Nah," said Alex. "He just doesn't take kids seriously. And adults will do anything to get on TV."

Rich was pacing the perimeter, studying the wiring, his face creased into a thoughtful frown.

"What?" said Darwen.

"This is all wrong," said Rich. "This cable is designed to handle massive power, way more than any PA or lighting rig could need, and most of it is going in the wrong direction. Look! Those black wires running that way go to the outlets on the wall."

"So?"

"That's fine," said Rich. "But what about those red ones? They go up the tower from that rack thing, as if the power source was up there, not down here."

Darwen looked where Rich was pointing. He was right. "Maybe they're for hanging lights?"

"No," said Rich. "The cable plugs into those transformer things there, then into the racks themselves. I don't know what they do, but when they are switched on, the racks themselves will be live. And where's the power source? Looks like it's up in the clock, but that doesn't make any sense. There are two completely separate systems here in addition to the power for the sound and lights, and I don't know what either of them do."

"Hey," said Alex from over by the clock tower. "Check this out."

There was another transformer, this one quite different. It appeared to be connected to the main electrical supply, though it also seemed to feed into the clock. On top of it, surmounted by lights and dials, was a control box with a single heavy metal lever.

"This has scrobbler technology written all over it," said Darwen.

Rich nodded. "What do you suppose it does?" he asked.

"One way to find out," said Alex.

And she pulled the lever.

Chapter Twenty-six
Shadows and Ghosts

Rich shouted for her to stop, but it was too late. The lever thunked home and there was a curious sigh, a long, slow gasp that seemed to come from all around them. Then nothing.

"Maybe it's not hooked up properly," said Alex.

"I don't know," said Darwen. "I felt . . . something."

"Most of the cables aren't attached," said Rich. "Whatever it tried to do took more power than the system had access to. Still, that was a really stupid stunt, Alex."

"We don't have a lot of time to play Sherlock Holmes," she returned, defiant. "And besides, no harm, no foul, right? It didn't do anything. Not getting enough power to the thingy."

"Guys," said Eileen. "Is it me, or is it getting darker?"

Rich checked his watch but then looked up into the sky. Darwen did too and was baffled to see the light thickening even as he looked. It was as if time had sped up and the sun had set, except that it didn't feel truly like night either. There were no stars. No moon. It was simply . . . dark.

Darwen gazed around him, and something else struck him. The shape and texture of the school buildings were shifting. Everything was roughly as it had been, but the hard angles were becoming rounded and irregular. Darwen turned slowly, peering at what was but somehow was *not* Hillside Academy. The roofline was growing craggy and the glass in the quadrangle windows was fading to nothing. It looked almost as if the window frames had become holes carved into ancient, natural rock by centuries of wind and rain. . . .

"It's the shadow school!" Darwen gasped.

"Two different worlds inhabiting the same space," breathed Rich. "Not good. Not good at all."

And that was when Darwen noticed that in one corner of the quadrangle, the darkness was deeper still. He stared at it and it shifted fractionally so that for a second it seemed roughly human-shaped, if large and crouching. He felt his mouth go dry as he watched it stand tall, far bigger than any living man, and then it moved like a shadow flashing across the walls and was suddenly thirty feet closer.

He had seen one of these before and knew what it felt to be inside its terrible embrace: the darkness, the silence, the sense of drowning in the airless space.

"A Shade!" Darwen cried, pointing.

Even as he said it, it moved, momentarily winking out of existence and appearing only a few yards from where Alex stood. She shrieked and ran, and the Shade rippled, a column-shaped hole in the night. It shifted again, fractionally this time, its edges blurring and re-forming like a shadow on water, and Darwen felt it watching them, sizing them up like a lion among lambs. Choosing.

"Any of that magnesium ribbon in your pocket?" Darwen asked Rich, recalling the dazzling light they had used to dispel the last Shade they encountered. That was the only way to fight them: light, brilliant to the point of being blinding.

Rich shook his head, his eyes on the impenetrable darkness. "I've got nothing," he said.

Without warning there was a bang and a flash: Eileen's blaster. The shot tore straight through the Shade, the light of the charge opening a hole in it almost a foot across. But as the shot exploded against the stone of the quadrangle, the hole closed itself and the Shade moved again. Eileen's action had succeeded in doing nothing but making the Shade's mind up. In under a second it was on her.

Another shot rang out, tearing through the Shade harmlessly and shooting up into the night.

"No!" shouted Rich, pounding across the grass toward where Eileen was now lost in the surging mass of empty blackness.

"Alex," called Darwen, "pull the lever back!"

He doubted it would get rid of the Shade, and it wouldn't save Eileen, but it might stop anything else from crossing over from the shadow school. As Alex stepped back toward the mechanism, Darwen watched in horror as Rich took a breath and leapt into the Shade. The creature seemed to hesitate as if surprised, and then began thrashing and flickering all the more. In the process, Eileen fell out and onto the ground, her eyes wide, face pale. Darwen ran to her as she gasped for air, but his eyes were on Rich—or rather—the surging black nothing where Rich had been.

A flashlight, he thought desperately. *Something. Maybe if the stage lights had been hooked up to the power?*

But there wasn't time for that. Rich had seconds left to live. The only thing Darwen could do to save his friend was distract the thing that was drowning him in the hope that they would get away. He did the only thing he could, the same thing Rich had done. He charged it.

He was entering the black emptiness of the Shade when he was thrown back by a blaze of light erupting from inside the monster. The Shade shrieked once as it was ripped into nothing, and there, on the ground, looking dazed and exhausted, was Rich, cradling the charred remains of Eileen's blaster.

"Overloaded the power cell," he managed. "Switched off the cannon so that all remaining energy emerged as a single pulse of light."

"Alex, did you—" Darwen began, but a look at her told him all he needed to know. No, she hadn't reset the lever, and he could see why. At the empty stone windows of the quadrangle, ghostly figures were collecting. Alex was staring at them, terrified.

As before, some were the merest smudges of gray light, others were more distinct and clearly human, clearly—now that he saw them properly—children. One whose outline was firmer than the rest was drifting toward them through the doorway into the quadrangle.

"Alex!" called Darwen. "Pull the lever!"

But Alex was staring at the pale figure gliding out to meet them. It was, without question, a girl, and when it drifted a little closer, making directly for Alex, Darwen felt almost sure that it was in fact . . .

"Naia!" gasped Alex. "It's Naia Petrakis! How is that possible?"

Darwen stared. Alex was right. The ghostly figure was none other than their classmate, hovering only feet from Alex now, one hand outstretched.

"Pull the lever!" Darwen called again, and this time, Alex blinked, as if waking up, and seized the metal arm of the machine and shoved it hard back to where it had been. Immediately the air around them seemed to shudder, then lighten, and the ghostly figures were fading to nothing. The last to go was the one closest to them, the one that looked like a pale, spectral version of Naia Petrakis.

"You think that means she's . . . ?" Rich hesitated.

"Dead?" said Darwen, watching with amazement as the Hillside buildings took their familiar, hard-edged shape around them. "I don't think so. I mean, they look like ghosts, but that doesn't mean they are, right?"

"She was wearing the owl bracelet," said Alex thoughtfully. She was still gazing at the space where the Naia apparition had been. "The one that was stolen to fuel the scrobbler generator, remember? She—the ghost thing—had it on her wrist."

"I think," said Darwen carefully, "that they're like the buildings.

They're, like, echoes of us, but some are stronger, more conscious than others."

"Why?" asked Rich.

"I'm guessing that it must have something to do with their contact with Silbrica. That's why the Naia we just saw was wearing her bracelet."

"But why would Naia attack us?" asked Alex.

"I'm not sure she was doing," said Darwen. "Everyone who has seen them has been scared because they look like ghosts, but no one has been hurt by them. Perhaps they aren't trying to do us harm at all."

"What about the one who raised the alarm when we were there last time?" said Alex, giving Darwen a shrewd look. "The ugly one? I'm pretty sure he wanted to hurt us."

"It looked like a scrobbler," said Darwen. "Or halfway to being one."

"Halfway from what?" asked Rich.

"From Chip Whittley."

He had expected disbelief, even indignation at the suggestion, but Alex was unsurprised. "That so figures," she snorted. "If anyone would side with Greyling, it would be him."

"He was actually in Silbrica only a couple of months ago," added Rich. "Maybe that's why he seems more solid than the others. But why does his echo look like he's partway to being a scrobbler?"

Darwen shook his head.

Alex formed her hands into fists. "That weasel. When I see Chip, the real Chip, I mean, I'm gonna take him out to the woodshed."

"You're going to take him where?" asked Darwen.

"Means I'm gonna give him a beating," said Alex. "It's an expression."

Darwen glanced at Eileen and this time she shrugged and nodded agreement, even if no one believed Alex could give Chip any kind of beating. "You should probably give that back to me," Eileen said, turning to Rich. She nodded at the burned-out blaster he still cradled in his arms.

"It's dead, I'm afraid," he said, handing it sheepishly to Eileen, "but I guess it did the job—"

He would have said more, but Eileen had thrown her arms around him and kissed him on the cheek. "Thank you," she said. "If you hadn't . . . I'll never forget it."

Rich didn't speak again for the next ten minutes, during which time his face was so red that Alex started calling him Rudolph and observed that if they were attacked by another Shade, they would be able to banish it by pointing Rich's head at it. Darwen laughed, but Eileen, for all her gratitude, still looked badly shaken and her smile was strained. The four of them sat on the grass and looked around at the Hillside quadrangle.

No one spoke, and despite the hot Atlanta night Darwen felt strangely cold. Something was coming to Hillside. Something new that involved the shadow school actually materializing on this very spot. Darwen did not need to wonder when. Greyling would strike as he had done at the Halloween Hop, when the whole school, their friends, their families would be in attendance, and they had no Mr. Peregrine to turn to for help.

"Whatever is going to happen," he said, "it's going to happen during the gala."

"Why?" asked Alex. "Wouldn't he want to be more sneaky? Why pick the one time when the place is packed with people?"

"I don't know," said Darwen, "but that window is going to be unveiled tomorrow night and it's at the heart of whatever he's planning. I don't know why, but my hunch is that he wants people to see it come online."

"It's not finished," said Rich, considering the equipment and the hanging cables. "Maybe we could sabotage the machinery. Stop it from happening."

"Would at least slow him down," Alex agreed.

"It also tells him we've guessed his plans," said Darwen, vetoing the suggestion, "and we lose the element of surprise. I think we go after him in his world first."

"That *would* be pretty surprising," said Alex. "Since it's likely to get us killed."

"I think that if we're here tomorrow night," Rich said, "when Greyling brings the shadow school to Hillside, we get killed anyway."

"If Greyling is going to bring his reality into ours," said Darwen, nodding his agreement, "we have to assume that, despite whatever technology is set up here, the controls will be largely at his end. I say we go after him there, and that means finding Mr. Peregrine and any allies we can get. Tonight."

He and Rich looked at Alex.

"Okay," she said at last. "Doesn't totally answer the question of how we're going to do it, but yeah, that sounds like one of our plans."

Rich took a breath, suppressing a smile, then nodded.

"I'm sorry," Eileen interjected. "But I"—she fought to say the words—"I don't think I can help you."

The others stared at her.

"It's just that I'm of no use to you. Without being able to open portals, I'm a . . ." Her voice broke. "A hindrance."

"What are you talking about?" said Rich. "I just learned how to open portals. And Darwen brought me to Silbrica loads of times before."

Eileen waved Rich silent. "That's sweet of you, but I'll just get in the way and slow you down like I did with the Shade. My time in Silbrica is done." She turned to face Darwen. "I'm sorry, Darwen, but I can't help. Not in that way . . ."

"No," said Rich. "You'll be really useful to us. Won't she, Darwen?"

Darwen looked at Eileen, searching for the right answer. Instinctively he felt they were stronger together, that she would be useful to have around, but her eyes were determined. He gave her a questioning look, and the shake of her head was final and strangely sad. "You know what?" said Darwen, trying to look upbeat. "You stay here. Maybe when the time is right, you could disrupt the technology here, yeah? An ally on this side will be dead helpful, especially if we get stuck on the other side."

"Thanks," Eileen replied. She looked down quickly, but not before Darwen saw a tear slide down her cheek. For a long moment she did not look up, but then she fished in her pocket and added, "You'll want this." She produced a round compact Darwen had seen her use many times. She flipped it open and showed Darwen the mirror inside. "There are two buttons on the side. Press this one"—she did a demonstration with her finger—"and you'll get me."

Her duffel bag chimed, and from it she plucked an identical compact, which she flipped open and held up to her face. When she spoke again, her voice came from the compact in Darwen's hand. He glanced into it and saw her face looking back at him. She managed a strained smile.

"A Silbrican phone," said Alex. "Cool."

"Who do I get with the other button?" asked Darwen.

"You used to get Mr. Peregrine," said Eileen briskly, stifling any further show of feeling. "But not anymore." She took a deep breath. "Try it."

Darwen did so and waited. A moment later a sleek snout and bright inquisitive eyes watching from a dark, furry mask appeared in the mirror.

"I was wondering when I'd hear from you," said Weazen in a matter-of-fact voice. "About time."

In spite of himself, Darwen smiled, then got right to business. "We have to get to Conwy castle tonight," he said. "How do we do it without attracting the attention of Greyling's hit man—the guy in the gas mask?"

"Conwy in Wales?" said Weazen, rubbing a paw across his face. "Figures."

"Yeah," said Darwen. "Why? What happened?"

Weazen scowled. "There used to be a portal in the castle, right? But it's been off the Guardians' grid for donkeys' years. Yesterday, somehow, someone used it again."

"That was us," said Alex proudly, peering into the mirror and beaming.

"Yeah, well," said Weazen, "right after that there was an explosion. Now the portals don't work."

"Maybe we can force our way through anyway," said Rich. "They weren't supposed to be active last time, but we got them operational."

"When I said they don't work," said Weazen, "that's what you might call an understatement. They're gone. Totally destroyed along with half the building."

"Greyling's assassin," said Alex. "The man in the gas mask. He must have done it right after we left to stop us from coming back."

"So Conwy's a dead end," said Darwen, shutting his eyes and trying not to scream in frustration. "We had one chance and we blew it."

"I had to get us out of there," said Alex firmly. "We had a fifty-fifty chance of picking the right one. We were unlucky. It happens."

"I know," said Darwen. "I don't blame you. I couldn't decide and we needed to leave. But now I don't know what to do. We're stuck."

There was a long silence and Darwen watched Weazen blinking back at him through the compact.

"We know Conwy was right," said Rich. "That it was part of the chain leading to Mr. Peregrine, or else they wouldn't have bothered destroying the portal. But that can't be the only way in, can it? We saw people in the watchtower mirrors, and scrobblers. They aren't mirroculists, so they can't go back and forth through the portals. There must be another way. An ordinary way."

"An ordinary way between worlds?" Alex mused doubtfully. "Like they hop on the scrobbler express from Gnasherville and shunt straight into Wales for a holiday by the sea?"

"The train! That's it!" said Rich. He began fumbling in his pocket. "Darwen, you have that ticket you found by the scrobblers that were killed by That Which Eats?"

Darwen plucked it out and showed it to Rich. It looked the same as the one Rich was holding up, the one he had found at Conwy castle. Rich's portion read "Blaenau–Ffe . . ."

Darwen held his next to it. It wasn't the other half of the same ticket, but it could well be the torn portion of a different ticket to the same place, which meant that *iniog* might be the end of the word.

"*Blaenau-Ffe* . . . something . . . *iniog*," said Darwen, hardly daring to believe they might be on to something. "Could it be a place name?"

"Best lead we have so far," said Rich.

"So we need a train that goes from Silbrica into our world?" asked Alex.

"There's only one railway line in Silbrica," said Weazen. "Not really my territory, so I don't know how to get there."

"I do," said Darwen, smiling again. "I've been on it before. So has Alex."

She gaped at him. "The night we went to the Jenkins house," she said. "My first visit to Silbrica."

"Exactly," said Darwen.

"How will we get out again?" asked Rich. "Assuming we can find Mr. P, I mean?"

"There will be another portal close to wherever they are holding him," said Weazen, "though I don't expect it will be hooked up to the Guardians' grid anymore. If you can find it, you might be able to force it open from that side."

"I can," said Darwen. "I will."

Alex shot him a curious look, but he pressed on so he wouldn't have to talk about it. "Eileen, can you get us home? We need to use the Great Apparatus, and I'd rather get there from my closet than risk going through the shadow school."

"Seconded," said Alex, eyeing the shrouded window above the clock tower platform warily.

"I'm parked out front," said Eileen. "I'll drop you at your place, then come back here."

Darwen felt a surge of energy. They finally knew what they were doing. He grinned at Rich, but his friend looked somber, even anxious.

"What?" said Darwen. "This is good."

"I know," said Rich. "But it just feels like . . . I don't know."

"What?" asked Darwen.

"Like we're going to war," said Rich.

Chapter Twenty-seven
Back to the Jungle

"**T**his is the one," said Darwen, checking the portal number once they reached the Great Apparatus.

"Once we go through there," said Alex, "once we reach Mr. Peregrine, things are going to happen fast, aren't they? I mean, assuming he's okay and all, we're going to want to leap into action with regard to Greyling and the Great Talent Show Fiasco."

"So?" said Darwen.

"So we won't have time to gather any more allies," Alex reminded him.

"Not been too chuffin' successful on that front so far, have we?" Darwen returned darkly.

"You had something in mind, Alex?" asked Rich.

"As a matter of fact," said Alex, flipping open the notebook to a page scrawled with tangled vines and overlarge flowers behind which catlike eyes watched, "I do."

Darwen peered at the image. It was a jungle locus. "Pouncels?" he exclaimed. "You want to recruit pouncels? They'll probably eat us on the spot!"

"They've helped us before," said Alex, "and no, they won't eat us. Not so long as you're with me."

"They do seem to be intelligent," said Rich, "for tree-dwelling half-cat, half-monkey pack hunters, I mean."

Darwen frowned and checked his watch. "I hate to delay going after Mr. Peregrine," he said.

"One trip," said Alex. "In and out. If we can't find them or don't make any progress, we come right back and go straight to the train."

Rich gave Darwen an expectant look, and after a moment, Darwen nodded.

"Okay," he said. "But let's make it fast."

Alex led them to the portal numbered 92 and they stepped through. Though Darwen had never been there before, the heavy, moist air on the other side felt familiar. It was like being inside a greenhouse: hot and damp and fragrant with the aroma of earth. Though they were in Silbrica, not Costa Rica, this was clearly jungle air. They could see nothing except a narrow, leaf-strewn path around which great trees grew, twined with heavy vines and surrounded by mounds of glossy, emerald green shrubs. Similar braids of vines formed the portal through which they had come, and they realized now that this was one of eight unmarked doorways arranged in a circle like some whimsical living gazebo. In the thick vegetation ahead, pendulous red flowers—as large and luxuriant as only Silbrica could grow—hung from branches, and fat, orange insects hopped delicately from blossom to blossom.

"Let's be fast," he said, not bothering to hide the unease he felt as the rainforest heat sent the sweat running down his neck. The last time he'd been in a jungle locus, he'd had to be constantly on the lookout for poisonous snakes.

"How are you going to find the pouncels?" asked Rich, pulling at his shirt collar. "You can't call them like they're dogs."

"Actually," said Alex, with a superior look, "I can." So saying, she cupped her hands around her mouth, took a deep breath, and emitted a raucous screech that made the hairs on Darwen's arms prickle.

Rich's eyes had gone very wide. "Wow," he said. "You sound like a mountain lion! How did you learn to do that?"

"I had a lot of time with them in Costa Rica, remember?" said Alex. "It's not a sound you forget."

She did it again, took a breath, and added a third, each one slightly different but all utterly animal. Darwen found that he was watching the jungle undergrowth around them with apprehension. He hadn't really believed that they would spot a pouncel, but he was having second thoughts now. Though they had seen the creatures mainly in Costa Rica, that wasn't their home. They came from Silbrica, from a place exactly like this.

Rich was studying the ground for the telltale claw marks the creatures left when they came down from the trees. As he turned to face the forest behind the portal they had come through, he paused.

"Guess Greyling has already visited," he said.

Darwen and Alex rotated to see what he was looking at.

While the jungle at their backs was lush and dense as could be imagined, the portion behind the ring of portals was a wasteland of smashed tree trunks and churned-up mud, the ground crisscrossed by the massive treads of giant bulldozers.

Alex was biting her lip, her hands still half cupped around her mouth, while Rich was glowering at the devastation, the color rising in his cheeks. And then there was movement in the corner of Darwen's eye, and he turned just in time to see the shadow of something large and graceful spring from one tree to the next. It landed deftly and turned to stare at them from the cover of a veil of waxy leaves.

Darwen immediately recognized the beast for what it was: a pouncel. Its piercing bright yellow eyes, unnerving though they were, were nothing compared to the knifelike teeth he knew came with them. "Now what?" he said, forcing himself to look away from the creature's long, razor-sharp claws. Pouncels were pack hunters. This one would not be alone.

Alex stepped forward cautiously, her eyes locked on the creature in the tree. She was making a different sound now, a low purring coo that was almost musical, into which from time to time she inserted a single word.

"Muffin."

Rich gaped at her. "You named one of those murderous brutes *Muffin*?" he hissed.

Alex merely glowered at him and continued to coax the pouncel in the tree. It didn't move, but then there were others up in the canopy and—more alarmingly still—on the ground only yards away, creeping stealthily out into the open. One of them had a distinct limp.

"Muffin!" exclaimed Alex happily. She took two hurried steps and then dropped to her knees on the jungle floor, arms outstretched.

The pouncel didn't move like a dog—it was altogether too stealthy and menacing for that—but it did come to her, circling, rubbing its head against her.

Alex stroked the animal with delight as if it was nothing more than an unusually fluffy house cat. The fact that the pouncel was almost the size of a mountain lion and had the long, rangy limbs of an ape didn't seem to bother her. Of less consequence to her still were the sounds made by its fellows still skulking in the underbrush.

Darwen and Rich, meanwhile, stayed rooted to the spot, unmoving, watching this bizarre scene and listening as Alex started interspersing her animal noises with remarks about Greyling and what he was going to do to the pouncels' jungle home. She said it all cheerily, in the singsong voice you might use to address a toddler, and Darwen and Rich risked skeptical glances between them. The idea that the creature could understand any of this suddenly seemed absurd.

Darwen was still thinking this when he became aware that "Muffin" had grown very still. His tiger-striped fur was bristling and his ears were erect. He was listening, and not to Alex, who, sensing his tension, had fallen silent. The other pouncels all looked the same: taut with apprehension and watchfulness, ears straining.

And then Darwen could hear it too: the dull rumble of machinery somewhere behind them, distant, but getting louder. He didn't want to turn his back on the pouncels, but he had to see. Slowly he turned to gaze past the circle of vine-framed portals and across the devastated patch of jungle to where a smudge of brown, greasy smoke rose from the trees. He took a step toward it, then another, peering for signs of movement. Rich came too, and then Alex and the pouncels, all moving as if entranced into the blasted clearing beyond the portals, drawn by the sound of devastation. He was straining to localize the noise exactly when the source came plowing through the shrubs no more than a couple of hundred yards away. The thing emitting the sound was metal and massive, less a bulldozer than a clumsy, boxlike tank. To Darwen it looked like it had driven out of the pages of a book on the First World War. It was rusty and pocked with rivets, and on top was a pair of helmeted scrobblers with some kind of huge gun behind an armored shield. As soon as the vehicle burst through the trees, it started shooting.

The energy weapon flashed once, emitting a bright green shaft of light like the beam of a laser. It speared the ground only yards to their right, which exploded in a shower of dirt and shredded leaves.

As the tank veered around to face them, one set of tracks spinning, the other stationary as the awkward vehicle slewed around, the pouncels scattered in every direction. For Darwen, Rich, and Alex, there was only one way to go.

"Back to the portal!" Darwen shouted.

They ran, ducking awkwardly as another laser blast tore through the air above them and crashed into a stand of trees in the as yet undamaged part of the jungle, tearing a ten-foot hole in the ground and leaving a standing cloud of bitter smoke where the shrubs had been.

"Which gate did we come through?" said Alex, who was the first to reach the portal ring. "They all look the same."

"That one," said Rich, pointing.

"You sure?" said Alex, considering the one next to it. "I thought it was that one. Darwen?"

Darwen had no idea. But even as he started to speculate aloud, the shaft of green light lanced the ground only feet from him and it burst into a fountain of dirt and smoke and noise. The impact blew him back, but he stayed conscious and was on his feet and pointing at the portal Alex had indicated in no more than a second. "That one!" he bellowed. "Go!"

Rich and Alex didn't need any further invitation. They jumped through so hard and fast that they tumbled headlong into the snow on the other side.

Snow? thought Darwen, his heart sinking.

"Uh-oh," said Alex. "I think I smell mammoth."

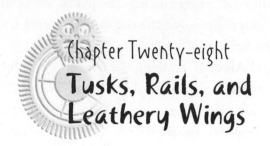

Chapter Twenty-eight
Tusks, Rails, and Leathery Wings

"**G**uess we picked the wrong gate," said Alex.

"Understatement of the year," said Darwen, considering the icy landscape that stretched out in all directions below them.

"Yeah," said Alex. "Sorry about that."

"Not your fault," said Darwen. "I panicked."

"Understandable, in the circumstances," Alex agreed wisely.

"Okay," said Darwen, rubbing his cheeks as the icy wind picked up. "Do we go back the way we came and try to get to the right portal before the scrobblers get us, or what?"

"I'm tempted by the *or what* option," said Alex, "but I'd like to know what it is."

"If only I'd picked the other gate," Darwen muttered, rubbing his face still harder.

They both gave Rich uncomfortable looks. Rich had identified the right portal. If they'd done what he said, they'd be back in the Great Apparatus and ready to get on with finding Mr. Peregrine. As it was, they were about to freeze to death unless the mammoth herders found them first and delivered on their murderous threats. Rich, however, did not seem angry. In fact, he was gazing fixedly off to their left.

"Might not be as bad as we thought," he said, stamping his feet in the snow. "I think I know where we are. I saw this bluff when we were here before. See that over there? That's the portal we came through last time." He was pointing down the rocky escarpment and across a plain covered in thick, blue-white snow.

"That would take us back to the gardens, and from there we can go to the Great Apparatus and on to that railway line you were talking about."

"Looks a long way," said Darwen.

"Three-quarters of a mile, tops," said Rich, his breath smoking. "If we're quick, we can be out before the herders know we're here."

Darwen hugged his meager clothes to his chest against the bitter wind, and—with a glance at Alex—nodded. Rich had made the right call last time and they had ignored him. This time they would do things his way.

Moments later they were making the awkward climb down from the bluff, Rich leading, forcing a path through the snow, which in places had drifted thigh deep. It was hard going, but the exertion kept them warm. By the time they reached the snowy plains below, Darwen found himself struck once more by the beauty and variety of Silbrica, so much so, in fact, that Rich's cry of desolation took him utterly by surprise. He and Alex scrambled on to see what Rich had found.

It was a mammoth, lying dead at the foot of the escarpment. Its thick white fur was blackened where it had been shot. There were oily tracks in the snow all around it: heavy boots and tank treads. It seemed that despite the mammoth riders' insistence to the contrary, the scrobblers had entered this locus after all.

"Oh no," said Alex. "When they aren't looking to kill you, they are really quite gorgeous animals, even if they do smell."

And so saying, she plucked from her pocket a tiny barrel-like container not much larger than an acorn. "Some of the zingers' military-grade perfume," she said by way of explanation. "Couldn't let a scent like this go to waste. I had kind of planned to save it for my high school prom, if I ever have one, but I guess I'll rely on my natural charm to knock the boys out." She pressed the container against one of the dead mammoth's glassy tusks till the barrel cracked open, and then she cast it over the shaggy corpse, allowing the aroma to spray everywhere. The air was suddenly full of fragrance so heady and exhilarating that Darwen felt a rush of warmth and happiness quite at odds with the situation.

Alex anointed the elephantine head just above the two trunks, as if she was performing some ancient ritual. Then, frowning, she turned to face Darwen and Rich. "Okay," she said. "We can go now, but if I ever find the scrobbler that did this or whichever of Greyling's lackeys was holding its leash at the time, I won't be held accountable. You got me?"

Darwen nodded, but Rich was once more gazing across the open plain. "Guys," he said. "We may have a problem."

Far across the snowfield but closing fast, churning up a cloud of white powder as they came, were four mammoths and their riders.

"Given what they said last time," said Darwen, "and the fact that we're standing around one of their dead mammoths, I think we get out of here fast."

Rich and Alex didn't even pause to comment. They just started running, trying as hard as they could to make it the few hundred yards to the portal without falling face first into the deep snow or skidding on the hard icy crust.

The mammoths were considerably faster and more sure-footed, and only moments after they had started to run, Darwen saw the first jet of blue flame that had been shot after them. They didn't have much time.

Alex had a knack for finding the quickest route, and she was light and quick. Rich had sheer, blundering power. Darwen was the weak link, lagging behind the others, sweating despite the cold, and close to exhaustion.

But the portal was only yards away now.

He didn't dare look back, but he could feel the earth shaking from the mammoths' pounding footfalls. He weaved left and right as another jet of blue flame dissolved the snow into a flaming pool only a few feet in front of him, and then Rich was grabbing him, pulling him into the portal.

The mammoth herders did not follow them through to the mansion gardens, but the three of them took a long moment before they relaxed. Their fear faded like the cold, and only when it had gone completely did they permit themselves a nervous smile.

"Still alive," said Alex. "That's good."

"Always," Darwen agreed.

They located the working portal, stepped through it, and found themselves in the heart of the Great Apparatus. They were only yards from where they had been before they'd ventured on what now seemed like a wild-goose chase, and a dangerous one at that.

"Sorry," said Alex. "I'm gonna shut up while you find the right portal."

"The jungle thing wasn't your fault, Alex," said Darwen, scanning the numbers above the vast ring of doorways.

"Kind of was," said Rich.

"It was worth a try," said Darwen pointedly, "and she wasn't to know the place was crawling with scrobblers or that we'd then go the wrong way out and wind up running from mammoth herders again."

"Thanks," said Alex.

"This one," said Darwen, choosing the portal numbered 25. He pushed a button, threw a lever, and waited for the curtain of energy to shimmer into place. "Here goes," he said, and stepped through.

He had been here before. He recognized the antique railway station with its iron footbridge and pearly gas lamps. He recognized the empty ticket office and the silence where there should have been the bustle of people waiting for their connections. He recognized the night, and even the train itself, a black steam locomotive covered in pipes and pistons and funnels.

Alex recognized it too and shivered. "I have nightmares about this train," she said.

"We aren't going to Woodvine," said Darwen, remembering the station where the Jenkins insects had attacked them. "We stay on till the end of the line."

"I'll bet," said Alex, gloomily. "The end of the line. That sounds about right."

"In our world," said Rich thoughtfully.

"It goes to a series of different Silbrican loci first," said Darwen, "but then, yeah, it crosses over into our world at a place called . . ." He hesitated and pulled the ticket they had found on the dead scrobbler beside That Which Eats. "Blaenau Ffe . . . something . . . iniog," he read.

"Weird," said Rich, following Darwen as he clambered into the nearest carriage and shut the door behind them.

"There are only a couple of places where you can cross between worlds if you aren't a mirroculist, apparently," said Darwen, taking a seat. "Unless you have the kind of technology Greyling used at Halloween to open that portal at school that his scrobblers could come through. This is one of those spots where the barrier between realities is very thin."

"Where do we get our tickets?" asked Alex.

"We don't," said Darwen. "It's automated, remember?"

"So why did the scrobbler have one?" asked Rich.

"I guess it was coming in the other direction," said Darwen.

"You're saying a scrobbler bought a ticket in our world that put him on a train to Silbrica?" said Alex. "Just, like, walked into a regular station in its goggles and grunted that it would like a return trip to another dimension?"

"Maybe one of their human allies buys the tickets for them," said Darwen with a shrug. "Something is going on in Wales. I don't know what, but it's important, and not just because that's where Mr. Peregrine is being held. Blodwyn wanted to tell us about it, remember? It's something bad, something I think we have to stop."

And with that ominous pronouncement the train began to move.

"What are the chances that we'll pick up a platoon of scrobblers at the next station?" asked Alex, but no one answered, and she let the question hang in the air.

They listened to the rhythmic clickety-clack of the wheels on the line, gazing out into the dark and misty Silbrican landscape. There was very little to see, and much of the time their view was blocked entirely by trees or the masonry of an embankment. They passed through three stations, all basically the same as Woodvine, all deserted, and Darwen found his unease increasing. He didn't know how he would recognize the point where they crossed into their own world, so he studied every signal box, every little bridge, every gantry that spanned the track, as if it might be a gateway out of Silbrica and into Wales.

But when he saw the tunnel up ahead, he knew.

"This is it," he said, staring at the black mouth in the hillside into which they were chuffing at full speed.

"How do you know?" asked Alex, regarding him carefully.

Darwen just shrugged, and then the locomotive entered the tunnel and light flickered up and down the carriages. The train rattled over a dozen unseen points, as if joining another rail system entirely, and then they burst out into an entirely different place, where the sun was already up and there were streets full of cars and familiar little houses with gray roofs just beyond the railway line. They crossed a flat coastal estuary, then climbed into forested hills and a little town nestling high above them, where the train pulled slowly into a simple station whose sign proclaimed it Blaenau Ffestiniog.

Darwen checked the two fragments of the scrobbler ticket and nodded grimly. This was the place.

"This is seriously strange," said Alex, gazing out of the window.

Next to them, waiting at the head of six old-fashioned carriages painted burgundy and cream, was a green-and-black steam locomotive with a funnel at each end and gleaming brass trim.

"This is Wales, right?" she asked. "Not Silbrica? They use steam trains here?"

"It's like the area around Hillside," said Darwen, though he wasn't sure how he knew. "We're in our world, but there has been a lot of movement from here to Silbrica over the years. There are echoes."

"How do you know that?" asked Rich, unlatching the carriage door and jumping down onto the platform.

"I can just feel it," said Darwen, shrugging.

Alex raised an eyebrow. "Like you can sense where the portals are? Like you can open some of them now without their being online?" she probed.

"Yeah, I guess," Darwen replied. But his thoughts took a darker turn. *Something is happening to me*, he thought. *Everyone knows. The gift is leaving me.*

He must have managed to conceal his fears from his face, however, because neither Rich nor Alex said anything to suggest that they recognized all was not well. If anything, they seemed only more determined to continue with their mission. Rich checked his watch. "We have maybe three hours," he said as they boarded the train. "Four, tops. If they haven't already noticed we're missing back home, they will then."

The whistle blew and they watched the locomotive belch thick black smoke as it pulled out of the station. The sky was heavy with rain, gray as the slate cliffs that towered over the buildings of the town.

"Now," said Darwen, "we walk."

But where they were headed was far from clear. They left the station and traipsed along a narrow road through the town, which climbed still higher into the stern and rocky hills. They walked till they got away from the houses, and then Darwen found a gate in a dry stone wall and went through it. When they had followed him, he sat in the damp bracken against the wall where no passersby might see them. From his pocket he drew Mr. Peregrine's tiny brass whistle, checked that no one was watching him, and raised it to his lips.

He blew it but could hear nothing.

"You really think there might be a flittercrake around here to summon?" said Alex. "And if there was, how would that help?"

"Just a hunch," muttered Darwen, putting the whistle back in his mouth.

Darwen blew another soundless blast on the whistle, then stood, expectant, staring up into the misty sky. He stayed like that for a minute or more and was about to raise the whistle to his lips again when something came hurtling through the air, plummeting like a diving falcon, its leathery wings almost folded until they splayed parachute-like at the last moment. The birdlike thing thudded onto Darwen's shoulder, clinging with its long claws. It was a flittercrake.

Darwen considered the creature's little bald head, its keen mannish eyes and cruel beak, and he felt sure his hunch was correct.

It wasn't *a* flittercrake. It was *the* flittercrake. The one he had first seen at the mall. The one that had led him to the old mirror shop. It fixed him with its beady eyes, its sidelong, knowing grin telling Darwen that he was right.

That first day, the day that changed his life, Darwen had thought he had simply noticed the flittercrake by happenstance, that his decision to follow it straight to Mr. Peregrine's shop was due to nothing other than sheer curiosity. But that hadn't been right. The flittercrake had been sent to find him, and then—later—to feign an attack on a rabbit-like creature on the other side of the mirror, in a way calculated to lure Darwen into crossing over into Silbrica for the very first time. Eileen had essentially told him as much, but only now did it occur to Darwen that the creature had been working with Mr. Peregrine more closely than anyone had guessed. If the flittercrake was somehow connected to the old man, and it had been able to creep through broken portal mirrors and any other little gaps between worlds, maybe it knew something about where he was.

He kicked himself for not thinking of trying to contact the flittercrake before.

Alex peered at the creature, her distaste evident as it flexed its bat-like wings then turned and stuck its tongue out at her.

"Oh, that's just wrong," she said.

"I remember you," said the flittercrake to Alex, in a high-pitched rasping voice that raised the hair on the back of Darwen's neck. "From the place with the mirror shop."

"The mall?" said Alex. "I don't remember you."

"Didn't see me, did you?" said the flittercrake. "You weren't supposed to. *He* was."

The little creature flicked a long-nailed thumb in Darwen's direction and rolled his eyes as if he was bored of dealing with such stupid people.

"You know where Mr. Peregrine was taken?" asked Darwen.

The flittercrake considered him thoughtfully, then nodded.

"Is it close by?" Darwen pressed.

"Close enough," said the flittercrake, his hard little gaze unflinching.

"Show us," Darwen concluded.

"You sure you want to go?" said the flittercrake, grinning maliciously. "Not a nice place. Dark and dangerous."

"If Mr. Peregrine is there, then yes," Darwen said, holding the creature's eyes with his own.

"He might be," said the flittercrake with a tiny shrug. It turned from him sulkily.

"You just said he was!" Darwen exclaimed, his patience growing thin. "Do you know where he is or not?"

"I know where he *was*," rasped the flittercrake, its voice like fingernails on a blackboard. "He might have been moved. He might not be alive. I haven't been anywhere but the portal itself. There are rooms."

"Show us," said Darwen, ignoring the suggestion that Mr. Peregrine might not be alive with an effort.

"All of you?" hissed the flittercrake. "Not just you?"

"All of us," said Darwen.

"Fine," sniffed the flittercrake, "but I'll be very surprised if you all make it out alive. Don't say I didn't warn you."

With one last leering grin, the creature shot straight up into the misty air like a skylark. Once up, it circled lazily, waiting for them to get back out onto the road, then flew up and into the rocky hills. There were few trees here, and the low vegetation broke through jutting slabs of splintered, gray slate. To the left they saw the mouth of an arched railway tunnel set into the scree-scattered hillside, from which a single track emerged. The flittercrake shot them a wolfish grin, then beat its wings into a long, looping flight past it.

"Is that a portal?" asked Alex as the creature vanished into the dark.

"No," said Darwen, conscious of the others watching him closely. "Come on."

Darwen wasn't sure how far they walked. A mile, maybe two, then they veered off to the right and into a complex of low buildings where a sign read LECHWEDD SLATE CAVERNS.

"It's a mine," said Rich.

"Of course," said Alex miserably. "I was hoping for a theme park or a mini-golf course, but it's a mine. Naturally." She watched as the flittercrake dived and settled, clinging to a piece of sagging gutter, following them with its ratty eyes. "You think we can trust that thing?"

"No," said Darwen, "but I don't think we have a choice. We're running out of time, and if I'm right, and his connection to Mr. Peregrine is real, then we need to take advantage of it."

The sun was still low in the sky, the parking lot cold and empty, and the buildings seemed deserted. The flittercrake paused, then leapt into flight again, alighting this time on a sign whose arrow read DEEP MINE. They followed it till they came to a turnstile and what looked a little like a railway line, except that it was tilted so that it descended steeply into the ground, the passenger waiting areas made up of stepped metal gantries. The "train" beside them was four yellow metal boxes with glass panels, also stepped to meet the pitch of the rails, each with seating for six.

As Alex gazed apprehensively down into the blackness below, Rich considered the controls dubiously. "It's operated from in there," he hissed, nodding toward an office building beside the track. There were lights in the windows, and as Darwen watched, he saw a shadow move across one of them.

Something was inside.

Darwen laid a finger on his lips and moved cautiously toward the door, which was, he now saw, slightly ajar. He could just make out a hum of machinery, but over the top he could hear voices. He flattened himself against the wall by the doorway and listened intently.

"Always the early shift, me," said one voice, a man. Welsh. Soft-spoken and bored-sounding. "I don't know why they bother. They aren't even using most of these anymore. Waste of my time."

"Easy money then, innit?" said another voice, also a man, but not local. A Londoner, perhaps, Darwen thought. It was a deep, rough-sounding voice: almost a snarl. "Don't see what you're complaining about. Sitting around 'ere, doing nothing, and taking home a fat check at the end of the week. Money for old rope, innit?"

"But what's it all for?" the other returned. "Science experiments, they say, but for what? And what kind of laboratory looks like that? And why is it in a mine? It doesn't make any sense."

"Don't have to," the other grunted. "I don't need to know so long as the cash keeps coming. And you shouldn't be snooping around either."

The other gave a sputter of protest, but his colleague talked right over him.

"Don't deny it," he said. "I've seen you poking around. Asking questions when the odd bods come. You'll mess it up for all of us. So cut it out."

"You're not curious?" said the Welshman. "You don't want to know why we're doing this?"

"Cloning, I reckon," said the Londoner. "Illegal, probably. It's like I said: asking questions will just ruin everything, so—just for once—shut your Welsh cake-hole."

"Charming, I'm sure," said the other. "Ever the sparkling conversationalist, aren't you?"

"They don't pay me to talk, and they don't pay me to push buttons and top off the fluids every four hours," said the Londoner, an edge of menace in his voice. "They pay me to keep an eye on things, and that includes you, so unless you want a knuckle sandwich, I'd button it."

Darwen shifted and found Alex on the other side of the doorway staring at him and mouthing soundlessly *What do we do?*

Darwen had no idea. It sounded crazy, but though he was used to the peculiar Silbrican perils of scrobblers and gnashers, people—ordinary men like these two—scared him.

The Londoner was talking again. "I'm looking to get promoted, anyway, me," he was saying. "No more sitting around this dump with you."

"You're not serious!" said the Welshman. "Just let them send you wherever and tell no one where you are or what you're doing? Sounds dodgy to me. They never come back, you know, the people they promote off-site. One day they're here, the next they're gone, and no one ever hears from them again."

"You should see the benefits package they're offering," said the Londoner. He whistled between his teeth. "I don't care where they send me or what I do. And it's not like I'd be leaving anyone behind to miss me, except you, Owen."

"Oh, yes," said the Welshman wryly. "I'd miss you terribly."

Darwen thought furiously. They couldn't just walk in and pretend they belonged there. And they certainly couldn't hope to overpower two men without a weapon of some kind. Darwen guessed it was these two he had seen through the observation mirrors in Mr. Peregrine's watchtower, and if so, the Londoner was a particularly big bloke.

Darwen felt an insistent nudge and, turning, found Rich at his elbow, eyebrows raised, hefting something carefully in one hand. It was a slab of slate the size of a book. Darwen knew what he was thinking. If Rich could get inside quickly or stealthily enough, could get behind the two men, preferably while they were still sitting, could raise that hunk of stone over their heads . . .

Darwen shook his head fiercely. The memory of what had happened to Blodwyn was too present in his mind.

"Checking the perimeter," muttered the Londoner, with a scraping of chair legs. "Try not to do anything stupid while I'm gone."

"Always a joy to work with," said the Welshman.

Darwen listened to the bigger man's receding footsteps, then the creak and clang of a heavy metal door. He waited barely a second before pushing the door open and stepping into the control room, leaving Rich and Alex gazing at each other, flabbergasted.

For a moment Darwen just stood in the doorway, his eyes flashing around the room. There were two chairs, close to a bank of old-fashioned controls: knobs, switches, and levers set into a slab of thick black metal whose wires trailed all over the room. Sitting in one of the chairs was the man in the white lab coat who Darwen had seen in the watchtower. He was reading a newspaper and sipping tea from a chipped mug. He hadn't noticed Darwen, who was standing quite still and silent only feet from him. Darwen probably could reach back to Rich, take that slab of rock from him, and cross over to the man before he got out of his chair. . . .

No. He would not do that.

"All right?" Darwen said.

The man in the chair started so violently that he spilled his tea all over the newspaper and leapt to his feet. "What are you doing in here?" he gasped, his Welsh accent even stronger in his astonishment.

"I came for the tour," Darwen answered simply, using the same excuse they'd fallen into back at the lighthouse in Conwy.

"There are no tours of the deep mine anymore," the Welshman began, but then he caught something in Darwen's eyes and his face became a mask of suspicion. "Who are you?" he said, rising.

"My name's Darwen."

He could almost hear Alex and Rich rolling their eyes behind him.

"Why are you here?" the Welshman replied, still suspicious. He was about forty, getting thick and soft around the middle, fair hair thinning fast so that the scalp showed through, pale blue eyes in a slightly chubby face. "No one comes in here. And if *he* catches you, you'll be in serious trouble. You need to get out before he gets back."

"He?"

"George. My co-worker, George Tomlinson. I say co-worker, but he's little more than a hired thug."

"And what kind of work do you do, Owen?" asked Darwen.

The man seemed taken aback by this use of his name, and he looked distracted as he replied, "Oh, this and that. I'm just a tech, really. Just, you know, monitoring the equipment, running the train, and making sure the current stays according to the protocols in the manual . . ." He caught himself, shaking his head as if to clear it. "Why am I telling you this? You need to get out before George gets back," he added, nodding to the door at the far end of the room. It was metal, unpainted, and dotted with reinforcing bolts. It looked like the kind of door you might see in a prison cell or a submarine.

"How long will George be?"

Owen shrugged and glanced at his watch. "Two or three minutes," he said. "Five if he goes to the bathroom."

"And can you lock that door from the inside?"

"I could bolt it," said Owen, looking increasingly uneasy with the conversation. "Why?"

"Buy me a little time," said Darwen.

"For what?"

"I need to go down into the mine."

"You can't do that!" sputtered Owen. "I'll lose my job."

"Good job, is it?" asked Darwen, meeting the man's eyes and holding them.

Owen shrugged and glanced away, so Darwen pressed on.

"The kind of job you're proud of? A job that makes you think you are doing something good for the world?"

The man's mouth opened and his eyes seemed to glaze.

"Or do you not want me to go down there because you know I'll find something I'm not going to like?" said Darwen, meeting Owen's eyes. "Something that shouldn't be down there?"

The man's mouth dropped open still further.

"That's what I thought," Darwen persisted. "I'm looking for an old man who's been hooked up to machines of some sort. He was kidnapped, drugged, and now you have him in that mine."

"They don't tell me anything, you know," said Owen, his resolve crumbling. "I just monitor the fluids and—"

"But he's down there?" Darwen exclaimed, his heart leaping. "He's there and he's alive?"

"Well, yes," said Owen, starting to rub his temples anxiously. "But I don't know what sort of shape he's in."

"Please, tell me what you *do* know," Darwen insisted. "He's my friend."

Owen had been shaking his head, but that last phrase stopped him.

He gave Darwen a long, worried look, then nodded. "He was alive, look you, at least till two days ago. But not conscious, exactly. It's like a coma, really, but part of him has to still be awake for the process to work. I don't know what it does. Some sort of medical experiment, I think. Cloning, George says. I just, you know, keep an eye on things so they don't die. I didn't know he'd been kidnapped or anything. . . ."

"The process keeps him alive so the thing that looks like him retains a little of his personality," said Rich, who had appeared in the doorway.

"The thing that looked like him?" Owen echoed, horrified.

"The flesh suit," said Rich. "It looks just like him even though what it's doing is the absolute opposite of what the real person—Mr. Peregrine—would want."

"What kind of things?" asked Owen, his voice faint now.

"Abducting children," said Alex, pushing her way in.

Owen stared at her, baffled.

"Murder," said Darwen flatly.

"What?" Owen managed.

"Look at this place, Owen," said Darwen, as calmly as he could. "Look at this equipment. You know that what we're telling you is the truth. So you had better make a choice before George comes back."

"Wait," said Owen. "I'm telling you he was alive two days ago. I was monitoring the tank he was in. But then they took him. Transferred him to a deeper part of the mine I've never even seen. I don't know why."

Darwen's heart sank. He had no idea what this meant. Rich and Alex looked at him, desperate and unsure, and Darwen resolved to go on anyway.

"Take us there," he said to Owen.

"I don't know exactly where—" Owen began.

"Then we'll find the place together," said Darwen firmly.

For a long moment—a moment they could not afford given George's imminent return—nothing happened, and Darwen watched the confused interplay of anxious thought on Owen's face. Finally the man took a great sighing breath.

"You'd better get on board," he said. "I'll transfer the controls to the train itself so I can come down with you."

Darwen nodded, showing only the briefest of smiles. "Do it," he said.

Owen pushed a button and turned a dial all the way around to zero. Immediately an alarm started ringing.

"That's torn it," Owen said.

Even as he spoke, they heard hurried footsteps beyond the metal door. Alex flew at it, hitting it hard with her shoulder just as it started to open. Owen ran to help her as a strong hand reached through from outside. The Welshman slammed into the door and the hand was snatched back with a grunt of pain. Alex shot the bolt home.

"How long will that buy us?" she asked, panting.

"Till George gets the oxyacetylene torch out of storage," said Owen. "Not long." He paused, pressed a button, and shook his head. "What am I doing? I'm going to lose my job!"

"Everyone here is about to lose their job," said Darwen. "My friends and me? We're shutting the place down."

There was an ominous clang against the door. Someone other than George was trying to force his way in. Or some*thing*.

"Odd bods," muttered Owen, and now he looked truly scared.

"Odd bods?" Darwen repeated.

"Big fellas," said Owen. "Strong. Foreign, we think. Don't speak English. They wear overalls and they always have their faces covered up, but some say they have big teeth and red eyes. . . ."

"Scrobblers," said Alex. "Great."

"Into the train," Owen exclaimed, leading the way.

There was another bang against the door, and then a tiny prick of blue flame started to open a thin red gash along the door where the bolt was. The four of them raced out to where the yellow train cars stood weirdly poised to drill down into the earth. Owen sat at the back and started thumbing on controls as the others took their seats and pulled the glass doors closed behind them.

"Quick," said Darwen. "They must be almost through." As he said it, Darwen heard the snap and tinkle of the bolt on the heavy door breaking cleanly in half and falling to the stone floor.

"*Diwdiw!*" exclaimed Owen in Welsh, staring at the flittercrake, which had been perching on the outside of the train but had flapped in with Darwen and now clung to his shirt. "What on earth?"

"The scrobblers are coming!" shouted Alex as the door to the control room kicked open.

And then they were moving.

Chapter Thirty
The Deep Mine

The yellow cars descended into the earth with a low whirring sound that set Darwen's teeth on edge. The flittercrake flattened its face to the glass and chortled malevolently, delighted by their evident discomfort.

"Can they come after us?" Rich demanded, peering back up the shaft.

Owen shook his head. "Manual override," he said, tapping the train controls. "A safety measure. Never thought I'd need to use it. Once we get out, they can call the train back up and come after us if they want to. You think they'll want to?"

Rich, Darwen, and Alex all looked at each other and said nothing.

"Right," said Owen. "Well, I'm not sure how we're going to get up again, but for now we're in the clear."

"If we can get Mr. Peregrine, we may not need to use the train again," said Darwen. "There's a portal down here," he added, recalling what Weazen had said.

"A what?" asked Owen.

Darwen shook his head. "I'll show you if we find it," he said.

Further and further down they went, so that the light from the sky behind them faded to nothing, and then there was only the soft glow of the lamps in the shaft. The walls were first concrete, laced with cable and braced with girders, then reinforced stone, carved out of the ground itself. From time to time they saw platforms where they might get off or glimpsed open passageways chiseled out of the rock, but still they descended, the air getting steadily cooler as they went. They saw one last set of signs aimed at visitors, then nothing as the train burrowed deeper and deeper into the ground, finally stopping in a silence Darwen could almost see.

They opened the car doors and clambered cautiously out. Low-wattage emergency lights glowed on the walls, and by them they could see the long tunnel with its side caverns. The slate had once been quarried there by men using little more than picks and candles. Where the ceiling was low, Darwen could see the black smearing of soot and felt a pang of pity for all those who had worked down here in the dark.

Owen brought two boxy flashlights from the front of the train and handed one to Rich. "This way," he said.

They passed through dank stone hallways flanked by square hollows marked by drill tips and strewn with refuse fragments of slate. Some of these rooms were small and regular, some cavernous, one with a broad and shallow pool that plinked from drops from the wet ceiling. They went up and down metal stairways, past still older wooden ladders that looked thoroughly unsafe, but just as they seemed to be following a well-trodden route, Owen pointed to the left.

Darwen didn't need telling. Wherever Mr. Peregrine was, he was close to another portal. Darwen could feel its presence swelling in his mind like the hum of electricity.

They climbed over the guardrail and entered one of the quarry chambers.

"A century ago," said Owen, his voice unwinding out of the gloom, "a man would work in a room like this his entire life. In the winter, he wouldn't see daylight at all, working from before dawn till after sunset under the ground. Sounds like hell, doesn't it?"

He was making conversation to calm his nerves.

"There is a portal down here," Darwen whispered to himself.

The flittercrake nodded its agreement.

"It won't help you now, though," it said, grinning. "They took it offline when they left." The flittercrake did a half loop, giving a simpering look from upside down.

"So we're stuck?" said Rich.

"Let's worry about that after we find Mr. Peregrine," said Darwen. He had managed to do it before, but the idea of having to force a portal open when it wasn't connected to either the Guardians' grid or Greyling's power supply sat like a great weight on his chest.

They rounded a corner and found themselves in a long tunnel like the main route through the mine. On either side were the same stone rooms, though there were no safety lamps here and it was only by the beam of Rich's powerful flashlight that they could see anything at all.

"This is where they transferred him," said Owen in an awed hush. "I've never been down this far before."

There were no tanks of liquid like the ones they had expected to find. Instead, the walls of the chamber were lined with metal objects the size and shape of oversized men, misty, greenish windows where the faces should be.

Darwen had seen this place before. "This is what the mirror in Mr. Peregrine's watchtower showed," he said to Rich. "I remember those weird pod things, except that then they were lit up from the inside. Why was he monitoring the very place they would take him?"

"They look like Egyptian sarcophagi," said Rich, sounding excited. "You think there are mummies inside?" He shone his flashlight into the nearest window and took a gasping step backward.

It was as Darwen remembered. The face inside belonged to a scrobbler—or very nearly—oversized tusks and massive, brutal features. Only the eyes were wrong. Behind the brass goggles they were blue, not red.

"I don't understand," said Darwen. "Where is Mr. Peregrine?"

"Over here," said Owen, standing beside one of the vertical pods. "These look to be the newest."

"You've never seen pods like these before?" asked Darwen.

"Never," said Owen. "I just worked with the fluid tanks. I knew there was another lab deeper in the mine, but no one talks about it and I don't have clearance to come down. Only the odd bods work down here. What's going on?"

"I'm honestly not sure," said Darwen, "but I don't like it."

"I haven't liked anything on this trip so far," said Alex, "but this place takes the creepy cake."

Darwen knew what she meant. Something down here in the dark was very wrong.

"Why are the pods plugged in?" Rich mused. "The lab—if that's what it is—has been abandoned, but something is still running. I can hear it."

"It wasn't when we came through," said Darwen. "It just started."

"You think we triggered it?" said Rich.

"Let's just get Mr. P and go," said Alex.

"That generator thing over there," said Rich. "The thing that has wires running to all the pods."

"What about it?" asked Owen.

"Was that little red light there before?" Rich asked.

"Quick," said Darwen, moving to the pods Owen had indicated. "Help me get these open."

Owen pried free a series of catches and Darwen yanked the door of the casket-like pod. It opened with a long, pneumatic hiss and a gasp of steam that took a moment to clear. When it did, Darwen stepped back in horror.

Inside was what had been Mr. Peregrine. The clothes were still his, and there was something familiar about the face. But the skin was thick and greenish, the teeth oversized, the whole body hulking and brutal looking.

"He's a . . . a . . ." Tears began to fill Darwen's eyes. He couldn't bring himself to finish the sentence.

But he didn't need to. Everyone could plainly see what Mr. Peregrine had become.

A scrobbler.

Chapter Thirty-one
Scrobblers Again

A s Rich and Alex gaped in horror, Darwen stepped back, revulsion rippling through him like nausea. Blindly he stepped to another of the pods and turned to see what he could through the greenish window. It also contained a scrobbler—a blue-eyed scrobbler, but a scrobbler nonetheless—as did the next two. The fourth was something different. It had something of the scrobbler to it, but where the monster's skin was green, this was pale, and the tusks were the merest extensions beyond the lips. It was obvious that it was, or had been, a man. There was a tracing of fair hair above the goggles, and the lips were slim. It wasn't an inviting face, and Darwen had a powerful impression that those lips and eyes could become cruel without further transfiguration, but it was certainly human. The next pod held a woman. The goggles over her eyes were the only thing about her that suggested anything of the scrobbler at all, unless it was a certain hardness in the face.

"She was just promoted!" Owen exclaimed. "She worked with me, like George, but she got promoted and transferred off-site a week ago. I saw her go down the deep mine for some kind of training session, but I haven't seen her since. What is happening to her?"

"A training session," Rich repeated grimly. "And she never came out."

Owen stared at him, then turned to Darwen for answers.

"She's being turned into a scrobbler," said Darwen. "What you call odd bods. I think I understand now. There are two separate processes. One of them makes and controls the flesh-suit disguises. The other does . . . this." He swallowed. "The scrobblers aren't born. They are made. Greyling takes people, ordinary people, and *converts* them."

The flittercrake's malicious grin had vanished. Instead the creature perched on top of the open pod containing Mr. Peregrine, glowering at them like a crow on a headstone.

Darwen looked into the greenish window at the top of the next pod and his stomach twisted again.

It was Blodwyn Evans.

And yet not quite. It had been her. Now it was a monster, a grotesque mockery of the person she had been.

"I should feel more relieved that she's not dead," said Alex, staring at the thing that had been Blodwyn.

"I know what you mean," Darwen agreed. Being transformed like this was almost worse than if she had been killed.

"Greyling is building an army," said Rich.

"No more sneaking bits of land from either world," Alex agreed. "He's going to invade both on a massive scale."

The great cavern felt even colder than before.

"Can we change them back?" Darwen asked.

"What do you mean?" asked Owen.

Darwen turned on him, furious, and grabbed hold of the lapels of his white coat.

"Are they gone forever?" he roared into the Welshman's face. "Or can we get them back to the way they were?"

"I don't know!" Owen protested. "I don't know what they become. This is a completely different operation from the one I worked on. The people who got promoted would go down and then they'd need new supplies and equipment."

"Regularly?" asked Rich.

Owen shook his head. "Sometimes there would be shipments of supplies going down every few hours," he said. "Sometimes it was days or weeks between deliveries."

"Could be that the amount of time the transformation takes varies from person to person," said Rich. "Maybe some resist it somehow."

Darwen's revulsion surged again. "Get him out of there," he said, nodding at the thing that had been Mr. Peregrine. "Turn the machine off and get him out."

"I don't know what that will do to him," Owen protested.

"I don't care!" Darwen exclaimed. "Get him out. Now."

Overwhelmed by Darwen's anger and certainty, Owen began unplugging leads and cables, throwing switches and releasing restraining clamps. A moment later, Owen and Darwen were dragging the limp and strangely distorted form of Mr. Peregrine from the pod. He was heavy, as if his clothes were soaking wet, and Darwen laid him down on the stone floor, panting. Owen opened the old man's mouth, exposing those terrible, tusk-like teeth, and pulled some kind of tube from Mr. Peregrine's throat.

"This is the same system we use in the tanks," he said. "Which means . . ." He looked around the pod and proclaimed, "Aha!" as he snapped a large syringe from a bracket on the back. He checked the label, then placed the needle directly over the old man's heart.

"What are you doing?!" Rich demanded.

"This is what we use for emergencies in the lab," said Owen. "If they're using the same method for keeping him in stasis, this should wake him up."

"Wake what, though?" Alex said.

Though it was wearing Mr. Peregrine's clothes, burst now at the seams, the thing on the floor was a scrobbler in almost every respect. Rich looked unsure. "I don't know, Darwen," he said. "Maybe he's gone. Maybe we were just too late and we should—"

"What?" Darwen demanded. "Leave him?"

"Look at him!" said Alex. "It's not Mr. P. Not anymore. And that means he's not going to help us fight Greyling."

Darwen looked down and for a second he thought they were right, but then he stooped to the greenish face and raised the right eyelid. "Blue," he said. "The eyes are blue. He hasn't changed completely. Wake him."

The flittercrake fluttered down and clung to Darwen's shoulder to watch. For once, the creature wasn't grinning. It looked worried.

Owen pushed the point of the needle into the old man's chest and depressed the plunger.

Nothing happened.

"Come on!" said Darwen.

"I don't think he's coming back, Darwen," said Rich.

"He has to," said Darwen, staring at the strange-looking figure on the floor.

Its eyes snapped open. They were still blue, but they were wild and uncertain, flashing madly around. The mouth opened and a great, hungry snarl emerged from the thing that had been Mr. Peregrine.

Everyone took a step back. And then it was sitting up, drawing itself into an awkward and menacing crouch as if it might be preparing to spring, looking around like the teachers at Hillside had when the lights dimmed. Its eyes found each of them in turn, lingered on them, and flicked on till they reached Darwen. Then they stopped and held him.

Mr. Peregrine—if that was still what the creature in front of them was—kept very still for a long time, and then, without warning, it lunged at Darwen, face-first, tusks bared as if poised to bite. Horrified, Darwen raised his hands to fight back . . .

But then it stopped. Its broad, greenish nostrils flared, and Darwen heard it inhale.

"It's smelling you," said Alex. "Why is it smelling you?"

Darwen kept very still and said nothing. He could feel the power of the thing inches from him. If it chose to attack him now, he would be powerless to stop it. He held his breath.

"Mister Octavius Peregrine," said Alex in a soothing voice. "Mister Octavius Peregrine."

"What are you doing?" hissed Rich.

"Reminding him who he is," said Alex. "Mister Octavius Peregrine."

And then the strangest thing began to happen: the creature's face started to change. Darwen wasn't sure if it was the name that did it, but the eyes lost something of their frantic, hunted look, the hunger replaced by something only humans could express: deep and lingering sadness. "Mr. Peregrine?" Darwen said hesitantly, the hope evident in his voice. He watched as the creature raised its huge, heavily nailed hands to its face and studied them, the grief in its eyes touched with horror.

"You are Mr. Octavius Peregrine," Darwen said, cautiously stepping closer and reaching for those massive hands.

"Darwen!" said Rich. "Be careful."

"Shh," said Darwen, taking another tentative step. When he was close enough, he took one of the creature's hands gently in his. Some of the green had even begun to fade from its cheeks. Darwen looked once more into its eyes. "It's okay," he whispered.

A flash of pain went through those eyes and the figure crumpled to the ground, grunting in obvious distress.

"What can we do?" Darwen asked Owen, still holding Mr. Peregrine's hands, but the Welshman just shook his head and shrugged.

"I've never done this before," he said.

"Darwen, look!" exclaimed Alex.

Darwen returned his gaze to Mr. Peregrine, whose back was arching in agony. The man who had been his mentor whipped back and forth with frenzied speed where he lay, moving impossibly quickly and emitting an awful screeching sound that changed, very slowly, into a simple, human sob. The body looked like it had collapsed in on itself, become smaller, as if part of it had melted away, until where the scrobbler had been there was what was clearly an exhausted and beaten-looking version of Mr. Octavius Peregrine.

He opened one eye, then his mouth, though it took several attempts before he could speak audibly enough for them to hear what he was saying.

"Hello, Darwen," he whispered. "I knew you would come."

Chapter Thirty-two
The Awakening

"**O**kay, this is weird," said Alex.

Owen gave her a look. It was clear from his face that he thought he had been having a very strange day for some time now, and the prospect that there was some *new* weirdness seemed to alarm him.

"What is weird?" Rich returned.

Rich, Alex, and Owen had moved away from Darwen, who was squatting on the stone floor beside Mr. Peregrine, as if by silent agreement that they needed a little space. The flittercrake was perched on Darwen's shoulder, holding on with its tiny bat-like claws, silently watching Mr. Peregrine. Alex was considering a curious piece of equipment.

"Looks like a conveyor belt," she said. "Runs all the way down the hall to that massive machine down there."

"Shouldn't we be leaving?" asked Owen. "You got what you came for."

"If Darwen's right," said Rich, "and this is some kind of scrobbler factory, then we need to free the people if we can . . ."

"And destroy the equipment," added Alex. "Greyling won't be taking over the world with this army. Not if I've got something to say about it."

"Do you ever *not* have something to say about, you know, *anything*?" asked Rich.

Alex just shrugged, unoffended.

"Come on, farm boy," she said. "Let's put those muscles of yours to good use."

The two of them strode purposefully off down the cavern, and Owen, apparently unsure what to do, followed them apprehensively. Darwen stayed where he was beside Mr. Peregrine with the flitter-crake. The old man was sitting up now, breathing carefully as if afraid he might lapse into some painful coughing fit. From time to time, he would consider his hands, as if puzzled by the memory of their greenish hue only a few minutes before. There was so much Darwen wanted to say, questions, challenges about why Mr. Peregrine hadn't told him of Greyling's mirroculist past, but for now he would keep them to himself. The old man looked far too fragile.

Darwen plucked the compact mirror from his pocket and pushed the button on the side. Eileen's face faded into view. Her hair was unusually disheveled and she looked tense. "What's going on?" she said.

"We have him," said Darwen, grinning. "Mr. Peregrine. He's alive. But he was being changed."

"Changed?" said Eileen, her momentary relief sputtering to a halt. "Into what?"

"A scrobbler," said Darwen.

"What?" Eileen exclaimed, her face pale. "How is that possible? I thought scrobblers were native to Silbrica."

"I'm not sure," said Darwen, "but as far as we can tell, scrobblers aren't born; they're made. They're just regular people until Greyling transforms them."

"But . . . why?"

"I don't know, but I think his plans are larger than a few conversions here. He's moved most of the operation out, but I don't know where he's taken it."

"You need to get back," said Eileen.

"Not till we've smashed this lab up," said Darwen. "We need to make it so Greyling can't build any reinforcements. Not here, anyway. I'll let you know when we're done."

He snapped the mirror shut and returned his attention to Mr. Peregrine. The old man looked tired and sick, but he was alive, and that seemed beyond anything Darwen had a right to expect. Darwen smiled again, wider this time, laughing with sudden relief.

"Enjoy the moment," said Alex as she marched back toward them. "'Cause our news? Not so much fun."

"What did you find?" asked Darwen.

"This," said Rich, holding out an iron helmet with a plate of heavy glass in the visor. To the back was fastened a box with a small green lightbulb and what looked like a coiled antenna. "The machinery back there produces these."

"Lots of 'em," said Alex. "Mass production."

"How many?"

"Impossible to say," said Rich. "There's a pile of them that were broken or misshaped. If those are the ones Greyling discarded, but we assume the rest worked . . ."

"Hundreds," said Alex. "Thousands."

"And they're not here," said Rich. "Which means they've been taken somewhere to be used."

"What do you think they do?" asked Alex, considering the helmet warily.

"Pretty much the same as these, I'd say," said Owen, nodding toward the pods.

"But faster and more efficiently," Darwen agreed. "He's refined the technology. I think," he said, finally committing to the idea, "that he's been testing some new version of the system at Hillside. Think about those weird moments at school when the lights dimmed and the teachers started acting all . . ." He sought for the word.

"*Argh,*" said Alex, pulling a monster face. "Scrobblerish."

"Right," said Darwen. "Take the machine that did that, add in the helmets, and you've got yourself an instant scrobbler army."

"Thousands of odd bods?" said Owen with a shudder.

"He's planning global conquest," said Rich. "Of both worlds."

"The man needs a new set of interests," said Alex. "Gardening, maybe."

"And we know where he's going to start," said Rich, his voice laden with dread.

"The Hillside gala," said Darwen.

"Our families will be there," said Alex, her face ashen.

"I know," said Darwen, rubbing his face with his hands as if trying to massage some focus into his mind. "We need to disconnect all the pods in this cavern from their power source and get the people out. Quickly. Owen, how much more of that stuff you injected into Mr. Peregrine do you have?"

"There's only one more shot," said Owen. "Looks like only the recently occupied pods are equipped with it."

"Okay," said Darwen, balling his fists. "So if we get the people disconnected from the pods but can't wake them, will they turn back into people?"

"Perhaps," said Owen. "If it's like what we did with the tanks, then the process has to be maintained through electrical impulse and a kind of chemical cocktail that they get daily. Without those, it will reverse, but it could take days, weeks."

"And I'd guess that if the transformation is complete," added Rich, "they might not change back at all."

"Better get to work, then," said Darwen. "Give the last dose to

Blodwyn: that woman there. Alex, you're on that side with Owen. He'll show you what to do. Rich, you're with me."

"What about me?" wheezed Mr. Peregrine with difficulty.

"Stay where you are," said Darwen. "Rest. You're going to need your strength soon enough."

"Why do I not like the sound of that?" asked Alex.

"Disconnect the power and get them out," said Darwen, adding with a glance at the flittercrake, "Stay with him." The creature nodded fractionally and crept closer to the old man. Darwen got to work.

It wasn't easy. Some of the pods seemed to have been there for ages and decades of rust had built up around their controls, ports, and locking mechanisms. Twice Darwen and Rich had to smash the fastening clasps off with a hunk of stone to get the pod open. One had, apparently, been damaged already, and the body inside was shrunken and lifeless, bone showing beneath the scrobbler goggles.

Darwen cursed under his breath. "Check the window at the top to make sure they are still alive before you start working to open the pod," he said. To Rich he added quietly, "We'll never get them all out. It's taking too long. And we need to make sure the pods can't be used again. Think you can wire them up so it would blow their circuitry or something?"

"I can give it a try," said Rich. "If we could cross the live wires with . . ." he mumbled to himself as he examined the machinery.

They worked for ten anxious minutes and in that time released eight people, all but one of whom was still alive, but immobile, as if in a heavy, drugged sleep. One of them was Blodwyn Evans, and though Owen had injected her, she still looked greenish and comatose, tusk-like teeth protruding from her lips.

"You think we could take her back with us?" Darwen muttered.

Rich gave the prone woman a look and frowned.

"Wouldn't be easy," he said. "We're going to have to practically carry Mr. P between us as it is."

He was right. Mr. Peregrine looked fully human now, but he also looked impossibly weary. He could barely stand, let alone walk unassisted, and he wasn't speaking, as if every breath was still too precious to waste on words. As Darwen watched, he saw the old man's eyes fall on the watchful flittercrake, and his thin lips crinkled into a dreamy half smile, as if he had been reunited with a favorite pet.

"I'd hate to leave Blodwyn down here," said Darwen. "She tried to help us."

Rich gave him a quick look and the two boys' eyes met.

"Will do what I can," said Rich. "But right now, Darwen, it's not her. She has the strength and instincts of a scrobbler. You need to give her some time to recover before we can start treating her like a person again."

Darwen nodded.

"Guys," called Alex. "We don't have time for this. We've got to get back to Hillside."

"Right," sighed Darwen. There was no way they could get everyone out of the pods before they left. "This is starting to feel like a diversion Greyling left to keep us from interfering with his plans."

Rich nodded seriously. "You know where the portal is?" he asked.

"Yes," said Darwen.

"You can just . . . feel it?" asked Rich. He was looking watchful again, and that slightly wary look was back in his eyes.

"Yes," said Darwen. "It's like a compass inside me. If I'm still and focused, I can almost see it."

"Maybe it's like one of those animals that can sense heat, like a pit viper," Rich mused.

"You're saying I'm a snake?" Darwen said, laughing in spite of himself. "Great."

"When we came in," said Rich. "I'm pretty sure those lights weren't on, but now . . ."

"How can you tell if they are scrobblers or people?" said Alex, snatching Rich's flashlight and shining it through the windows of the pods.

"I told you," said Darwen, craning over her shoulder to see in. "Scrobblers have red eyes. See? These have . . ."

But as he said it, the blue eyes of the person in the pod closed briefly. When they opened again, they were a deep, burning crimson. At the same instant, there was a burst of steam from the edges of the pod, a slow hiss like a basket of snakes, and the metal case began to open. It wasn't the only one.

"How do we get out?" yelled Alex.

All along the chamber wall, pods were starting to open. The conversion process was, apparently, complete.

Even the flittercrake looked scared.

As Darwen made it out into the stone corridor, he could see why. It wasn't just the pods in that one chamber that were opening. It was all of them. Darwen felt the vague pull of the portal, but between him and it were dozens of waking scrobblers.

"Come on!" he called. He and Rich hoisted Mr. Peregrine to his feet. The man still felt like he was half asleep, and as his full weight landed on their shoulders, Darwen and Rich exchanged an anxious look. They couldn't go far like this, and no distance at all at any speed. Alex was pulling Owen along. He looked dazed and stricken with terror.

The flittercrake sped ahead and the others followed. They were already halfway along the chamber when Darwen realized they had left Blodwyn Evans behind. "We have to go back!" he sputtered, turning awkwardly to where the woman lay on her back, her mouth opening and closing like a fish strangling in air. "Owen! Come and help us carry her. . . ."

"We can't!" said Rich. "Even if we could carry her, look!"

Dazed scrobblers were spilling out all around her. She looked completely helpless.

"When they see she's not one of them," Darwen gasped, "they'll kill her."

"But she still *is* one of them, Darwen," Rich reminded him. "If we go to her now, she's likely to turn on us, but the scrobblers will probably leave her be. With luck she'll change back gradually and be able to get away from the others before they notice."

Darwen glanced back into the room they had left. Over half the pods were open and their occupants were shambling out, looking dazed and angry. One of them roared, flexing its great jaws so that the lips pulled back from the tusklike teeth, all trace of humanity gone.

They just didn't have a choice.

He gave one last pained look at the scrobbler that had been Blodwyn Evans, and then he began to run, catching Mr. Peregrine's arm and dragging him along. Ahead, more scrobblers were emerging, some of them picking up rocks or tearing pieces of twisted metal from the pods from which they had emerged. It seemed that the first thing the scrobblers did on waking was search for a weapon and someone on which to use it.

The flittercrake was dashing ahead, careless of whether the others could keep up or not. Alex was a few steps behind it with Owen at her heels, but Darwen, Rich, and Mr. Peregrine were way behind. Another scrobbler blundered into the hall from a side room on the right, blocking their way. They weren't going to make it.

The scrobbler turned to face them, hunching and spreading its arms to catch them. Its movements were still a little slow, and at the last second Darwen skipped to the left, yanking Mr. Peregrine and Rich after him. The old man stumbled, but the scrobbler's swinging snatch missed them, and the monster faltered, as if disoriented by its own movement. Before it could turn to find them, Darwen was pulling Mr. Peregrine on. Behind them, the stone hallway was filling with scrobblers. They were waking now, getting faster, more alert.

Rich stopped and picked something up. As Darwen ducked, Rich flung a chunk of slate into the mass of scrobblers. It thudded against one of them and the scrobbler turned wildly, furious, but unsure where the projectile had come from. As Darwen pressed on, looking back over his shoulder, he saw the scrobbler punch one of the others in the gut. The second stumbled back, colliding with another, and before Darwen had gone more than a few yards, they had turned blindly on each other, kicking and clawing and shouting.

"Should buy us a few seconds," said Rich, businesslike.

"Nice one," said Darwen.

But it was only seconds. Many of the scrobblers behind them weren't involved in the melee at all and there were still more spilling out ahead.

"Where's that portal?" Alex roared over her shoulder.

Darwen half closed his eyes and it was almost like he could see the gate, like he was picking it up on some kind of radar in his head. Fifty yards ahead and twenty to the left. But the scrobblers seemed to be everywhere, erupting from every alcove and hollow, half blind still, confused but bent on doing the only things they really understood: destroying, terrorizing, killing.

"You remember when we could stop them just by touching them because people loved us?" remarked Alex as she ran, pulling a speechless Owen along by the hand. "Good times. Next time I take a trip with you, Darwen Arkwright, I'm bringing a machine gun."

Thirty yards ahead. Fifteen. Five.

Darwen rounded the corner, still pulling the struggling Mr. Peregrine, but Rich was helping again and the old man's feet barely touched the ground. There was the gate, flanked by pods. Two were open, another was starting to steam at the hinges, and three were dormant. Two scrobblers were already in their way, flexing their fingers thoughtfully as if discovering what their new bodies could do.

"You can sense where the portals are?"

The question was so quiet that, in the confusion and panic, Darwen almost missed it. It was Mr. Peregrine who spoke, and for all his exhaustion he had fixed Darwen with a particularly level stare.

"Yeah," said Darwen, self-conscious. "I suppose all mirroculists can."

Mr. Peregrine's brow contracted into a frown, and though he said nothing, Darwen could almost hear his answer: *No, Darwen, they can't. This is different. New.*

"It's no big deal," said Darwen. "I can just feel it, especially if it's close or if it . . . is . . ."

"What?" asked Rich urgently. Darwen had tailed off, and was now gazing up the cavern to where the portal had flickered into life.

Someone was coming through.

For a split second Darwen thought the Guardians had sent reinforcements, that there would be a team to help them disarm the pods. Maybe it was Weazen.

But then he saw the face.

"It's the man in the gas mask!" he yelled. "Take cover!"

Chapter Thirty-three
Revelations at Devil's Bridge

Greyling's agent moved as before, slow and deliberate, turning methodically as he aimed his gun—a different one this time, with a wide muzzle like a rocket launcher—and began firing: three quick shots at Alex, which she avoided by diving behind a bank of pods. One of them exploded in a burst of electricity, shattered rock, and twisted metal. The scrobbler inside blundered out, burning, bellowing in rage and pain. It took three steps, then fell heavily to the ground.

Darwen and Rich hid behind another pod with Mr. Peregrine as the man in the gas mask began his slow advance into the cavern. A scrobbler blundered into his path, and he blasted it aside, almost casually, without breaking stride.

Darwen risked a look across to where Alex and Owen cowered. They were all pinned down and the man in the gas mask was moving to where he would have a clear shot. Darwen gave Rich a frightened glance.

"Ideas?" he asked.

"Nothing," said Rich. "Right now, our best hope is the scrobblers."

But though the scrobblers looked angry, they also looked confused, far from clear who their enemy was. The man in the gas mask, by contrast, was a picture of deliberation. He came on, shooting at the scrobblers only if they got in his way, and even then it barely took his attention from his real targets. Darwen could feel the invisible eyes behind the gas mask fastened on him. Another few steps and his shot would be unobstructed. Darwen risked a look at Mr. Peregrine. The old man's face was a mask of horror that went far beyond fear for his life.

"What?" asked Darwen.

"They sent him!" said the old man, aghast.

But just as it seemed that the man in the gas mask had them, he stumbled and took a step backward. Some powerful arm had launched a chunk of slate at him and it had caught him a clear blow in the chest. He hesitated, and another rock came hurtling through the air. Greyling's agent sidestepped it, but he looked suddenly uncertain. As a third piece of stone was thrown, Darwen peered back to see where it was coming from.

A lone scrobbler had stepped out into the center of the hallway and was staring the man in the gas mask down with a single-minded purpose that matched his own.

"That scrobbler," said Rich. "What is it doing?"

"Not it," Darwen answered. "She."

It was Blodwyn Evans, still caught between woman and scrobbler, but somehow tapping into her human memories and emotions. She took a quick step and hurled another piece of stone, hard and fast as a javelin. Greyling's agent misjudged it, and it caught him high on the head, so that one lens of the gas mask cracked. The impact snapped his head back, and when he righted himself, his body seemed unsteady, woozy.

"Now!" shouted Darwen, lurching out from behind the shattered pod, pulling Rich and Mr. Peregrine after him. "Get to the portal."

Another chunk of stone hit Greyling's assassin squarely in the chest and this time he sank to one knee, just as Darwen reached him. They passed each other within inches, Darwen using all his strength to keep moving, Mr. Peregrine's deadweight half spread across his shoulders. But the portal had closed again, and Darwen knew the man in the gas mask's daze wouldn't last much longer. And there were still dozens of scrobblers that were steadily shaking off their grogginess.

Darwen had no choice.

"Take Mr. Peregrine," he said to Rich, and, finding a little more speed and determination, he leapt past them and up to the wall where the portal was. He slammed one palm against it, reached with his mind, and felt the energy leave him. He sagged to the ground, vaguely conscious that the scrobblers were turning to look at him but also certain that the gateway had not opened.

No, he thought. *Not now. Let me be a mirroculist just five minutes more.* This was not the time for his gift to fail him.

He tried again, standing, both hands to the wall this time, reminding himself that he should have several years as a mirroculist. That was what Lightborne had said. He might have it till he was sixteen.

But then again he might not. Others lost it earlier and Darwen's gut continued to tell him he was one of those. He focused on the portal, but as if to prove all his doubts, the flicker of life he produced in the gateway was even less than before.

He felt a hand on his shoulder and flinched, though he knew it wasn't nearly big enough to be a scrobbler. Alex's face swam into view.

"You okay?" she said.

Darwen shook his head. "Can't open it," he managed.

Panic flashed through Alex's face, but she mastered it almost instantly.

"Rich," she said, still looking at Darwen. "Little help."

Rich blundered over. Mr. Peregrine was behind him. He looked as shattered as Darwen felt.

Behind them, three scrobblers were watching, and as Darwen looked, they started moving toward them with grim purpose.

"Hands," said Alex.

"We don't need—" Rich began.

"HANDS!" Alex demanded. She seized Darwen's hand in one of hers and Mr. Peregrine's in the other. Rich took Darwen's and Owen's.

"Okay, Darwen," she said, her face leaning in so close that their foreheads touched. "Gotta do it."

"I can't. . . ."

"You can," she said. "We'll help. Now."

Darwen's eyes closed in concentration. He felt the pressure of Alex's hand in his and focused. He saw the portal, felt the power leave his body, but this time, just as it seemed the gateway would flicker into nothing again, he sensed it catch like the motor of an old lawn mower. There was a whisper of energy that went though him, something that came from his friends, almost lifting him to his feet.

The portal stabilized.

"Go!" shouted Alex, and Darwen, who was too weak to see what was happening, was pulled through by the others. The energy hum of the portal became something else, though it took Darwen a moment to realize what he was hearing.

Water. A lot of it.

He opened his eyes just as Rich's grip on his hand became vise-like, and he heard Alex's sputter of "Whoa!"

He immediately saw why.

They were standing on the ledge of a rocky cliff facing what looked to be an ancient stone bridge spanning a narrow and heavily wooded gorge, at the bottom of which ran a churning torrent of water. The portal they had come through was a narrow but towering waterfall, plunging through the dense green shrubs and bracken that clung to the rock.

"How did we . . . ?" Owen was saying. "How *could* we . . . ?"

Darwen realized that it wasn't, in fact, one bridge that he was looking at. It was three, each slightly different and built directly on top of another with only the narrowest of gaps between them.

Darwen's gaze strayed back to the waterfall. He was close to blacking out, but he had to see if anything followed them through.

Nothing did.

"I know this place," Owen gasped. "It's Devil's Bridge! But that's miles from Conwy."

"Devil's Bridge?" Alex repeated. "Don't like the sound of that."

"That bridge at the bottom," said Owen, pointing. "The one we were under. That's ancient, that is. Built by monks in the Middle Ages, I think, though the story is that it was so difficult to build only the devil could have done it, in return for which he got the soul of who-ever crossed it first. An old woman tricked him by sending a dog over before any people could cross."

"More folktales to explain fissures between worlds," said Rich.

"The other bridges were built later to handle heavier traffic," said Owen. "The second is eighteenth century, the top one—the metal one—early twentieth. I came here as a kid. Never forgot it."

"Climb up!" called Rich over the roar of the water. "There's a path over there." He pointed to where a railed walkway snaked its way up one side of the ravine.

The wet stones were slick to the touch and Darwen moved cautiously, feeling like he was dragging sacks of rocks with each exhausted step.

"Mr. Peregrine," Rich was hissing. "Mr. Peregrine! You are going to have to walk. Climb if you can. Can you hear me?"

The old man nodded absently, but his eyes looked vague and un-focused. Alex led the way, but she looked uneasy. "If he falls," she whispered to Darwen, "I won't be able to stop him."

Darwen nodded. Rich was big for his age, strong too, but even with Darwen's help, he couldn't be expected to carry the old man's weight on so precarious a route.

"I'll do it," said Owen. "It's partly my fault that he's in this state, isn't it? You go ahead."

"Wait," said Darwen. However much his strength had left him, he could still feel the energy of another portal close by. He scanned the area and his gaze fell on the glittering water of the falls. There was no question what it was, and he felt both exhilarated that he had found a route out of here and weary beyond words at the prospect of trying to open it. "There's another portal in the waterfall," he said. "We should use that. But I need a moment."

"What if the man in the gas mask follows?" asked Alex. "He came through the portal like he was a mirroculist himself."

"Yeah," said Rich. "How is that possible?"

Darwen shook his head. "I don't know," he sighed, "and I don't know how long Blodwyn and the scrobblers can keep him busy, but I really need a moment."

He sat down and put his head in his hands.

"Blodwyn and the Scrobblers," Alex echoed. "That sounds like the worst rock band in history."

For a moment, Darwen just sat there, listening to the roar and splash of the waterfall, arranging his thoughts. He didn't want to say it, but he had to. He needed to know.

"I have a question," said Darwen, turning to Mr. Peregrine.

"He's really tired, Darwen," said Alex. "Can't it wait?"

"No," said Darwen.

"What do you want to know?" asked the old man with an attempt at a smile.

"Who was the last mirroculist?" asked Darwen. "The one before me."

Mr. Peregrine hesitated. "Well, Darwen," he said between shallow breaths, "that is confidential information. The Guardians feel it is best to preserve the secret identity of anyone who serves the council. . . ."

"It was Eileen, wasn't it?" said Darwen.

Rich gaped, then turned to Mr. Peregrine, expecting him to deny it. But the old man just frowned thoughtfully.

"I thought so," said Darwen. "I could tell. I could see it in her eyes when we crossed over, how much she missed it, how sad she was. *My time in Silbrica is done*, she said. Lightborne told me about how mirroculists grow out of their gift. Have you any idea how hard it is to lose something that special?"

He caught himself before the halt in his voice stopped him from going any further.

"I should have said," Mr. Peregrine replied wearily. "I should have warned you that you would not be a mirroculist forever. As for Eileen, I thought that if she worked for me, it would be easier for her, if she stayed close to Silbrica, that the sense of loss would not be so great."

"Yeah," said Darwen, still angry. "I don't think it worked that way. Replace the ability to cross into another world full of beauty and wonder with spying on some kid and his friends? I don't think that really cut it. But I guess that when you're no use to the Guardians anymore, no one worries too much about what happens to you next."

"Dude!" said Rich. "He said he was trying to help her. What's got into you?"

"Greyling was a mirroculist," Darwen shot back. "Lightborne told me that too."

Rich had opened his mouth to protest, but no words came and he just stared. Alex gave Mr. Peregrine a searching look, and at last the old man nodded slowly.

"I didn't want to confuse you," said Mr. Peregrine. "I thought that—"

"Yeah, I know," Darwen retorted. "You were trying to protect me, right? From the truth."

"I just assumed . . ." Mr. Peregrine began.

"Yeah, you Guardian types do that a lot," Darwen snapped.

"Darwen, I know you're upset," said Rich, "but give the guy a break, okay?"

"One more question," snapped Darwen, ignoring him.

"You are way out of line, Darwen," said Alex. "The man has been through a serious ordeal. . . ."

"I said," Darwen repeated, his voice rising, his teeth clenched. "One. More. Question."

Mr. Peregrine seemed to brace himself, then nodded.

"Tell me about the man in the gas mask," said Darwen. "The man who just tried to kill us."

"What do you mean?" said Mr. Peregrine, hesitant.

"You recognized him," said Darwen. "I saw it in your face. Blodwyn knew him too. I wondered how you could know one of Greyling's henchmen, but then I remembered what Moth and Weazen said about this terrible agent called the Fixer: a killer who worked not for Greyling, but for the Guardians."

Rich and Alex looked baffled and uneasy.

Mr. Peregrine met Darwen's eyes and, for a long moment, said nothing. "The Fixer is not so much a person as a role," he said at last. "The job is passed on. But you are right. The assassin in the gas mask is indeed the Fixer, and I can hardly imagine a more terrible development. No one is more"—he sought for the word—"*efficient*. If he is trying to eliminate you, then it seems, unfortunately, that this Fixer has now turned rogue or, more likely, has simply joined with Greyling."

"When did he join Greyling?" Darwen asked.

"I don't know," said Mr. Peregrine.

"In the last few months?" Darwen pressed. "The last few weeks? Or is it longer? A year or more?"

"I don't know," Mr. Peregrine repeated.

"You do," said Darwen, his voice hard, his eyes starting to burn. "When was it?"

"I've told you I don't know," said Mr. Peregrine. "What difference does it make?"

"You're lying," said Darwen, getting to his feet. "You know."

"Easy, man," said Alex, concerned. "He was in those tanks for months, remember? And besides, he said he doesn't know."

"It's okay, Darwen," said Rich soothingly. "It doesn't matter anyway."

"It does," Darwen spat back.

"Why?" said Rich. "The Fixer is our enemy now. Who cares how long he's been working for Greyling instead of the Guardians?"

"I do!" Darwen yelled.

"But why?" asked Alex.

"Because he killed my parents," said Darwen.

There was a horrified silence.

"No," said Alex. It wasn't a denial or an argument. She said it as if she couldn't bear for what Darwen had said to be true, as if she could push the sentence away and it would vanish from her mind forever.

But Mr. Peregrine just closed his eyes tight and said nothing. It clearly pained the old man to have the truth brought into the light like this, but that did not make it any less true.

"So it was the Guardians after all," said Darwen. "I saw pictures of the man in the gas mask at the road accident where my parents died, and I figured he was someone who worked for Greyling, but he wasn't, was he? The Fixer does what the Guardians tell him to and the Guardians don't look too closely into how he goes about it. That's what Moth said. 'The Guardians do not ask enough questions about how the Fixer gets the results they want.'"

Darwen's voice was quiet and cold as he strung it all together, and no one else made a sound.

"The Guardians could see trouble coming in the form of a powerful and disgruntled former mirroculist called Greyling," Darwen went on, "and they knew they needed someone on their side who could open portals. But there wasn't one to hand. So they decided to make one, like Greyling makes his scrobblers. They killed my parents to trigger my mirroculist gift. An emotional trauma, right? *Killing his family ought to do the trick*, they said to themselves. *Just what we need to give us a weapon against Greyling. So yeah, send out the Fixer with his gadgets to arrange a car crash. No one would suspect a car wreck, right? Happens all the time. And those people in it, the Ark-wrights, they were nobody, right? Not compared to what we got out of it: our pet mirroculist.* They were NOBODY!"

He was shouting now, the tears running down his face.

"*You* did it!" he yelled, his fists balled. "Maybe the Fixer pushed the button, but you people gave the order. You killed them!"

Mr. Peregrine reached up with sudden speed, shrugging off his exhaustion, gripping Darwen's arm and pulling him down and into his arms. Darwen fought to free himself, but the old man was stronger than he looked, and the grip was viselike as he pressed Darwen to his heart.

"I didn't know," Mr. Peregrine whispered. "I swear it. I'm so sorry, Darwen, but I didn't know."

Darwen squirmed and fought for breath, then collapsed, sobbing his rage and despair into the old man's chest.

Chapter Thirty-four
Battle Plans

It was a long while before Darwen was fit to move, and the others spent most of the time watching the portals in the waterfall anxiously, but, for whatever reason, the Fixer—the man in the gas mask, who had killed Darwen's parents and joined with Greyling—did not pursue them to Devil's Bridge. Rich caught Darwen looking at him as he checked his watch and gave an apologetic shrug.

"Sorry," he said. "I was trying to calculate the time back home. The gala . . ."

"Yes," said Darwen, getting slowly to his feet. "We should go. For the record, what we're going to do tonight—or try to—is because it's right, because Greyling must be stopped, not because the Guardians want it."

Rich and Alex nodded, their faces stern, and Darwen concluded, "Okay. Let's do this."

He felt impossibly tired, as if he had aged at some extraordinary rate over the last hour. For most of that time, the others had avoided his eyes, half embarrassed, half trying to give him a little privacy with his grief and outrage. Only Mr. Peregrine did not leave his side. The old man sat rigid beside him, one arm around Darwen's shoulders, his face set and his eyes closed, oblivious to the fine spray of water from the falls.

"I should go back," said Owen. "I want to help you, wherever you are going, but I have a family. . . . I don't know what is happening back in Blaenau Ffestiniog."

"Yes," said Darwen. "You're right."

"I don't know," said Rich. "We're going to need all the help we can get."

Owen looked pained.

Darwen took his hand and shook it. "You've done enough," he said. "We would never have got this far without you. And we're grateful. But now you should be with your family."

Alex and Rich exchanged uneasy looks, but Darwen held Owen's eyes and gave him a final nod. "He can't go back to the mine," he said. "It's overrun by scrobblers."

Darwen didn't want to admit that he doubted he could open the portal anyway.

"That's fine," said Owen hurriedly. "I'll call a taxi from the village and take the train."

Darwen nodded, too tired to speak.

"Thank you," said Owen. "You helped me make a choice."

"I knew you would do the right thing," said Darwen, managing a self-conscious smile. "Go."

When Owen was safely on his way, they made their way to the second portal reflected in the cascading water of the falls. Darwen reached out to open it, but found he could do nothing until Rich and Alex helped. They watched him sidelong, but he didn't say anything, so neither did they. Once the portal was open, they stepped through the water.

The others seemed none the worse for wear, but Darwen collapsed on the other side before he could even look around. He lay, panting and exhausted on cool stone, his eyes still closed, only just awake enough to hear Rich's muttered, "Oh no. Not here."

"What?" Darwen managed. "Where are we?"

He rolled onto his side and, with an effort, opened his eyes.

It was almost as dark as the mine had been. But he soon realized why his friend sounded so scared. Around them loomed familiar walls as if shaped by wind out of the living rock. There were stone doorways and windows and a stone quadrangle with a stone approximation of a clock tower. . . .

"It's the other Hillside," said Rich. "The shadow school."

"This is where Greyling brought all those helmets," Alex mused. They were stacked on racks all around the edge of the quadrangle, and there were cables and pieces of scrobbler equipment humming all around them.

"Darwen's right," said Rich, his voice leaden as the reality sank in. "Greyling is going to use the gala to convert everyone there. Parents, teachers, students. He's going to make them all into scrobblers."

"Stuggs," said Alex. "He has the personality of a scrobbler already. I bet it wouldn't take much to push him into being all green and tusky."

"We have to stop the gala from going ahead," said Darwen, dragging himself upright. "Make sure no one is there when Greyling's forces go through."

"Too late," said Rich, checking his watch, whose hands were spinning as they had the last time they were in this locus. "Time has sped up again. The gala has already started."

Darwen pulled the compact from his pocket and pressed the button for Eileen. She answered looking pale, her whispered "Yes?" sounding strained.

"We're at the shadow school!" Darwen blurted.

"Shh," Eileen hissed. She looked startled and her hair was uncharacteristically messy.

Darwen lowered his voice.

"Something is about to happen at the Hillside gala. We need you and anyone else who might help there."

"Already in place," Eileen muttered. She rotated the mirror fractionally, and Darwen could see Aunt Honoria sitting stony-faced in the folding chair beside Eileen. Her lips were so thin they had almost completely vanished. "I had to convince your aunt that you would meet her here after you've done your part in the talent show," Eileen whispered, "and for that conversation, Darwen Arkwright, you owe me big time."

In spite of their predicament, Darwen smiled. He could only imagine how hard that meeting must have been. He wanted to tell her that he knew what she had been, what she had lost, wanted to share that his own gift was, it seemed, leaving him, but he couldn't. Terrible things were about to happen. He could sense it. Now was not the time.

"What's going on there?" he asked.

"Everyone is gathering in the quadrangle under the clock tower," she whispered back. "Looks like the weather is going to hold."

"Great," said Rich bitterly. "The one time we could use a real Georgia gulley washer and it stays fine."

"How long till the speeches and stuff start?" asked Darwen.

"Could be any moment now," said Eileen. "They are just waiting for everyone to get into their seats."

"It's okay," said Darwen. "We'll be right there."

"What are you going to do?" Eileen hissed.

Darwen shrugged.

"Just . . . I don't know," he said. "Have you spoken to Weazen?"

"Yes," she said. "He's on his way."

"Good," said Darwen. "Though to be honest, we have no idea what we're doing. Okay, just . . . give us a minute, okay?" he said, and snapped the compact shut.

"So what's the plan?" asked Alex.

"Theirs or ours?" asked Rich.

"Either," said Alex.

Darwen thought furiously. "If we're right," he said, "then Greyling has technology that will convert everyone at the gala into scrobblers. To do that, he'll bring the shadow school into the same space as Hillside, and then he'll have to keep the people in the quadrangle from escaping. We should assume he'll have forces to keep them corralled: more scrobblers, probably, gnashers too, but maybe other things as well. They will have to come from this side: from here in Silbrica, so we should expect company soon. They may already be in other parts of the shadow school or waiting just inside the perimeter fence."

Mr. Peregrine eased himself up and started scanning the empty windows of the uneven quadrangle walls anxiously. The flittercrake clinging to the torn shoulder of his jacket flapped but did not let go.

"As soon as we reach Hillside, we have to disable Greyling's equipment," Darwen continued. "Rich, that's on you."

Rich nodded, his face pale.

"You said the cables ran up to the tower, right?" said Darwen. "So when we cross over, you'll have to get up there. Somehow," he added with an apologetic shrug. "We'll have to get the people out," he continued. "Mr. Peregrine, that's your job. Adults respond better to other adults."

Mr. Peregrine looked rattled, but he just nodded.

"Alex," Darwen concluded, "we have to assume Greyling will use the window as a portal. Smash it into a million pieces as soon as we're through it."

"That," said Alex approvingly, "I can do."

"And you?" said Rich to Darwen.

"Greyling will be there," said Darwen. "He's bound to be. And he's mine."

Rich opened his mouth to protest, and Alex had a thousand questions on the tip of her tongue, but Darwen glared at them both, and they let it go.

"Well," said Alex. "I guess we know what our gala talent is."

"What's that?" said Darwen.

"We save the world," she answered.

"Or we appear—very briefly—in the bloodiest, most horrible school play ever," said Rich.

"Yeah," said Darwen. "Let's call that Plan B."

He paused, then turned to Mr. Peregrine. "One more thing I need to understand," he said, "and I'd like a direct and honest answer."

"I told you, Darwen," said Mr. Peregrine, "I knew nothing about the circumstances of your parents' death."

"I know," said Darwen, "and I believe you. This is different."

Mr. Peregrine's eyes narrowed warily, but he nodded for Darwen to proceed.

"Darwen," said Rich, pointing. "I can see lights out beyond the quadrangle. Something is coming!"

"So Greyling was a mirroculist," Darwen said.

"Yes," said Mr. Peregrine, "and I'm sorry that I didn't tell you—"

"I know," said Darwen. "It's fine. But I need to understand."

"Getting closer, Darwen!" said Rich, his voice urgent and anxious. The flittercrake on Mr. Peregrine's shoulder flapped its wings distractedly, craning its neck to see what might be coming.

"But he grew out of the gift," Darwen continued.

"As all mirroculists do," Mr. Peregrine said. "But because he had been useful, the Guardians granted his wish to stay in Silbrica rather than returning to his ordinary life."

"They put him on the council," said Darwen.

"Eventually, yes," said Mr. Peregrine, sounding defeated.

"There!" shouted Rich, pointing through the glassless windows and through the craggy approximations of classrooms beyond the quadrangle. "Scrobblers for sure and other things. They are coming this way."

"Darwen!" shouted Alex, getting hold of his arm and yanking it. "We really don't have time for this."

"But that wasn't enough for him, was it?" Darwen persisted, his eyes fixed on Mr. Peregrine. "Because being on the council means staying in one place most of the time, and it means never leaving Silbrica."

"Indeed," said Mr. Peregrine, and even though the shapes of the scrobblers were clearer now beyond the uneven walls of the shadow school, he seemed resigned to the conversation. "No one could have known how hard that would be for him. Being a mirroculist is about the ability to travel, to step between worlds. Not being able to do that anymore . . ." He thought for a moment, looking old and strangely frail. "It damaged him. He felt, I think, cheated. That sense of injustice, of power lost, has driven him ever since."

Darwen nodded, strangely calm now. It was not news, and though the confirmation weighed on him like sadness, he felt clearer in his mind.

"Okay," he said as the first of the scrobblers appeared in the classrooms only yards away. "It's starting."

Chapter Thirty-five
The Invasion of Hillside Academy

"**T**o the portal," said Darwen.

They clambered up the iron gantry to the window, conscious that it was humming with electricity, but Mr. Peregrine moved slowly, and the quadrangle corridors were filling with scrobblers and gnashers. Darwen hesitated. "You two go on ahead," he said to Rich and Alex. "I'll be right there."

He reached back for Mr. Peregrine's thin hand and pulled him up the steps, conscious of the scrobblers marching evenly through the corridors. They weren't coming out into the central square but were lining the walkways on all four sides. They moved as one, like the army that Darwen knew them to be, and they were equipped with every kind of weapon Darwen had seen in Silbrica and many he hadn't. It was the gnashers that came loping into the grassy area, bounding on their knuckles like great headless baboons.

"It won't open!"

It was Rich's voice. Darwen turned, still pulling Mr. Peregrine.

"What do you mean?" he said. "The portal's online? Why won't it open?"

"Just won't, man!" said Alex, whose eyes were on the gnashers crossing the grassy enclosure at an alarming speed. "Get up here!"

"Go," wheezed Mr. Peregrine. "I can manage."

Darwen let go of his hand and leapt up the last of the stairs. "Hands!" he barked.

Alex and Rich grabbed his, and Darwen braced himself for the strain of opening the portal, vaguely aware that Mr. Peregrine was still struggling up to join them.

He could hear the pounding of the gnashers' paws, could almost hear their probing tongues testing the air as they sought blindly for the intruders. And then there was only the gateway to Atlanta, rising up like a wall of bright water before them. He pressed Rich's hand into Alex's and reached back for Mr. Peregrine, fingers splayed, searching. He found the old man's slender wrist, seized it, and stepped through just as Mr. Peregrine cried out.

The reason for the cry became clear as soon as they reached the other side, but the strangeness of the scene still acted on Darwen like paralysis.

They were standing on the stage that had been erected beneath the great window. Principal Thompson, his back to them, was standing at a podium overlooking the quadrangle, whose grass was almost completely obscured by a mass of upturned faces. Even in his panic, Darwen scanned the crowd for Aunt Honoria. He couldn't see her, though she was surely out there. Teachers, the lunch staff, janitors, students, their families, and anyone with even the slightest connection to Hillside were there, gazing up at the platform on which Darwen, Rich, Alex, and Mr. Peregrine had just materialized. But amazingly, the ripple of surprise, the outbreak of sudden chatter, was not about them, and it took the first scream for Darwen to realize what everyone was looking at.

The gnasher that had been chasing them had caught hold of Mr. Peregrine just as they crossed over, and it now stood, hulking and savage, on the stage beside them.

"Ta-da!" sang Alex, striking a pose.

A woman in the audience, sitting in the front row, began to clap, but as the uncertain ovation began to course through the audience, the gnasher's chest split open to reveal its awful shark mouth, and as the snakelike tongue lolled out, the screaming recommenced.

The principal turned on his heel and gave them a long, baleful look. "Fine," he said, taking a step toward Darwen and staring down at him. "Fine. We begin a little earlier than scheduled. Mr. Stuggs," he said, turning to the side of the stage, "if you will?"

For a moment Darwen thought the principal was talking about the gala, but there was a grim determination about the man that suggested something darker. Even so, Darwen was too slow to realize what the command to Mr. Stuggs actually meant. The PE teacher waddled across the stage and, before Darwen realized what was happening, took hold of the lever that Alex had pulled to inadvertently bring the two schools into the same space.

"No!" Darwen shouted, but the PE teacher just gave him a wide, satisfied grin and leaned on the long metal handle till it shifted. Whether or not Stuggs knew what he was doing, Darwen couldn't possibly guess, but that hardly mattered. There was a familiar droning sound and the clunk of something mechanical locking into place, and then the shadow school began slowly to materialize around them.

"Rich!" shouted Darwen. "The tower."

But the only way up to whatever Greyling had installed above the clock was through the door at the foot of the stairs to the stage.

"Wait!" said Alex. She stepped forward, seized the microphone stand from under the principal's nose, and with a rush of feedback that had everyone slapping their hands to their ears, sent it crashing through the stained glass window. As it shattered, the hum of energy around it buckled and vanished, leaving only an irregular hole giving onto the stairwell inside.

"You're welcome!" shouted Alex as Rich clambered through and up.

But breaking the window clearly had no effect on the larger process. All around them, the school was changing, its edges becoming rougher, more approximate as the precise brick gave way to something more like the irregular stone of the shadow school. The two places were occupying the same space. The sign above the stage proclaiming the Hillside gala was fading, becoming insubstantial, and the light was dropping fast. Pieces of equipment they had seen in that Silbrican no-place that had seemed disconnected appeared precisely aligned with other components that were already here, locking into place and powering up, their circuits complete.

The crowd's faintly amused bafflement had been replaced by something altogether different, something more deeply unsure and fearful, but they were also hesitant, too busy muttering and standing up to get a better view to realize that what they should have done was run for the exits. Darwen scoured the crowd for his aunt, but there was too much uproar and bustling aimlessly about for him to spot her.

Darwen glanced over to where Mr. Stuggs stood, the confusion on his fat face turning to horror as the gnasher made its decision and lumbered murderously in his direction. It would guard the lever till Greyling's forces arrived, Darwen realized, and they were already on their way.

The windows looking onto the quadrangle where the Hillside community sat in their Sunday best were suddenly full of masked faces sprouting tusks from their heavy, greenish jaws. Parents rose and pointed, demanded explanations or expressed their outrage, while others watched affably, as if this might all be part of some kind of theatrical stunt to kick off the gala. Somewhere among them was Aunt Honoria, but he still couldn't see her.

Everyone had to get out of here, and fast.

But how? The scrobblers lined the quadrangle. And now they were moving, marching out and around the edge of the square, armed to the teeth. The gnashers, by contrast, made for the racks of visored helmets, which had faded into place with the rest of the shadow school. The process was about to begin.

Someone, a man in a dark suit, his face indignant, got to his feet and began fighting his way out of the row of chairs in which he had been sitting. One of the scrobblers at the perimeter took a step toward him and leveled his energy weapon.

"Stop!" shouted Mr. Peregrine, but there was too much going on for anyone to hear him.

"Yo, Mr. P!" shouted Alex. "Catch."

And so saying, she tossed him the microphone.

"Don't move!" Mr. Peregrine commanded the man in the suit. "Take one more step, and that creature will kill you where you stand."

He said it with such earnestness that the man froze, frowning, while the murmur of unease from the rest of the crowd increased markedly.

"I realize that this is probably part of the show," said a blond woman in oversized shades, "and your special effects are really quite impressive, but you are actually starting to frighten people."

It was, Darwen was sure, Princess Clarkson's mother, the movie actress. Darwen gaped at her. Special effects? Could they still believe that this was all just part of the gala?

"This is not part of any show," Mr. Peregrine said firmly. "You are in grave danger and must do as I say."

Some of the students recognized Mr. Peregrine as their former world studies teacher, and they waved confusedly. Darwen looked out over the anxious faces and, at last, found Aunt Honoria. She was close to the back, sitting on the side so she could slip out to make a business call if necessary. Eileen was beside her and they were leaning in to each other, talking urgently. She looked not so much upset or worried as simply angry, and it occurred to Darwen that she had looked a lot like that recently.

Your fault, he thought. *She says it's work, but it's really you, all the pressure and stress you've brought into her life, none of which she could have imagined, none of which she ever wanted. And now she's here, for you, and she'll be forced into one of those helmets and then . . .*

Darwen turned away from the horror of the thought, and as he did so, something happened behind him.

"Okay, gosh darn it!"

It was Rich. Clearly the apparatus in the clock tower had been guarded. He was now being dragged bodily out of the tower by two scrobblers and shoved onto the stage. Rich's eyes met Darwen's and the bigger boy framed an apologetic shrug: *I tried*, it said. Darwen nodded his understanding, but he was starting to see just how badly things had gone wrong. What had they been thinking? And then the broken window frame pulsed with energy. For a second, Darwen thought the portal had somehow come back online, that someone was coming to help, but then the image clarified, and his blood seemed to freeze in his veins.

It was a face, contained within the window frame but somehow with depth and shape, like a hologram or an image from a 3-D movie. The eyes were small and sunken, but the irises were hot and red. The nose was hawkish, not far from the flittercrake's beak, and the mouth was thin, but a dark pink inside and lined with sharp, yellow teeth. Darwen had never seen the face before, and assumed it was yet another disguise, but he had no doubt who it was.

Greyling.

The face looked down over the quadrangle and the slim mouth smiled mirthlessly.

"Welcome," it said.

The mouth moved, but the sound seemed to come from speakers

to the side of the stage. Some of the anguished muttering from the crowd stopped, but there was something callous in the face that unsettled them still further. Something hungry.

"While I explain the great experiment these good people are about to be a part of," said Greyling's ratlike face, licking his lips, "let us begin distributing the headgear."

Gnashers all around the quadrangle grabbed helmets from the rack and forced their way into the seated audience, which shrank back, wincing and crying with panic. Darwen watched as a woman cringed away from the monster's wavering tongue, arms huddled to her chest, eyes tight shut. When the gnasher simply crammed the helmet onto her head, the people around her seemed positively relieved.

"There now," said the face of Greyling from the window. "Nothing to worry about. Resist, however, and my soldiers will have to deal with you terminally. Far better to just play along."

Mr. Peregrine seemed poised to argue, but when Principal Thompson wordlessly demanded the microphone with a single outstretched hand, Mr. Peregrine reluctantly gave it to him.

"Excellent," said the principal, as if he was addressing a school assembly. Darwen had never suspected the principal of being involved with Greyling, but it now seemed unavoidable that he was. He probably had no idea just what he was helping Greyling do, and he had probably been promised all manner of things that would somehow benefit the school, but in Darwen's eyes that only made him stupid rather than evil. "Now it might save time to just pass the headgear along the rows," the principal continued, smiling with something like pride. "As you get yours, put it on your head and keep it there. Under no circumstances should you remove it. This is a brave new day for Hillside as we lead the world in crossing new educational thresholds."

A lot of people did as they were told, some laughing uneasily as if this all might still be part of the show. Others hesitated.

"This is ridiculous!" exclaimed the man in the suit, slamming his helmet down and making to get out of the row. This time the scrobbler at the end did not hesitate. An amber streak like lightning from the scrobbler's weapon caught the man squarely in the chest. He gave a long, constant shriek as his body was thrown backward and landed, smoking, on the grass ten feet away.

Even the principal looked shocked, and some of his former enthusiasm was lost in a sudden uncertainty that flooded his face.

"Tut, tut," said the face of Greyling. "Someone doesn't want to play. My scrobblers have an array of equipment to make you more compliant. My power supply is wired through every portal in Silbrica, and my communication system can reach every corner of a world you people don't even know exists, a world on whose colossal energy I can draw at will. That scrobbler just used the lowest possible setting on its discharger because—believe me—I would rather keep you alive. Dead you are no use to me, but I will not permit interference. So . . . would you like to see what the next setting does?"

A woman had leapt from her chair and dropped to the body of the man in the suit.

"He's alive," she said. "Barely."

The mood of the crowd had shifted in an instant. Where there had been uncertainty, even an impulse to make light of the situation, there was now a deathly hush and the air felt charged with dread that Darwen could almost smell. It hung there, like electricity in the unnatural night. In unison, the scrobblers took a step forward, hemming in the crowd and raising their weapons so that soon everyone who had not yet put a helmet on had some kind of blaster trained on them.

"There now," said the face of Greyling. "That makes life simpler, doesn't it? Choice is really overrated. And you'll thank me. Those helmets will bring you power and purpose. They will bring you clarity uncluttered by human doubt or weakness. You will never worry about a single decision ever again, and you will be free to wield your new strength without fear, without conscience."

There was a silent pause, through which Darwen caught a scattering of sobs, and then they complied. All the people in the front row put the helmets on. Some merely looked scared of the scrobblers, but others seemed curious, even eager. Mr. Stuggs pressed his helmet into place. He looked excited at what might happen next, so that for a second Darwen was reminded of Alex's observation that the man was—at least in spirit—half scrobbler already. Darwen stared, then turned back to the seated crowd, watching in horror as Aunt Honoria lifted the helmet over her head. As she lowered it into place, his aunt's face was completely unreadable.

For a second, Darwen couldn't breathe. He saw her eyes vanish inside the dark visor of the helmet and he could think of nothing, even when a scrobbler behind him shoved a helmet into his own hands. He looked around and saw that the same thing was happening to Mr. Peregrine, to Alex and Rich. Their eyes met briefly, desperately, and they shared the obvious truth that they had failed. Indeed, their resistance had been so useless that the scrobblers weren't even paying them attention anymore. Alex stood looking lost, but beside her Rich was suddenly considering the microphone, which the principal had set down on the stage.

Darwen knew that look. "What?" he asked under his breath.

"The communication system," said Rich. "It's wired to everything in Silbrica, Greyling said."

"So?" asked Darwen. "You can divert the power away from his machines?"

"No," said Rich. "But if I plug this microphone into that transmitter there, you can send a message through every portal in Silbrica. The energy surge may even lock the portals open for a while so anyone can pass through them. But the key is the message. Got anything you'd like to say?"

Darwen thought quickly. It wasn't much of a plan, but they didn't seem to have any other options. He nodded and stooped to the microphone as Rich casually reached for the jack plug on the end of the cable, plucked it out of the PA system, and, without raising his eyes, took three steps to where the scrobbler generator stood humming. He put the plug behind his back, facing the assembled people and their scrobbler guards, clicked it into place, and gave Darwen the smallest of nods.

Darwen took a breath, raised the microphone slowly to his lips, and said, "These are the mirroculists, Darwen Arkwright . . ."

"Alex O'Connor," said Alex, leaning quickly in.

"And Richard Haggerty," Rich concluded.

"On behalf of all the peaceful inhabitants of Silbrica," said Darwen, "we summon all allies to Hillside Academy to stand against Greyling and the destruction he will inflict upon your world."

There was no amplification. His voice sounded as it always did. But one of the scrobblers spun around and snatched the microphone from his grip.

Nothing else happened.

Darwen waited, staring at the blank face of the helmet he was holding with its little antenna in the back. He shot Rich a desperate look, but the bigger boy just shrugged. Had anyone heard? Would anyone come? It seemed unlikely, and they were already out of time. Any moment now, the device up in the clock tower would emit some kind of pulse and the transformation would start. He had no idea how long it would take or if he could reverse it once it had begun.

The scrobbler behind him nudged him with the business end of his energy weapon and the helmet chinked against something in Darwen's pocket. Eileen's compact. Darwen thought fast. They had never needed Weazen more than they needed him now. Maybe he was already here and watching, waiting for the right moment. . . . It was now or never.

Darwen dropped the helmet, snatched the compact from his pocket, and flipped it open, hitting the second button on the side as he did so. He didn't wait to see the hairy muzzle and bright, masked eyes. He just shouted, "Now!" and hoped that would be enough.

For the second time in as many minutes, his hopes were dashed to pieces by silence. The face of Greyling turned its rodent smile on Darwen, but nothing else happened.

Then, out of the unearthly stillness, Darwen heard a tiny noise somewhere beneath him, then a considerably larger sound, an electric bang, which was accompanied by the door into the clock tower blowing right off its hinges and flying in fragments all over the silent crowd, so that bits of wood rained down on their helmets. Then there was a blur of fur and brass and Weazen was out and shooting, a series of hard, precise flashes that sent scrobblers doubling up and collapsing where they stood. The others shifted their aim, trying to pick out the Peace Hunter as he returned their fire. The darkness was suddenly lit by a dozen arcing streaks of light and the firework explosions that came with them.

Darwen leapt forward, elbowing Principal Thompson in the back as Alex, neatly sidestepping the scrobbler that was guarding her, stepped up to the edge of the stage and shouted, "Run! Everyone, get out of those helmets! And yeah, it's a cliché, but for once it's really true: run for your lives!"

But as she said it, the clock face high above them burst into an eerie, greenish glow, so that everything below was cast in strange, leaping shadows. Darwen heard the hum of the broadcast rising in pitch and, in the same instant, saw tiny lights on the backs of the helmets burning glowworm green.

It was too late. Even those who had been in the act of removing their helmets stopped as if momentarily unsure who they were or what they were doing. They hesitated, and then they began to move again.

But now they were different.

Darwen could see it in their slow deliberation. Then, before his very eyes, some of them started getting bigger, their shirts and jackets tearing across the shoulders as their arms got longer and more apelike, the skin taking on a drab, olive hue, the fingers thickening and growing clawlike nails.

No, he thought, but there was nothing they could do but save themselves.

"Come on!" he shouted to Rich and Alex, leaping down from the stage and bolting toward the first set of glassless windows that might get him out of the quadrangle.

But his path was blocked.

It was Eileen. She looked confused. She had a bruise above her left eye and there was a trickle of dried blood in her hair. She was holding the compact in her hand and it was pulsing softly. Darwen's mind raced and a terrible possibility occurred to him.

No, he thought, gazing at the wound on her head.

"Eileen," he managed. "Open your purse."

She cocked her head on one side as if mildly surprised, but she smiled as if nothing was happening, unsnapped the bejeweled purse she always carried, and held it open. Darwen looked and squeezed his eyes shut to keep the tears in.

"What's the matter?" demanded Rich. "Eileen, help us get these people out!"

Eileen looked slightly baffled, gazing blankly at the compact as if she was listening to something far away.

"She won't help," said Darwen.

"Sure she will," Rich protested. "Won't you, Eileen?"

"You remember we couldn't understand how the Fixer moved through the portals?" said Darwen.

"Yeah, so?" said Alex.

"The Fixer can move through portals because the Fixer was once a mirroculist," said Darwen, his words leaden with despair. "Isn't that right, Eileen?"

"What?" said Eileen, still sounding confused.

"The Guardians find work for their former mirroculists," said Darwen, weary beyond anything he had ever felt. Weary and desperately sad. "Show them your purse," he said to Eileen.

Eileen smiled and showed them the open purse. In it was a construction of leather and rubber and metal with green lenses, one of which had been cracked by a slab of stone flung by a scrobbler that had once been Blodwyn Evans. It was a gas mask.

Eileen drew it out, gave it a quizzical look as if she had never seen it before, then, as the compact in her other hand gave a single earsplitting beep, swept it over her head and became a completely different person, became—there could be no doubt—the Fixer.

Chapter Thirty-six
Changes

Darwen had suspected it, had wondered about the way the Fixer had arrived in the mine just after he told her what they were doing, about the wound on her head caused by Blodwyn Evans in her half-scrobbler form. But suspicion isn't the same as really knowing. Now the fact of the thing chilled him to the bone and he was slow to respond, so that before he could reach for her, she had pulled that flintlock blaster with the mesh around the long barrel from her purse and was pointing it at each of them in turn.

"Eileen!" Rich protested. "It's us!"

"She can't hear you," said Darwen. "Not really. It's not Eileen anymore. She's under some kind of mind control."

The thing that had been Eileen tipped its masked face slightly to one side, sighting along the blaster's barrel straight to Darwen's chest. She showed no emotion and Darwen gritted his teeth, braced for the shot that would come, wondering vaguely if it would hurt to die.

There was a flash and a pop, and the weapon flew from her grasp. She clutched her hand to her chest in pain. To his right, Darwen saw where Weazen crouched, his own blaster still aimed at the Fixer. But then she was reaching into her purse for something else she could use against them.

As Darwen stood there, almost mesmerized by the Fixer's soulless mask, Rich closed fast behind her, holding one of the folding chairs in both hands. He swept it up and across with astonishing force, catching the Fixer on the back of the head. She went down like a sack of potatoes, and as Darwen stared, Rich snatched the mask from Eileen's face. He studied it, then put it on the ground and stamped his heel through the transmitter built into the back, then did the same with her tiny compact mirror.

"Nice one!" said Darwen, impressed.

"Come on!" shouted Alex, pulling at him. "Gotta go."

Escape, however, looked unlikely. Where there had been only a couple of dozen scrobblers moments before, there were now hundreds. They were dressed as teachers and parents, but they were scrobblers nonetheless.

"Wait!" said Rich. "Look. The signal isn't affecting everyone."

He was right. While many of the scrobblers were engaged in the firefight with Weazen, some of those in the audience were cautiously removing their helmets.

Genevieve Reddock had already taken hers off and was glancing around uncertainly, while two rows ahead, Simon Agu had slipped out of his and was gazing, devastated, at the scrobbler that had been his father.

"Come with us!" shouted Darwen, but Simon's eyes were wild as he tugged at his father's suit, trying to get some sign of recognition from the thing that was wearing it. "Simon! That's not your dad. Get away from it!"

But Simon didn't—or couldn't—pull away, and a moment later the thing that had been his father took him roughly by the arm and jammed the helmet back on his head.

"We've got to get to that machine!" Darwen shouted, knowing even as he said it that their only chance of escape was in the opposite direction.

Weazen was ducking and scurrying through the quadrangle corridor, leaping and shooting through the glassless window frames. Once in a while, he got a lucky shot off, but he was really no more than a diversion, and the longer he tried to keep it up, the more likely it was that he would get hit. Darwen's face stung from the grit that flew every time one of the blasters hit the stone walls. Weazen was fast, but there were just so many scrobblers shooting at him. It was, Darwen knew, only a matter of time. . . .

Up on the stage, Mr. Peregrine was backing away from the particularly large and brutish scrobbler that had been Mr. Stuggs. It would have had him already except that the flittercrake was flapping around the monster's head, looping and diving, scratching at its green skin with its talons.

Another delaying tactic that would buy only a few seconds.

The scrobblers and gnashers were everywhere, grabbing whoever was closest to them, or picking up rocks and chairs to use as weapons, and looking to come after Darwen, Rich, and Alex.

"Get out of the quadrangle!" Darwen shouted, blundering past a hesitant scrobbler and making for the door.

"Oh no," said Alex.

In the circumstances, it didn't seem that things could get worse, but then Darwen followed her gaze to the ragged windows of the perimeter corridor and he could see them: pale, phantom faces fading in from the shadow school.

The ghosts.

Despite the adrenaline surging through his body, he felt himself go suddenly cold as wet stone.

Some of the other students who hadn't yet been caught were spilling out of the rows of chairs and looking wildly for somewhere to go, but now their attention was seized by the spectral apparitions at the windows. Melissa Young screamed. Bobby Park covered his face and slumped against the wall, sobbing.

"Crybaby," sneered a voice behind him.

It was Chip Whittley. His face was impossible to read, like he had put on a mask to conceal whatever might be running through his mind, the fear, the excitement, the wild, brutal delight, but he was still cradling the scrobbler helmet he had been given in one casual hand.

Yes, thought Darwen. *Delight. He's glad. He can feel the power Greyling is bringing and he wants it. . . .*

"You knew this was coming, didn't you, Arkwright?" he said, smirking, but oddly calm in the chaos. Nathan Cloten, helmetless and looking frightened, was just behind him, and a few yards back was Barry Fails. Unlike the others, Barry was wearing his scrobbler helmet, the visor up so that his baffled face was just visible inside. Was Darwen imagining things, or was Barry's face starting to develop a greenish tinge?

"You need to help us," said Darwen. "We can stop it if we can just—"

"Why would I want to stop it?" said Chip, amused. "Time to step up and be a man. This is the world, Arkwright, and I'm going to take my place in it."

"What are you talking about, Chip?" asked Nathan. "What's going on?"

"The future," said Chip, considering the helmet in his hands. "What do you say, Nathan? Stay a kid all your life, or grow up right now?"

"This isn't growing up," said Darwen. "It's becoming a monster. Look at Barry!"

Chip did. Darwen was right. Barry's skin was definitely green and the features of his face were thickening. His shoulders had spread so that the fabric of his Hillside blazer had torn at the seam down the back, and his arms seemed to have gotten longer.

"What's happening?" said Nathan, horrified, but Darwen's eyes were on Chip.

"Let's just get out of here," said Darwen, "and then we can talk."

He turned and took a hurried step through the door into the cave-like echo of the perimeter corridor, trying not to look at the pale ghost faces that were out there. Rich and Alex were already there, stock-still and terrified.

"What is happening to Usually?" gasped Nathan. "And what are those other . . . things?"

"Ghosts," said Chip, at his elbow.

"No," said Darwen. "More like shadows cast by us into the other world. I think . . ." he said, putting the ideas together as he spoke, "I think they are a side effect of Greyling's machines. He's the man whose face you saw on the clock tower. As he tries to change the adults and bring the two realities into the same space, he's creating a kind of echo. I don't think he intends it to happen. What he's trying to do is turn the grown-ups into scrobblers—his monster servants and soldiers—by drawing on whatever darkness or cruelty is inside them, but it's doing something different to the kids. I don't know why. The ghosts are like spirit echoes. They are images of our essences, our souls."

"Other world?" sputtered Nathan. "What other world? What are you talking about?"

Darwen turned to say something back but found himself face-to-face with a scrobbler that was blundering after them. It was wielding a length of metal pipe discarded by the workmen when they built the stage. Darwen looked around. Unless they were to mingle with the ghosts that crammed the hallway, gazing rapt at what was happening in the quadrangle, they were cornered.

Nathan cried out. Alex took Rich's hand.

The scrobbler took a wide stride, raising the pipe over its shoulder to strike, its masked eyes fastened on Darwen's. He backed into the rough stone on the far side, huddling into a protective crouch, and braced himself, hands up over his head. He shut his eyes, held his breath, and waited.

Nothing happened.

Cautiously, Darwen opened his eyes. The scrobbler was still there, looming over him, the pipe raised to strike. But while the thick fingers of its greenish left hand flexed and unflexed, the right, the one with the weapon, held quite still.

"Darwen!" exclaimed Alex. "Oh God, Darwen. Look at its clothes!"

Darwen dragged his gaze from the blank mask and as they traveled down the scrobbler's body, a new feeling took hold of him, a feeling mixed of equal parts horror and grief. The monster was wearing a recently torn but once elegant black business suit and a silver chain around its neck.

Her neck.

It was—or had been—Aunt Honoria.

For a second, Darwen could not breathe, could not think. His arms, upraised to protect himself, sagged. Faced with what his aunt was about to do, his body and mind just gave up.

They had lost, and fighting back no longer mattered or made sense.

How long he stayed there he couldn't say, but he gradually realized that Alex had extended a cautious hand toward the scrobbler's left arm, that Rich was reaching slowly, inch by careful inch, up to its face. He hesitated, then took hold of the visor and raised it.

Beneath the glass the strange hybrid was revealed. It was and was not a scrobbler. The skin was green. The teeth burst from the heavy lips like tusks. But the eyes . . .

Darwen shifted, trying to get a better look. They were not so much red as a deep and fiery chestnut, and as he watched, they seemed to fluctuate, first toward the crimson, then to their original brown and back. It was like looking into the energy pool in the Guardian chamber when the life of Silbrica had been dying, like some terrible struggle was going on inside.

"Aunt Honoria," he managed. "It's me. Darwen."

The red eyes blinked, staying closed for a second, and Darwen kept very still, aware of that massive fist with the pipe raised over its head. A tear squeezed out from under the greenish eyelids and ran down the scrobbler's cheek, and then the eyes were open again, and they were brown, a deep, rich brown that Darwen knew.

Darwen stood slowly, grasping the scrobbler's left hand, and slowly, almost imperceptibly at first, the right hand with the pipe came down. The weapon slipped from its grasp and clanged heavily on the stone floor, but almost immediately an awful change came over the scrobbler's face. The mouth opened, the eyes squeezed shut, and the hands flew to the sides of the helmet. It rocked back and forth, producing a groan that rose in pitch and volume as the scrobbler doubled up.

Rich caught its shoulder, but it was too heavy for him and crumpled to the ground.

"What's happening?" Alex asked. "What's wrong with it?"

"It doesn't know what it is," said Rich. "Or it realizes what has happened and can't undo it. Either way, it's in terrible pain."

"Get the helmet off!" gasped Darwen.

"It's connected to her brain!" Rich answered. "Taking it off might kill her."

"It's killing her anyway," said Darwen, reaching for the helmet and pulling.

It took both of them, but they got it free. Aunt Honoria collapsed to the floor.

"Still breathing," said Alex, dropping to her side, "but I don't know. . . ."

"We have to get to that machine!" Darwen said. "The signal is still in her head. In all of their heads."

"It's too heavily guarded," said Rich. "There were half a dozen scrobblers and a couple of gnashers up there when they caught me. They have strict orders from Greyling. No kind of diversion will move them."

"Then we need to interfere with what it's doing," said Darwen.

"Why?" said Chip.

Darwen turned. He had forgotten the other boy was still there. Chip still looked cocky, as if he was relishing the situation, but there was a caution in his face that he couldn't hide.

"Because this is what Greyling does," Alex shot back at him. "He captures. He steals what people value most and he kills. You of all people should know that."

Chip was still smirking, but his eyes were wary.

"What does she mean?" asked Nathan. "Why you of all people?"

"Talking nonsense," said Chip, his eyes on Alex. "Just the usual O'Connor crap."

"You saw it!" she exclaimed. "Back in Costa Rica. You know what he does. What he's doing right now!"

"Doesn't seem so bad," said Chip, picking up the length of pipe the scrobbler-Honoria had dropped.

Rich was talking to himself. "The machine works on adults, but not kids, or not as well at least," he reasoned. "And it works faster on some adults than others. Why? It has to be about who they are as people, what they want, how they see themselves. And if so, then it's not just about electricity or other kinds of power. It's not just wires and machinery. It's about thought: theirs and—"

"Greyling's," Darwen completed for him.

"Right," said Rich. "So if we can disrupt Greyling's thoughts, we might be able to break the machine or at least slow it down."

"That's on me," said Darwen, hauling himself to his feet and picking up Honoria's helmet.

"Looks like your little ferret friend is about to get fried, by the way," Chip remarked.

Darwen glanced back into the quadrangle, aware that the noise of battle had suddenly stopped. He caught a flash of fur as Weazen ran from one shattered rock to another. He was clearly out of ammunition and the scrobblers were closing in.

But before Darwen could see what happened next, Nathan blundered into his line of sight, pointing horrified into the mass of silent specters. "Chip!" he exclaimed. "That's you!"

He was right. Gliding toward them through the throng of ghosts was one more solid than the others, one that was recognizable, but twisted with malice so that the face had almost ceased to be human. It was, in fact, the face of something more than half a scrobbler, a face Darwen had seen before.

"What is that?" said Chip in a low voice.

"It's you!" Nathan repeated.

"It's your echo from the shadow school," said Darwen. "It's stronger than the others because you have spent time in Silbrica. It's like . . . a footprint, I guess, an impression that you made by being there."

"An impression of me?" said Chip, staring at it.

"Your . . . true self," said Darwen, struggling to find the words. "It's as you appear on the other side."

"It's horrible," Nathan gasped, his eyes still fixed on the dreadful apparition that was coming toward them, its mouth gaping in a dreadful parody of a scream.

"Why does it look like that?" said Chip, holding the metal pipe out in front of him as if warding the apparition off. "If that's me, why is it so . . . ?"

He couldn't find the word, and Darwen was astonished to see revulsion in his face.

"That's what they think I am?" he said, and the sneer was gone now.

The apparition was getting closer, moving directly toward its counterpart from Hillside. It was cruel, vengeful, petty, destructive, a vessel of hatred.

"Chip!" Darwen shouted. "Don't let it touch you!" He didn't know why, but he was sure that would be bad.

But the scrobbler phantom leapt forward before Chip could move. For the briefest moment it was like they were wrestling, and then the two merged and the shadow turned around and its face was Chip's own.

The wrestling continued, but now it was inside. The shadow fought with Chip and Darwen guessed that they'd know who won by what he did with the heavy length of pipe still gripped in one hand. His face contorted, rippled, then stabilized as it turned to Darwen, who shrank back against the stone.

For a moment, in spite of the confusion around them, there was stillness. At last the thing that had been Chip Whittley spoke.

"I," Chip began, straining to find the words. "I am. Not. That. I won't be."

Darwen stared, not daring to believe it.

"Okay," he said. "Good. Help us."

Chip—if that's who the glowing figure still was—just stood there, as if thinking, but then he put the scrobbler helmet down and turned away from it.

"I have to go," said Darwen, not sure what had happened to the other boy or what he might do. "Now."

Darwen ran back into the quadrangle, dodging scrobblers and gnashers till he was far enough forward to be able to look up into the face of Greyling that glowed sourly down from the shattered window. If only he could break Greyling's concentration, disrupt the way his mind was channeling the power of his machines, maybe that would help. . . .

"You!" he shouted, waiting till the glassy eyes found him, holding the helmet in one hand, pointing squarely into the ratlike face with his other. "I know what you are."

Chapter Thirty-seven
Talents

"I should say," said Darwen, "I know what you *were.*"

The face flickered, and for a moment several different expressions were all visible—confusion, unease, curiosity—and then the image resolved again into its original bland expression, the hard eyes peering down the long, rodent nose.

"This is an unusually futile gesture, even for you, Darwen," said the face. "What do you believe you have learned that could possibly make a difference to what I am already achieving?"

"You know," said Darwen.

The face flickered again, and this time there was doubt in the eyes before the smooth mask slid back into place.

"Indeed?" said the face.

"You," said Darwen, very carefully, "were a mirroculist."

The ripples through the face lasted much longer this time. In them was wild, shrieking anger and a terrible anguish, though both slid back into fury and hysterical laughter. The laughter of insanity.

"I know what happened to you when you lost the gift," said Darwen. "I know why you are here and what you are trying to do to replace it."

"And you fear you will become me when your own gift leaves you," said Greyling.

"No," said Darwen. "I would miss it. But I would never kill and destroy to get it back. I'm stronger than that."

"Stronger than me?" sneered Greyling. "You have seen my power, the forces I can command. You are just a child who can open a few doors."

"I might be a kid," said Darwen, "but I don't need to command anybody. I have friends. We work together for each other and that makes us strong."

"You think this sentimental nonsense will distract me," said Greyling, amused. "It will not work. My mind is focused. I have an army poised to do my slightest whim and nothing you can muster will stand against them. You and your so-called friends have nothing—"

Greyling did not finish the sentence. Somewhere at the back, a confusion of noise had broken out. First came the earthshaking bellow of a terrapod, and Darwen's heart sank. If Greyling had brought those monstrous turtle creatures with him, then fighting back looked pretty futile. But when he glanced back to see the thing with its scrobbler escort, he saw they were swatting at something: tiny green lights that hovered about them.

Moth had come after all!

"Dellfeys?" scoffed Greyling, unimpressed. "That is all you could manage?"

But it wasn't. If Moth and her dellfeys were no more than an irritant to the scrobblers, the zingers that had begun swooping from above dropping their perfume bombs, the snorkies with their sabers, and the pouncels, which were suddenly leaping from the window arches and the rocky ledges, were rather more of a problem.

"They came!" Darwen gasped. "We called, and they came!"

Scrobbler weapons were being discharged in showers of sparks and belches of smoke, and the terrapod roared so the ground trembled, but then an entire wing of the quadrangle caved in, and through what had been the rock of the wall itself came a massive white shape with tusks of glass and trunks that shot blue fire. Two of the great white mammoths and their riders blundered into the quadrangle and even the terrapods shrank from them in terror. Greyling's scrobblers were falling back, firing defensively, and the gnashers were running wild.

The face of Greyling was shifting at great speed now, flicking through the snapshots of its uncontrollable sadness and rage, and as it did so, Darwen could sense a shift in the air around him. The scrobblers were slowing, and Mr. Iverson, who had been standing motionless, as if entranced, tore the helmet from his head and looked around bleary-eyed. Mrs. Frumpelstein had hers off too. And Miss Harvey. Even Mr. Sumners was slowly, uncertainly sliding his off.

Good people, after all, thought Darwen. Whatever Greyling had forced into their heads, whatever he had offered them, they had resisted.

"No!" yelled the face of Greyling. The flitting images slowed, stabilized, as the blank look of unconcern was forced back into place. "None of this matters," said the face. "It will not stop me."

But that momentary break in the signal had made a difference. Darwen could tell. There was a new hesitancy to those the machine had converted. The scrobbler that had been Simon Agu's father relaxed his grip on his son and slowly released him.

"A momentary delay," snarled the face of Greyling. "For which you and your friends will pay dearly." The face tightened into focus again, but it was dwindling now, and as it shrank, it became more real. And it wasn't just a face. It was a man up there on the platform framed by the shattered window. This was no apparition. Greyling himself was standing before them, trying to hold his victory together.

Darwen had seen him in other forms—the silvery figure at Halloween, the clown manikin in Costa Rica—but he had never laid eyes on the real Greyling before. He was a thin-faced youngish man with overlong hair and hunted eyes, but he also looked unexpectedly average, a conjurer stripped of his costume and magic tricks.

The barely audible drone of the conversion machine swelled again, but there was something else, a sudden and curious silence behind him. Though Darwen dreaded taking his eyes off Greyling, he had to see. He turned.

The hesitant scrobblers were parting, cringing away, and through them flowed a sea of ghosts.

They were pouring in from the quadrangle corridor, slipping through the empty windows and streaming toward the clock tower. At their head was one who walked on the ground, who pushed his way past the dazed, uncertain scrobblers and mounted the stairs to the tower with a sense of grim purpose.

It was Chip Whittley. All trace of the scrobbler that had haunted the countenance of his Silbrican ghost form was gone, and Chip's face glowed with a silvery light. At his heels were Alex and Rich, their faces bloodless in the pearly glow of the ghosts around them.

They moved directly toward the ragged hole where the stained glass window had been and, behind it, the stairs up to the clock mechanism.

Greyling hesitated, spreading his arms to block the column of specters, but baffled and unnerved by them. His eyes were desperate. "They cannot stop the machine!" he shouted. "They have no bodies, no force. They can do nothing."

"They have will," said Darwen. "Determination. Sometimes that is enough."

Greyling stared with something like horror.

The thing that was and was not Chip Whittley stepped through the hole and up, but now the other specters were pouring on ahead and Greyling had shrunk away from them. Darwen could hear the frantic bellows of the scrobblers on the top of the tower, their weapons flashing harmlessly as the ghosts streamed through. The blasts tore part of the stone cladding away from the tower and suddenly Darwen could see the machine itself, a great crab-like mass of black iron squatting up there in the ruins of the clock face, its green lights blinking.

He saw it and watched as the figure he still thought of as Chip threw something open on the device so that a blinding blue flash tore out like a sheet of lightning. Chip screamed, but he held on, and suddenly the ghosts were flowing directly into the machine, their energy mixing with the signal it was producing, diluting it, changing it, blending it with their own essence.

"No!" roared Greyling.

There had been nothing to fear from the ghosts, Darwen realized. Not even, finally, from Chip.

The machine rocked and groaned, then emitted a pulse of amber light that coursed out across the remains of the school, halting every scrobbler in its tracks. It lasted only a second, but it was, Darwen knew, enough. The process had been reversed.

Principal Thompson blundered across the stage and leaned on the lever till it thunked home. For a moment everything seemed to swim, and then the shadow school was fading out, leaving the scarred wreckage of Hillside behind. The gnashers and scrobblers, and all their equipment, everything that had come from the other side, all winked out in a blink of light. The ghostly phantoms that had haunted the shadow school had all gone into the machine. The parents and teachers who had been subject to the conversion process now stood befuddled, but fully human.

"No!" shouted Greyling again, and now he was small and pathetic-looking in his furious disappointment, no more than a thin ordinary man staring into the face of his own failure. He snatched up a fallen blaster and aimed it squarely at Darwen. "You have disrupted my plans for the last time," he said.

He squeezed the trigger.

Darwen closed his eyes and winced at the explosion of sound, feeling dust and grit hit him in the face. But then he heard screaming that was not his own, and he opened his eyes.

In front of him, having burst from the very earth itself, was a colossal crimson serpent, which loomed over Greyling as if suspended from high in the air. Part of its throat was smoking from Greyling's shot, but it would take more than a weapon such as that to bring down so powerful a creature. Greyling resighted his blaster on the snake, but it was far too quick for him. With one lunge, the man—if man Greyling still was—was snatched screaming into the monster's dreadful jaws and was gone.

There was a sudden and total silence. The great snake turned to consider Darwen, and Darwen felt the word Rich had used blossom in his mind: *Space.*

The great snake just hung there and Darwen felt its thoughts like music that raged like an ocean or a brushfire, but overlaid with rich and complex harmonies that filled his mind with joy almost like the perfume of the zingers.

We won, thought Darwen, considering the great crimson serpent that loomed over everything, still and watchful. *We won.*

But at a cost. He knew it before he saw Rich and Alex climb down, before he saw their stunned faces, before he could get close to the body they carried between them, assisted by a dazed-looking Mr. Iverson. The person they were cradling so carefully, the person who had, when it finally counted, sacrificed himself to save the others, was Chip Whittley.

Chapter Thirty-eight
Sacrifice

Darwen stared at the boy's body, his eyes burning. Chip had given himself to the machine, to save the others and to prove to himself that he was not what the shadow school thought him to be. Darwen blundered over to them but could think of nothing to do or say. They laid the body on the stage and just stood there, staring. It was a moment before Darwen realized that Mr. Iverson had brought Chip's parents forward.

What happened next was the strangest and most terrible thing yet. Mr. and Mrs. Whittley were both tall and elegant, his father wearing a crisp business suit, his mother in a gold summer dress, though both sets of clothes had been torn by the conversion process. Chip's father studied the arms of his ravaged suit, his face baffled and indignant. When his eyes fell on Chip's body, his expression did not change, and he glanced around with the same affronted confusion.

"He doesn't recognize him," Alex whispered, her tears running freely.

"He will," said Rich.

And he did. The effect of the conversion gradually fell away from him, but his bewilderment seemed to deepen as his hauteur melted. Darwen could see it in his face: *This boy? Who is this boy?*

And then, without warning, his wife began to scream. She fell on the body, hugging it to her, and finally he knew.

"Chip?" he whispered. "Chipper?"

Grief broke over him. Broke him. Husband and wife clung desperately to each other and nothing Mr. Iverson could say would calm or satisfy them. At last, Chip's father turned his face up to the sky and howled. There was no other word for it. It was an appalling sound, raw and bitter and pained, as if he had been torn open and they were seeing—hearing—the very heart of the man, all his achievements, his wealth, his power stripped away.

And then something happened, something stranger than anything Darwen had experienced in all his time in Silbrica. That Which Eats lowered its serpentine head to where the boy's body lay and then, with sudden and incalculable speed, threw its coils around him.

"What is going on?" someone demanded, but Rich stepped forcefully through the crowd.

"Back off!" he shouted. "Let it be. Can't you feel it? It's not going to hurt him."

And now Darwen could feel it too, something that came off the snake like warmth. But the snake itself seemed to shrivel slightly, and its skin was dulling like autumn leaves withering.

"It's giving some of its own life to save him," said Rich. "Out of gratitude."

Darwen wanted to ask how that was possible and how Rich could possibly have known as much, but he sensed his friend was right. He could feel it, waves of soothing energy like light or music. Darwen felt a glow of pleasure, the kind of feeling he got from shooting a soccer ball into the top right corner of the net, from his first trip to Silbrica, or from his friends returning from the tower alive and well and Greyling defeated.

And then Chip was stirring, waking, and—finally—shrieking in panic at being locked tight in the embrace of a massive snake. For its part, the great serpent released him, shot a look at Rich and Darwen and Alex, so that they felt the word: *Balance.*

It glowed in their minds, and they knew that not all the healing energy had come from the snake. It had drawn on their thoughts too. Balance: a life restored for the one the snake had taken from Greyling, and a gift to them for all they had risked. The immense creature hesitated just long enough for them to feel Rich's final thought—*Grateful*—then That Which Eats dove straight into the ground, its long, scarlet body sliding into the earth like some kind of train, and was gone.

Chip's parents clutched him to their breasts, sobbing with relief, and Darwen caught the boy's eye over his mother's shoulder. He looked shocked and uncertain, but Darwen held his gaze for a moment, then gave him a nod of acknowledgment. They had all done their part.

The sense that something impossibly strange had happened spread through the other parents like panic, pushing them back into themselves. They snatched out cell phones but found that nothing electrical was working. They ran for their cars and called for police and paramedics.

Darwen, meanwhile, just watched from a quiet corner, lost in his own thoughts.

Eventually it was Eileen who led Aunt Honoria to him. Darwen considered his former babysitter, but there was no trace of the Fixer about her now, and he felt as sure as he could be that that part of her identity had died when they smashed the transmitter in the gas mask.

Both women looked unsteady on their feet and far from clear on what had happened, but when his aunt saw Darwen, something about her changed. Her eyes met his and there was a new clarity in her face. She rushed to him and snatched him into her embrace, where he stayed, sobbing, finally giving in to his exhaustion.

"I thought I'd lost you," she said.

"Yeah," Darwen whispered. "Me too."

Darwen glanced back to where Chip stood with his parents. They were clinging to him as if letting go might mean somehow losing him again forever. For Darwen it was like seeing a boy he had never known. He had not liked Chip Whittley. For almost as long as Darwen had known him, the boy had been a bully—mean-spirited, smug, and casually cruel. None of those things had gone from Darwen's mind, but in what he must have thought were his final moments, Chip had made a choice that redeemed everything else he had ever done and more.

Darwen wondered if he would have done the same.

Later, when the police had arrived and the school grounds were once more lit by the strobing blue lights of their cars, as the parents and teachers were shepherded away to waiting EMTs with blankets, Darwen sat on the grass with his back to the wall, Rich on one side, Alex on the other.

"Any sign of Weazen?" asked Alex.

Darwen shook his head. He had lost sight of the little creature long before the machine had exploded. Alex stared at the ground.

"They don't remember," said Rich. "Our families, I mean. And the teachers. They know something happened, but the conversion process took them out of themselves. They have no idea what took place after they put the helmets on and are pretty fuzzy about how they came to do that in the first place."

"The kids remember," said Alex. "They weren't affected in the same way. Most of them, anyway. No one will believe them, of course, 'cause they're just kids, but they will remember. If the school stays open, next year is going to be pretty interesting."

"What are the cops saying?" Rich asked.

"An explosion." Alex shrugged. "The new broadcast system over-loaded or something. No one seems very sure."

"I can't believe we got out of this alive," Rich mused. "Can't believe we saved them."

"Oh, I'm not surprised at all."

It was Mr. Peregrine. He was hobbling toward them across the quadrangle, smiling wearily.

Darwen got up, and when the old man reached them and offered his hand, he shook it.

"Well done," said Mr. Peregrine. "A terrible business handled far better than could have been reasonably expected."

"I couldn't have done it without Chip," said Darwen, still amazed by the truth of the thing.

"Perhaps not," said Mr. Peregrine. "And when I become the teacher you said I was, I'll manage to find a lesson in that. But tonight is a time for celebration."

"Not for me," said Darwen.

The others looked at him, hesitant and unsure.

"My gift is burning out," said Darwen. "I can feel it. Soon I won't be a mirroculist anymore. It's on you two," he added, with a glance at Rich and Alex.

"Let us not be too hasty on that score," said Mr. Peregrine.

"What do you mean?" asked Darwen.

"Did you see what Greyling's machines did?" asked Mr. Peregrine. "All that hatred and selfishness and cruelty pumped directly into people's brains?"

"It turned them into scrobblers," said Alex.

"Well, it started to," said Mr. Peregrine. "But not evenly. Some embraced the transformation, while others resisted it. Some—your aunt for one—were able to shut down the change by sheer effort of will. Your friend Barry Fails, who is your age, became a scrobbler. Chip Whittley did not."

"Usually isn't our friend," said Alex.

"Mr. Stuggs became a scrobbler immediately," Mr. Peregrine continued.

"No surprise there," Rich muttered.

"He was . . . susceptible," said Mr. Peregrine carefully.

"You can say that again," Alex agreed.

"But Miss Harvey did not," Mr. Peregrine concluded, smiling.

"So?" said Darwen, who didn't see what any of this had to do with his gift.

"So," Rich inserted, "the success or failure of the process wasn't about the age of the people targeted."

Mr. Peregrine beamed at him. "Precisely so, Mr. Haggerty," he said. "Despite what the storybooks tell us, not all children are sweet, giving, and imaginative, while some adults have those qualities in spades. Assessing people's character is a tricky matter, and it is not reducible to figuring out how old they are."

"I don't get it," said Darwen. "What does this have to do with me?"

"I think the old assumptions about the mirroculist losing his or her gift as they cross over into adulthood are, to put it simply, wrong," said Mr. Peregrine. "I think it depends on the individual and what they plan to do with the gift they have been given."

Darwen just looked at him.

"There is much that I do not understand about your particular talent, Darwen, but I think you will bear it for a while longer yet. You have already achieved things no mirroculist has been able to do before."

"Opening portals that aren't on the grid, you mean?" said Rich.

"And being able to sense where they are?" added Alex.

"Both of those things, yes," said Mr. Peregrine. "But your greatest achievement is one I think you have not yet recognized."

"Yeah?" said Darwen. "What's that?"

"Your ability to share," said Mr. Peregrine, smiling kindly.

"Share?" Darwen repeated. "Share what?"

"Many things, I suspect," said Mr. Peregrine, "But in this case, I mean your gift."

He paused as Darwen gaped at him, clueless, and the old man nodded first at Alex, then at Rich.

"Wait," said Alex. "You mean, we're not really mirroculists?"

"In the strictest sense," said Mr. Peregrine, "no. You have the ability to open portals to Silbrica because Darwen has given it to you. He has done what no mirroculist I know of has done before. He has divided his talent between his friends, a process that, though I do not understand how, has somehow intensified his ability. A remarkable thing, generosity of spirit. Never underestimate it."

"Huh," said Rich, to Darwen. "Thanks, man."

Darwen didn't know what to say.

"Yeah," said Alex, rather less enthusiastically. "Thanks."

"I didn't do it on purpose," said Darwen, shrugging apologetically, not sure whether he should be proud or embarrassed.

"Nah," said Alex, cheering up. "It's all good. 'Course, I'd rather be a mirroculist on my own talent and in my own right, as it were, but still . . . this works."

She shrugged and beamed, already past it.

"My point," said Mr. Peregrine, "is that you have already broken many of the old assumptions about mirroculists, and I see no reason why you shouldn't break this last about how children must grow out of their gift. Tonight, I think, suggests the opposite. Children can be spiteful and selfish, while adults are capable of all the best qualities their children possess. They just have to remember how to use them. I don't know why this surprises me. Many of the most interesting grown-ups I know are still about twelve years old in their hearts. I am confident, Darwen, that you can retain whatever is necessary to hold onto your gift well into adulthood." Mr. Peregrine paused and eyed Darwen carefully. "What? Is this not good news?"

But Darwen couldn't speak; he just nodded emphatically and looked down so that they could not see his shining eyes.

"Hey, Octavius."

It was Eileen. She looked young and dazed and a little embarrassed. "Good to have you back with us," she said.

"The pleasure, believe me," said Mr. Peregrine, "is all mine."

"Darwen," said Eileen, "your aunt is waiting for you in the parking lot."

Darwen nodded thoughtfully. "One more minute," he said. "I just need to . . . I don't know, let it all sink in."

Eileen bobbed her head in agreement.

"Listen," said Rich, looking very sheepish and as pink as Darwen had ever seen him, "I'm sorry about hitting you. Kind of had to be done, but still . . . sorry."

"Hitting me?" said Eileen.

"You don't remember?" asked Alex. "He popped you with a chair but good. It was like the WWF, man. POW!"

"Okay, Alex," said Rich.

"You hit me with a chair?" said Eileen, one hand straying to the back of her head. The question wasn't outraged so much as baffled, as if she was straining to recall something just beyond her reach.

"You don't remember," said Rich. "Any of it? You don't remember what you were doing? What you did before . . . ?"

"It's okay," Darwen inserted. "It was an accident—right, Rich?"

Rich gave him a look, saw the determination in his eyes, then shrugged. "That's right," he said. "Just an accident."

"That's okay then," said Eileen, massaging her scalp and smiling. "I'd hate to think I had made a fool of myself and couldn't remember what I did."

Darwen held his smile as long as he could, then looked away, blinking back tears. It wasn't her fault. Telling her what she had done as the Fixer, particularly to his parents, would only devastate her. That wasn't fair. Her body but not her mind was guilty. She had been under the control of first the Guardians, then Greyling, but that control had been broken, and with it that part of her past had died. Darwen would not resurrect it.

On the other side of the square, chair-strewn lawn, something small and dark stirred, shaking off a pile of rubble and sitting up, its eyes bright.

"Weazen!" Alex exclaimed, running over and snatching the creature up. "I didn't think you'd made it!"

"Took a bit of a tumble," muttered the Peace Hunter. "And got more than a little singed by . . . hey! Watch it! Stop! Put me down!"

But Alex was dancing around the quadrangle, Weazen held tightly against her chest, kissing his scorched and matted fur, till even Darwen found himself grinning. As she cavorted around, he gave Mr. Peregrine a sidelong glance. The old man was beaming too.

Darwen returned his gaze to Alex, who was still dancing with a struggling Weazen, and he began to laugh outright.

"Check it out!" shouted Alex, in between croons and kisses. "This right here? This could have been our bit in the talent show."

Chapter Thirty-nine
Endings

The semester concluded without another class meeting. The school was closed pending "structural remodeling" and various investigations over exactly what had happened the night of the end-of-term gala. For a few evenings, the story made local headlines, but as the true nature of events failed to emerge, the TV reporters seemed to lose interest. Every time it came on, however, Darwen would find himself watching his aunt's face, trying to see what she remembered. She still worked long hours, but she had taken to turning her phone and laptop off while they sat together for meals, and when the news items about Hillside started, she would become strangely still and focused. The pattern was always the same. She looked confused, like she was straining to recall something important from long ago, and then she would offer to make him a sandwich, or bring him a Coke, and would wind up sitting silently next to him on the couch with her arm around him. Her embrace was always a little too tight for comfort, a little desperate, and she avoided his eyes, but Darwen was glad of it.

Mr. Peregrine was somehow a teacher again, or so he said. Principal Thompson had been placed on administrative leave indefinitely, whatever that meant, and the new principal was Mr. Sumners, the math teacher. He had reinstated Mr. Peregrine without ever trying to get a solid explanation for why he had been absent so long. It seemed that with all the negative publicity the school was getting, he could not afford to turn any teacher away who wished to stay on. He never knew that Mr. Peregrine—the real Mr. Peregrine rather than the Jenkins creature that had worn the Mr. Peregrine flesh suit—had never actually taught a class at Hillside.

Two nights after the abortive gala, Darwen, Rich, and Alex went through the oven door to the Great Apparatus and up to the council chamber, where they found Lightborne, Jorge, and the others seated as if they had been expected.

"Mr. Arkwright," said Lightborne, rising. "I believe we owe you a debt of gratitude."

"You do," said Darwen, with such simple certainty that he felt them suddenly tense. "And I will tell you how you are going to repay me."

Lightborne's benevolent smile flickered. "You have our undivided attention," he said.

"Good," said Darwen quietly. "You have shown yourselves unwise. You have been deficient in your governing of Silbrica. Worse, you have made alliances with the enemies of Silbrica to preserve your own power and have resorted to treachery and murder. . . ." His voice faltered. Everyone in the room looked at him. "Murder," he repeated, "including that of my parents, to give yourselves tools against those who might oppose you."

"Darwen, there are things you do not understand," said Lightborne. "I see how our methods must seem extreme to you—"

"Seem?" Darwen interrupted. For a moment he thought he would rage at them, scream and point, accuse and bellow till his lungs bled, but those, he suddenly felt, were the actions of a desperate and powerless child, which he was not. He smiled thoughtfully. "You may explain your actions any way you like, but it will not excuse them. I am suspending the council immediately. You are all fired."

"On what authority?" gasped Lightborne, genuinely surprised now.

"That of the mirroculists," said Darwen, "and their allies, who, as you know, will come if we call them."

That silenced them.

"The boy has a point!" called a voice from the stone seats lining the chamber. It was Weazen. He was eating pizza again, his muzzle shiny with oil. Beside him, as if suspended in the air, was a tiny but constant green light. Moth was with him.

Darwen smiled and felt his conviction grow.

"If you think you are worthy to join the new body that will replace you," he added, "you may apply to Mr. Octavius Peregrine, the dellfey called Moth, Weazen—the Peace Hunter—and Ms. Blodwyn Evans, who, you will be pleased to know, is fully recovered and back to her old self. They will be in charge of the process. Consider carefully how much of your past you want exposed before applying."

Lightborne looked thunderstruck, but he also knew when he was beaten. He shrugged off his formal robes and let them lie where they fell, then he walked away, up the long stairs and out of the chamber. The others followed suit.

Jorge went last, and he did so after first smiling at them and nodding. "This," he said, "is good. Silbrica is a wondrous place, Darwen Arkwright. Pay attentions to its health."

When they had all gone and Darwen, Rich, and Alex were alone in the great chamber, Alex approached the shimmering energy dome. "So you've gotten rid of the old guard," she said. "Who will take over? Silbrica requires a group who will be bound together mentally to oversee the good of the world. Where are you gonna find people who will get it right?"

"The Guardians aren't from here, remember?" said Darwen. "They ruled over the place, but it wasn't really theirs. It's not surprising that Greyling was once one of them."

"So what's the alternative?" asked Rich.

"We turn Silbrica over to the people who live here," said Darwen. "We build a council of dellfeys and mammoth herders, pouncels and zingers, snorkies and whatever else can think and communicate and share a vision for what Silbrica is."

Rich whistled. "That's a pretty tall order, Darwen," he said. "They have lived separately for a long time. Not sure how well they'll work together."

"That's for them to determine," said Darwen. "They came together to protect not just their own loci but the whole world. I think they can keep it up. Mr. Peregrine will help."

"And you?" said Alex. "What about you? What about us?"

"We did what we had to," said Darwen. "Greyling is gone and our fight is over. Now we get to explore, to enjoy the world we helped save. I don't know if Mr. Peregrine is right, if I'll be able to open the portals forever, but I, for one, intend to use the gift as if I might one day lose it."

"Me too," said Rich.

"Try and stop me," said Alex, grinning. She took each of their hands. "Mirroculists together forever, whatever happens."

"The Peregrine Pact," said Darwen, pulling them a little closer.

"I told you," said Alex. "First day you arrived, I knew we'd be best friends. You didn't believe me, but I was *so* on the money."

"That's right," said Darwen, grinning at Rich. "I didn't believe you."

"Yeah, whatever," Alex sneered. "Laugh it up. You didn't see it coming, but now I'm the most important person in both of your lives. It was inevitable, really."

"That's right," Rich agreed, rolling his eyes. "You are the star of the show."

"And don't you forget it," Alex shot back. "So what do you say we pick a locus we've never visited before and see what it has to offer?"

"Maybe tomorrow," said Darwen. "I promised my aunt I'd bring you guys over for dinner tonight."

"She still feeling just guilty enough to give you whatever you want?" asked Alex.

"Pretty much," said Darwen. "She's not sure why, but she can deny me nothing."

"You should ask for pulled pork," said Rich. "With Texas toast and baked beans."

"Seriously?" said Alex as they began to walk down to the Great Apparatus and the chute up to Darwen's room. "She's reeling from nearly killing him and you want to exploit that by asking her for barbecue? That's just sad. You should ask for a car. Something sleek and fancy that I'll look good in. Heck, Rich can already drive, so long as we don't have to cross any bridges in traffic. . . ."

"I did just fine on the bridge," Rich inserted.

"Whatever, tractor boy," Alex returned. "If I hadn't been navigating and yelling every time you almost bashed a cop car, we would have been in the ocean."

As Rich sputtered his protests, Darwen smiled to himself, casting a long look over the circle of portals in the center of the room, all leading to strange and astonishing places, a near infinite network of wonders to explore. Without him and his friends, none of this would be here. They had stood their ground against Greyling and his scrobbler army and they had won. Silbrica at last knew peace and freedom.

"You coming, man?" Alex shot back from the chute. "I thought we were having dinner."

"I'm coming," said Darwen. "Just taking it in."

"It will all still be here tomorrow," said Alex. "You can check it out then."

"Yes," said Darwen, turning his smile upon her. "Yes, I can."

THE END

Acknowledgments

Thanks to my wife and son, who read early drafts of the manuscript and provided invaluable feedback, to my agent, Stacey Glick, to Ben Schrank, Sarah Van Bonn, Natalie Sousa, Kristin Logsdon, and—especially—Gillian Levinson at Razorbill. I am also particularly grateful to the teachers, students, and booksellers whom I have met in the last couple of years as I toured schools. You remain a constant inspiration.